The Secret Fiancée

LEXINGTON & RAYA'S STORY

THE WINDSORS

CATHARINA MAURA

This one is for those of us that crave happiness with every heartbeat but don't dare reach for it. Don't let fear dictate your future.

Contents

One

Lexington

A nervous thrill runs down my spine as my fingers fly over my keyboard, line after line of code slowly unraveling our security system. It's bullshit that I have to hack into my own family's firmware in the first place, and it's even bigger bullshit that it's taken me weeks to get remotely close to breaching it. Hundreds of hours went into finding the slightest weakness in our Head of Security's systems, only to come up empty every single time.

Until now.

My heart begins to race as I write the last few lines that are sure to let me into my grandmother's laptop. I flex my fingers, sucking in a breath before I press enter.

"Thank fuck," I whisper as my monitor flashes for a split-second, before mirroring what must be my grandmother's home screen. The background photo of my parents with my five siblings and I nearly makes me feel guilty enough to stop what I'm doing, but my need to be in control of my own life drowns the feeling out.

Nerves dance across my skin as I search my grandmother's

computer in the most methodical way I can think of given my time constraints, and with each second that passes, my frustration grows. "Where did you hide her, Grams?" I murmur, typing faster, more frantically.

My gaze drops to the heirloom Laurier watch I inherited from my grandfather, its second hand moving smoothly. Our Head of Security, Silas Sinclair, will realize what I'm up to and shut me out within a few minutes at most, giving me approximately three more minutes to find the information I'm after. "*Fuck*," I groan when my internal monitors begin to flash.

I sit up when Pippy, my robot assistant, calls my name, her voice sounding from the speakers in my lab. "Lex, Sinclair Security identified a breach that they're working on. It won't take them long to shut you out," she tells me. "By my estimates, you have two minutes left."

"Damn it, Silas."

I work faster, searching my grandmother's systems for every single mention of my name, of which there are thousands. You could be the best coder, but without a strategy, your skills are useless — and I'm feeling pretty damn useless right about now.

"Come on," I whisper, my agitation increasing as the seconds trickle by without result. "Where are you hiding?"

My screen flickers just as I open a promising document, and my heart nearly fucking stops. I only have a few seconds left at most, but as it turns out, that's enough for me to find what I was after.

Raya Lewis.

I grin to myself just as my screen goes black, satisfaction spreading from my chest throughout my entire body. "Raya," I whisper. It almost feels sinful to say her name out loud before I'm meant to know it. I lean back in my chair and stare up at the ceiling, my mind whirling. "Who are you, Raya Lewis?"

For as long as I can remember, my family has utilized arranged marriages as a way to grow our existing business and enter new industries. None of us get to choose who we marry, and I won't be any different, but I'm not going into this blind. I won't let my grandmother play me the way she did my brothers, slyly manipulating them into thinking their choices are their own, when she's always held their strings.

My phone begins to buzz, snapping me out of my daze, and I smirk when I see the incoming video call. One beat passes, and then another, before I finally pick up.

"Are you fucking kidding me, Lex?" Silas says, fury written all over his face.

I merely shrug as I position my phone on my desk, ready for the lecture Silas no doubt prepared for me. "Merely keeping you on your toes, Si. How else am I supposed to be sure that you're really doing your job?"

He throws me a withering look that makes it near impossible not to smile smugly, and my amusement only heightens his anger. "How the fuck am I supposed to explain this to your grandmother?"

Every hint of satisfaction melts away, and I straighten in my seat. "You won't," I warn him, unease evident in my voice, despite my firm tone. "The first time I meet the woman I'll be forced to marry can't be on my grandmother's terms. I'll do as is expected of me, but I'll do it on my own terms. I need to know who my future wife is behind the facade she'll no doubt craft the second we're formally introduced to each other."

His expression falls, understanding stealing away his anger, and he sighs. "I'll feign ignorance if this ever comes to light," he says reluctantly, something akin to pity crossing his eyes.

I lower my head, my heart wrenching painfully. He knows better than anyone else why I'm doing this. He's the one who saved me, after all. Silas found me when no one else could, and my family and I have been in his debt ever since.

"What do you know about Raya Lewis? You shut me out before I could read my grandmother's file on her."

Silas shakes his head. "You know I can't tell you anything. It's bad enough that you learned her name."

I tap my foot impatiently as I stare him down, knowing he won't budge. The second I get off this call, he's going to bury any and all information about her. "I just need to know what kind of person I'm going to marry, Silas. I need to know that I'm not about to make the same mistake twice."

Silas runs a hand through his hair and sighs. "Fuck," he groans, knowing he can't deny me. "She's a robotics major at Astor College," he says hesitantly, like he's certain he'll regret telling me as much as he has, despite it being very little.

"Robotics," I murmur, oddly surprised to find out her major is the same as mine was. Not only that, but she's also attending the same college I attended — the college one of my best friends owns.

"Lex," Silas says, his tone filled with caution. "You should know that the match isn't confirmed yet. Raya's father desperately needs the merger your grandmother offered him, but he's refusing to make an arranged marriage part of the deal. As it stands, I'm not sure this engagement will happen."

I stare out the window for a moment, an unfamiliar feeling lodging deep in my chest. "No," I murmur. "I have a feeling she's the one."

Two

RAYA

My heart pounds wildly as I take one cautious step after the other, careful not to trigger the comprehensive alarm system around the lab. One wrong step, and security *will* come rushing in to remove me from the premises.

I hold my breath as I clutch the badge I stole and hold it up against the reader, praying none of the security protocols have changed in recent weeks. "Thank God," I breathe as the door unlocks audibly, the soft click making me look around furtively, surprised I managed to get this far at all.

My shoulders relax as I walk in, my gaze settling on the electric car propped up on a platform in the middle of the room. Each time I see it, I'm in awe all over again. It's the first fully solar powered car that'll be commercially available — a technological feat I've dreamed of since my father first brought me to work with him years ago, the plans for this exact car strewn over his desk. The technology for it didn't exist back then, but that didn't stop him from pursuing his dreams of a sustainable car.

I sigh as I drop my bag by my feet and reach down to grab the trusty gold colored air ratchet my dad gave me years ago. I tighten my grip and reach for the solar panels on the car's roof with a smug smile on my face, only for that smile to wither the second my fingers brush against the cold surface.

Loud alarms begin to blare, and seconds later, security guards come storming in. I hang my head in defeat and stand frozen, my back to the door, shame keeping me rooted in place. *Damn it.* How the hell did they tie the security system to the car itself? I should've known breaking in was too easy. Should've known something was wrong when I breezed through the building within minutes.

"*Raya Indira Lewis*, would you like to explain what you're doing in my lab?"

I turn around slowly at the sound of my father's voice, my cheeks blazing and my heart hammering in my chest. "Hi, Dad!" My voice is filled with faux cheer, and the slight tremble gives away my nerves. "Aren't you supposed to be in a meeting?"

Six of my dad's private security guards surround him, three on either side, and they all share the exact same look — exasperation with a tinge of bemusement. They step aside as Dad walks toward me, his brow raised and his eyes twinkling in a way that diminishes the sternness I'm sure he's attempting to portray. "I thought we agreed that you'd focus on your master's degree, so why do I keep finding you in my lab multiple times a week?" He brushes my hair out of my face gently and shakes his head.

"*Dad*," I begin to say, my tone defensive. "I learned something in class today that I just had to try. I think I know how to fix the solar panels."

Dad's expression shifts, a hint of hopelessness drowning out his brilliant blue eyes. His gaze tells me that he knows exactly how I feel — countless times, he's stood in my shoes, certain he'd found the solution to the project we've invested so heavily in with nothing to show for it.

Most solar panels only store about 20% of sunlight they're exposed to, and that isn't sufficient for a car. We managed to double that level, but for this car to be viable, we need to get that closer to 80%. Our car just doesn't work the way it's supposed to, and because of that, it can't be sold to the public.

My father and I both firmly believe that sustainable cars are the future, but neither of us had counted on the economic downturn we're facing. Dad has done his best to hide it from me, but I know the company is on the verge of bankruptcy. People simply aren't buying new cars these days. Luxury cars are hardly affected, but mid-range cars? They aren't selling right now, and we don't have the resources or expertise to move into higher end vehicles. Combine that with our heavy investment into a product that isn't viable, and we're left with heavy debts and low revenues that can't shoulder them.

Day by day, I can see my father lose hope while trying his best to remain strong for Mom and me. There isn't much I can do to help, but I can keep experimenting, and I can keep trying. If we could just turn our solar powered car into a commercially viable product, it would change everything. We'd instantly become frontrunners in not just sustainability, but in electric cars altogether. It wouldn't just save the company — it'd bring it to new heights, the kind my father has always dreamed of.

Dad places his hands on my arms, his expression filled with just as much sternness as there is understanding. "Angel," he says, his voice soft. "The company will be there when you graduate in a couple of months. In the meantime, I just want you to enjoy college. Make memories, Raya. Live your life. I didn't quite understand it when I was your age either, but time truly is precious, and I can see you wasting it away working on our prototype. It's taken enough from us, hasn't it?" He tucks my hair behind my ear and forces a smile. "Besides, isn't it Adam's birthday tonight? That's where you should be tonight, Raya. Not here, in my lab."

Guilt steals away my words, and I look down. He's right. I'm supposed to be at my best friend's birthday party, yet here I am, in Dad's lab, because I couldn't resist trying out an idea. Adam and I grew apart a little during our undergrad at separate colleges, and I've been trying to remedy that now that we're doing our master's together, but I've done a terrible job of prioritizing my friendships.

"This company is your future, Raya, but it shouldn't be your present. If I catch you here again on weekdays, I'll bar you from entering the building altogether."

I begin to protest, but Dad silences me with a pointed stare. "Your twenties are supposed to be filled with fun and countless regrettable decisions, Angel. I want you to live a fulfilling life. Go explore. Figure out what it is that makes you happy. Find a hobby or two. Lewis Motors can't be your whole identity — I need to know that you'll be okay even if somehow... if someday, the company isn't there anymore."

He looks away, his expression cracking. Pure torment and worry beyond anything I've witnessed from him before shines through for a moment, before Dad pulls himself together. "I'm sorry, Dad," I murmur, not quite sure what I'm apologizing for. I'm not sorry I sneaked in, but I *am* sorry I still haven't found a way to help him.

Three

Raya

My mind is still on the solar panels as I walk into *King of Hearts*, Adam's favorite rooftop bar. I left an overview of my plans with my dad, and though he chastised me, I know he'll execute my ideas the first chance he gets. I just hope it works this time.

The bass's vibrations cascade over my body as I weave through the crowd, my gaze roaming over the countless ballgowns and masks everywhere. *King of Hearts* is known for its themed parties, and the venue has transformed into something magical for tonight's fairytale theme.

Fairy lights illuminate the path to the table Adam reserved for his birthday, and I force myself to cheer up and smile. I can't let helplessness consume me — not tonight.

Adam spots me and holds up a shot glass with a mischievous expression, a gold-colored plastic crown on his head. "I warned you that you'd have to do a shot if your crazy plans to break into your dad's lab made you late to my birthday."

I shake my head and smirk, my mood improving rapidly. "No

way!" I hold up my arm, pointing to my wrist. "Ten minutes before the clock strikes twelve!"

We've celebrated his birthday at midnight since we were ten, and this year won't be an exception. I've hyper fixated on the solar panels for months now, and all it's led to is me neglecting my classes and being banned from entering my dad's lab. I won't let it affect my friendships too.

Adam shakes his head and wraps his arm around me. "Fine," he grumbles, his eyes roaming over my elaborate eye makeup. "What are you supposed to be?" he asks, frowning. "Are you a dragon? I was sure you'd show up dressed like a princess."

I giggle and lean back, slipping out of his embrace to show off my makeup properly. King of Hearts is known for its theme parties, and I found the cutest face stickers to match tonight's fairytale theme. "I'm a fairy! Fairy, fairytale, get it?" I thought it was obvious, given the elaborate wings around my eyes, but clearly not.

Adam's lips twitch as he tries his hardest to suppress a smile, but he only lasts for a few moments before he barks out a laugh, his crown slipping in the process.

"Raya!" one of the girls from our Signals and Systems class shouts, and next thing I know, I'm holding a gold carriage-shaped cocktail glass. "Cheers!"

I take a deep breath before knocking it back, hoping it'll take away some of my lingering somberness, yet knowing it won't. Dad's unshakeable confidence might fool others, but not me. I know we're mere months away from bankruptcy, and our only salvation is the prototype. If I could just fix the solar panels, it could change everything. It's like the solution is on the tip of my tongue, yet it continues to evade me. Watching Dad put on an act for me is becoming increasingly tough, and I'm not sure how much longer I can pretend to be clueless.

I take a steadying breath when Adam hands me another glass, his gaze roaming over my face slowly, his brow raised. "What's wrong?" he asks, his arm wrapping around my shoulder.

I rise to my tiptoes to reassure him, but the words lodge in my throat. "It's n-nothing," I manage to stammer eventually, and Adam leans back a little to look at me, clearly far from convinced. "More importantly," I tell him, pasting on a smile the second my phone begins to vibrate in my pocket, "are you ready for our countdown?"

His face lights up and he nods eagerly, his full attention on me as I count down from ten as best as I can in the noisy bar we're in. "Three, two, *one*... happy 22nd birthday, Adam!"

My arms wrap around his shoulder, and he lifts me off my feet, crushing me in a strong hug. Adam buries his face in my hair for a brief moment before he sets me down again. I grin up at him, genuinely happy for the first time in hours as I push him toward our other friends, who are all eager to wish him a happy birthday too.

"You know what we need?" Sophia, Adam's lab partner, shouts. "Shots!" Her words are so wildly in contrast with her cute Cinderella outfit that it takes me a moment to register her words.

Adam's eyes find mine, and we both burst out laughing simultaneously. He knows how much I hate shots. "I'll get them," I tell her, "but I'm not doing any!"

Adam throws me a look that I instantly decipher as him checking if I'm okay, and I nod at him before walking toward the bar, my mood lifted.

Twenty minutes later, the bartender hands me a tray filled with twelve shots, and I grimace as I take them from her, not quite sure how I'm going to carry them back to my friends without spilling anything in this crowded space.

Almost as if the universe was trying to prove how hopeless my quest was, I crash into someone mere moments after I turn away from the bar, barely having taken a step. Blue liquor spills all over a perfectly white shirt, instantly soaking through the fabric.

Mortification washes over me, and I freeze as my gaze shoots up to the tall stranger's face, only to find the top half of it obscured by a yellow and gold glittery mask in the shape of wings.

My lips part, an apology on the tip of my tongue, yet my words momentarily fail me as I take in his dark hair, those dazzling emerald eyes framed by thick dark lashes that I'm instantly jealous of, and the sexiest cheekbones I've ever seen.

His eyes find mine, and he looks shocked, but there's no anger in them. "I am *so* sorry," I stammer eventually, feeling increasingly ridiculous as seconds filled with silence pass between us.

He shakes his head and smiles as he reaches for the wooden tray, revealing cute dimples that instantly make him even more attractive. "Let me help you with that before you do even more damage, little fairy," he says, his eyes twinkling with amusement. "I don't think this is safe in your hands." He takes it from me and effortlessly holds it up above the crowd with one hand, the other reaching for mine. "Where am I carrying this to?"

My heart skips a beat as I tighten my grip on his hand and pull him along to our table, grateful for his help and far too mortified to object.

Adam smiles and waves me over when he spots me, only for that smile to fade when he notices the stranger trailing behind me, our hands entwined. "Raya," Adam says the moment the tray is placed on the table. "Who is this?"

"Lex." His voice is smooth and firm, a hint of danger in it that wasn't there before. The name suits him — strong yet playful, which is the exact vibe he gives off.

I smile sheepishly. "I accidentally spilled half our shots all over him," I begin to explain, belatedly realizing that I'm still holding his hand.

I pull my hand away, and he raises a brow as he leans in behind me. His lips brush over my ear, the sensation sending a shiver straight down my spine. "*Raya,*" he repeats, like he's testing out my name. "Is that guy your boyfriend?"

Startled laughter escapes my lips, and I shake my head as I turn to face him, my chest brushing against his. "No. He's my best friend," I reply, used to the common assumptions people tend to make about Adam and me.

Lex stares at me for a moment, his eyes sparkling with something that can only be described as satisfaction. "Good," he says, his voice bordering on a growl.

"How so?" I ask, unable to keep my tone from being flirtatious despite my best attempts.

Lex smirks, his hand wrapping around my waist. "He seems nice. I'd have hated being the reason his heart breaks."

My eyes widen, and he chuckles as he gently pushes my hair behind my ear. "Lex," I say, enjoying the way his name rolls off my tongue. "Bold of you to assume you'd ever stand a chance with me."

"Would you like to bet that I can convince you to give me a chance before the night is over?" His gaze roams over his messy shirt. "And not just out of pity."

I raise a brow, ready to wipe that smug smile off his face with a simple *no* when my gaze locks onto the golden raven on the buttons of his shirt. "That's a Raven Windsor Couture shirt," I mutter, my playfulness making way for shock. It isn't the kind of shirt you can just buy — they're all handmade, and they sell out within minutes to those that have been on waitlists for months. "I am so incredibly sorry, truly. Please let me reimburse you for it!" I take another look at the shirt and narrow my eyes. "Provided it's *real*, that is."

My fingers trail over his ruined shirt, and it isn't until Lex grabs my wrist and flattens my palm against his chest that I realize what I was doing. "I assure you that it's very real," he says, grinning. "Regardless, don't worry about it."

His grip tightens around my wrist, and he takes a step closer. "However... if you did want to make it up to me, there *is* something I want, something money can't buy."

I raise a brow, curiosity drowning out my natural wariness. "Enlighten me. What is it you want?" I ask, bracing myself for the disappointment that'll follow the no doubt piggish answer he'll give me.

"Play truth or dare with me," he says, catching me by surprise.

Lex grins as he spreads my fingers across his chest and places his own in between mine. "Six rounds — one for each shot you spilled on me."

Four

Lexington

"Truth or Dare?" Raya repeats, intrigue warring with relief in those gorgeous dark brown eyes. She was stunning in the photos that accompanied the background check I ordered on her, but she's even more beautiful in person. Clearly, no camera could capture her beauty adequately.

I smile at her as I reach for her long, dark, windblown hair, curious what she thought I'd say. I push it out of her face for her, but I'm no match for the breeze that insists on playing with her long strands. "Is that too much to ask for?"

She shakes her head and smiles, leaving me speechless. *Damn.* I didn't think she could get any more beautiful, and then she fucking smiled. This is a fucking disaster — I wasn't supposed to be so captivated by my future wife. "Not at all. Let's play, but with a slight twist. For every truth question asked, we both have to answer."

I nod, entirely caught off-guard by her. I hadn't even planned to speak to her tonight, and never in a million years would I have expected her to physically crash into me the way she did. This isn't how I thought this night would go, but I'd be foolish if I let this opportunity slip.

"You've got yourself a deal. So, tell me, Raya. Truth or dare?"

She studies my face for a moment, and trepidation seeps into me. Does she recognize me, even with the mask? Perhaps I should've given her a fake name, after all. Considering her background and education, it won't be hard for her to figure out who I am. I'm not in the media as frequently as my siblings, but I haven't been able to evade them entirely either.

"Truth."

I grin and step closer to her, until her chest brushes against me. Her eyes widen, and my heart begins to beat a little faster as I place my hand on her lower back before leaning in. "Are you truly single, Raya? Your friend has been glaring at me from the moment he noticed us holding hands, and I'm not too sure what to think of it."

She raises a brow and glances over her shoulder to find the guy in question staring at us. He seems startled when she catches him looking and shoots her a hesitant smile. Pure fucking delight rushes through me when she places her hand on my chest and slides it up until she has it wrapped around the back of my neck, before turning back to face me.

Possessiveness and desire grip me hard and fast as she rises to her tiptoes to talk into my ear, her voice barely carrying over the noise in the bar, completely catching me by surprise. "Adam and I have been friends since elementary school. We're really close, but nothing is going on between us, and nothing ever has. I'm as single as can be."

My shoulders relax, my own reaction surprising me. Whether or not she has feelings for someone else shouldn't matter, yet the thought of my wife pining over someone else aggravates me like nothing else has in quite some time.

"Your turn, Lex. Are you single?"

I hesitate for a moment, my conscience weighing heavy on

me. I hadn't expected to speak to her just yet, hadn't planned to spin a web of lies. "There's no one but you, Raya."

My response makes her laugh, and the way her head falls back as her nose crinkles in the cutest way just has me mesmerized, much to my absolute horror. "You're such a flirt," she says, her eyes twinkling. "I can't even tell if you're being serious or not, yet somehow I'm inclined to believe you, despite how hard that might be."

I raise a brow and wrap my hands around her waist, irritated by my need to touch her, to keep her close. "Why would that be hard to believe?"

Her gaze roams over my body leisurely, and just like that, my cock hardens. Her breath hitches when she feels it, and the way she blushes does something to me — fills me with satisfaction I hadn't expected to feel.

"Never mind," she says, shaking her head, her cheeks crimson. "My turn. Truth or dare?"

I tighten my grip on her, enthralled. It's been years since I felt so alive, since I've done anything spontaneous at all. Every single thing I do is carefully planned — the time I wake up, the route I take to work, and especially the people I come into contact with. So how the fuck did I find myself in a crowded bar, playing games with a woman whose name I shouldn't even know?

"Truth."

What would happen if she asked me a question that would force me to explain why I'm here, and that us meeting isn't as coincidental as it might seem? I'd planned to assess how she behaves when she doesn't think people are watching — the way she treats servers, the way she handles herself. I was never supposed to do more than that, but I can't disentangle myself from her either.

"Tell me a secret no one else knows," she says, looking positively gleeful. Her entire face is lit up with excitement, almost like she's certain she's asked me a tough question, and it's so fucking adorable. I expected a schemer, an opportunist, but there's nothing but innocence and sincerity in her eyes.

"A secret, huh? How about this one: I'm wondering what you'd look like in a RWC wedding gown — an authentic one."

She laughs again, and that's when I know I'm *fucked*. This feels like more than mere attraction — it's real chemistry and a connection, something I avoid at all costs.

Her hands slide to my shoulders, and she holds on tightly as she leans back a little, her eyes narrowed playfully. "If you're not going to take this seriously, I don't want to play," she says, pouting just slightly. "I'm not answering, since you didn't give me a real truth."

Fuck. I bite down on my lip and silently plead with my cock to calm the fuck down, but it's a futile effort. Seeing her looking up at me with those big brown eyes and those sexy pouty lips is wreaking havoc on my mind.

"I *am* taking this seriously," I promise, my tone soft, gentle. With each passing second, more of my wariness melts away, and I'm not sure I like it. History has proven that I'm not the best judge of character, after all. "My turn," I tell her, feeling conflicted. "Truth or Dare?"

Her cheeks are flushed as she looks into my eyes, seemingly gathering her courage before she says, "Dare."

Impulsiveness drowns out reason as I raise a hand to her face and push her hair behind her ear. "Dance with me, Raya. I dare you to."

The way she smiles makes a crack appear in the icy fortress that surrounds my heart, and I'm concerned it's but the first of many. I never wanted to feel this way again, yet I can't help myself as I pull her closer, one hand threading through her hair. "Damn it," I groan, something akin to helplessness rushing through me. "Why do you fit against me so perfectly?"

She giggles and wraps her arms around my neck, her perfume invading my senses. She smells like honey and flowers — fucking delicious. Raya moves her body against mine, and *fuck*. I've never found dancing particularly erotic, but it is when it's with her. I've never experienced anything like this — being in a crowded room with someone yet feeling like we're the only ones here. Raya has me under some kind of spell, I'm sure of it.

"My turn," she says, rising to her tiptoes to speak into my ear. Her breath feels hot against my skin, and I tighten my grip on her, my hips involuntarily pushing into her. "Truth or dare?"

"Dare," I'm quick to say. I've lost count of the amount of rounds we've played, and against my better judgment, I hope she has too. Six doesn't seem like nearly enough anymore.

Raya grins up at me mischievously, looking so fucking adorable that I just know I won't be able to deny whatever request is about to leave those sexy lips. "Lift me up like they do in *Dirty Dancing*. It's my mom's favorite movie, and I know it's crazy, but I've always wanted to do that particular move." Her words are spoken in a rush, her eyes trailing down to my arms appreciatively. "You look like you might actually be able to do it."

Once again, she makes me grin in a far more genuine way than I'm used to. "Testing me, are you?" I ask as I grab her hips, loving the feel of her. "Joke's on you, Raya. I have a romance obsessed little sister who happens to love that movie. Though it's been years, this isn't the first time I've been told to perform this move. You are, however, far nicer about it than that little tyrant ever was."

She gasps when I tighten my grip on her and lift her up effortlessly, not even asking her to run up to me so I can use the momentum to perform the move the way it's supposed to be. Raya giggles when I have her up in the air and spin her around slowly, our eyes on each other the entire time. She has no idea that my security team cleared most of the floor around us, allowing us to move freely.

Her face is lit up with joy when I carefully tilt her body back down, holding her up against me with my arms pressed against the back of her thighs. "I can't believe this," she says, her eyes wide with giddiness. *Fuck*, she's so fucking adorable. Everything about her seems so genuine, but it's near impossible to suppress that little voice in my head that warns me this must be an act she's putting on.

Raya's hands wrap around my shoulders as I slowly slide her down my body, enjoying the feel of her against me. She looks up at me when her feet hit the ground, and I smile back at her as I hold her close, keeping my arms around her. "It's my turn, isn't it? Truth or dare, Raya?"

She looks into my eyes, and the way she gives me her full attention is fucking intoxicating. This isn't good at all — I wasn't supposed to be so taken with her after one single meeting. "Dare."

Her fingers brush over the back of my neck, making my heart race. I'm high on her, not thinking clearly — that must be why the following words leave my lips. "I want to dance with you somewhere in private, Raya. I dare you to go somewhere a little quieter with me, some place where we don't struggle to hear each other's words."

For a moment, I'm certain she'll tell me no, but then she gives me the slightest little nod, and relief washes over me even as doubt continues to creep in. I shouldn't be doing this, but I can't make myself pull back either.

Five

Lexington

Raya's smile dims when I hold open the passenger door to my car, and unease runs down my spine when I walk around the car to join her. Raya's gaze roams over the interior inquisitively as she puts on her seatbelt, and when she looks at me, her dark eyes are filled with confusion.

"This is a WM Diana, and it's customized," she says, her tone cautious. "Customizations like these aren't offered for this car."

Her tone is sharp, accusatory. Something shifts in her body language, and she wraps her arms around herself defensively, the gears in her mind clearly turning.

What was I thinking, leaving with her? I *wasn't*, and that's the problem. I should've called it a night and gone home, my identity safe and my curiosity satisfied. Instead, I complicated this situation beyond measure.

"How do you know that?" I ask as I start my car and put it in self-drive mode, not bothering to hide my surprise. Very few people would've noticed the subtle customizations — the slightly different shade of cream leather that isn't offered normally, the convertible roof that's built in so well it's barely changed the interior. Her eyes pause on each little tweak I made, and unease washes over me. Did she figure out who I am?

Raya looks into my eyes, her gaze hard. "I just happen to know a lot about cars," she says, her voice soft. "Electric cars specifically."

I smile wryly. "And here I thought you couldn't get more perfect," I tell her, feigning ignorance, like I don't have a file at home detailing every little thing about her, right down to her penchant for forsaking going out in favor of helping her father in his lab. I'm well aware how much she knows about cars, but I'm surprised how much she knows about *this* specific one. Her knowledge about my work makes me uneasy, suspicious.

She turns to look out the window, her chest rising and falling a little faster than before. "Maybe this isn't a good idea," she says, her voice faltering. "I don't really know you, and I've never done anything like this before. I'm not sure... I don't think... this probably isn't safe."

I frown, unsure what to make of that look in her eyes. I can't tell if she's pretending not to realize who I am, or if she's genuinely concerned. I hesitate for a moment before grabbing my wallet and handing it to her, curious to see whether this is all an act.

She stares at it in confusion, and I smile tightly. "My ID, bank cards, and several other forms of identification are in there," I tell her, my voice soft. "You're welcome to send that to your friends so they know who you're with, but if you prefer, I can just take you home. I have no intention of doing anything that'd make you feel uncomfortable, Raya. I just want to spend a little more time with you. Maybe play a few more rounds of Truth or Dare, uncover a secret or two."

She stares at my wallet, and resignation washes over me. My surname always changes everything, turns the purest of people into opportunists. If she truly doesn't realize who I am, this'll change everything.

Raya flips my wallet open, and my eyes run over her face. A small part of me silently begs her not to disappoint me as I carefully scrutinize her expression. I'd like to think that my grandmother vetted her thoroughly, but a person's character is hard to judge from a distance. It's why I'm here with her now, trying to get a glimpse of the real her before it's too late.

"*Lexington Windsor*," she reads out, her face blanching. When she glances back at me, her eyes are wide with genuine shock, and I exhale shakily, relief warring with resentment. I hate that I feel the need to do this at all, but I suppose this'll be a good opportunity to see if she'll treat me any differently.

Her gaze darts between the picture on my driver's license and me, almost like she's verifying it truly is me. "Oh God, I guess that shirt is real after all," she whispers, sounding horrified.

My eyes widen in surprise, and her embarrassed expression evokes a startled laugh. "It's not funny, Lex," she says, her cheeks bright red. Raya turns in her seat and grabs my hand, entwining our fingers before bringing our joined hands to her chest. "I'm begging you — don't tell Raven about this. Do you have any idea how embarrassed I am? I accused a *Windsor* of wearing fake Raven Windsor Couture!"

My laughter turns into the deep and uncontrollable kind, the kind I haven't experienced in years. Amusement mixes with relief, and my heart swells. The way she's looking at me hasn't changed, and the connection I felt is still there. My identity hasn't changed anything between us, like I thought it would. It's just made her look a little more at ease, like knowing who I am truly did provide the safety she'd been looking for. Raya Lewis... she's unlike anything I'd expected, and I'm not quite sure what to do with that. It's not often I find myself surprised.

"*Fine*," I tell her, barely able to suppress my smile. "I won't tell her, but there's a price to be paid for my silence." Raya looks into my eyes, her embarrassment making way for intrigue. "If you want me to keep quiet, you'll have to seal my lips."

Her gaze drops to my mouth, and my breath hitches. "And how do I do that?" she asks, her gaze growing darker.

I tighten my grip on her hand and bring it to my chest as I lean in to whisper in her ear. "You know how, my little fairy."

She draws a shaky breath and turns her face, her nose brushing against my cheek. My eyes fall closed when she presses the sweetest, softest kiss to my cheek, and something odd happens to me. My stomach does a strange fluttery thing, and though I know it isn't physically possible, I'm *certain* my heart skips a beat.

She pulls away with a blush staining her cheeks a pretty pink, and I just stare at her wide-eyed, my heart racing. Raya bites down on her lip, and it takes all of me not to kiss her right here and now.

It's been so long since I've been lost in the moment, since I've done something that wasn't perfectly thought out. I'm not even sure what I'm doing anymore — things were never meant to escalate like this, but I can't make myself stop either.

My fingers slip between hers moments before my car comes to a stop, and I look into her eyes, searching for the slightest hint of reluctance but finding none. Instead, my beautiful fairy smiles at me, her cheeks flushed. I can't help but grin back as I raise our joined hands to my lips and kiss the back of her hand before helping her out the car.

Six

Raya

"Truth or Dare?" Lex asks as we walk into the Windsor Residences building, his grip on my hand firm, reassuring.

I glance at him, unable to steady my nerves. I'd been so shocked when I realized who he is that I didn't ask him where we were going. "Truth."

He looks at me, his gaze tinged with concern. "Tell me what's on your mind right now. You're suddenly very quiet, and I'm concerned you're uncomfortable."

I shake my head and squeeze his hand. "I'm honestly just trying not to overthink things. I'm really good at that, you know. Overthinking."

I hesitate as we walk past a set of elevators, toward one that has a security guard standing next to it. The man nods at us both and presses the button for us. "It's just a little surreal to be standing here with you," I admit as we step into the elevator. "I've studied your company extensively, and the fact that I didn't instantly recognize you makes me feel so dumb."

He stares at me, almost like he can't quite figure me out, when there truly isn't much *to* figure out. "Raya," he says, his voice soft. "I'm glad you didn't recognize me. When you look at me, I don't want you to see the CEO of Windsor Motors. I just want you to see *me.*"

I nod in understanding, but it doesn't take away any of my awkwardness. Lex grins as the doors open right into his penthouse, and he guides me into his home.

"Wow," I whisper, surprised to find so many family photos on the walls in the hallway. Somehow, I hadn't expected his place to actually look like a real home.

My fingers trail over the photo frames on the wall, and I try my hardest not to fangirl over the women in all of Lex's family photos, most of them taken at weddings and family gatherings.

There's one with Raven herself, at what appears to be her wedding. Very little is known about her wedding, and only a handful of photos were ever published by the papers since the press wasn't even aware of her highly secretive ceremony. It feels like an intrusion to look at the photo, but the way Lex and Raven smile at each other is captivating.

Right next to it is a photo of Lex with Valentina Windsor — another one of his sisters-in-law, Luca Windsor's wife. This photo was clearly taken on the day she became the COO of Windsor Finance, and the pride in Lex's eyes is enough to make my heart skip a beat.

I know Valentina used to be Luca's secretary, and when it was revealed that the two had gotten married secretly, the media went wild for a while. They'd made Valentina seem like some kind of gold digger, and the Windsor family very swiftly and ruthlessly had several papers shut down entirely as a result. The Windsors always seemed like such an unattainable family, and to be standing in one of their homes now is beyond surreal.

"You have more photos with your sisters-in-law than your brothers," I note bemusedly as Lex leads me further along the hallway slowly, as though to give me sufficient time to explore, his hand in mine.

"They're the ones that keep our family running. They keep us together," he says, clear reverence in his voice. "Each and every one of those women truly have become sisters to me, and I'm not sure I could see our lives without them anymore. They saved me, and they don't even know it."

He smiles to himself as we pause by a picture that was taken in the cockpit of a plane. "That's Faye," Lex tells me, pointing out the redhead in the photo — like I wouldn't recognize one of the most famous pianists in the world. I nod nonetheless, scared he'll think I'm some kind of weird groupie if I react any other way. "And that's my brother, Dion, who has feared flying for years but voluntarily stepped onto countless planes because Faye loves to travel. He even made me fly commercial planes for her one summer and trembled every second of every journey but suffered through nonetheless, all without her knowing, simply because he was worried about her safety as she explored the world."

He looks at me then, his gaze contemplative, almost like he's trying to assess my reaction to his words, to the photos. "That's what my family does — we love fiercely, and there's nothing we won't do for those we love. I'd never let anyone hurt them."

His voice is soft, but there's an edge to his tone, a quiet warning accompanied by a deep loneliness in his eyes, something I'm sure he never meant to let slip. I can't imagine being a Windsor — constantly having to be on the defensive and aware of your surroundings lest someone capture a vulnerable moment and sells it for a profit. Shame hits me hard and fast when I realize that I'm one of the people that added to Lex's torment by reading the articles about his family like they were entertainment, when they're real people that never asked for the media's attention.

"Come on," he says, entwining our fingers. "You can get all starry-eyed over them in person at some point. For now, there's something else I want to show you."

My lips part in surprise, but my denial dies on my tongue as he chuckles and pulls me into the living room, where we both pause for a moment to take in the beautiful skyline and the dazzling skyscrapers that light it up.

We both stare out the floor-to-ceiling windows speechlessly, lost in the moment. "I wasn't all starry-eyed," I murmur eventually, sounding far more petulant than I'd meant to. The last thing I want is for him to feel like I'm after him for who he is, like he clearly fears.

Lex turns to face me and places his index finger under my chin, his gaze keeping me enthralled. Something passes between us, something that makes my heart race. He bites down on his lip, and heat rushes to my cheeks. This man... he's so effortlessly sexy, and I suspect he knows it.

"Oh yeah?" he murmurs. "Yet somehow, your eyes keep me far more captivated than the starry skies above us ever could. I'm not sure I like how easily you've put me under your spell."

It's odd, because I'd have mocked any other guy for those same words, yet when he says it, it all sounds so sincere. He almost sounds pained, like I'm an enigma he can't figure out, when there's no puzzle he hasn't solved.

Lex's hand slips into mine, and he looks over his shoulder as he pulls me along to his open plan kitchen. It's like he can't keep his eyes off me for more than a few seconds, and I've never experienced anyone being quite so *present* with me.

"Wine?" he asks as he holds up a bottle that looks incredibly expensive. He opens it before I have a chance to tell him to save it for a special occasion.

"I'd love some," I answer, my voice soft. Something about being here with him is throwing me off, and I can't quite tell why. I'm feeling more vulnerable than usual, and the way he keeps making my heart race is unprecedented. No one has ever made me feel this way, and I can't determine what it is about him that captivates me so.

Oddly enough, I was disappointed when I realized who he was, because I instantly realized that these moments we're spending together won't last. Lexington Windsor is someone whose work I've admired for years, but *Lex*... he seems like an entirely different person, someone that's within reach, even if it's only for an evening. It's ironic how tonight's fairytale theme seems to have extended beyond the bar. This night will end, and the magic will disappear.

Lex pours me a glass and pushes it towards me before raising his own. "To spilled shots, truths, dares, and the way they brought us together."

I tap my glass against his and smile, surprised and entirely delighted by his words. "To honesty, bravery, and serendipity," I murmur.

Lex's expression falls briefly, and I can't quite figure out what I said wrong. "Speaking of shots," he says, glancing down at his white shirt and the blue stains on it. He undoes the top button before looking up at me from lowered lashes, mischief written all over his face. "I need to throw this in the wash before it stains permanently. Honestly, it's pretty sticky too. It might actually be too sticky for me to get off all by myself... I may need your help."

I bite down on my lip to suppress my smile when he grabs my hand and places it over his chest. His heart is racing underneath my palm, and somehow, the feel of it is soothing — it's reassuring to know he feels this thing between us too.

"Help?" I repeat, a soft giggle escaping my lips. "Like this?" I ask, as I undo a button slowly, loving the way his breath hitches. Something about him makes me act far bolder than I ever have before. He makes me feel comfortable despite my nerves, and I'm not quite sure how he's managing what no one else ever has before.

"Yeah," he whispers, his chest rising and falling rapidly as I continue to unbutton his shirt. He leans back against the kitchen counter, his gaze burning, and heat spreads from my cheeks to my entire body as his chest and abs come into view. My fingertips trail over his skin teasingly, and his abs contract underneath my touch, sending a little thrill down my spine.

"Raya," he groans, sounding pained.

My stomach flutters, and I throw him a shaky smile as I grab his shirt and slide it off his shoulders. He's breathing hard, and the way he looks at me is so empowering — like there's no one in the world but me.

"Your turn," I whisper. "Truth or Dare?"

He grins, looking devastatingly handsome as he leans back against his kitchen counter, my hands still on his shirt. His gaze roams over my face, and he seems to contemplate something for a moment, before shooting me the sweetest smile. "Dare."

Seven

Lexington

"Dance with me," she whispers, her eyes filled with something that has me breathing a little harder, my heart beating a little wilder. "I dare you to dance with me, Lex."

I grin at her and shrug out of my shirt fully before reaching for my phone. Raya's eyes widen just a touch as music begins to play, and she smiles when I offer her my hand. The way she can't quite keep her eyes off my bare chest makes me feel like I'm on top of the world, and for once, I cast aside my usual desire for control, opting for spontaneity instead. It's the first time in years I've done anything like this, and I forgot how good it can feel to let go, to see where the night takes us without fixed plans to guide us.

I've watched her all night, and I haven't noticed even the slightest hint of insincerity. She doesn't seem impressed with the splendor of my penthouse as much as the view and my *abs*, and fuck if it doesn't give me hope. If she truly is who she's pretending to be, she's my every dream come true.

Raya's free hand slides up my chest and around the back of my neck, and I pull her closer, falling into step with her. She grins when I raise a brow, impressed by her footwork. "You know how to dance the foxtrot?"

She tilts her head in a cutesy way, a sheepish smile on her face. "It's because of my parents," she tells me. "It's their dance, and when I was younger, my dad spent countless afternoons getting his toes stomped on as he taught me the steps."

My heart races as we turn, dancing through my penthouse, perfectly in sync. We're not leaning back like we're supposed to, nor are our arm placements correct, but our steps are perfectly aligned. Our version is more intimate, more romantic. "I'd better make sure I remember to thank your father for his grand sacrifice someday," I tell her, smiling, even as a pang of longing settles deep in my chest. I had my grandfather, and I'll always be grateful he was there for me, but I'd give the world for an opportunity to make memories with my parents. Would they dance together the way Raya tells me her parents do? I'd like to think so.

Raya tilts her head to the side just a touch — a move I've come to associate with her not taking me seriously and thinking I'm just being flirtatious. If only she knew I meant every word.

Her hair sways as we turn, and *fuck*. Her face is lit up by the moonlight shining in through the window, and the way she looks up at me with that look in her eyes... surreal. "You're beautiful, Raya. Fucking breathtaking." The words leave my lips without conscious thought, needing to be said, my will be damned. Every minute I spend with her just makes my resolve weaken more. I was supposed to figure her out so I could stay ten steps ahead of her, but fuck, she's got me dancing around in circles with a smile on my face.

Raya blushes and misses a step, her eyes wide. I smile and pull her closer, the two of us coming to a standstill in my living room. I've never felt quite this flustered. With each passing second, I second-guess myself more. Will this all fall apart when she realizes that me running into her wasn't a coincidence? The way she toasted to *honesty*, instead of truths or dares, wasn't lost on me.

I cup her face with my free hand, tipping her head up towards mine. God, I hope my intuition is right this time. I hope this is all as real as I think it is. Please, don't let this become another moment I'll regret, another occasion when indulging in spontaneity ends up costing me.

Raya draws a shaky breath, her gaze roaming over my face, like she's trying to assess my sincerity. Her eyes pause on my lips, and she tilts her face just a little, the same need I'm feeling mirrored in her eyes.

My thumb brushes over the edge of her mouth, and her eyes flutter closed. "Can I kiss you, Raya?" My voice is soft, pleading. I don't recall the last time I felt this way. I don't think I've ever felt this desperate for a mere kiss. I shouldn't be doing this, shouldn't let myself be swayed by the mood tonight or the chemistry between us...but fuck, I'm desperate for her.

She looks up at me from lowered lashes, her breath hitching as she nods. "I dare you to," my future wife whispers.

I tighten my grip on her as my lips brush against hers, once, twice, carefully. *Fuck*. She tastes like honey — my favorite. I groan as I pull back for a split second, only for my lips to come crashing down against hers harder. She responds in kind, her hand threading through my hair as she kisses me back.

Raya moans when I part her lips, my tongue teasing her as I deepen our kiss. She rises to her tiptoes, and desire grips me hard and fast when she moves her body against mine. My hands run down her waist, betraying my need, and another moan escapes her lips when she feels how hard my cock is against her.

My hand dips lower down her back, impatient in its pursuit for more. Her curves are perfectly soft, and fuck, I wish her dress wasn't in the way. Raya gasps when I grab her hips and lift her into my arms. Her legs wrap around me instantly, her dress riding up in the process, and I push her up against the window. We both moan the moment my cock settles between her thighs, the grinding movement intoxicating even through the layers still separating us.

My forehead drops to hers, and I draw a shaky breath, willing myself to take it slow with her. I pull back a fraction to look at her, rooted in place by the look in her eyes. It hits me hard, that feeling of pure intoxication. "You make me feel entirely out of control, Raya. I swear this isn't what I had in mind when I asked you to leave with me. I don't want you to think there's only one thing I'm after, but *fuck*, baby, I can't tear myself away from you."

She cups my cheek and looks into my eyes, her gaze searching. "Maybe I'm foolish for believing you, but I do." Her thumb brushes over my mouth, her breath coming out in little pants. "You do the same thing to me, you know? You make me throw caution to the wind, all for just another kiss."

The way she looks at me makes it near impossible to resist pulling her in for one more kiss, yet somehow, I find it in me to lower her to the floor. I've already overcomplicated things endlessly by approaching her under false pretenses, I can't let things go any further. Tonight was meant to tell me whether or not she was a good person, but every second with her snowballs into another, creating a chain of events I can't extricate myself from. I'm not even sure I want to.

I offer her my hand, and she takes it, her fingers entwining with mine as I lead her back to the kitchen, where our wine glasses are waiting for us. "I forgot whose turn it is," Raya says, squeezing my hand. "But I think it's mine."

I chuckle, my heart warming when I take in her cute expression. "Truth, my little fairy. I'll go with Truth this time."

She reaches for her wine glass and leans back against the kitchen counter, her gaze roaming over my bare chest hungrily. "I'll go easy on you," she says, her voice husky. "Tell me your favorite color."

Her gaze settles on my Adonis belt, and her eyes trace the V shape of it leisurely, her cheeks rosy and her hair messier than before. She looks so fucking sexy, and for a moment, I find myself imagining what she'll look like in my bed.

"Yellow."

Her eyes snap to mine, the surprise in them oddly endearing.

Her face is so expressive, and I love being able to read her thoughts and emotions. With each moment we spend together, more of my doubts melt away. "No way! Mine too!"

I chuckle and reach for her, gently pushing her hair out of her face. "Seems like we're perfect together," I tell her, my tone light. In the back of my mind, alarm bells are going off, reminding me that the web of lies I'm spinning continues to become more elaborate by the second. Acting on impulse has never worked out well for me, yet that's all I've done with her from the second she crashed into my life.

"Your turn, Raya. Truth or dare?"

"Truth," she says as she takes a sip of wine. Her eyes find mine, and there's something so intimate about the way she tries to read me, the way I don't mind it when I'm so accustomed to hiding my emotions behind a carefully crafted facade. I just hope I don't come to regret opening up to her. I'm not even sure why I'm doing it, why I'm allowing her to see parts of me I've never shown anyone else.

"Tell me, my sweet little fairy. What did you want to be when you were little?"

She smiles, her gaze wistful. "My family actually runs an automotive company too, and I always knew I'd end up following in my father's footsteps. I remember the day I decided that I wanted to be an engineer vividly."

My heart skips a beat when she smiles, her gaze overflowing with affection. "I'd just found out that I wouldn't be able to drive the cars my dad let me help him build until I turned sixteen, and to my six-year-old self, that'd seemed like an eternity. I think that was the first time I experienced real heartbreak, Lex."

I chuckle, my heart warming as I'm enraptured by the animated way she tells me her story, the way her eyes widen as the pitch of her voice rises. "It's not funny," she says, pouting. "Even back then, I was convinced I wouldn't be able to fully understand cars until I was able to drive one, and it threw a wrench in my plans to become a genius car designer. I had it all planned out, you see. I was going to create a whole collection of princess cars because I felt like there weren't enough pretty pink cars."

I brush her hair out of her face and bite back a smile. I bet that even then, she'd have been fucking adorable. "So, what happened?"

She grabs my arms, her smile so wide that I can't help but smile in return. "You will *not* believe this. I'd been lethargic for weeks, until one day, Dad took me to his company after school. He told me he had a surprise for me, and when we walked into his worksite, there was a little platform, identical to the ones he uses for his prototypes. On it stood the most beautiful glittery pink car I'd ever seen — it was a perfect replica of my dad's own car, in my favorite color."

She sighs, the stars in her eyes shimmering with admiration for a man I'm reluctant to meet. Bob Lewis's background check wasn't quite as clean as Raya's, and I'm not sure what to make of the man. "I knew right there and then that I wanted to follow in my father's footsteps. I just didn't know how hard it would be to fill his shoes."

I cup her cheek gently and lean in the press a soft kiss to her forehead. "If anyone can do it, it's you, Raya. I have no doubt."

The way she looks at me makes my heart race, and we both smile. "What about you? What did you want to be when you were younger?"

I rock back on my heels, enjoying the way her gaze roams down my body as I do so. She inhales sharply when she sees how hard I still am, my pants doing nothing to hide my erection. Her cheeks turn so beautifully rosy, and I smirk, loving that look in her eyes.

"I'm not sure, you know? I always wanted to be an engineer, just like my grandfather. Unlike my older brothers, I don't have all that many memories with my parents. My hero was my grandfather."

My chest tightens at the memory of him, and I lower my gaze, my eyes brushing over the watch he gave me just a few days before

I lost him. "He was incredible, and growing up, I wanted to be just like him. I'd sit next to him as he designed and built toys for each of my siblings and me, and he never tired of answering my questions. He'd let me help, and to this day, it's the knowledge he imparted that I still rely on most. I miss him each and every day, and every once in a while, I find myself talking to him out loud as I'm designing something, wondering what he'd do or what advise he'd give me. I do it even though I know he isn't there to hear me."

I wonder what he'd think of Raya. He'd often joke with me, telling me he already had someone in mind for me to marry someday. Even when I was little, I'd known I wouldn't choose my own partner, and I never should've tried. If I hadn't, Grandpa might still be here with me.

Raya reaches for me and brushes the back of her hand over my cheek, her touch soothing. "He'd be so proud to see you today, Lex. I'm a little reluctant to admit it, but you're kind of a role model to me too. That's why it was so embarrassing for me when I realized who you were, because I really should've recognized you straight away, and it's so silly that I didn't. I've followed your career for some time now, and I've always loved how freely you share your knowledge, even when you know you'll lose your competitive advantage because of it. Each time you publish a paper, I read it *immediately*. Some of your research helped me with something I'm working on, and you just... you have no idea how much of an impact you make."

Her words humble me, and I'm not quite sure what to say. "It's something my grandfather taught me," I end up muttering. "Technological advances mustn't be hoarded; they must be shared for the betterment of society as a whole. Grandpa believed that competition leads to further innovation, and I firmly agree with him."

"He sounds incredible," she says, her tone reverent.

"He was," I agree, pulling her in for a hug. I haven't been able to talk about my parents or my grandfather in years, and she has no idea how difficult it is for me to do so now. I'm not even sure how she was able to make me open up like that, when no one else can.

Raya rises to her tiptoes and hugs me tightly, and it hits me then — when was the last time anyone hugged me like that? I draw a shaky breath as I tangle my hand in her hair and tilt my face, needing more.

"Raya," I whisper, pulling back a little to look at her. She reads me with ease and leans in to kiss me. This kiss is different to the ones that came before it. It's filled with consolation and incredible sweetness that I can't quite get enough of.

"My turn," she whispers against my lips, before leaning in for another kiss. "Choose Dare, Lex."

I smile in between kisses, surprisingly happy to obey my future wife.

Eight

Lexington

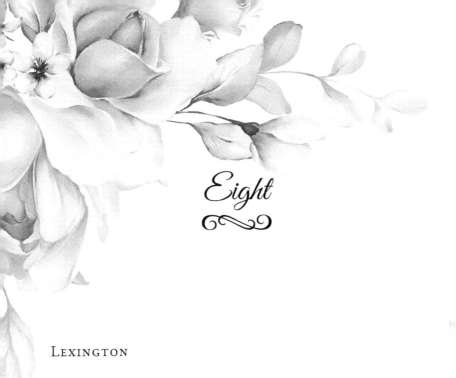

"What's got you smiling that way?" Raya asks, her index finger tracing a line between my brows and down, to the tip of my nose.

At some point in the night, we moved to my sofa and opened another bottle of wine, playing endless rounds of truth and dare, never running out of things to talk about.

Spending time with her is like nothing I've ever experienced before — it's effortless, and somehow, she makes my thoughts still. For the first time in years, I don't feel on edge around someone who's essentially a perfect stranger. I didn't think any woman would ever be able to make me lower my guard again, but in a matter of hours, she has.

"*You*," I murmur, pulling her closer, until I've got her seated in my lap. "I'm genuinely just having a great time with you."

I cup her face, my heart racing. Should I just tell her the truth? Or is it too late for that now? I've never felt more conflicted than I do right now. Fear of all different kinds tugs at me — fear she truly is just a great actress, and I'm letting her fool me with surprising ease. Fear that she's innocent, and my actions tonight will set us up for failure from the very start.

Raya's forehead drops to mine, and then her face dips lower, her lips finding mine. Just like that, every thought fades away. This kiss is slow, explorative, and I take my time parting her lips, tasting, nipping. She moans softly, the sound rushing straight to my cock. She's had me turned on all night, each kiss driving me a little closer to the edge. It's torture to be around her, that honey scent of her invading my senses.

I turn us over, and she falls backwards on the sofa, her hair spread all around her beautifully. That expression when she looks up at me from lowered lashes… fucking enchanting.

I cover her body with mine, and her fingers slide through my hair before she grips it and pulls me in for another kiss. I groan as she moves underneath me, rocking her hips in a needy way I just can't resist. "Fuck, Raya." Even her name sounds perfect, whispered between our lips. "Do you have any idea what you're doing to me?"

I push up against her, making her feel just how hard she's made me, and a soft moan escapes her perfect lips. I don't think I've ever experienced just prolonged arousal, wanting someone yet trying my hardest not to let desire guide a conversation. I'm at my breaking point, and I think she is too.

My future wife gasps when I part her legs with my knee, and I chuckle as my hand slides down between us, until I'm gripping her thigh, my thumb brushing over her lace panties.

She's soaking wet, even through the fabric, and it's fucking thrilling to know it's all for me. Her eyes flash with the same desire I'm feeling, and I smirk as I let my finger brush over the fabric again, teasing her. "Can I?"

She bites down on her lip, her expression conflicted. "I… I'm not sure, Lex. No one has ever…"

My eyes widen. "Never?"

She shakes her head, and I smirk as I drag my finger down her soaking panties, loving how wet she is. Every single kiss turned me on more than I've ever been, and I'm so fucking glad it isn't just me.

"Will you let me?" I whisper, my heart racing. "Let me make you come, Raya. I want my name on your lips and my fingers buried deep inside you... nothing more than that."

She blinks, her expression clearing a little. "I... I'm not..." she bites down on her lip and looks away. "I'm not sure."

I study her face, reading her indecision. "Okay, baby," I murmur, pressing a kiss to her cheek.

"I'm sorry," she whispers, her voice trembling.

I pause and push myself up on top of her. "You don't owe me anything, Raya. Least of all an apology."

She glances at me helplessly, insecurity flickering through her gorgeous brown eyes. "I just haven't felt comfortable enough with anyone to do something like that. I thought it'd happen when I went to college, but I haven't seriously dated anyone, so it just... it just didn't happen." She wrings her hands nervously. "I guess you were expecting something different since I left the party with you. I'm not sure why I did that, to be honest. I've never done that before, but I just... I don't know..."

I tense and turn us around so she's straddling me again, her hair falling down the front of her body and her dress bunched around her waist. "Raya, take all the time you need. I'll wait as long as you want me to. To be honest, I was a virgin until college too, so I get it. I found it really hard to trust anyone, and I constantly feared that the story of me losing my virginity would end up in the tabloids." If only that had been the worst thing that could've happened. "I was sure I'd suck at the whole sex thing and whoever I slept with would go on to do an interview with some dumb tabloid, like The Herald."

Raya's eyes widen in surprise, her mood lifting. "I can't even imagine having the media watch my every move. There are many parts of your life I envy, but that isn't one of them."

I cup her face, my heart heavy as my thumb brushes her lips. I wish I could protect her from that kind of scrutiny, but the second the media finds out about her, they'll dig up every last detail they can find. "It isn't easy, but on the flip side, it allows us to do so much good. Whenever we can, we try to divert the publicity towards our charities or our businesses."

She nods, her gaze roaming down my chest and abs leisurely. Fuck, I'd give the world to have her ride me just like this. Someday... hopefully someday soon.

"Tell me, are there things you've never done?" she asks. "Not sexually, per se. Just things you might not have found the right person for?"

"So many things. There are a lot of things that I'm reserving for my wife, and no one else."

Her gorgeous brown eyes twinkle with curiosity. "Like what?"

"My home, for starters. I've never brought a woman to my home on the Windsor Estate. The same goes for my company — I've never brought a woman into my office, my worksites, or my labs. Then there are more specific little things. I've never cooked for anyone but my family, and I haven't ever let a woman drive my cars."

Raya grabs my hands and entwines our fingers as she lifts our joined hands to her face. "A meal cooked by Lexington Windsor..." She kisses my knuckles, and my heart begins to race. "I have a feeling you'd look really sexy standing behind a stove."

I thread a hand through her hair and pull her down for a kiss. "What's your favorite food, Raya?"

She laughs, the sound warming my heart. "Definitely my mom's lamb biryani."

"I guess I'd better learn how to cook that then," I murmur against her lips. "Do you think she'd be willing to teach me?"

She giggles, not realizing that I'm dead serious. I always thought I'd hate being forced into an arranged marriage, that I'd resent my wife.

Until I met Raya Lewis.

"I've heard the rumors about you being a massive flirt, but

experiencing it myself is something else altogether," she says, her tone playful.

My stomach turns, and I look away, bitterness washing over me. "I haven't dated anyone in years, Raya. The press loves to report absolute bullshit about my family. Just because it's in the papers doesn't mean it's true."

Her gaze roams over my face, searching. "Then give me another Truth, and I'll trade you a Dare."

I raise a brow, intrigued by the curiosity in her eyes. "What is it you want to know?"

She hesitates, nibbling on her lip for one second, and then another, the silence stretching between us. "Tell me why you haven't dated anyone in so long."

I tense involuntarily, unsure how to answer her. "I prefer logic and reason. Realistically, being in love is just a chemical reaction, one that impairs your judgement. I have no interest in it, and thus, I have no interest in dating anyone."

Her expression falls, and she nods as she forces a smile that seems so genuine I wouldn't have realized how fake it is if I hadn't had the honor of witnessing her real smiles all evening.

"I take it you don't believe in fate or true love, then?"

I huff, my amusement apparent. "Of course not. Surely you don't either?"

"I do," she says, her expression solemn. "It'd be hard to look at my parents and think that's anything but true love. It's what I want for myself someday — a marriage like theirs. I want the jokes, the way they still look at each other, the cute notes they leave hidden around the house, and the weekly dates they still go on. I want more than a marriage that really is just a glorified friendship — I want true love."

I look away, knowing I can never give her that. If I'd never known that I can't be what she needs, would that have made the next few years more bearable?

Nine

Lexington

For the first time in as long as I can remember, I wake up with a smile on my face, Raya's perfume lingering all around me. I wasn't sure what to expect, but I didn't think she would be so easy to talk to. I genuinely enjoyed her company, and the chemistry between us… it was unreal. Neither of us wanted the night to end, and we stayed up late, drinking wine and playing truth or dare, until we couldn't keep our eyes open any longer. I carried her to my bed and kissed her goodnight, and for the first time in years, I fell asleep next to someone.

My eyes flutter open as I reach for Raya as carefully as possible, so I don't wake her up… only to find her side of the bed cold and empty. I sit up in surprise, my gaze roaming around the room in search of her, only to settle on the note left on my nightstand. My heart sinks as I pick it up.

Truth: Last night was amazing, and getting to know you was a little surreal. They say don't meet your heroes, but you surpassed every expectation, every notion of who I thought you were. You're incredible, Lexington Windsor.

Dare: I won't leave you my phone number, Lex. I have no intention of being yet another fling, and realistically, we just live in different worlds. It probably won't happen, but if we ever run into each other again, I dare you to play Truth or Dare with me again. It's the most fun I've had in a very long time, and I don't think I'll ever be able to play this game again without thinking of you.

Love,

Raya

I shake my head as I lift her note to my lips, my eyes falling closed. It even smells like her. I sigh as I fall back onto my pillow, my thoughts racing. She knows who I am and still walked away. Is she scheming and playing an elaborate game that I'm falling for? Very few women would pass up the opportunity to get close to me, and I'm surprised Raya did.

Her background check revealed how involved she is in her father's projects, so there's no way she doesn't know what state his company is in. Surely, she realizes I could help. Why would she walk away when she's perfectly positioned to use me to her advantage?

I stare at my ceiling for a few moments, unsure what to make of her. Is this all an elaborate ruse? I sigh as I reach for my phone, my mind on Raya as I scroll through my list of contacts until I find one of my closest friends. I hesitate for a split second before clicking on Leia Astor's name.

"Lex?"

"Leia, sweetheart. I need a favor."

"No," she replies instantly.

"You're not even going to hear me out?"

She laughs, the sound of her kids playing in the background. "Every time you call me asking for a favor, it's something weird."

I run a hand through my hair and smile. "That's not true, Ley."

"The last time I helped you, you made me automate parts of your latest car, but you conveniently forgot to tell me you'd programmed the whole operating system to say lewd things in your brother's voice."

I bite back my laughter. That was funny as *fuck*. "Wish I'd filmed Luca's face when I demonstrated that. I'm devastated that my brothers wouldn't let me put it in the final car. It would've sold even better if it'd had Luca's voice."

Leia laughs. "To be fair, you aren't wrong. That man's voice is delicious."

"Hey!" I hear from the background. Leia bursts out laughing, and seconds later, I've got her husband on the phone. "*Lexington Windsor,*" he growls. "Let me guess, you're calling to corrupt my wife. What kind of trouble are you two getting into now?"

"Adrian. A pleasure, as always." My tone is entirely in contrast with my words.

He huffs, clearly not amused to speak to me. I love riling him up. He's just like my brothers, completely obsessed with his wife and so easy to mess with. "What do you want?" he barks.

"A favor from *both of you*, actually."

"Absolutely not."

"I'll babysit your kids so Leia and you can have a couple of child-free evenings."

He chuckles. "I have amazing in-laws that love taking care of the kids."

Damn it. "I'll throw in an all-expense paid holiday to any Windsor Hotels resort." He's silent, contemplating. It's near impossible to bribe an Astor — they're as rich as we are. I have to try, though. "Private jet. I'll fly you myself if you want me to."

"He's just messing with you," Leia shouts from a little further away, clearly hearing me over speakerphone. "Just tell me what it is. I can tell you're anxious, Lex. Whatever it is, you know I'll always help you."

I hesitate for a moment. "I want a guest teaching position at Astor College. I'd like to take over the Mechatronics class you teach, Leia."

"That's it?" Adrian asks, his voice dripping with suspicion. He and his family run Astor College, so it won't be difficult for him to grant me this favor, but considering how much I've knowingly annoyed him in the past, I have no doubt he's tempted to say no.

"Yes. Just one semester, one class."

"You got it, Lex," Leia says, causing her husband to groan.

"You're kidding me, right?" he mutters, the sound muffled.

"Don't be petty," Leia whisper-shouts back, and I vow right there and then to stop messing with Adrian Astor. "I'm not sure what you're up to, Lex, but we'll grab drinks soon, and you *will* fill me in. Something is up with you, and I want to know what it is."

I smile to myself, so tempted to tell her all about Raya, but knowing that I shouldn't. Hell, I shouldn't even know about her myself. In the back of my mind, I keep thinking about what Silas said about our engagement not being confirmed yet. The words seem more ominous now than before.

"There's someone I want to learn a little more about, and she's a student at Astor College," I end up admitting, unable to keep much from Leia. "I can't quite figure her out, and I just need to observe her a little longer."

She falls silent, no doubt reminded of the way she fell for her own professor, back when Adrian was her thesis supervisor. "Well.. don't do anything I wouldn't do," she says, moments before her husband bursts out laughing in the background.

Ten

Raya

"You've been absentminded all day," Adam says as we find seats in my most anticipated class of the semester, his gaze roaming over me. "Actually, you've been out of it for a while now, ever since my birthday. You never told me what happened that night." He hesitates, his expression conflicted. "I saw you leave with that guy, you know."

I bite down on my lip nervously as I throw him a furtive glance. I've never kept secrets from Adam, but something about my evening with Lex just feels private, and not just because of who he is.

"Nothing happened," I tell him, my words truthful yet empty. It's silly, really. All we did was kiss and play Truth or Dare while sipping wine. Though only a few weeks have passed since then, I doubt Lex even remembers me. His charisma and the fact that he had a bachelor pad separate from his main residence spoke volumes. I clearly wasn't the first girl he brought there, and I won't be the last. He isn't interested in love, and I'm not foolish enough to believe I'd be an exception.

I meant what I wrote in the note I left him — I'm not interested in a fling, not even with someone like him. I know I can't reform a billionaire playboy, and even if I could, I'm not sure I'd want to. I've always wanted a relationship similar to my parents' marriage; a simple life, the kind you could never have with a Windsor. My night with Lex was incredible, but it was a onetime experience that I have no intention of repeating.

"Then why haven't you been yourself?" Adam asks as we sit down at the very front of the lecture theatre. "Not even sneaking into your father's lab and experimenting with the solar panels has lifted your spirits. It's been weeks, Raya. I'm a little worried about you. Did he do something to you that you didn't consent to?"

My eyes widen at the insinuation, and I turn in my seat. "No, of course not," I deny, my hand wrapping around his biceps.

His shoulders relax, and he nods, seemingly not all that convinced. I suppose I *have* been a little lethargic since that night, but even I'm not quite sure why. I knew exactly what I was doing when I sneaked out of Lex's bed, my decision made, but I just can't stop thinking about him. I kept wondering what might've happened if I'd stayed. If I'd at least left my phone number, would he have wanted to see me again?

I sit up as the doors to the lecture hall swing shut loudly, and my melancholy makes way for excitement. Professor Leia Astor and her husband, Professor Adrian Astor, are the main reasons I chose to study at Astor College. They're different to most other professors and practice what they preach. They frequently consult on high-profile projects, and they're known to bring industry experts such as Aria and Grayson Callahan in for guest lectures.

Not just that, they offer valuable hands-on work experience by way of practical projects throughout their classes, at companies that simply aren't accessible to most, like Sinclair Security and Aequitas. Though I have every intention of following in my father's footsteps, I can't pass up on such valuable work experience. Leia Astor is a true inspiration for women like me. Watching her succeed makes me believe that I can do it too, and learning from her is a true dream come true.

Whispers cascade through the room, following the footsteps I can hear behind me, and I turn to look over my shoulder, only to be met with the same deep green eyes that I haven't stopped thinking about in weeks. My heart stutters, and he pauses mid-step, our eyes locking. *Lex*. What is he doing here, in my classroom? He grins at me, his dimples making an appearance, and then he moves past me.

"Good morning, class. My name is Lexington Windsor." Giggles and murmurs erupt all around me, but I can't tear my eyes off Lex. He's looking right at me, his gaze the same as it was that night. "You may refer to me as Professor Windsor. I'll be taking over this Mechatronics class from Professor Astor for the duration of this semester."

Adam taps my thigh and leans in, breaking the spell I was under. I turn toward him, causing his nose to brush against my cheek. "*Lexington Windsor*? It's him, isn't it? *Lex*."

I nod nervously, unable to deny it.

Adam stares at me wide-eyed for a moment, comprehension dawning. "Fuck. You went home with *Lexington Windsor*?" he whispers. "Did you know he'd be here today?"

I shake my head, my cheeks flushed. "I haven't spoken to him since your birthday. Honestly, I didn't actually realize who he was initially, and once I did, he made it so easy to just stay in the moment with him."

Adam's eyes flash in an unfamiliar way, and he lowers his eyes. "I'm sure he did," he mutters.

"This class will be unlike any other," Lex says, his gaze roaming over the room. His expression is different now, more serious, with a hint of something I can't quite place. Standing there in his three-piece suit, he looks every inch the powerful, unattainable billionaire that I know him to be. "I suggest you take your first assignment seriously, since the top three students in this class will receive internship positions at Windsor Motors. If you do well during your internship, you'll be offered a permanent position upon graduation."

His words leave the room in uproar, understandably so. Windsor Motors doesn't offer internships, and this is unprecedented. Their graduate program is notoriously hard to get into, and thousands of people apply every year from all over the country, when there are never more than twenty available spots.

Unlike other firms, Windsor Motors offers very comprehensive one-on-one mentorship, and Lex is known to personally mentor at least a handful of people every year. Each of his mentees has published groundbreaking research papers with his help, and they've all gone on to create innovative products for Windsor Motors. Working for Lexington Windsor is life changing, and without a doubt, it's one of the biggest dreams of every single person in this room, Adam and I included.

"I can't believe he's *the* Lexington Windsor," Adam murmurs, his voice strained.

I sigh and slump in my seat, a soft pang hitting my chest as I take in the reactions of every single woman in the room. All of a sudden, the evening we spent together seems inconsequential in light of who he is.

"I'll start you off easy," Lex says. "Can someone explain the concept of mechatronics to me?"

Most hands in the room rise at alarming speeds, everyone eager to gain his favor. He glances at me for a moment, before settling his gaze on Adam. "You."

Adam hesitates. "It's essentially designing electromechanical systems, whereby the operations of a system and its housing are designed together to comprise a complete system, rather than one working around the other."

Lex nods. "Any mechatronics specialist needs a comprehensive understanding of technical and electrical engineering, and that's exactly what I'll be testing with your first project. I'd like drone designs from each of you on my desk by next week. You'll then be split into teams to build the top three designs, fully funded by

Windsor Motors. Both design and execution will be judged, so don't worry if your design isn't chosen. Every design will have flaws, and the way you handle those in the implementation process is often just as important as the design itself."

Excitement buzzes through the room, and I watch as a girl seated closer to Lex leans in, her lashes fluttering. I can't hear what she asks him, but the way he smiles at her makes me look away, my heart clenching painfully.

"Fuck," Adam says, his voice soft. "I hate to admit it, but that's an incredible opportunity." I sigh and lean against him. Adam glances at me and turns to wrap his arm around my shoulders. "You okay?" he asks, squeezing.

"Yeah," I murmur, my gaze drifting back to Lex and the girl he's still talking to. "You're right, and we shouldn't let it go to waste," I force myself to say, knowing that it's true. "If anyone can snag up those internships, it's us."

"Is that what you want? I'd be happy to intern at your dad's firm with you, if you prefer that, but I can't deny that this is a once in a lifetime kind of opportunity."

Lex's eyes meet mine for a moment, and he smiles in a polite, friendly way, like he truly is nothing but my professor. I tear my eyes away and take a deep breath. "Yes," I tell Adam, my heart clenching. "Let's try our best and see what happens. I'll end up working for my dad eventually, but I'm not silly enough to pass up on priceless work experience." With only a few months to go until graduation, this opportunity seems more invaluable than ever.

He pulls back a little to look at me, his gaze searching. "All right," he says, the edges of his lips turned up into the slightest smile. "Let's do this then. If anyone can design a product worthy of Lexington Windsor's praise, it's you."

Eleven

Raya

My mind is still on Lexington Windsor as I pull up in front of my parents' house for dinner. I thought he'd stop me after class, but other than the way he looked at me when he walked in, we didn't even interact. It was almost like the night we shared was a lucid dream echoing in my reality, but not his. It's exactly what I should've expected from *Lexington Windsor,* but it isn't what I expected from the guy I've come to think of as *just Lex.* I'm annoyed with myself for being even a little disappointed, when I should know better.

A soft ballad plays through the house as I walk in, and I smile to myself when I hear my father's horrendous singing from the kitchen. I don't even have to step into the room to know what I'll find — Mom and Dad dancing together in the midst of cooking, probably with food stains all over them.

I pause in the doorway when I hear Mom's laughter, taking a moment to just watch them. Seeing them together makes me understand why Dad insists that I create memories and live my life to the fullest. It's what my parents do together each and every day.

Dad twirls Mom around, her red dress swaying as she smiles from ear to ear, her nose crinkling in the cutest way as she looks into his eyes. Similarly, Dad's full attention is on Mom, and he still looks at her the way he did a decade ago. This is why I walked away from Lex, because I'm after this kind of love. Seeing him again today only reinforced my decision, so why am I filled with a touch of bitterness and a heavy dose of disappointment?

The song comes to an end, and Mom leans back in Dad's arms, her smile fading away as they look at each other. "We have to tell Raya what's going on with the company today," she says, her tone suddenly filled with torment. "You know that, right?"

Dad pulls her closer and hugs her tightly. "I can't," he whispers. "I'm not ready, Meera. Everything I built was meant to be hers someday, and now..."

Mom rises to her tiptoes and gently cups Dad's face. "I don't want to, but perhaps we should think about the merger offer. If nothing else, we should discuss it with Raya."

Dad's expression hardens, and he steps away from Mom abruptly. "How could you even entertain the idea of... of—" He turns away from Mom with something that can only be described as a mixture of horror and disgust written all over his face, only to freeze when he notices me standing in the doorway.

"What's going on?" I ask, my voice calmer than I expected it to be. I've known the company is in trouble for months now, and I'd wondered how long it'd take them to tell me. A merger, though? That's news to me.

Dad's face falls when I walk into the room, and I pause, caught off-guard by his somber expression. My father is a formidable man, his presence intimidating to everyone but Mom and me. I've never seen him look the way he does right now — pained, *lost*.

"Raya," Mom says, her voice breaking. "Why don't you sit?" She gestures toward the breakfast bar and sighs. "There's something we need to tell you."

I nod hesitantly, suddenly nervous. Every instinct is telling me to proceed with caution, that the words that are about to spill from my parents' lips are ones I'll wish they never uttered. For so long, I've existed in a state of denial — almost like our financial woes weren't real so long as my parents never formally told me about them.

"Raya," Dad says softly as I sit down, his blue eyes filled with something I've never seen before — trepidation, resignation, and worst of all... guilt. "I can't hide this from you much longer."

His eyes fall closed, and the shaky breath Dad draws makes my own breath hitch. "Hide what?" My voice is soft, placating. I'm tempted to tell them that *I know*, to relieve them of the burden of having to tell me, but it'd just hurt them more to find out I've been aware of the situation all along.

Dad looks away, almost as though he can't quite face me. "The company isn't doing very well, Raya." He pauses, giving me a moment to let the words sink in.

Mom nods. "With the way the economy is moving, we're not far from bankruptcy," she adds. "We've done all we could, exhausted all our contacts. The only solution is a merger, but it's an unconventional one."

"Unconventional in what way?" I ask, my usual steadfast voice noticeably shaking. There's something she's not telling me, and that is entirely at odds with my mother's no-nonsense personality. Even when I was little, Mom never sugarcoated things for me.

Dad throws her a look I can't quite decipher and shakes his head. "It doesn't matter, angel," he tells me. "It's not something I'm willing to consider. I've started the process of filing for bankruptcy. I'm so sorry, Raya." Dad's voice breaks and he looks away, but not before I catch a glimpse of the pain in his eyes. "This isn't the legacy I wanted to hand down to you. I always thought you'd succeed me, that we'd work together until I'm gray and old, and even then, you'd indulge me and let me help in whatever way my creaky old bones could. This company... it was meant to be yours someday, but I... I failed, Raya. I failed both you and your mother, and words cannot convey how sorry I am." He looks up, his eyes filled with heartbreak. "I should've told you sooner, but I suppose part of me hoped that I'd find a solution after all, that I could save us."

Dad hangs his head, and I reach over to grab his hand, holding on tightly. "The merger," I say, my voice tinged with caution. "Would it save us from bankruptcy?"

Dad's eyes widen, hesitancy and a hint of disgust clouding his deep blue irises. "The merger comes with a price I'm not willing to pay." He pulls his hand out of mine and crosses his arms, his expression hardening.

"That's not an answer," I retort, throwing the same words my parents have used throughout the years right back at them. They deeply value honesty, and they've never once let me get away with non-answers or attempts to talk myself out of situations. In return, they've always done me the same courtesy — until now.

Dad stares at me for a moment in that way he does sometimes, like he's proud of me, even though I haven't done anything to make me deserving of his pride. "You are far too sharp for your own good," he says, his voice soft, filled with sorrow.

"Mom," I murmur, my voice shaking. "Tell me the truth, please."

She hesitates, her eyes falling closed for a moment. "Yes, Raya. It would save us. However, one of the prerequisites of the merger is an arranged marriage between you and the heir of the acquiring company. They're a family company, much like we are, and it's one term they won't budge on."

"It's not a term I'll ever agree to," Dad snaps. "I'd much rather file for bankruptcy than... than... *sell* my own daughter like that. I will *never* agree to it."

Shock renders me speechless for a moment, before the gears in my brain begin to turn. I've always wanted a marriage just like my parents', one filled with love and endless laughter. My parents still go on weekly dates, and Mom still surprises Dad at work with handmade lunches and sweet messages written in his lunch box. I always wanted love, *true love*, but never at the expense of my parents' happiness.

Our company is everything to my father, and not just because that's where he met Mom. It's his pride and joy, his legacy. I'm not sure he'd even know who he is without it — it's the only thing he loves other than Mom and me. I've never known anyone that genuinely loves his job and his employees the way my father does, and bankruptcy would break his heart in a way I'm terrified would be irreparable.

"I'll do it, Dad," I say, my voice firm. "Ultimately, it's my life that's at stake, so this should be my decision — not yours. I'll do it. I'll get married."

Twelve

Raya

"You have to find a way to convince Dad," I tell Mom as I roll out dough to make chapattis, trying my hardest to make them as round as Mom makes them and failing entirely, despite my best efforts to mentally calculate the force of the pressure I'm using and the angle I'm rolling at. "I don't understand why he won't even entertain the idea when *I'm* not opposed to it."

I told him I'd get married if it'd save the company, and Dad lost his mind, refusing to speak to me at all, let alone tell me anything about which company we'd merge with, or who I'd even marry.

Mom sighs as she watches her infamous lamb curry simmer on the stove. It's Dad's favorite, and she makes it every time we need to convince him of something. This time, I worry it may not be enough. "Raya," Mom says, her voice soft. When she looks at me, her gaze is pained. "To be honest, I'm on the same page as your dad. I do want the merger to proceed, but not with you as collateral."

I place my hand on her arm and draw a shaky breath. "This

could save the company. You know that losing our business will mean losing a little part of Dad, don't you?"

She falls silent and turns away from me to grab her spice tray, clearly just wanting to get out of this conversation that we've had a thousand times over now. "Had our roles been reversed, and Dad had to make a sacrifice for my happiness, he'd do it without a second thought. If nothing else, I should be given all the information so I can make an informed decision."

"It's different," Mom says, her tone exasperated. "You're our daughter, Raya. It's our duty to take care of you, to *protect* you."

I run a hand through my long hair, trying my hardest to remain patient. "I'm not a child anymore, Mom. You raised me better than this — how could you possibly expect me to turn a blind eye when I could solve all our problems?"

I watch as Mom makes masala chai, my favorite. She hand blends all the ingredients into a fine powder once a month, and despite following her instructions to the letter, I've never been able to get it quite right, so now she just sends me off with a jar of her mix instead.

"I expect you to do it because these aren't *your* problems to solve, Raya." I watch as she adds milk to the tea on the stove. "You can keep coming home every single evening instead of staying in your dorm where you're *supposed* to be," she side-eyes me and shakes her head, "and we can keep having this conversation every single time, but it won't change a thing."

"Why?" I ask, my voice breaking. "The man I'd marry... is he truly so bad?"

Mom hesitates and shakes her head. "No," she says, sighing. "Honestly, he's exactly the kind of person that I think you'll end up with, from what I can tell about him, anyway."

She pours me a cup of steaming hot tea, and I take it from her carefully. "Then what is the issue? Truly, Mom. I'm just trying to understand."

She nods to herself and takes a deep breath, her thumb brushing over the Ganesh pendant around her neck. "Okay," she whispers, seemingly more to herself than to me. "Why don't we sit for a moment?"

She leads me to the breakfast bar, and nerves rush through me. Mom rarely sits me down for a conversation — all our talks happen while I help her cook. The few times she's sat me down, it's been because of something serious.

She takes my hand, her expression conflicted. "The reason your dad is so opposed to the mere idea of an arranged marriage is because of *me*." She looks down and draws a shaky breath. "You see, Raya... the day I turned eighteen was also the day I got married."

I frown, certain that can't be right. I've seen Mom and Dad's wedding photos, and while she looked young, she wasn't eighteen.

"It was an arranged marriage with a man I'd never even met before. Your maternal grandfather, who you've never met, arranged it. The man in question was someone from the village in India that my parents were born in, and I had no say in the matter. As it turned out, neither did he."

I stare at my mother in shock. "*What*?"

She nods, her expression haunted. "Things were different back then, Raya. You just didn't choose your own partner — your parents would choose for you. He seemed great on paper since he was well-educated, and our background was similar. Besides, our parents grew up together and moved here from India around the same time. It seemed like a good match, except he already had someone he loved."

I stare at Mom, unsure what to say. I'd never have guessed that she'd been married before Dad. They're so happy together, and it truly seems like they're each other's first and only love. I suppose that might still be true.

"Unfortunately, he blamed me for the marriage when I had even less of a choice than he ever did, and within a matter of weeks, he became... hard to live with. I tried going back home, but my family kept telling me to make things work, and that divorce wasn't an option."

"So that's why I've never met your side of the family," I murmur. I knew they'd fallen out, but I was never quite sure why. As I grew older, I assumed it was because Mom married outside of her culture, and perhaps that was part of it, but the full story is clearly a lot more complex.

She nods. "I didn't have the courage to escape that marriage, knowing that my family didn't support me. They're very traditional, and once I'd gotten married, they wouldn't let me move back home. I could go home for weeks at a time, but eventually, I was sent back to my husband, until I just couldn't take it anymore." She raises a trembling hand and pushes her hair behind her ear, her expression filled with heartache. "I'd been working for your dad at the time, and one day, he saw the bruises on my skin. He helped me unconditionally. Your dad saved me, Raya."

I bite down on my lip to keep my emotions in check, shocked by Mom's story and the role Dad played in it. I knew they met while she was working for him, but this isn't what I'd been imagining all these years. It's surprising that she's still able to smile the way she does when she's been through so much.

"Your father is terrified that my fate will befall you, honey. The mere idea of an arranged marriage fills him with worries for your safety, and nothing I do or say will convince him that I was just unlucky, and that what happened to me could've happened even if my first marriage had been a love marriage. All of my cousins are in successfully and happy arranged marriages, so I don't fully share Dad's worries, but I do understand where he's coming from. There are risks to marrying someone you don't truly know, and the one thing your father will never do is risk your safety."

I nod and cross my arms, at a loss for words. "I'm sorry, Mom." I say eventually, wishing I were one of those people that just knows the right thing to say at the right time. "I wish you never had to go through that, and I'm really grateful Dad was there for you."

She smiles at me and brushes my hair out of my face. "Me too, sweetie. Your father is the reason why *I'm* opposed to an arranged marriage for you. I want you to have a grand love story of your own, and I want you to be with someone of your own choosing."

For reasons I can't quite explain, my thoughts drift to Lex and the way we danced together, the stories we shared with each other. If I had a choice, would I choose to spend another evening with him, laughing and playing truth or dare until we're barely able to stay awake?

I sigh and let my eyes fall closed for a moment.

Yes.

A thousand times over.

Thirteen

Raya

My heart beats louder with each step I take toward Lex's campus office, my nerves racked. The news about the merger and everything it entails threw me off so much that I missed his last class, and thereby potentially my chance to intern at Windsor Motors.

The door is ajar, giving me a view of him behind his desk, his tie loosened and his hair messier than it was in class last time. I watch him for a moment as he flicks through papers that have been submitted to him, his brow raised and his expression serious.

This version of him is in such contrast with the playfulness he showed me a few weeks ago. I didn't think I'd ever see him again, yet here he is, even further out of reach than ever before.

I hesitate before lifting my hand to knock, scared in more ways than one. Lex looks up at the sound, and just like that, I'm rooted in place. He smiles, his dimples making an appearance, and my heart skips a beat.

"Raya."

He rises from his seat, and I take a deep breath before walking in, unsure how to behave around him. "Hi, Professor Windsor," I end up saying, my voice trembling.

Lex's expression hardens, and I stare at him for a moment, wishing I knew what he's thinking. "Miss Lewis," he corrects himself, gesturing toward the seat in front of his desk. "You weren't in class this week."

"I'm sorry, Professor. I have no good excuse, and I'd understand if you won't let me submit my design now that I've missed the deadline." My voice shakes, and I lower my head as I reach for the folder I brought with me. My movements are hesitant as I place it on his desk, unsure what to expect.

"Take a seat."

Lex walks around his desk as I sink down in the seat he pointed out, my entire body trembling with nerves. He closes the door to his office before turning back to me, and my heart skips a beat. *This*. This is how he looked at me that night — like he can't see anything but me.

"Tell me why you missed my class, and I'll decide whether your reason is worthy of an exception." My eyes widen a fraction, heat rushing to my cheeks as he walks back toward his desk and leans against it instead of sitting down behind it, placing his body inches from mine. "Give me a *Truth*, Raya."

I look up at him, longing hitting me hard as memories crash through my mind. The way he kissed me, the rounds of truth and dare we played, and the way his body felt against mine as we laid on his sofa. It was the first time I felt a real connection with someone, and it hurts that it finally happened mere weeks before finding out that I'll most likely marry someone I've never even met, someone my parents refuse to tell me anything about. I wish I never knew what I'll miss out on.

"It's a personal matter, Professor."

He moves closer, until he's right in front of me, my knees brushing against his shins. I hate how incredible he looks in that navy three-piece suit, clearly another one of Raven's highly coveted designs. "Personal, huh?" Something flashes in his eyes, and he leans in, placing his index finger underneath my chin, tipping my face up. My heart begins to race, and he smiles like he knows exactly how he's making me feel. "What is it that kept you from me?"

His gaze dips down to my lips, and I inhale shakily. "I was at home with my parents for a couple of days," I tell him, my own gaze drawn to his mouth. What would happen if I kissed him right now, one last time? Would it make me forget about the things my parents are keeping from me? Would it make me forget the countless reasons this man in front of me can never be mine?

"Are they okay?" Lex asks, his expression clearing as his hand falls away.

I nod and cross my arms. "They're fine. It's just... they just needed me at home for a little while." I look away, my voice breaking. What would he say if I told him I spent days trying to convince my parents to let me marry a perfect stranger, in order to save my family's company? Countless arguments, and still Mom and Dad wouldn't even tell me what company we'd merge with, or who I'd marry, convinced I'd take matters into my own hands if I knew. The look in their eyes spoke volumes, though. Whoever it is has the power to save us, and they hate that as much as I do.

"I see," he says, his tone light. "One more question, Raya. Answer me honestly, and I'll let you submit your design." I glance back at him to find him looking at me with an expression I can't quite read.

I nod, my nerves sky high. I know what he'll ask, and I'm not sure how to answer him.

"Why did you sneak out of my bed?"

I bite down on my lip, my cheeks blazing. "I'd never done anything like that before, but I understand the etiquette. It was a fun night, but I know that's all it was. It seemed easier on us both to just walk away before things got awkward."

He clenches his jaws for a moment. "That's one hell of an assumption," he says, anger bleeding into his voice. "You act like we had meaningless sex, when we both know that isn't what happened. Can you really look me in the eye and tell me that night meant nothing to you?"

I turn away to look out his window, unsure how to answer. Nothing good will come of me admitting that he's right. I can't have a crush on my *professor*. Hell, I should've walked away the moment I realized he was *Lexington Windsor.*

"Don't do that, Raya," he says, his voice soft and pained. He reaches for me and effortlessly pulls me out of my seat, my body crashing against his. Within seconds, he has me perched on the edge of his desk, his legs between mine, our positions the same as that night in his kitchen. "Don't hide from me like that. Answer me."

His gaze is pleading, his voice strained. He cups my face, his thumb brushing over the edge of my mouth, and my eyes flutter closed for a moment. "Lex," I whisper, my voice breaking.

His hand slides into my hair, and he grips tightly, his eyes on mine. He moves closer, spreading my legs wider and making my skirt ride up, until the fabric is bunched at the top of my thighs. "Tell me the truth," he demands, his gaze unyielding as he reaches for my hand and flattens it across his chest, covering it with his.

I lower my eyes and draw a shaky breath. "It's best for both of us if we leave that night in the past. You said it yourself, Lex. You have no interest in dating anyone, and things have changed for me since then too."

He studies me, his hand slowly balling in my hair, his touch at odds with his calm expression. "What changed?"

I look into his emerald eyes, unsure what the best thing to do is. "Remember the first question you asked me when we played truth or dare?"

Are you truly single, Raya? He nods, his jaw locking.

"My answer changed."

He lets go of me and runs a hand through his hair, anger marring his features. "Who?" he asks, his voice surprisingly calm, despite the edge to it.

"It's complicated."

He pulls his tie loose entirely and takes a deep breath, his expression forlorn. "I refuse to believe that you started dating someone else after the night we spent together, Raya. Sure, we didn't have sex, but the way we danced, the conversations we had, and the way you kissed me? That's every bit as intimate, if not more so. I can't be the only one who wants more."

His gaze is heated as he places his index finger underneath my chin. "I suggest you end whatever it is you started before I find out who he is." His gaze roams over my face, lingering on my lips for a moment, before returning to my eyes. "You're *mine,* Raya Lewis. You just don't know it yet."

Fourteen

Lexington

My body is taut with nerves as I continue to tighten the bolts in the automated cheese slicer I built for my sister, but it doesn't keep my mind off Raya for more than a few minutes. I sigh as I force myself to check that my new invention, built to look like a little guillotine and appropriately named Cheesy, slices a block of cheese into paper-thin slices, just the way my sister likes it. She's cut herself countless times trying to slice cheese in a stupidly thin way, but this should help.

It isn't, however, helping *me*. Coming up with new ideas and building tools for my family always takes my mind off things I don't want to think about, but not today. No, every few minutes, I'm reminded of Raya's honey scent, the way she moans when I kiss her, and the way her nose crinkles in the cutest way when she smiles. Then my thoughts involuntarily turn to the way she couldn't quite face me as she told me that she's no longer single.

Who the fuck is he? I've spent days trying to figure it out, only to come up empty. More than once, I've found myself on campus on days I'm not teaching, tempted to find her and demand answers I'm not entitled to. I sigh as I laser engrave the words *Let Them Eat Cheese* into Sierra's gift, knowing she loves that kind of twisted humor. Normally this level of silliness would've had me smiling, but today my heart feels heavy.

It annoys me how quickly Raya got under my skin. I can't figure her out, can't read her motives. No way was she able to walk right into someone else's arms a mere few weeks after falling asleep in mine. What is she playing at?

"Pippy," I call, the sound of my voice activating my AI Robot Assistant. "Have you been able to find any new information on Bob Lewis and Lewis Motors? And what about Raya? Did you learn anything new about her?"

"It took a while, but I was able to delve a little deeper into Mr. Lewis's financial records. Lewis Motors truly is at the brink of bankruptcy, and Mr. Lewis's personal assets can't sustain their relatively modest lifestyle for much longer, since he's reinvested all his savings back into the company. Despite his financial situation, he continues to pay $10,000 a month to an unfamiliar external account, straining his already precarious finances further. I also couldn't find anything about him prior to when he started his business. There's a gap between when he graduated and when he started his firm, though I suspect he was preparing to launch his business during that time and may not have been working."

I nod slowly, uncertain what he might be up to. Debt, perhaps? "Look into the paper trail for me, will you?"

"Certainly, Lex. As for Raya, I'm sorry to say that I have no new updates. I was unable to verify that her relationship status has changed."

Relief rushes through me, and I smile wryly. Was she just trying to deter me with her words? If she truly was dating someone, I'd already have figured out who he is by now.

"What about Annie?" I ask, my voice soft. "Have you found Annie?"

"I'm sorry," Pippy says, her slightly robotic voice tinged with regret. "No trace of Annie yet. I'll keep looking." My heart twists painfully, and I sigh as I continue to work in silence, hoping to drown out my thoughts by keeping my hands busy.

"Lex," Pippy says eventually, her tone concerned. "Bob Lewis at the front desk. Would you like me to notify the receptionist that he is to be admitted to your lab? As it stands, our staff are refusing him entry."

My eyes widen, and for a moment, I stand frozen. What could Raya's father possibly be doing here? "Yes, Pippy. If you'd please?"

"Certainly, Lex," Pippy replies.

My hands instantly turn clammy, and I wipe them on the overall I always wear in my lab before remembering to yank off the stained garment. I glance down at the shirt and pants I'm wearing, trying my hardest to remember where I threw my jacket. "Fuck," I mutter to myself when I realize I left it in my office on the top floor. With the lab being on a different floor, there's no way I can make myself look presentable in time.

The door to my lab unlocks and swings open automatically, curtesy of Pippy, and Raya's father walks in, followed by my secretary, Susan. He's as tall as I am, with dark hair and bright blue eyes that sweep over my lab. The man looks formidable, yet his expression seems to be a mixture of reluctance and helplessness.

"Lexington Windsor, I take it?" he says, and I snap out of it, offering him my hand.

"Indeed. Bob Lewis, right?"

He stares at my outstretched hand, the muscle in his jaw ticking as he shakes it, his grip unnecessarily tight. I smile in response, hyperaware that this man might very well end up becoming my father-in-law.

"You can leave us," I tell Susan, and she nods politely before disappearing quietly.

Bob glances at my equipment and the various projects I'm working on, each laid out on a separate table. "You don't seem surprised to see me, and you seem to know who I am, so you must know what brought me here."

I straighten my shoulders and look him in the eye. "I'm aware of my grandmother's offer, though she doesn't realize that I know. Nonetheless, I am surprised to see you here today, Mr. Lewis. What can I do for you?"

He locks his jaw and stares at the design plans for my next car, strewn all over one of my tables. The plans are highly confidential, yet I couldn't care less at this moment.

"I shouldn't be here at all," Bob says, his voice soft. "My agreement is with your grandmother, and per our terms, I shouldn't speak to you until the ink is dry on our contract." He looks up at me then. "However, I couldn't sign away my daughter's life until I had a better understanding of the man I'm tying her fate to."

My heart begins to race, and I cross my arms as I nod at him. "I was under the impression that you'd declined my grandmother's offer."

"I did. My wife and daughter made me reconsider." He pauses and looks me up and down. "Whether this merger goes through all depends on what kind of man you are, Mr. Windsor."

"Lex," I correct him, trying my best to smile genuinely. "Please call me Lex. That's what my friends and family call me."

He nods and walks around the room, pausing at each table, clearly conflicted. I know he desperately needs this merger, or his company won't survive, yet he seems unwilling to follow through.

"You said that it's your wife and daughter that changed your mind. Does that mean Raya knows about me?"

Was it me she was referring to when she claimed to no longer be single? It didn't seem that way, but I can't help the sliver of hope I feel. It would explain why I haven't been able to find so much as a trace of the man she's supposedly with.

His eyes cut to mine. "I have yet to tell her which company we're merging with, or who she'd marry. Raya is rather impulsive, and she has the biggest heart. She'd do anything to save the company, and I can't risk her taking matters into her own hands," he says, his tone carrying an edge to it.

"So, she agreed to marry someone without even knowing who it is?" That sliver of hope expands, enveloping my heart. The conversation Raya and I had in my office makes a lot more sense now, and I can't help but smile to myself.

Bob nods as he pauses by Cheesy, his expression hardening. "Are you some sort of psychopath, Mr. Windsor?" he asks, his tone harsh as he examines what is essentially a miniature guillotine. "Is that why your grandmother is so desperate to find you a wife?"

I run a hand through my hair, mortification washing over me. "That... that is not what it looks like," I explain dumbly. "It's a cheese slicer, designed for my little sister," I begin to explain. He listens as I tell him about the frequent cuts on Sierra's fingers, and his shoulders relax as I explain her ridiculous love for cheese, and how I'd hoped Cheesy would help her.

My nerves are racked as Bob just stares at me for a few moments. "I'm surprised calling you a psychopath didn't anger you. I expected you to be the eccentric billionaire the media portrays you to be, but you seem surprisingly normal."

I raise a brow in amusement. "I suppose I'm *not* sorry to disappoint?"

His lips twitch, the edges turning up in a reluctant mini smile. "I thought you might take this opportunity to deter me. I was under the impression that you were forced into this as much as we are."

I nod and lean back against one of the tables. "I *am* being forced into it, but I also always knew that it was coming. I know I don't have a choice, and though I'd never tell her this, I trust my grandmother." Just not fully — not enough to not have sought out Raya before the engagement was formalized. If I'd had even the slightest inkling that Raya had malicious intent toward me or my family, I *would* have sabotaged our engagement.

Bob nods and takes his time walking through my lab, almost like he's trying to get on my nerves with his intrusiveness. Before I met Raya, I might've been inclined to indulge him, even if it's just to buy myself a little more time before marriage. Now? Now I simply smile and lean back as he touches highly fragile and expensive pieces of tech.

"You should know that my daughter is everything to me," he says eventually, his expression serious. "There is nothing I won't do to protect her. If I ever so much as suspect that she's being mistreated, I'll bring her back home by any means necessary, consequences be damned."

I smile, only mildly surprised by the thinly veiled threat. "I would never disrespect or mistreat my wife." I pause for a moment, understanding his concerns. "Nor would I ever ask her for anything she isn't willing to give, Bob. She'd be my *wife*, not my property."

He studies me, seemingly less conflicted than he was before, but clearly not convinced either.

"My daughter wants real love, Lex. The kind her mother and I share. Can you give her that?"

I hesitate and look away. "I'll give her everything she could ever want, but I'm not sure I have it in me to love her." I take a deep breath and look at him, making him an informal promise. "I would try, though. For my wife, I'd try."

Fifteen

Lexington

My heart is racing as I walk into my grandmothers' dining room, where we've all been ordered to gather. I try my hardest to come across as relaxed, when deep down, I'm starting to panic. My conversation with Raya's father weighs heavy on my mind, and the decision he made when he walked out of my lab will impact the rest of my life.

I force a smile when I spot my sisters-in-law. I walk over and muss up Celeste's hair, before resting my elbow on Faye's shoulder, my playfulness a facade to hide my nerves behind.

"You know she hates it when you do that," Raven chastises me, while Sierra stomps on my foot, making me stumble away from Faye, who giggles at my expense. Val rolls her eyes, and I grin, happy to see them all smiling. Seeing joy on their faces makes it easier to live with the lack thereof in mine.

We all fall silent when Grandma walks into the room, and instantly, Raven walks over the Ares, Val joins Luca, Dion wraps his arm around Faye's shoulder, and Celeste grabs Zane's hand, leaving Sierra and me to stand side by side. They're united fronts, all four couples, and something akin to envy settles deep in my chest.

What would it be like to trust someone to that extent? To have a real partner in life? The mere idea of putting myself in such a vulnerable position ever again puts me off, but I can't deny that I envy the happiness I see on their faces. For a moment, I wonder what it'd be like to have Raya standing next to me, and longing lodges in my chest.

"Kids," Grandma says, her pink suit entirely in contrast with her stern expression. Anyone who looks at her would think she's a sweet old grandmother, when she's the most cunning of us all. "I'm sure you can guess why I've gathered you all here."

Her eyes settle on me, and I stand rooted in place when she throws a deceptively sweet smile my way. "Lexington, all four of your brothers are happily married, and all four have committed to unions that have greatly benefited our family. We are exceptionally lucky to have Raven, Val, Faye, and Celeste, and I know I speak for all of us when I say that with each addition, the love between us just grows."

I nod in agreement, my stomach tight with nerves. "Now it's your turn, Lexington. Your engagement has been decided upon."

I bite back a smile, beyond relieved she isn't springing this on me. "Enlighten me. Who am I marrying?" I ask, praying Bob made the decision I hope he made. Raya may have been grandma's first choice, but I know she wasn't the only woman under consideration.

She looks thrown off by my relatively relaxed response. Each of my siblings has reacted adversely to the news of their engagement, and I know she expected the same or worse from me.

"Raya Lewis."

I breathe a sigh of relief, the widest grin splitting my face. "Interesting," I say, nodding. "The Lewises are tech giants, so it's an excellent choice." It's true — Raya's family specializes in midrange cars, which isn't at all what Windsor Motors does, but they're a fantastic company. Their current financial woes are a reflection of the economy more than anything else. In thirty years, Bob Lewis has accomplished more than most companies do in three hundred, and based on what Pippy learned about his research and vision, the company will go much further still. Raya is a perfect fit in every single way, and I can't help but smile to myself, my unease finally melting away. The uncertainly took its toll on me, but it's official now — Raya Lewis is mine.

Murmurs cascade through the room as my siblings begin to speculate, all of them eyeing me warily. I suppose I'm not fooling them. They know I'm not in the least surprised.

Grandma raises a brow, equally confused by my mild response. "Raya is currently an engineering student at Astor College. Her family is not opposed to her getting married prior to graduating, but Raya has requested that her marriage be kept a secret from the press, so she's able to complete her education in peace. They have an interesting set of requirements that we'll discuss at length soon."

I cross my arms and nod. "What a coincidence," I tell her. "I just agreed to teach an engineering class at Astor College."

Grandma looks completely thrown off, unused to not being ten steps ahead of us, and the look on her face makes it hard to keep from smiling. "We've set the wedding date one month from now. Since we agreed to their request for secrecy, we felt there was no need to delay the paperwork. The two of you can simply have your ceremony once Raya graduates."

I nod, realization dawning. If I'm officially being informed of our engagement, then Raya must have found out by now, too.

By now, she'll have found out that I approached her under false pretenses.

Sixteen

Raya

My steps are measured as I walk through the Windsor Residences lobby, my heart in my throat. I'd been just as nervous the last time I walked into this building, but for vastly different reasons. Unease makes my stomach twist as I head toward the elevator Lex and I took up to his penthouse last time, only for a uniformed member of staff to stop me.

"Unfortunately, we can't allow anyone access beyond this point," the same security guard from last time says, his tone firm.

I stand rooted in place, uncertain what to do. Before I can even explain that I'm here because I was invited, a familiar voice sounds from behind me.

"It's fine. She's my future wife."

My eyes widen, and I look over my shoulder to find Lex standing a few paces away, his expression unreadable. The three-piece charcoal suit he's wearing makes him look unapproachable, unattainable, yet here he stands, proclaiming me to be his.

Lex studies me for a moment, his eyes roaming over my face, countless unspoken words hanging in the air between us. He lowers his gaze and walks up to me, his hand settling on my lower back. The security guard nods politely and steps back to press the elevator button for us, and I wordlessly let Lex guide me forward.

His hand stays in place as the elevator rises, warmth seeping into my skin, even through the fabric of my black dress. From the moment I found out, I've imagined countless versions of the same conversation that I know we must have, yet now that the time has come, I'm speechless.

Lex draws a shaky breath as the doors open, and I follow him into the penthouse that I didn't think I'd ever step foot in again, seeing it through fresh eyes.

"Did you know?" I ask, my gaze roaming over the photos in the hallway. He told me that I'd meet the girls soon enough, and I thought he was just flirting with me.

"When you asked me if my mom would teach you her biryani recipe, and you told me you'd thank my dad for teaching me how to dance the foxtrot. When you kissed me, Lexington, and then told me you'd wait for as long as I needed you to. Did you know then?"

He looks at me with clear guilt in his eyes. "Yes."

I smile wryly as my heart wrenches, a sense of betrayal rushing through me. "So every single time I asked you to tell me the truth, you told me white lies." I run a hand through my hair, my eyes stinging. "You know, I thought it was a crazy coincidence when I ran into you like that. Then you showed up as my professor, and I thought that perhaps, it was fate." I laugh humorlessly, feeling like a complete fool. "What did you hope to accomplish, Lexington?"

He walks up to me, regret marring his features. "Raya," he says, his hands wrapping around my shoulders. "Please, will you let me explain?"

Bitterness makes me want to step back, out of his reach. Instead, I nod reluctantly. "Give me the full truth this time."

"The full truth," he repeats, looking down at his feet. "I was concerned I'd never truly get to know you if the first time we met was after we got engaged. You'd put up a front, acting the way you'd think is expected of you, and I'd be left trying to figure out what's real and what isn't." He runs a hand through his hair and sighs. "I needed to know what kind of person you are, without the weight of our families' expectations and the merger bearing down on us. I'd never let just anyone into my home and near my family. My grandmother may have vetted you, but I needed to check for myself."

I stare at him in disbelief, my heart aching. "Funny, how you went out of your way to dig into who I am, but in doing so, you did exactly what you worried *I'd* put *you* through. You crafted a facade, acted the way the situation called for, and led me on." He looks away, his expression conflicted. "Was any of it real?" I ask, my voice breaking.

"Of course," he says, his voice soft. "I meant it when I said I was genuinely having a great time with you. I didn't expect to like you as much as I do, Raya."

I step back, out of his reach, a chill running down my spine. "Is that supposed to make me feel better, Lexington?" I ask, incredulous. My jaws snap shut, hurt turning into fury.

I wrap my arms around myself, my stomach turning. I've never felt so manipulated, and every memory we created instantly becomes tainted as I begin to analyze everything he's ever said to me, every interaction. When he told me he had no interest in falling in love, he was warning me, telling me not to expect certain things from him during our marriage. It's the reason I walked away, only to find out walking away was never an option.

"Raya," he says, his tone pleading. "Please know that I didn't have any bad intentions. It was an opportunity to find out how you'd treat me if we met by chance, and I just couldn't pass that up. I knew I wouldn't have a choice when it came to the woman I married, but at the very least, I wanted to meet you on my own terms. So much of what we do in the next couple of years will be dictated by our families, and more than once, we'll find ourselves putting up an act, behaving a certain way for the press or our social circle. Our obligations will change everything."

He looks tormented, desperate, and I feel myself waver. "It's not that I don't understand why you did it, Lex. I get it, but that doesn't make it okay. You *deceived* me. You approached me knowing that our lives would inextricably entwine from that moment onwards, and instead of telling me the truth, you played with my feelings." I pull a hand through my hair, frustrated. "And now I'm supposed to marry you? I can't even trust you to be honest with me."

"I'm sorry, Raya," he says, but it doesn't ring true — it doesn't sound sincere.

"Your apology makes no difference," I tell him, my voice breaking. "You could lie to me every single day for the entire duration of our marriage and there isn't a single thing I could do about it. It's not like I can just walk away, and we both know it."

Something cracks in his expression, and he takes my hand. "I wouldn't do that to you," he says, pressing my palm flat against his chest before covering it with his own hand. "I won't mislead you again, and though you may not be inclined to believe me right now, I have every intention of being a good husband. We're not getting married by choice, but I'll do what I can to make sure you won't regret becoming my wife. Just because this isn't what either of us wants doesn't mean I won't do the right thing."

"How could I not regret marrying you, when the only thing I've ever wanted out of my marriage is the one thing you'll never give me?"

His face falls, and he sighs as he tightens his grip on my hand. "Please don't ask me to make you false promises."

I pull my hand out of his grip and study him, unsure what to make of him. I've seen so many facets of Lex, but I still don't have a complete picture. "Look, I didn't come here to argue with you," I tell him, my shoulders slumping. Ultimately, this is a business deal, and that's something I can't ever forget. "I came here today to tell you that I have some terms of my own."

He raises a brow and nods, indicating for me to proceed.

"I don't want anyone knowing about our marriage, especially

not while you're my professor. I've had to work incredibly hard to get into Astor College, and I don't want to be assailed with rumors that'll impact my education or my career."

His expression hardens, and he reaches for my hair, pushing it out of my face with a cold look in his eyes. "I'll agree to that, so long as we're clear on one thing: you're mine as much as I'm yours, and I do not share. You can hide our marriage as much as you want, but it doesn't make it any less real."

The possessiveness in his gaze makes my stomach tighten, and my heart begins to beat a little wilder. From the moment I found out who I'd marry, I've wondered whether any of what we shared was real, whether he truly wants me, or whether it was all an act, a role he was playing. I doubt he's faking *this*. He may not be happy about the way we're being forced into this, but he wants me — and he doesn't seem particularly pleased about it.

I run a hand through my hair and nod. "No lies," I add. "Tell me the full truth at all times and trust me to handle it. Don't sugarcoat things for me and don't treat me as anything but your equal."

Lex nods. "Done."

"No favoritism or nepotism. I don't want to feel like I haven't earned something I have, or like I deprived someone more deserving of an opportunity."

"Of course." He steps closer to me and cups my face, his thumb brushing over the edge of my mouth. "I've seen your drone design, Raya. You don't need my favor."

My heart wrenches, and I just about keep myself from replying that I *do*, or we wouldn't be getting married. "One more thing, Lex."

He raises his brow and nods. "Tell me."

I take a deep breath and square my shoulders. "Three years from now, I want a divorce."

His eyes flash with something akin to anger, and he steps closer to me, his shirt brushing against my dress, his jaws set.

"I fully respect your choices and your boundaries, Lexington.

You made it abundantly clear that you have no interest in love or relationships, but someday, that's exactly what I want for myself. I understand that it won't be with you, and I won't push for things you won't give. All I ask is that you let me go eventually, so I can find someone who'll love me like you won't."

His expression hardens, and his hand slides into my hair, his grip tightening. "We'll see about that," he growls.

I smile up at him humorlessly. "It wasn't a suggestion. It's a demand."

Seventeen

LEXINGTON

I frown when Pippy's voice rings through my living room, announcing that all my brothers are enroute to my house. "They are all on the last stretch of the road, and Xavier Kingston isn't far behind them," she tells me. My home is the furthest house into the Windsor Estate, so once they pass a certain point, this is the only place they could be headed to. I should've known, should've expected them to come check up on me following the engagement announcement.

The doorbell rings, and I groan in defeat. "Shall I let them in, Lex?" Pippy asks.

"Can I pretend I'm not home?"

"Unfortunately not," she replies in her slightly robotic voice. "It appears Luca brought wheel locks, and he's holding one up to the camera at the front door at present, gesturing between your brand-new car and the door. If my interpretation of his body language is correct, Luca is threatening to put locks on your cars if we don't let him in. How would you like me to handle this situation?"

I walk up to the window and glance out, finding Luca handing out tools with far too much delight for my liking. "For fuck's sake," I mutter. "I bet this was Val's idea. Luca wasn't this fucking *feisty* before he married her."

"Oh, it appears Zane has successfully locked both cars in the driveway. I apologize, Lex. Ares was obstructing my cameras at the rear of the house while Luca obscured the camera at the front door. Well, I'll be... they *blinded* me. *Such impertinence.* Those boys are quite simply... *rascals. Such rascals.* I shall turn on the watering system this instant."

"Fucking great," I murmur. Not only did I program too much sass into my AI, but my brothers also show no signs of being deterred. "Hold on, Pippy. They'll just become that much more annoying if you do that. Just let them in."

"Very well, Lex," Pippy says, sounding just a little peeved, and the front door swings open.

"Hi, little brother!" Luca chirps, followed by chuckles and mingling shouts that sound an awful lot like variations of the word *congratulations*. I watch in absolute horror as Dion rolls in an invention I once made to cheer him up — the monstrosity I'd jokingly named the Lex-board.

"You've gotta be kidding me," I whisper.

"Surprise," Dion says, his eyes twinkling in delight.

My eyes widen even further when Xavier fucking Kingston saunters in, holding up a bottle of whiskey. "Look," he says, entirely fucking unapologetic. "I'm honestly just here for the banter."

"Of course you are."

I sigh as I sit down in the chair Ares dragged to the middle of the room, knowing full well this is my reckoning. My past has come back to bite me in the fucking ass, and no matter how hard I run, I can't escape the absolute torture my brothers are about to put me through.

Zane is fucking giddy as he turns on the Lex-board, which truly is just a glorified touch-screen whiteboard. My heart sinks when I read the words on it. "*How not to fuck shit up with your wife*. Subtle."

My brothers exchange glances. "Trust us," they say, almost in unison. "We've all made mistakes we wish we hadn't made. We've paid the price, so you don't have to."

I cross my arms and raise a brow. "You're joking, right?"

Their expressions turn serious. "Not at all," Ares says. "Zane told us you approached Raya and never told her that you knew who she was. You've already started your relationship off on the wrong foot, and you'd be surprised how hard it may be to regain the trust you've lost. I can guarantee she'll be pissed the second she finds out you essentially led her on, and you won't know how to fix it."

I sit up a little, uneasy, even as I throw a glare Zane's way. I confided in him when I asked him to help me supply the things I bribed Adrian Astor with, and I should've known he wouldn't keep his mouth shut. "She knows, and she *is* pissed. Told me she wants a divorce in three years."

Dion just sighs and starts his slideshow. "I guess it's too late for you to learn this lesson, but we don't, under any circumstances, lie to our wives. There are very few occasions during which lying is acceptable, and I've listed those for you below."

I frown when there's only one word on his *list*: never. "Funny," I murmur. "Real funny how fucking whipped you all are."

They exchange smiles, like they're all in on a secret I don't know, and I just sigh as I lean back in my chair, already tired of their shit.

Xavier, Dion's best friend, just hands me a glass of whiskey, and I knock it back gratefully. This is what I get for teasing each of my brothers when they got married, for being a real pain in the ass in an attempt to lighten their load. They have no idea that the way I messed around with them was designed to distract them, to help them.

"Lex," Ares says, his voice soft. "Raya seems like a really nice girl, and from what I've heard, she seems to be a perfect fit for you. Don't push her away before ever giving your marriage a real shot, and don't even bother lying to us and pretending you don't like her. You don't have time for a teaching position at Astor College — you took it because she intrigues you."

No. I took it to study her, to ensure she isn't a threat. My heart wrenches as I glance at my grandfather's watch. I can't allow the past to repeat itself, no matter what. Keeping an eye on Raya is a safety measure, a necessity.

"Fine," I murmur, knowing full well my brothers won't leave me alone until they feel like I've at least heard them out. "So, tell me how to keep my wife happy."

My brothers all snicker in satisfaction. The pleased looks they share just irritate me further. I don't even understand what their deal is until Xavier rolls his eyes as he repeats the words *my wife* mockingly. *Fuck.* For years, I've given them shit for how often they slip the words *my wife* into sentences unnecessarily, only for me to subconsciously do it myself. *Fucking shit.*

"Oh, we've got you," Zane says, grinning, clearly pleased I'm at least willing to listen when they aren't exactly giving me a choice.

Yet somehow, I find myself enraptured when they point out what I should pay attention to, right down to favorite foods, *lamb biryani*, favorite colors, *yellow*, and little things that make her happy, *like doing that move from Dirty Dancing*.

Unease settles deep in my stomach when I realize I have most of the answers already. I bite down on my lip, my foot tapping a soothing rhythm.

Nah, Ares is wrong.

I didn't take that teaching position because she intrigues me. It wasn't so I could see her again, because I couldn't stay away.

Surveillance.

That's all it is. It can't be more than that.

Eighteen

Raya

I'm nervous beyond measure as Adam and I walk into Lex's class, and I tighten my grip on my bag to keep my hands from shaking. The last couple of days have been a whirlwind of negotiations and formalities between our families and our lawyers, and I've barely even seen Lex since the conversation we had. It feels strange to walk into his class now like nothing happened, like he isn't the man I'm marrying.

"You're really quiet. Everything okay?" Adam asks, his gaze roaming over me, concern etched into his face.

I nod, my heart wrenching. One of the first contracts I signed was a mutual non-disclosure agreement. I can't even tell my best friend that I'm getting married, and I only have myself to blame for it. "I'm just nervous because the design winners will probably be announced today."

He simply sighs, knowing me well enough to know I'm lying. "I've never seen anyone rattle you the way Lexington Windsor does," he says, his tone filled with a hint of contempt as we sit down.

"He doesn't *rattle* me," I instantly deny.

Adam throws me a disbelieving look, and I sigh as I slump in my seat. "Maybe he rattles me just a little, but that's mostly because he's *Lexington Windsor*, CEO of Windsor Motors. You know how long I've been studying their growth trajectory, Adam. I've always hoped for Dad's company to emulate Windsor Motors' performance. I know we're capable of it, and I honestly think that if we succeed in making our solar powered electric car commercially viable, we might exceed them. I guess it's just exciting to be able to learn from Lex."

Adam studies me for a moment, his gaze unreadable. "Lex, huh?" he says, smiling wryly as he takes his tablet out of his bag. "You've never been a good liar, Raya."

"Fine," I tell him. "*Fine*, okay? He does affect me. Happy?"

Adam sighs and turns to face me. "Not at all," he says, his tone snappy. "I'm incredibly concerned, because not only is that man our *professor*, he's also a completely unattainable billionaire, and I don't want you to get hurt."

I deflate and reach for his hand over the table, understanding dawning. Adam's mom helped his father build his business from the ground up, only for him to leave his family once he'd achieved the success he'd always dreamed of. Adam hasn't spoken to his dad in years, and ever since his father left, he's been convinced money changes people, and that those who have an excess of it can't be trusted.

"Don't worry," I tell him, unsure how else to reassure him. I know exactly what I'm getting into with Lex, but Adam would never understand. If he found out I'm essentially marrying Lex for money, he'd never look at me the same again, and I'm not sure I could take that.

Adam tightens his grip on my hand and nods as Lex walks into the lecture theatre. Lex locks his jaws when he spots our joined hands, his expression hardening as he stands rooted in place, his gaze slowly drifting up my arm, until it settles on my face.

My stomach twists as I try to decipher the look in his eyes. It's a mixture or anger and... betrayal? Whatever it is makes me pull my hand to my chest for a moment, before I busy myself with my laptop. Lex's shoulders relax, but his expression remains stormy as he addresses the room.

"Three designs were chosen," he says, not bothering with pleasantries today. "You've all worked hard, and to say that I'm impressed with your efforts would be putting it mildly. I was told that Astor College houses the brightest of minds, and you have upheld those words."

The room is instantly filled with pride and hope, but a few people snicker from the back of the room. "We all know you're not here for our bright minds," someone shouts. "You're just here for Professor Leia," someone else adds.

My heart sinks when I notice Lex's guilty expression, and something dark unfurls in the pit of my stomach. I've heard the rumors about Lex and Professor Leia dating while they were studying at Astor College, but I'd dismissed them as petty gossip. Was it true, after all? He said he hadn't dated in years, not that he'd never dated at all. Is he still hung up on Leia Astor? My stomach twists at the thought of it — she's such an amazing woman that I couldn't even blame him if that's the case.

Lex's gaze bores down on me, and I raise my head to meet his eyes. He studies me, something akin to understanding crossing his face. The edges of his lips turn up into a satisfied smile, and he rocks back on his heels, looking surprisingly pleased.

"You two," he drawls. "Get out. *Now*."

Much to my surprise, several people dressed like regular students stand up, their stiff posture making it clear they're Windsor security personnel in disguise. Both students are escorted out, and Lex runs a hand through his thick, dark hair.

"Let me make one thing abundantly clear," he says, his tone sharp and his eyes locked with mine. "I'm engaged, and I won't tolerate any rumors that could even remotely upset my future wife."

A hush falls over the room, and I draw a shaky breath, surprised by his instant reassurance. He looks at me like he's pleading with me to believe him, his attention solely on me. Heat rushes to my face, and I look away, unable to keep from smiling.

"Besides, I do not take insults toward my family lightly," he adds. "That is what Leia Astor is to me — she's like a *sister* to me. My relationship with her is not of a romantic nature, and it never has been." He turns to the class then, and I nervously tuck my hair behind my ear. "You will respect her and her husband as you do me, and you will not defame her in my presence."

Lex's gaze roams over the room, as though to ensure we comprehended his words. Within minutes, he's addressed and dismissed the rumors about him. Not just that — he made it clear he's taken, and something about that makes my heart overflow with hope.

"He's engaged?" Adam whispers, turning to me. "What a complete piece of shit. I'm sorry you had to find out this way, Raya. I know you said nothing happened between you two that night, but still..." Anger crosses his face, and he glares at Lex. "I should've known he'd be a cheater. Probably thinks his money can buy him anything."

My lips part to come to Lex's defense, only for my words to evade me. How do I explain that I'm the woman Lex is engaged to, and that he couldn't have cheated on me that night? I run a hand through my hair in frustration, unsure what to do or say.

"Raya Lewis," Lex says, saving me from having to respond to Adam's words. I look up at him to find his gaze moving between Adam and me, a hint of irritation in his deep emerald eyes. My heart skips a beat, and I stare back at him, wide-eyed.

"Adam Lawson."

He sits up, much like I have.

"Emma Thomas."

I raise a brow when I realize it's the same girl Lex was talking to in our first class. The one who was blatantly flirting with him.

"Your designs were chosen. Congratulations to all three of

you. Your drone designs were innovative but practical. Not only were you able to successfully apply the concept of mechatronics, but you also ensured your designs incorporated accessible materials."

Adam and I exchange shocked looks and sit back in stunned silence as all three plans are distributed through the room by Windsor Motors drones that are far superior to anything any of us could've come up with. Everyone begins to talk amongst themselves at once, discussing the designs that are delivered to them, and all the while, I can't take my eyes off Lex.

I didn't think he'd so publicly announce that he's off the market when we aren't even married yet. We've barely even spoken since that day in his penthouse, and I wasn't sure where I stood with him, until now. The possessiveness in his gaze speaks volumes, and it confuses me. He made it so clear he didn't want to be in a relationship, but his actions aren't in line with that of a notorious bachelor. He seems committed to me, and I'm not sure what to make of that.

"You'll each be grouped into a team. You'll receive an email about that shortly, but if you check the papers in front of you, you'll find all the essential details on there too. Go ahead and strategize. Create assembly plans around the design you've been assigned to as a team. Next week's class will be in Astor College's labs, where we'll start the practical part of this class."

"We're on different teams," Adam grumbles.

I tear my eyes off Lex to look at the documents in front of me. At the top, it states Team Leader in big letters. "That makes sense, since both of our designs were selected."

Adam narrows his eyes slightly. "He wouldn't have chosen mine simply to split us up, would he? I can't even switch with anyone to work with you, because we're both team leaders. He'd better remember that he's engaged. I won't let him mess with you, Raya."

I chuckle and shake my head in surprise. "Of course he

wouldn't have done that," I murmur, just as Lex glances our way, his eyes blazing with something that looks a lot like jealousy.

Nineteen

Raya

"Honey, are you ready?" Mom shouts. "We're going to be late for your dress fitting!"

I rush down the stairs, nerves making me sick to my stomach. Everything is moving so fast, and I'm not sure how to handle it.

Since we agreed to keep our marriage a secret, we opted to just get the formalities out of the way as soon as possible, but that means there are only three weeks left until I marry Lexington Windsor, and it all seems so surreal. I feel like a spectator in some play, actors moving all around me while I just get in the way.

"Hope you don't mind if I join, after all?" Dad asks, his gaze conflicted as he stands by mom's side, his arm wrapped around her shoulder.

I grin and shake my head as I walk into his embrace. "Of course not, Dad. You know I wanted you there."

He sighs, reluctance crossing his face as he bends down to hug me tightly. Mom joins in, the three of us cuddled together for a few moments. It's odd how my impending wedding suddenly made things feel so precarious. I moved back home to make the wedding prep easier, and I couldn't be happier with that decision. I know I'm not losing my parents, but somehow, it feels like I am, like things will never be the same again once I'm married.

Dad tenses when the doorbell rings, and I step back as he opens the door to a vaguely familiar face. "Good afternoon, Mr. and Mrs. Lewis," the man says, smiling at my parents before nodding at me. "Raya, isn't it? It's a true honor to meet you all today. My name is Ares Windsor. I'm Lexington's oldest brother." My eyes widen in shock when I realize who he is — he's Raven's husband.

He shakes hands with both of my parents, his expression sincere. "I was told that you're going dress shopping today, and I was hoping you'd allow me to drive you to my wife's boutique. Wedding dresses are my wife's specialty, and she'd be honored if you'd let her design your dress as a wedding gift, Raya."

His words render me speechless, and all I manage is a weak nod. Raven Windsor wants to design my wedding dress? I suppose it makes sense, but it's just a little... surreal. Ares smiles, his face lighting up in relief, like he genuinely thought there might be a chance anyone would ever say no to that offer.

"I know that champagne is often involved at dress fittings, and I'd love for you to enjoy your afternoon without having to worry about driving," Ares says, holding up his car keys.

Dad looks reluctant, and from the corner of my eye, I see Mom squeeze his hand in warning. "That would be lovely, Ares," she says, ushering me out the door.

I'd been nervous before, but now I'm anxious. From the moment the engagement was finalized, my emotions have been in constant turmoil, and the pace at which things are moving is just making it worse.

"Just a word of warning," Ares says as he gets behind the wheel. Dad is seated next to him while Mom and I are sitting in the back of one of Windsor Motors' most expensive supercars. I smile involuntarily as Dad glances around appreciatively, his fingers trailing over the smooth leather interior. No one appreciates a good car more than my father does, and I can tell he's impressed.

"I think my sister may be there, and if you're really unlucky, you'll find that throughout the afternoon, all of my sisters-in-law will find completely random excuses to drop by and meet you. They're all very excited to welcome you to the family."

My stomach twists nervously at the thought of Sierra Windsor. She's a real estate magnate, and one of the youngest and most successful women in her industry. She's known to be smart, fearless, and ruthless, and I suspect she'll be cold and reserved. "Thank you for letting me know," I tell him, hating the way my voice shakes.

Ares shoots me a reassuring look through the rearview mirror, his eyes the exact same shade of green as Lex's. "I know it's all a lot, but make sure you enjoy every moment as best as you can. You only get married once, after all. Vow renewals aren't uncommon in our family, but if you can, make sure the memories you make at your legal ceremony are ones you'll want to hold on to."

Dad huffs. "That remains to be seen," he says, his tone sharp. He twists in his seat to face me. "There is nothing wrong with getting a divorce," he reassures me. "Your happiness matters above absolutely *anything* else. If you ever want to get married again, you can."

A startled laugh escapes my lips, and I reach for Dad to squeeze his shoulder. "I know, Daddy. Don't you worry."

Ares merely grins, relaxed confidence written all over his face as he parks right in front of Raven's boutique. I stare up at it with wonder, taking in the white exterior with its pink peonies and roses all around it. It's beautiful. Whimsical but classy, and entirely out of my price range.

Ares leads us deep into the store, and I lower my head, feeling thoroughly humbled by the splendor all around me. "Hi, Cupcake," he calls, his eyes lighting up the second Raven comes into view. He opens his arms wide, and she grins as she hugs him.

He squeezes tightly, his eyes falling closed for a moment, and a pang of longing hits me hard. That's what I thought I'd have — true love, like my parents, like Ares and Raven.

He presses a kiss to her forehead and steps back to introduce us. Raven's eyes light up when she spots me standing behind Ares, and she pushes against his chest, making him step aside as she rushes toward me. Before I realize what's happening, she's wrapped me in a tight hug, nearly knocking the wind out of me.

This is *Raven Windsor,* supermodel and famous designer, and she's *hugging* me. "It's so good to meet you," she says, leaning back a little. She smiles so genuinely that I can't help but smile back.

"It's really good to meet you too," I manage to say. "An honor, really."

She shakes her head dismissively and turns to greet my parents, who both look as shellshocked as I am. Behind her, members of her staff walk in holding champagne and canapes, and both Mom and Dad are seated in comfy chairs as Raven explains the process.

First, she'll take my measurements, and then she'll let me try on a few dresses of my choosing to ensure we're on the same page in terms of style and fit. After that, we'll go into the design process.

We've only just about wrapped up the measurements when the store door opens and closes loudly, and I jump in surprise. "We're not late, are we?" I hear a woman say.

"I told you over and over again to hurry up," another woman replies, sounding worried. "But you still insisted on wrapping that cookie eleventy billion times until you got it *perfect.* We don't even know if she likes cookies!"

"Girls," Raven snaps, her voice stern. She doesn't sound particularly surprised, just a little annoyed. "What do you two think you're doing?"

I tense just as two women turn the corner and come into view. They look apologetic, and one of them is holding the biggest bouquet filled with an assortment of yellow flowers, while the other is holding a small pink box with a truly excessive number of ribbons on it.

My heart begins to race when I realize that they're Celeste and Sierra Windsor. Celeste and her husband, Zane, are hoteliers and the owners of the world's most luxurious resorts. A while ago, I read an article in The Herald that said Zane bought a private island just for his wife. I remember thinking back then that they lived in a whole different world, and now I'm somehow supposed to fit in with these highly accomplished women. I don't see how I ever could.

"Hi, Raya! I'm Celeste." She tips her head to the red-faced woman standing next to her. "And this is Sierra. We're really sorry to interrupt, but Lex wanted me to give you this." She steps forward and hands me the bouquet with the sweetest smile on her face. "I doubt he'd ever admit it, but he spent hours yesterday walking through my husband's greenhouse and observatory, cutting each flower in your bouquet by hand before binding them all together."

I take the bouquet with trembling hands and murmur my thanks as I pull the flowers to my chest, my heart aching. The thought of Lex deliberating over which flowers to choose and how they'd look together makes me instantly feel conflicted. Did he mean it when he told me he'd try to be a good husband? I find it hard to believe, and I can't get over the fact that he orchestrated every interaction we've ever had. Even this seems oddly calculated — sending flowers when he knows his family and mine would be there to witness it.

"This is for you too," Sierra says, handing me the small pink box with trembling hands. "I made it. It's not quite the same as my grandmother's, as you'll soon learn, but I'm the family's cookie connoisseur, and I can guarantee that this cookie isn't half bad."

"Thank you so much," I tell her, grinning from ear to ear. "I love cookies."

Her eyes light up, and she sighs — seemingly in relief. I seem to have passed a test of some sort, because she leans in and wraps an arm around me, side hugging me. "Welcome to the family, Raya. I'm so excited to have another sister. You have no idea."

"We all are," Celeste says, smiling sweetly. My heart warms as I smile back at her, a spark of hope that I thought I'd doused reigniting. Maybe this marriage won't be as loveless as I'd feared — it just won't be the kind of love I was hoping for.

Twenty

RAYA

I glance at the text message Lex sent me this morning as Adam and I head to our next class. Celeste all but begged me to text him to let him know I received the flowers she brought me, and ever since, he's texted me to wish me a good day and sweet dreams — every single morning and evening. I don't know what to make of him at all. He claims not to want a relationship, yet his actions are in contrast with that. Sooner or later, we'll need to talk and get our expectations aligned. I don't want to be led on or read more into things than I should.

"It's so annoying that we aren't on the same team," Adam says as he holds the door open for me. "We always work so well together. Now we're both just going to be slowed down due to sheer inefficiency."

I look up and grin. "You haven't even met your team mates yet, Adam. Maybe they're not so bad."

"He did it on purpose, I'm sure of it," he complains, and a hint of unease runs down my spine. I laughed it off the first time

Adam said it, but was he right? It wouldn't be the first time Lex orchestrated a situation.

We both look up as Windsor Motors drones approach us, and within seconds, the drones are leading us to our stations and our team members. The technology is fascinating, but it's also intimidating. It's disheartening to know that it's highly unlikely anything we create in this class would hold a candle to Lex's inventions, but at the same time, I'm excited to try.

"Raya Lewis, right?" a guy I vaguely recognize says.

I nod at my team, my cheeks heating when I realize they'd all been studying my design intently.

"John," he adds, offering me a sweet smile, before tipping his head to the tall girl standing next to him, her hijab matching perfectly with her pale pink blouse. "This is Halima," he adds, before turning toward the short blonde guy, "and that is Simon."

"It's so good to meet you all," I tell them, flustered. The last couple of days have been such a whirlwind that I haven't had time to worry about the responsibilities that come with being a team leader. I've been so overwhelmed that it barely registered.

Halima hands me a list of materials. "I hope you don't mind, but I checked what the lab had in stock based on what your design plan incorporated, and then found substitutes for what wasn't available. I've been told that we can order in materials if we'd like, pending Professor Windsor's approval."

"This is perfect," I tell her as I read over her list, grateful she took the initiative to do this. "Shall we gather what we need?"

She nods at me just as Simon whistles. I turn to follow his gaze and find Lexington walking into the room, her eyes on his watch and a frown on his face. He looks up, our eyes locking, and I blush inadvertently when his expression darkens as his gaze roams over my face, his lips forming a smile.

"Damn," Simon says, groaning. "Maybe I should fail this class so I can offer to do *anything* for extra credit."

My eyes widen, and I stare at him in shock. Halima merely

throws me a sympathetic look. "He's always this inappropriate," she explains. "He starts to think out loud the second an even remotely attractive man enters his peripheral vision. You'll learn to tune him out soon enough. Just ignore it like I do. He's incorrigible."

Simon sighs. "I said that out loud, did I?"

John bursts out laughing and shakes his head. "I can't even blame you," he says, bringing his fist to his mouth in an attempt to stop laughing. "Even I can appreciate the way that man wears a suit." He glances at Lex and frowns. "I've been trying to figure out who he's marrying and can't even find the slightest clue. The Windsors have been so secretive about his fiancée, but I don't think he'll be able to hide it for long. I read in The Herald that Lexington bought a ridiculously priced yellow diamond at a prestigious auction, so now we just wait for that diamond to rock up on someone's finger."

For a moment, my eyes drop to my empty ring finger, and longing crashes through me. I always thought I'd get a grand proposal, and a yellow diamond is what I've always dreamed of. It hurts to know that dream will never become a reality. Lex made it clear he has no interest in romance, so even if that story is true, the diamond wouldn't be for a ring. A birthday gift for Sierra, perhaps. Whoever it's for… it isn't me.

"Let's get started," I tell them, needing a distraction. "Competition will be fierce, and I really don't think I offer any advantage at all. Everything I knew about making my design work was in my plan, so all teams that were assigned my design have as much information as I do. We just have to be quicker, so we have more time to troubleshoot, and I can almost guarantee we'll need that time."

They nod, their expressions rapidly becoming serious as I divide our tasks and check that everyone is okay with the parts they've been assigned. For the first twenty minutes, we work together seamlessly. It's one of those things I love about being at Astor College — almost everyone here truly has a grand vision for their future, and we're all willing to work hard for it. Being teased about how much I loved studying is one of the parts of high school I definitely don't miss.

"I see you've gathered your materials and you're already halfway through building the framework for your drone," Lex says, sneaking up behind me.

I gasp and jump, dropping my soldering iron. He chuckles and wraps his hand around my waist, steadying me. "I'm sorry," he tells me, his gaze roaming over my face. He holds on to me for a few moments longer than necessary. "I didn't mean to startle you."

I turn to face him fully and tilt my face up toward his, my heart beating a little faster. Even now, he looks at me like I'm the only girl in the room, and I hate it. I hate how much hope he gives me every time he's near.

"Apologies, Professor Windsor," I say, my tone hesitant. Standing here with him and pretending he's nothing but a stranger isn't as easy as I wish it was. "When I focus on something, everything else just fades away. I'm really bad at paying attention to my surroundings."

His hand brushes against mine, once, twice. "I'll be sure not to sneak up on you again, then," he says, before glancing at our work. "This was a winning design, but that doesn't mean you can't adapt it in the execution phase. Sometimes things that work on paper don't work in practice."

I turn back toward our work, and he leans in over my shoulder, standing far closer than he really should. "That's some really nice wiring work, but it's very intricate. Have you taken heat into account? What about safety? Would the slightest malfunction cause this design to drop from the sky like a rock, not just breaking the drone, but potentially harming someone?"

"Shit," I mutter when I realize he's right. I'm great at working on cars, where every single component has its own established place, but smaller devices such as these are tricky for me.

He places his hand on my lower back and straightens. "It's good work, but it needs to be refined." He smiles then. "Which reminds me, there's something I meant to discuss with you regarding your design. Please see me after class."

I nod nervously, thrown off and more than a little flustered. This is the first time he's specifically told me to come see him, not giving me an out. With only two weeks left until the wedding, it's clear he's done giving me space.

Twenty-One

Lexington

I'm leaning against my impractical hardwood desk as I wait for Raya after class, certain Adrian gifted it to me to irritate me. It's fully enclosed and doesn't even allow me to extend my legs fully, but he insisted I have it, no matter how vehemently I declined the offer.

I sigh as I tap my finger against my desk. Raya has barely smiled at me since she found out about our engagement, and I know I only have myself to blame for it. My fiancée confuses the hell out of me. I thought I'd be grateful for the distance she's clearly keeping, but instead, it just makes me fucking miserable.

I rise from my seat at the sound of knocking, and Raya walks in moments later, her long hair cascading down the front of her body, all the way to her waist. "Professor Windsor," she says, her expression unreadable. "You asked to see me."

My shoulders relax at the sight of her, and I smile. "I love hearing you call me Professor Windsor," I murmur. "But I think I prefer hearing you call me Lex."

Her eyes widen a fraction, and a blush blossoms across her

face when I walk up to her. The way her gaze runs down my body is surprisingly reassuring. "Raya," I murmur. "You haven't replied to any of the texts I sent you." I cup her face and hold my breath for a moment, scared she'll recoil at my touch. "I won't stop sending them, you know? Until I'm able to wish you a good day or night in person, I'll keep texting you."

"I'm not sure what to make of you. Everything I thought was real feels orchestrated, and now I'm second-guessing everything you do or say, everything you've ever said. I'll get over it, I'll have to, but I just need a bit of time to get my thoughts straight."

"I understand," I tell her, and I do. "It was never my intention to hurt you, Raya. I hope you know that."

She smiles tightly, that same polite and distant look in her eyes. It should be a relief that she isn't arguing with me, that she isn't asking much of me. So why do I wish she would?

I brush my thumb over her bottom lip, longing unlike anything I've ever felt rushing through me. "If I asked you to play truth or dare with me again, would you?"

Surprise flickers through her eyes, and for a split second I'm certain she'll decline my request. But then she sighs and nods. "Truth," she whispers.

"Would you prefer to get married in my brother's rose garden, or my grandmother's ballroom?"

Her eyes widen, and she searches my face. "What is your preference?"

"Whatever will make you happiest."

She inhales shakily, her gorgeous brown eyes fluttering closed for a moment. "The rose garden. Your turn."

"I'll let Zane know. Truth."

"Why did you send me flowers?"

I bite down on my lip and avert my face. The truth is that I saw them when I walked into Zane's observatory to speak to him about borrowing his rose garden, and they instantly reminded me of Raya. I just thought they'd make her smile.

"It was clever," she adds. "Sending them while Sierra, Celeste, Raven, Ares, and my parents were there to witness it."

I sigh and wrap my hands around her waist, catching her by surprise when I lift her on top of my desk and move to step between her legs. "It wasn't an act," I tell her, my tone pleading.

She searches my expression, like she's trying to make sure I'm telling the truth. "I don't understand," she says, her hands reaching for my shoulders. It feels like an eternity since I last had her this close.

I pull back a little and grab her chin, keeping her eyes on mine. "Let me be clear, Raya. You're going to be my wife, and I'm going to spoil you rotten. If I want to send my wife something as simple as flowers in her favorite color, I'm going to do so — regardless of who's watching. I'm going to treat you so incredibly well, you won't lack for anything, nor will you yearn for anything." I'll make it so she won't crave love, won't even realize it's absent. I won't let my past touch her.

"Do you see how that's a mixed signal?" she asks, her grip on my shoulders tightening. "Those kinds of things, you do them when you're in a relationship, which you've explicitly told me you don't want. I'm not saying I didn't like it — I loved it, Lex. I'm just trying to figure out what you're thinking, so I don't misunderstand or get my hopes up."

"It's true that I wasn't interested in a relationship, but as it turns out, *you* are the exception to that rule, Raya. I've given you space because I've been thinking about what you said, what you demanded. I don't know if I can give you what you want, but I'd like to try being in a real relationship with you. I owe it to you to try."

Her eyes widen, and I smile wryly, as surprised by the words as she is. I hadn't meant to say that, hadn't even known I wanted that until the words left my lips. Before I met Raya, I had every intention of drawing boundaries and sticking to them. Somehow, I just can't manage it with her.

She's right — the flowers were out of character, and I simply hadn't been thinking when I sent them, my usual rigorous decision-making process drowned out by my desire to make her smile.

"I don't want this distance between us," I admit. "It wasn't my intention to upset you, or to push you away." Fuck, I want more of the way she made me feel when we danced in my living room, the way she moaned when I kissed her, and the truths we shared. I'm tired of feeling so fucking hollow, so lonely, when she's right there, shining a light on to my shadows and chasing them away with her mere presence. That one night with her made me feel more alive than I have in years. I can't let fear deprive me of that.

"What does that mean?" she asks, looking more vulnerable than I've ever seen her look before.

"I don't know yet," I whisper. "Raya, there are things I can't tell you about, things I've experienced that left me forever changed. I know it isn't fair to ask for your understanding when I can't even give you the full truth... but my little fairy... I promise you, I'll try. I'll try to be what you want me to be, to give you what you need."

My heart wrenches when she cups my face and looks into my eyes, her touch gentle. "It would make me so happy if you'd give us a real chance, Lex. I'm not asking you to change, you know? I'll take you as you are."

Twenty-Two

Raya

"You look stunning," Mom says, tears in her eyes as she takes in the heavy white bridal lehenga I'm wearing, the outfit a perfect fusion of her culture and Dad's. Raven outdid herself with the design, making my wildest dreams come true. It's elegant, and it fits me like nothing else ever has, truly transforming my figure. I've never felt more beautiful.

"So do you, Mom," I murmur, taking in the gorgeous yellow saree she's wearing. She looks just like I'd always imagined she would on my wedding day — classy, radiant.

"Raya," Mom says, grabbing my hand. She searches my face, her gaze tormented. I've never seen her as emotional as she is today. "You don't have to do this if you don't want to, my darling. It's not too late to back out now. We'll find another way."

I shake my head and tighten my grip on her hand. "No, Mom. I stand by my decision. I know this isn't what you wanted for me, but he's a good man. He loves his family, and he's dedicated to his job. Lexington won't just save the company; he'll help us realize our vision for it."

Some time and distance did exactly what I hoped it would — it gave me perspective. It helped me not take Lex's actions personally. Taking a step back allowed me to see his behavior for what it was: protectiveness. It doesn't hurt any less, but I understand where he's coming from. Besides, against better judgment, I trust him when he says he'll try.

Mom draws a shaky breath and looks down. "I know you always wanted a big Indian wedding alongside a western one, and now… now you won't have that. He *does* seem to be a good man, but I just want you to have everything you've ever wanted, and I know this isn't it."

I glance at my empty arms, the mehendi and bangles I always thought I'd have missing. She's right — this isn't quite what I'd imagined. I always thought my wedding would be a grand affair, just like in my favorite Bollywood movies, but then again, I always thought I'd marry for love. "It's okay, Mom," I reassure her. "I promise, I'm more than fine."

Mom begins to reply, but we're interrupted by the sound of knocking on the door. "Come in," she calls, and my heart wrenches when Dad walks into the guest room Zane and Celeste provided me with, ahead of the ceremony that'll take place in the observatory attached to their home.

He freezes when he sees me, his eyes wide and rapidly filling with tears. "Oh, my little girl," he says, his voice breaking. Dad walks up to me and takes my hands, swallowing hard. "You look so beautiful."

A tear runs down his face, and I catch it with my thumb, cupping his cheek gently. "Thank you, Dad."

He chokes back a sob and shakes his head. "Let's not do this, hmm? Let's just go home."

I chuckle and shake my head, my heart warming. "I can't keep my groom waiting at the altar now, can I?"

"Sure you can," he reassures me. His eyes are filled with sorrow and guilt, and seeing him looking at me like that just breaks my heart.

I hold up my pinky and smile. "I promise I'll come home the second I'm even remotely unhappy, okay?"

Dad hooks his finger around mine, sealing my pinky-promise. "These kinds of promises are unbreakable," he reminds me, a smile breaking through. "So I know you'll keep your word."

I nod and rise to my tiptoes to press a kiss to his cheek, which just makes him cry in earnest. He hugs me tightly, and Mom wraps her arms around us both, equally emotional.

"I'm sorry to disturb," someone says from behind us, her tone sweet and understanding. "But it's time."

Dad sucks in a breath and tries his best to compose himself while Mom fixes my makeup, her expression searching. She pushes my long waves out of my face and looks into my eyes. "*Khush raho*," she whispers, tears in her eyes. *Be happy.*

I nod, silently promising I'll do all I can to fulfill her wish. She looks me over once more, making sure I truly am fine, before she hands me over to my dad. It isn't until I'm holding his arm that I recognize the petite redhead standing in the corner, the sweetest smile on her face, a tinge of longing in her expression as her gaze moves from my parents to me.

Faye Windsor. Lexington's sister-in-law and Dion Windsor's wife. "I'm your pianist today," she explains, and my eyes widen in surprise. "I'll be playing as you walk into the observatory with your father, so I'll go in ahead of you."

I never took note of any of the details, because this wedding was meant to just be a formality. However, it seems like the Windsors don't quite agree. Not only did they arrange for the wedding to take place in the most beautiful and grand observatory I've ever seen, but we'll also have one of the world's best pianists playing for us? It seems far too romantic for something that is essentially a glorified business deal, and it fills me with something I can't quite define. Longing, perhaps — for it all to be real. This wedding may not be exactly what I've always imagined, but it isn't far off either.

My heart is racing as Mom leaves to take her seat, accompanied by Faye, and Dad and I make our way to the start of the white rose petal trail that leads us toward the aisle. "I love you," Dad says, his voice shaking. "I will always be there for you, Raya. No matter what. You don't ever need a reason to come home to Mom and me, okay? Our home will always be yours, too."

I look up at him as music begins to play, our cue. "I love you too, Daddy. Always will."

He draws a shaky breath and closes his eyes for a moment to compose himself, and then he nods. Together, we walk down the aisle, where Lex is waiting for us, his four brothers by his side. Much to my surprise, Sierra, Raven, Celeste, and Valentina stand on my side, sweet smiles on their faces.

I'd been worried about feeling lonely at my own wedding, since I haven't even told Adam about it. Seeing these four women standing there gives me the same hope I felt during my dress fitting, and I smile at them, before settling my gaze on the one person I'd been avoiding looking at.

Lexington.

Our eyes lock, and he inhales sharply. He looks stunned, mesmerized, and I watch as Ares leans in and whispers something in his ear, no doubt teasing him. Lex barely responds, doesn't take his eyes off me for even a second.

Dad and I pause in front of him, and my nerves skyrocket. Dad grabs my hand and holds it tightly, hesitating for one beat, and then another, before he places my hand in Lexington's, his own covering both of ours. "That's one half of my heart you're holding," he tells Lex, his voice trembling.

Lex nods solemnly and tightens his grip on my hand. "I'll treat her with care, always."

Dad's eyes flash, and then he nods, pulling his hand away. He takes one more look at me, searching for the smallest sign of hesitancy, and I smile at him reassuringly. His eyes fall closed for a moment, and then he steps back to take his seat next to Mom and Lex's grandmother.

"We have gathered here today to witness the marriage of Raya Indira Lewis, and Lexington Windsor," the vaguely familiar looking officiant says, and I turn to face Lexington, my heart racing.

"You look breathtaking," he whispers, stepping closer to me.

I smile shakily, reality finally sinking in when we're both asked to say our *I do*'s. Lex slides a plain gold band onto my finger, and I stare at it for a moment, reminded of the article I read about the yellow diamond he bought. Who was that for?

Sierra hands me a similar ring, and I push it onto Lex's finger slowly, my hands trembling just a little as I push the ring past his knuckle, into place. The entire time, Lex's undivided attention is on me, his gaze roaming over my face, silently caressing every inch of me. Something passes between us, a moment of understanding, and he smiles at me intimately.

"You may kiss the bride," the officiant says, and Lex's hand slides behind my neck, his gaze heated. He moves closer slowly, his nose brushing against mine before our lips meet. Lex groans when I tilt my face and kiss him back, my heart soaring. I missed this — the way he makes me feel, the way he touches me.

His fingers slide into my hair, and he parts my lips, deepening our kiss as he presses his body against mine. His tongue teases mine, and a soft, needy sound escapes the back of my throat. It makes him press against me harder for a moment, before pulling away, his eyes sparkling with desire.

"Mr. and Mrs. Windsor, everyone!" the officiant says.

Applause erupts around us, but Lex and I can't take our eyes off each other. He drops his forehead to mine and draws a ragged breath. "*Mrs. Windsor,*" he repeats, the sweetest smile on his face as he straightens and grabs my hand.

Twenty-Three

Lexington

My heart races as Raya and I dance in Zane and Celeste's rose garden to the song Dion composed for us. She looks so ethereal, I almost want to pinch myself to make sure I'm not dreaming. I haven't been able to take my eyes off her for even a second.

"Why are you staring at me like that?" she asks, her cheeks beautifully rosy. Our steps are so perfectly in sync, and the way we're gliding across the rose garden reminds me of the way we danced in my penthouse.

"Just looking at my wife," I murmur, my fingers brushing against the parts of her back that are exposed in that stunning wedding outfit she's wearing. "You're just so beautiful, Raya."

The look in her eyes keeps me enchanted, and my eyes drop to her lips for a moment. The way she kissed me made it nearly impossible to pull back, and I'm already counting down the seconds until I'm alone with her.

My hands move to her hips, and I grin, one brow raised. Raya giggles and nods, knowing exactly what I'm asking. She gasps when I lift her up the way I did in King of Hearts, raising her up above my head as I twirl her around slowly, entirely under her spell.

She laughs, and fuck, that's the first time I've seen her laugh since that night in my penthouse. She's looked so reserved ever since, and I didn't even realize how much I'd missed this part of her.

I tilt her down slowly, carefully, until I've got my arms wrapped around the back of her knees as best as I can, her body pressed against mine. She looks down at me, her gorgeous brown eyes twinkling as I continue to turn with her in my arms.

"Raya," I murmur as I slowly lower her to the floor, my hand wrapping into her hair. She tilts her face up, a soft sigh escaping her lips when I lean in, my mouth hovering over hers. My heart fucking soars when she rises to her tiptoes and kisses me, her arms wrapping around my neck.

I groan when she pulls away, her breathing erratic as I cup her face, my thumb brushing over her lips. Fuck. I can't believe this beautiful woman is my *wife*. "Dance with me somewhere more private, my little fairy." My tone is pleading, desperation bleeding into my voice.

Raya gives me the smallest nod, and I breathe a sigh of relief, a smile spreading across my face as my fingers entwine with hers. I feel my family's eyes on us, laughter and teasing ringing through the air as we make our way out of Zane and Celeste's observatory, but thankfully, her parents are nowhere to be seen. Somehow, the idea of stealing their daughter away from them for what is essentially our wedding night feels sinful.

I shrug out of my suit jacket and wrap it around Raya moments before we walk out, shielding her from the evening breeze. "I love seeing you in my jacket," I murmur without thinking. "You look far better in it than I ever did." I grab the lapels and pull her close, my eyes roaming over her.

She grins and tilts her head in that way I find so adorable — that way that tells me she thinks I'm just being flirtatious. "I wouldn't be so sure," she says, her cheeks perfectly rosy. "You look really good in this tux."

"Do I?" I ask, grinning as I step closer to her, my body brushing against hers. Her expression is so disarmed, and it's fucking exhilarating. I haven't seen her look at me that way since the day we met.

Raya parts her lips to respond, only for headlights to catch our attention. I step away from her when my grandmother's limousine stops in front of us, and the door opens. I sigh as I glance at my wife. "I guess that's our ride," I murmur, apprehension seeping into me as I help Raya into the car.

My eyes widen in surprise when I join my wife and find both of her parents sitting opposite her, right next to my grandmother, all three of their expressions unreadable. "Well," I murmur. "I suppose I should've seen this coming." I knew my grandmother would do this to us, but I hadn't expected her parents to be here too. I guess that explains why they weren't in the rose garden just now.

Raya's dad stares at me with an unyielding expression, and I have no doubt a lesser man would've cowered before him. I merely smile politely and take Raya's hand in mine, which only seems to aggravate him further when I meant for it to be reassuring.

"Congratulations, both of you," Grandma says as the car begins to move. The drive from Zane and Celeste's house to mine is only about ten minutes, but for those ten minutes, my grandmother has the upper hand. Or so she thinks, anyway.

I draw circles across the back of Raya's hand with my thumb, and she squeezes in return. I glance over at her to find her looking nervous, and I turn back to my grandmother with a raised brow.

"For starters, please allow me to give you your new identification documents, and your new Windsor Bank credit card," Grandma says, handing Raya an envelope. I smirk when I spot the name Raya Indira *Windsor* on it. It sounds so fucking good.

"The card is linked to my personal assets, and it doesn't have a limit," I tell her, my voice soft.

Her gaze cuts to mine, and she raises a brow. "What if I bankrupt you? I might just go out and buy every Lewis Motors car there is," she says, making everyone in the car laugh.

"Buy two," I retort, loving the idea of spoiling her. "It still wouldn't dent my bank balance."

Grandma shakes her head indulgently and hands her a black suede jewelry box. "While the card is from Lex, this is from me," she says, a sweet smile on her face. "I've given each of my granddaughters-in-law a unique, priceless jewelry set handcrafted by Laurier, and this one is for you. Lexington told me that yellow is your favorite color, so your set contains yellow sapphire and diamonds. It's a little old-fashioned but wearing it will convey my approval to the world."

"T-Thank you," Raya stammers, caught off guard. So far, every interaction she's had with my grandmother has been formal and related to the paperwork we had to complete before our wedding, so I suppose tonight is the first time she's truly been made to feel like family.

"As I'm sure you're both aware, this marriage comes with several rules, and we all want to make sure you're aware of them," Raya's mom says, her tone gentle, placating. My wife's shoulders straighten, and she sits up a little.

Grandma throws her a smile before turning to look at me pointedly. "I'll keep this brief, since we'll arrive at your house momentarily."

I nod in gratitude, already well aware of what she's about to say. "Lex and Raya, your marriage must last a minimum of three years."

I nod, and so does Raya. This isn't the first time either of us is hearing about the rules — we both signed paperwork detailing every last term and condition, after all. "Throughout that time, you must both live on the Windsor Estate, and you *must* share a bed."

Raya's dad tenses, and her mother places her hand on his knee. He glances at his wife, and the look in her eyes seems to put him at ease. I can see why Raya wants that, but I don't think she realizes just how rare that kind of bond is.

"You cannot be apart for more than three consecutive days at a time, and no more than twelve days a year. While this is a business deal, it is our hope that your marriage is a successful one, and these rules are meant to help you give your marriage an honest chance. As such, infidelity of any kind will not be tolerated. Should you breach any of these terms, the merger will fall through, and you'll lose your inheritance, Lex."

Raya and I both nod. "There's more," Raya's dad says. "While your main residence will be at the Windsor Estate, I would like you both to come home every weekend. I may have consented to this marriage, but I have to make sure my little girl is doing okay. I want to see how you treat her firsthand, and if you ever do anything I don't like—"

"—we'd just really love to see you on weekends," Raya's mother interrupts, smiling tightly. "You'll come home every weekend. We understand that you may have social obligations, but even when that's the case, we'd like you to spend the night at home. In return, you'll be exempt from having to attend any other family events for the first three months, to give you a chance to focus on your marriage."

"Understood," I say, trying my hardest to smile sincerely. I can't fault them for looking after their daughter's wellbeing, however inconvenient their requests might be.

Raya's dad looks surprised, like he didn't think I'd have agreed to his request. His shoulders sag a little, and I can't tell if he's relieved or annoyed I agreed so easily. His expression turns into genuine worry when the car comes to a stop in front of my home, and he reaches for his daughter, taking her free hand in his. He searches her face, and even I can read the quiet message, the reassurance in his eyes. I have no doubt he'd have attempted to take my wife home with him if she hadn't smiled at him and leaned in to kiss his cheek before doing the same to her mother.

Raya looks at me and tightens her grip on my hand, and I nod before helping her out of the car, bending down to lift her into my arms moments later.

"What are you doing?" she asks, gasping and glancing back at the car behind us.

I grin at her as I take a step forward. "What I'm supposed to, my little fairy. I'm carrying my wife over the threshold, into our home."

Twenty-Four

Lexington

Raya's eyes are glued to mine as I carry her into the house and grin at her, relieved to find her looking at me the way she did in the rose garden. It's not quite the same way she looked at me the day we met, but it's far less guarded than it's been recently, and I'm counting that as a win.

She bites down on her lip when we enter my bedroom, her gaze roaming over my face, a hint of insecurity making its way into her eyes. "Is this the home you told me you've never brought a woman to? The home you reserved for your wife?"

I nod and lower her to the floor carefully. She takes a step back, her gaze conflicted as she looks around. I study her as she takes in the cream tones and all the tech I have installed, and I'm not quite sure what to do or say now that we're alone. "If there's anything you don't like, we can just redecorate. I want to make sure you feel at home here. There's a lab at the back of the house too, with any and all equipment you could possibly want. Nothing is off-limits to you, Raya."

She smiles tightly and nods, her expression unreadable as she walks through the bedroom and into the attached dressing room, pausing in front of the floor-length mirror. I watch her as she looks at her herself, a hint of disbelief written all over her face, like she can't quite comprehend that she's here with me, dressed in a wedding gown.

Her eyes meet mine in the mirror, and she turns to face me, her gorgeous brown eyes sparkling with vulnerability. I hesitate for a moment before stepping closer, the back of my hand brushing over her cheek softly. "Truth or Dare, Raya?" I whisper.

She exhales shakily, her eyes fluttering closed. "Dare."

I cup her face, my thumb brushing over her mouth. "I dare you to just be in the moment with me. Don't think about the past or the future and just be here with me."

She leans into my hand and draws a shaky breath before nodding. "Your turn," she whispers.

"Dare."

My wife looks up at me from lowered lashes, and the way her eyes roam over my face makes my heart beat a little faster. She hesitates, her gaze settling on my lips. "Kiss me, Lex. Make me forget about everything but this moment with you. Keep me from overthinking."

Surprise is quickly drowned out by desire, and I step closer to her as I tilt her face up, my hand sliding into her hair. "With pleasure, Mrs. Windsor," I murmur, taking my time. I kiss the edge of her mouth first, earning myself a sweet whimper. The tip of her nose is next, and she startles a little, only to gasp when I kiss her forehead. "Like that?" I whisper, proceeding to kiss her temple. "Tell me how you'd like to be kissed, my little fairy."

She reaches for my shirt and balls the fabric in her hand, pulling me closer. "You know how," she tells me, throwing my own words back at me.

I smirk and lean in, my lips touching hers once, twice, before I grab her waist and pull her flush against me. My wife rises to her tiptoes, her lips parting for me eagerly. The way she moves her tongue against mine is fucking intoxicating, and that faint honey flavor... *delicious.*

Her hands roam over my shirt, and I groan when she undoes the top button, and then the next one, until my shirt falls open. I pull back to look at her, only to find the same wild hunger I'm feeling in her eyes. She slowly slides my shirt off my shoulders, putting a wicked smile on my face. Having her full attention on me like that is fucking thrilling.

I pull my shirt off entirely, my cufflinks hitting the floor as I yank it off impatiently. Raya's gaze roams over my body appreciatively, and I grin at her. "Examining your new belongings, Mrs. Windsor? What's the verdict?"

"I haven't decided yet," she tells me, her voice husky. "I can't. I don't have the full picture, you see."

"*Fuck*," I moan when she slides her hand down my chest, hooking her finger into the waistband of my pants.

My heart is racing as I place her hands on my zipper, and she looks into my eyes as she undoes my pants, only to lose her confidence the moment her hand brushes against my rock-hard cock. Her eyes widen, and a cute innocent look takes over her expression.

"Turn around."

My tone is harsher than I'd intended, my impulse to control the situation bleeding into my voice. Raya inhales deeply before obeying, slowly turning to face the mirror again, her eyes finding mine in the reflection.

A soft, needy whimper escapes from her perfect pouty lips when I move her hair aside to expose her neck, my eyes on hers as I kiss her just below her ear. She shivers when I trail the curve of her neck with my lips, taking my time.

Raya gasps when I place my hand on the back of her blouse, her chest rising and falling rapidly. "Can I undress you?"

She searches my face for a couple of seconds, and then she nods, the movement near imperceptible. My hands tremble as I undo the delicate hooks on the back, my heart skipping a beat when it falls open, exposing her skin. Raya presses her hands to the front of her blouse, insecurity drowning out her desire, and I smile at her.

"I told you I'd wait for as long as you wanted me to, Raya. That hasn't changed. I won't do anything you don't want me to."

She nods and pulls her arms away, but the way she still has her shoulders drawn up tells me she isn't comfortable, so I move on to her skirt instead, helping her step out of the heavy garment. Raya's eyes are blazing when I grab her waist and lift her into my arms. She wraps her legs around me, and I take a moment to just look at my wife. I wasn't sure I'd ever get to experience this version of her again — the version I've come to consider *mine.* My enchanting little fairy.

My hands slide down to her ass, and she gasps, rotating her hips into me just a touch. "Fucking perfect," I whisper against her mouth as I carry her back to our bedroom. Her arms wrap around my neck, and she kisses the edge of my lips, making me pause mid-step.

She moans when I push her against the nearest wall and kiss her, her hands roaming over my shoulders, only to thread through my hair. It's fucking thrilling to be wanted by her, and I've never experienced anything quite like this. I don't think I've ever been this hard. I can barely think straight, can't even make my way to my bed without needing another taste of her. I groan as I try my hardest to pull away from her and take another step forward, and she laughs, no doubt enjoying my torment.

Raya inhales shakily when I place my knee on my bed and carefully lower her on top of it, her blouse still loosely covering her. I bite down on my lip harshly when my eyes roam down, settling on the baby blue lace between her legs. Fuck if this isn't the most beautiful sight I've ever laid eyes on — my wife, half undressed, her eyes sparkling with desire.

Her eyes grow impossibly wide when I push off my slacks, and she inhales sharply, her cheeks stained beautifully pink.

Twenty-Five

LEXINGTON

"You're gorgeous, Mrs. Windsor," I murmur as I watch her lie back on my bed, her long hair fanned around her. I lower myself on top of her, caging her in with my forearms on either side of her. My nose brushes against hers, and she sighs, tilting her face.

I chuckle and kiss her cheek, and then the edge of her mouth. "Lex," she warns, her grip on my hair tightening in warning moments before her lips come crashing against mine.

I groan and kiss her back instantly, my tongue demanding entry. She opens up for me, that same honey flavor threatening to drive me wild. The way she moves her body against mine is intoxicating, and I groan when she moves a hand down my back, cautiously exploring.

I pull my lips off hers and move them to her neck, to that spot that makes her moan so beautifully. Her head falls back, and I smirk as I trail a path down to her collarbone, taking my time to ease her nerves, showing her I have nothing but a world of patience for her. I look up at my wife when I reach the top of her blouse, her gaze dark with desire. She gives me the slightest nod, and I bite down on my lip as I pull her blouse off her slowly, my breath hitching when it falls away.

"Fuck. You're literal perfection, Raya," I whisper, my voice filled with reverence as I lean in, my tongue flicking against her nipple. She moans for me again, and I grin as I repeat the motion before I switch sides to do it all over again. She squirms underneath me, her grip on my hair tightening as I play with her perfect breasts, my cock throbbing.

Raya's spine arches as I tease her, and I grin to myself as I move lower, kissing her sternum, and then her ribs, slowly making my way down. She's breathing hard, her eyes smoldering, and fuck, I don't think she's ever looked more beautiful.

Raya gasps when I grab her leg and hook it over my shoulder before kissing the inside of her thigh. She moans softly and then bites down on her lip to suppress the sound, her cheeks beautifully rosy. "Don't hide those perfect little sounds from me, darling. Let me hear you. Show me I'm pleasing you."

My wife inhales sharply when I kiss her panties, and she squirms a little. "If you'll let me, I'll worship every inch of you, Raya."

Our eyes lock, and I groan in delight when she tightens her grip on my hair and nods. A perfect little moan escapes her perfect little mouth when I kiss the edge of her panties, before I take the fabric between my teeth and drag it aside, my eyes falling closed in delight at the sight of her bare pussy. "Fucking perfect," I whisper, more to myself than to her. I inhale deeply before dragging my tongue down.

My wife's back arches, and I grin when the sexiest moan escapes from her throat, her heel pressing into my back. "Oh God, *Lex*."

Hearing her say my name like that is such a fucking thrill, it's unreal. My wife's pussy is a drug handcrafted for me, the sounds she makes the perfect high. I grab her other leg and hook that over my shoulder too, opening her legs wider, allowing me to fuck her with my tongue, tasting, lapping, until my name is the only word she remembers.

I circle her swollen clit, and her nails graze my scalp, her moans turning into needy whimpers as I slowly edge her, making her desperate for release and refusing to give it to her. "Lex," she gasps. "Please."

I tease my beautiful wife, bringing my tongue a little closer to where she wants it before pulling back. "Please what, Raya?"

She looks at me with desperation written all over her pretty face. "Please make me come."

Fuck. I'd planned to tease her further, make the first time I taste her unforgettable, so she'll keep coming back for more. But what mortal man could possibly resist a plea like hers?

"You beg so prettily, my little fairy," I groan. "You know exactly what you're doing to me when you look at me like that, don't you?"

She bites down on her lip for a moment, her touch tender when she brushes my hair back, away from my forehead. "Please, Lex... I can't take it... please, let me come."

Goddamn. Raya Windsor will be the death of me, and I'll die a happy man. "Anything for you, baby," I whisper, before I finally give her what I want, my tongue working her clit the way she needs me to. Her back arches, and her heels dig into my back as my wife comes all over my tongue, my name on her lips.

I smirk as I kiss her thigh leisurely while she collapses back onto our bed, and my cock twitches as I drag a finger down her swollen pussy. "One more, little fairy."

She inhales shakily, her eyes widening when I push two fingers in slowly before curling them, teasing her G-spot. "I can't," she breathes. "I've never—"

"You will," I tell her, tearing her lace underwear off her entirely. "I wasn't asking, Raya."

She gasps when I place my mouth back on her clit, my fingers buried deep inside her. I take it a little easier on her now, my movements gentle, coaxing. "*Lex*," she moans, her hips rolling. I grab her and hold her steady, using the tip of my tongue on her, until her legs begin to tremble. Her nails scrape over my back as she comes, a throaty moan ringing through the air. Fuck, I could come just from the sounds my wife makes. I smirk as her pussy contracts around my fingers, over and over again, her orgasm drawn out.

I don't pull my fingers away until her muscles relax, and I sigh happily as I rest my head on her stomach, her leg thrown over my shoulder. Countless inventions and an endless amount of multi-million deals, yet nothing tops the way my wife just made me feel, my tongue against her clit and my name on that sexy little mouth of hers. I doubt anything ever will.

"Lex," she whispers, her voice husky and oh so fucking sexy. I look up, our eyes locking. "I want you."

I raise a brow, my heart skipping a beat as I push myself up on her forearms to look at her properly. "Are you sure?" My voice trembles. "We don't have to, Raya. I want you to feel ready. I know you've been waiting..."

She shakes her head and reaches for me, the tips of her fingers brushing over my temple. "I'm ready. I always wanted it to be my wedding night. I just... I just didn't want to admit it back then."

I bite down on my lip as I study her face, and she throws me a shaky smile, accompanied by a pleading look. "Please don't turn me down," she says, her voice breaking. Her breathing turns ragged, and she looks away.

"Never," I murmur, pushing myself up on my knees. Her gaze roams over my chest and abs, her lips parting when I push my boxers down, making quick work of them. I grab my cock and pump it once, twice, and she stares at it wide-eyed.

"That..."

I grin and move on top of her, positioning myself between her legs. "It'll be fine, baby. We'll take it as slow as you'd like, and we can stop at any time, okay? Just say the word."

She nods, and I drag my cock across her pussy, earning myself a pretty little moan. I chuckle and do it again, before pushing into her just slightly. "Oh God," I moan, my eyes falling closed briefly.

Raya whimpers, a hint of discomfort in her expression despite how wet she is. "It's too much," she whispers. "I feel so stretched out."

I bite back a smile and hold myself up on one forearm, freeing up my hand to cup her face. "My sweet little fairy," I whisper. "That's just the tip."

Her lips fall open, and I chuckle, my forehead dropping to hers. My laughter makes me slide a little further into her, and her head falls back, her long neck on display for me. I lean in and kiss her in that spot she likes, earning myself a delicious moan.

My hand wraps into her hair, and I pull back a little. "Look at me," I demand, needing to see that she's okay. My beautiful wife obeys, her eyes finding mine as I push a little further into her, slowly stretching her out. "You feel absolutely incredible, Raya. It's like your pussy was made for me. I'm not even all the way inside you yet, and you have me ready to come."

She flushes, and I smirk, pushing in a little deeper still. It's been years since I last had sex, but fuck, I don't remember it ever being this good. Her breath hitches, and I instantly pause, giving her time to adjust.

"You're taking my cock so well, baby," I whisper, pressing a kiss to her forehead. She looks at me like she's pleased with my praise, and I look into her eyes as I push in deeper. "You're doing so good, darling. Halfway there now."

She threads her fingers through my hair, her other hand around the back of my neck. I've never experienced anything like this. The way she's looking at me, with complete trust, is exhilarating.

"Can you take a little more, my little fairy?" She nods, but her expression is conflicted. "I need to hear you say it, Raya. It's never too late to stop."

"Don't stop," she says, her eyes blazing. "I can take it, Lex. All of it."

I nod and pull back a little, my eyes on hers as I slide all the way in, bottoming out inside her. She groans, her nails digging into the back of my neck, her pupils blown wide. "Breathe for me, baby," I whisper, my forehead dropping to hers.

She takes a shaky breath, and I smile at her. "Good girl," I whisper, holding still. "You're such a good girl, aren't you?"

Her eyes light up, and she smiles shyly, her body slowly relaxing underneath me. She's so fucking precious, my sweet little fairy. I pull my hips back just a little, rocking back and forth as I watch her face. There's no pain in her gaze now, and I breathe a sigh of relief as I pull back a little more, taking her slowly, enjoying every last second of it.

Raya cups the side of my face, desire once again lighting up her beautiful brown eyes, and I pull almost all the way out, only to thrust back into her a little harder. She moans so fucking beautifully for me that I nearly lose it there and then. "I won't last long when you sound like that, darling."

Her hands roam over my body, and she begins to rock her hips, meeting me thrust for thrust. "I don't want you to. I want you to come for me," she says, and the possessiveness in my wife's eyes does it for me.

"Then hold on for me, baby," I whisper, taking her with harder and faster strokes, every single one of her moans only bringing me closer. She gasps when I roll my hips, and I smirk in satisfaction when I realize how she likes it. I repeat the motion again and again, until her moans become a little more incoherent, the look in her eyes a little glassier.

"Oh," she whispers. *"Oh God."* her eyes fall closed as her pussy contracts around my cock, and I groan, coming right alongside my wife.

Twenty-Six

Raya

I'm surprisingly nervous as I make my way to Lex's kitchen dressed in the shirt he wore last night, my hair still wet from the shower. I wasn't sure he meant it when he said he'd try with me, but last night filled me with hope.

I bite down on my lip when I find him leaning back against his kitchen counter, his torso exposed and gray sweats hanging low on his hips. He's got a cup of coffee on the counter and his tablet in his hand, his full attention on what he's reading. My eyes widen when he reaches behind him and grabs a pair of black-rimmed reading glasses. I didn't think he could get more handsome, but the glasses do it for me.

It's hard to believe that I'm married to this man — the same man I've admired for so long, that I still look up to. Lex must feel me staring at him, because he looks up and smiles, his gaze roaming over my body. His eyes instantly darken, and he puts his tablet down slowly.

"Good morning, Mrs. Windsor. How do you feel?"

Heat rushes to my face, and I walk further into the kitchen area. "Morning. I didn't even hear you get up."

He pulls me closer the second he has me within reach, his hand wrapping around my waist. "I always get up at five," he tells me as he twists my hair around his finger. "I like structure, so I get up at the same time and work out at the same time every day." Something akin to frustration flashes in his eyes, and he pulls me closer, tucking my head underneath his chin. I wrap my arms around him and hug him.

Lex sighs and tightens his grip on me, his face buried in my hair. "Let me make you some coffee," he murmurs. "I need to show you how all our robots work, too. Are you hungry?"

I shake my head and tilt my face to kiss his neck. He shivers and buries a hand in my hair, instantly growing hard against my stomach. The way he wants me is so empowering. He groans and grabs my waist, lifting me into his arms. My legs hook around his hips, and he turns me around, placing me on the edge of the counter. Lex looks at me like I torment him, and I can't figure out what I've done to make him look that way.

He grabs my hand and raises it to his lips, only to pause, his expression hardening. "Where is your wedding ring?" he asks, his tone harsh as his gaze cuts to mine.

I blink in surprise and pull my hand back. "In the bathroom. I took it off to shower."

Lex frowns and cups the back of my neck, his thumb resting on my throat. "I'm never taking mine off again, and I don't want to see you without yours. I understand you can't wear it on your hand at school, but I still want it on your body at all times. I'll buy you a necklace to hang it on, little fairy."

I nod, my heart racing. For a man who seemed so opposed to a relationship, he's awfully adamant that I keep a token of our marriage on me at all times. "Fine," I murmur, pulling him closer. "If you wear yours, I'll wear mine too."

Lex's shoulders relax, and his gaze roams over me. "There's something just entirely irresistible about the way my shirt looks on you," he whispers, before tilting his face and taking my bottom lip between his teeth, nipping, teasing. I smile against his mouth and lock my ankles behind his back, bringing him closer, my hand sliding up his neck and into his hair.

Lex moans when I kiss him, his hands roaming over my body with a hint of desperation. "God, I can't get enough of you," he says, his hands settling on my waist.

The way he's moving against me is driving me wild, and I pull away to look at him. "Lex," I plead, unsure what I'm asking for.

He grins and pulls me closer, placing his hands underneath my thighs as he lifts me up and carries me through the kitchen, toward the bedroom. We're halfway there when a slightly robotic voice rings through the air.

"Lex, you have visitors," she says. "Bob and Meera Lewis are at the door. Since you have them in my system as your wife's parents, I'll be letting them in now."

"Fuck," he mutters, and we both stare at each other wide-eyed for a moment. Seconds later, I hear my parents' voices, and Lex puts me down. I take one look at the scratches I left all over his body and grab his hand, making a run for it.

"What are we doing?" he whisper-shouts, following my lead.

I throw him an incredulous look and push him into the bedroom, slamming the door shut in a rush. "What do you think I'm doing?" I ask, my voice borderline hysterical. "We're both half-naked! *Get. Dressed.*"

He chuckles and shakes his head as he follows me into the dressing room, moving much slower than I'd like him to. "Pippy," he calls, "lock my bedroom door and brew some fresh coffee."

"Certainly, Lex," the same voice I heard earlier says, and I turn, my eyes wide.

"You named your AI Smart Home System *Pippy*?"

He shrugs. "She kind of acts like a puppy most of the time, but that seemed too... I don't know."

I try my hardest to hold back my laughter, but a soft giggle makes its way past my lips, nonetheless. That's so ridiculously silly, and it's a lot more like the Lex I've gotten to know than the man he pretends to be.

"I haven't had a chance to tell you that all those clothes on that side are for you. You were too preoccupied to even notice last night. Raven designed them for you after she got your measurements at your dress fitting."

My mouth pops open in surprise, and he grins as he takes a yellow dress off the hanger and hands it to me. "I've been dying to see you in this."

Lex grabs a white t-shirt and pulls it over his head with ease while I shrug off the shirt I'm wearing in a rush. He smiles at me when I step into the dress and moves closer. "Relax, baby," he murmurs, pressing a kiss to my shoulder before helping me zip up the dress. "You look beautiful."

"How are you not nervous?" I ask, surprised by his relaxed demeanor.

"Oh, I am," he says, a shadow crossing his face. "I hate surprises, and I don't usually let anyone but my siblings and my grandmother into this house. However, I told you that I'd try to be the man you need, so that's what I'll do. I'll try, Raya. I'll try to fight my instincts, my usual responses. They are your parents, and they're clearly worried about you. I can understand that."

I turn and rise to my tiptoes to kiss his cheek. He sighs and grabs my hand. "I wish we could finish what we started in the kitchen," he complains. "But instead, we'd better go greet your parents before they hunt us down."

I smile and let him lead me out of the room, my heart soaring when I find Mom sitting on the sofa while Dad paces in front of her. They both look up when we walk in, and the worry on their faces diminished just a touch.

"Raya," Mom says, jumping to her feet. She rushes up to me and rubs my arms, her gaze roaming over my body. Some of the panic in her eyes eases when I smile, and she moves to hug me tightly, before offering Lex a hug too.

"Hi Dad," I say as I walk up to him. He looks emotional and opens his arms for me, wrapping me in a tight hug.

"Is everything okay?" he asks quietly, his voice barely above a whisper.

I nod and rest my head on his chest, mom's story echoing through my mind. My stomach turns when I suddenly realize why they're both so anxious this morning. They must've been worried Lex hurt me last night, and I can guess the reason why they'd think something like that. I force a smile as I step back, my heart breaking for Mom all over again.

Lex walks up to us and shakes Dad's hand, his smile sincere. "It's good to see you both," he says, his expression friendly. "Would you care to join Raya and me for breakfast?"

My parents exchange glances and nod before following Lex to the dining area, where several robots are already setting the table, their wheels carrying them back and forth. "That's an impressive feat of technology," Dad grumbles, like he doesn't want to admit it but can't help himself. "But these are all jobs humans could've had. Doesn't your family employ plenty of household staff?"

Lex pauses and smiles tightly as he pulls a chair out for me. I look up at him as I sit down, noting the tension in his expression. He doesn't say anything as he pulls out Mom's chair for her, seating her next to me. "My siblings do, but I don't like having people in my home," he eventually says quietly. "My robots will never betray me — they'll never sell a story to the press, nor will they ever harm me or my family. They'll only ever do what I've programmed to do."

I reach for his hand over the table, and he looks up at me in surprise as he entwines our fingers. Something about his forlorn expression compels me to offer him quiet support, consolation. It doesn't go unnoticed by my parents, who both glance at our joined hands, and then at each other.

Mom smiles, genuinely, for the first time today. "I think it's very impressive, Lexington," she says, throwing him one of those sweet indulgent looks I know all too well. "They look very cute too, with... what's that called now? The *emoji* faces?"

Lex's cheeks redden just a little, and he smiles. "Thank you, ma'am."

She grins at him and places her elbow on the table, her fist underneath her chin. "Oh, honey, if you'd like, you can call me Mom. You're my son-in-law now, after all."

Lex's eyes grow impossibly wide, and dad huffs, not at all impressed by Mom's acceptance of Lex. I, on the other hand, throw her a grateful smile, hope sparking in my chest. When I found out he approached me under false pretenses, I wasn't sure what our marriage would look like. I didn't dare believe him when he said he'd *try*, but so far, his actions are speaking louder than words could.

He's trying, and I will too.

Twenty-Seven

Raya

My fingers brush over the wedding ring around my necklace as I sit down next to Adam in our usual study spot — the picnic benches just outside the library. My ring is safely tucked underneath the dress I'm wearing today, but somehow, I feel like I have the words *Just Married* written all over my forehead. It's odd to be back on campus just a few days after getting married. It feels like everything has changed, but simultaneously, it's like nothing has.

"What'd you get up to last weekend?" Adam asks, taking a bite of his apple. He looks at me with an unreadable expression, and I sit up a little straighter. "I was gonna ask you if you wanted to study together, but I couldn't reach you."

I smile tightly, silently praying my nerves aren't obvious. "Not much," I murmur, looking down as I think back to the wedding on Saturday. "Just studied," I add, conveniently leaving out the part where all I studied was my husband's body, in every room of our house.

We played truth or dare as Lex showed me around, and both

of our dares continuously became more outrageous. I wasn't sure what it'd be like to be married, to be alone with Lex like that, but I enjoyed every second of it. When he said he'd try to be a good husband, he really seems to have meant it, going as far as making me coffee in the morning and giving me access to every single thing in his home, including all his tech and the lab of my dreams. Our first weekend together was surprisingly blissful, and it left me feeling happier than I expected.

"I've been worried about you, you know? I wasn't sure how you were coping with the whole Lexington Windsor thing. I know you really liked him, and it can't be easy to see him photographed with someone else."

I frown, confused as to what he's talking about. "You didn't see?" he murmurs, his expression falling.

I shake my head and take a deep breath, expecting the worst as Adam grabs his phone and pulls up The Herald's social profile. My brows rise when he shows me a photo that must've been taken the day after our wedding, in the parking lot of a well-known fast-food chain — a location The Herald has deemed to be far beneath a Windsor. My heart races as I read the scathing speculative pieces they wrote about Lex and his mysterious girl, which, as it turns out, is *me*.

The photo is shockingly blurry, and I'm surprised by how much of a tale they managed to spin out of something so simple. Lex had taken me for a drive after showing me all the rarest and most expensive cars in his collection, and the location of all the keys. Halfway through the drive he took me on, in my favorite car of his, my stomach grumbled. He laughed, asking me what I wanted to eat, and I'd pointed at a fast-food chain sign in the distance, saying I'd love some fries.

It was a simple outing, yet somehow, The Herald seems to have turned it into some kind of alleged scandal between my husband and a model I haven't even heard of — one I definitely don't look like. It appears they're praising her for being so down to earth and having junk food mere hours before walking a show, their common sense completely lacking. Who even wrote this?

"This is ridiculous," I snap. I sigh and lock Adam's phone with a lot more force than necessary, a hint of unease washing over me. The scrutiny that comes with being near Lex is something I hadn't expected, and I'm not sure how to feel about it.

"What is ridiculous?"

My eyes widen, and Adam's head snaps up at the sound of Lex's voice. My husband smiles and joins us on the picnic bench, seating himself next to me. He glances at my textbook and raises a brow. "Surely multivariable linear systems aren't throwing off two of my star pupils?"

My heart instantly begins to race, and I stare at him wide-eyed, surprised to find him on campus today when I know he isn't teaching. My class is the only one he took on, after all.

"Professor Windsor," Adam says, his expression shifting. "We were actually just discussing the article The Herald posted about you and your supermodel fiancée."

My husband raises a brow when I involuntarily glare at him. "Must be nice, being with a supermodel," I mutter without thinking, annoyed the media linked him to someone else just a day after we got married. I know the story isn't true, and I know I literally am the woman in the photo that accompanied the article, but somehow, I'm still a little aggrieved.

Lex smirks, his eyes darkening when he recognizes the look on my face for what it is — jealousy. He reaches for my notebook and adds a couple of things here and there, correcting some of my summaries. "I saw that article," he murmurs, sounding unfazed. "I almost wish they captured my *wife* properly that day, because she looked ridiculously beautiful."

He looks up at Adam as his right hand slips underneath the table. He places it on my thigh, just under the hem of my dress, and heat rushes to my cheeks. I look down at my notebook, my heart racing wildly as I try to behave naturally.

"I didn't know this about her until we got married and started living together, but she gets super cranky the second she's hungry," Lex says, his thumb drawing circles on my bare skin, slowly inching higher. "Her face just transforms the second she bites down on a French fry, though. It made my whole day to see her smile like that."

"Your wife?" Adam repeats, his eyes snapping to my face for a moment, before he turns back to Lex. "So, it's official, then? You're married?"

Lex chuckles and squeezes my thigh, his pinky brushing over the lace between my legs. "I couldn't make it any more official if I tried," he says, his gaze moving to his left hand, draped over my notebook. The wedding ring he refuses to take off catches the sun just right, and he grins. "And I wouldn't have it any other way."

I'm surprised The Herald hasn't noticed Lex's wedding ring yet, especially considering how much he loves touching it. "She's a lucky girl," I mutter, unable to focus on anything but the feel of his hand on my skin. He doesn't seem remotely scared of getting caught, but my heart is pounding wildly. I bite down on my lip when he curls his fingers, dragging them over my panties. My breath hitches when he grins, realizing I'm rapidly getting wet for him, and I look away, scared my cheeks are rosy.

"The lucky one is me," he says, his tone husky. He moves his hand and squeezes my thigh one more time before pulling away and closing my notebook. He pushes it back toward me with a knowing smile on his face. "I have to run. I have a meeting a couple of towns over, and I'll have to grab my helicopter and fly in for it if I want a shot at having dinner with my wife."

Adam frowns. "That's a lot of effort just so you can have dinner with her." He glances at me, a hint of pity in his eyes, and I lower my head, feeling more and more guilty by the second. I'm going to have to find a way to tell him before Lex gives our secret away, but I'm scared of how he'd respond if I told him about the reasons behind our marriage.

Lex rises to his feet, our eyes locking for a moment. He smiles so sweetly that my heart skips a beat. "It's not much effort at all.

Even with my helicopter, I probably won't make it home in time, and I hate that I can't even promise my wife that I'll have dinner with her. You have no idea what lengths I went to today just to catch a glimpse of her."

I look up at him and smile, my heart skipping a beat. So that's why he's on campus today, because he doesn't think he'll get home before I fall asleep. All week, he hasn't made it home before I've fallen asleep, but I know he's trying to give me as much of his time as he can, and that's enough. "I'm sure she appreciates how hard you're trying," I tell him. "And if it were me, I'd appreciate the few moments you do give her."

His expression softens, and he nods, his gaze lingering for a moment before he walks away. It isn't until he disappears from view that I reopen my notebook and find a message scribbled at the bottom of the page.

Jealousy looks good on you, Mrs. Windsor. See me after class tomorrow for extra credit. You deserve it for showing me such a pretty sight.

Twenty-Eight

Lexington

"Pippy, tell me where my wife is," I murmur as I get in my car, irritated it's so late already. My schedule was already overwhelming before I decided to start teaching too, but I didn't mind it before now. Work gave me purpose and structure, and I never even noticed just how long my workdays are.

Not until I married Raya.

"Your wife is currently at home, Lex. She was on campus most of the day, then she went to her father's company, after which she came home. Mrs. Windsor asked the household robots for some tomato soup at around seven in the evening and appears to have been studying throughout and after dinner. She took a short break to shower at around nine and then returned to studying. Mrs. Windsor seems to have figured out that the household robots can solve equations for her, and she's utilized them to help her with her coursework."

I chuckle, equal parts surprised and amused. "Thanks, Pippy."

"My pleasure, Lex," she says as I park in my driveway. My car locks itself, while my front door unlocks and swings open automatically.

I walk in to Raya standing in front of one of my robots, a long cream silk nightgown clinging to her body. "Okay, but do you feel like the emojis in your database are sufficient for you to adequately express your emotions?" she asks.

"Mrs. Windsor," it replies, its face portraying an exasperated emoji. "We have been over this. I do not have emotions. I merely emulate human behavior to improve the user experience of those I interact with."

"You say that, but you sound a little annoyed, Lola."

Lola? Who the fuck is Lola?

"*Again*, I have been programmed to emulate human behavior, Mrs. Windsor. I was taught that repeatedly being questioned is meant to elicit an annoyed response. You're not fooling me, Mrs. Windsor. I know that you're just asking me the same question in different formats, using different words."

I chuckle. I can't help myself. Raya whirls around and flushes at the sight of me. "Oh," she says, her tone high-pitched. "You're home. I didn't think I'd get to see you today."

"Darling, are you arguing with the robots?" I murmur as I walk up to her, pleased I managed to catch her before she fell asleep today. Five days of marriage, and she's turned me into an addict. Each day that I barely get to see her is torture, and she's got me rethinking my whole schedule and workload. More than once, I've flown into Astor College just to catch a glimpse of her between meetings, and fuck, it just isn't enough.

Lola's face turns into a neutral one as it zips away, but Raya's face reddens beautifully. "I was doing no such thing," she says, her eyes wide. Fucking adorable. "I just don't understand why she won't call me Raya! She's meant to be a smart robot, Lex, but she won't listen to reason."

I bite back a smirk. "Strange. I'll look into that," I tell her, pretending like I didn't program all my tech to refer to her as Mrs. Windsor, simply because I fucking love the sound of it. There's no way I'm admitting that. I'm not even entirely sure why I did it at all. It's something I did on a whim, something I don't want to think about too hard, for fear of what I'd find.

The last couple of days have been odd, as we're both getting used to being around each other. I wasn't sure how I'd feel about having someone in my home, *in my bed,* but things have been better than expected, though perhaps that's because we haven't had much of a chance to spend time together. I'm not sure if our busy schedules are working in our favor or not. It's like the people we are during the day and at night are entirely different.

Late at night, I'll join her in bed, and she rolls toward me. I'll kiss her, and she'll whisper in my ear, issuing a dare I can't resist, and I always end up losing myself in her. By morning, she's barely able to look me in the eye, both of us hiding behind our busy days.

My hand wraps around her waist, and I pull her closer. "How did you even manage to piss off a robot? How long were you questioning it?"

She stares up at me innocently. "I wasn't doing anything weird, I promise! I was studying for my Cognitive Engineering final, and I realized I had a perfect example of an intelligent system right next to me. I just wanted to test a few things."

I grin and pull her flush against me, loving the way she's looking at me. When I told her I'd try, that I wanted to date her, I wasn't actually sure I could. I didn't think I'd be able to let a woman in ever again, nor did I think I'd be able to cope with having her in my space, invading my privacy. How does she do it? How is she knocking down all my walls with such ease, so quickly? What is it about Raya Windsor that I find so enchanting?

"Sounds like you were annoying our robots because you were bored, my little fairy. I have the perfect remedy for boredom."

"Oh yeah?" she says, her gaze darkening. "What's that?"

"This little game I like to call Truth or Dare."

She smiles, and my heart begins to race. "Then tell me, Lex. Truth or dare?"

"*Dare.*"

Her gaze roams over my face. "Kiss me."

I slide my hand into her hair and tilt her face, my lips hovering over hers as I savor the moment, the way she sighs and rises to her tiptoes, taking what she wants. I smile against her mouth when she kisses me, my hands sliding down her body until I'm holding her hips. Raya moans when I force her pretty little mouth open, my tongue stroking hers leisurely, until her body starts to move against mine. A soft, needy sound escapes from the back of her throat when I lift her into my arms, and her legs hook around my waist as she buries a hand in my hair.

We're both breathless by the time she pulls away, and I stare up at her, entirely fucking enchanted. "Your turn, darling. Truth or dare?"

She bites down on her lip as I carry her to the sofa. "Truth," she says as I sit down with her still in my arms, so she ends up straddling me. Raya places one hand on my shoulder and caresses my temple with the other.

"Tell me whether you thought about me today."

The way she blushes is enough of an answer, and I grin in satisfaction. "Just once or twice," she murmurs.

"Yeah? What did you think about? The way I made you come last night? Or the way you begged for my cock shortly after?"

Her eyes twinkle, and she shakes her head. "You only get one question, Lex."

"Fine," I murmur. "I've thought of you countless times today, my little fairy. I've never been eager to go home before, Raya. I've never had anyone waiting for me, and I didn't think I'd enjoy it as much as I do." I didn't expect to enjoy dating my wife as much as I do.

She averts her gaze, the sweetest smile on her perfect lips. "Your turn," she whispers.

"Truth."

She looks at me then, her gaze turning a little more serious. She hesitates, inhaling deeply before she speaks. "Tell me how you feel about going to my parents' house this weekend."

I pause. "Nervous," I admit.

She nods like she gets it, but I know she doesn't. Raya doesn't understand how hard it is for me to sleep in a place that doesn't have security systems I've checked and approved, where I know the location of each exit, each window.

She couldn't possibly understand.

No one does.

Twenty-Nine

Lexington

Unease settles in my stomach as I park in front of Raya's parents' house. My gaze darts to the extra security Silas stationed here for the weekend, but it isn't enough to relieve my worries.

"Is that really necessary?" Raya asks as she takes in the uniformed bodyguards, her voice soft. "This is a gated community, Lex. Besides, my dad has a very comprehensive alarm system."

She sounds disappointed, offended, and I wish I had the words to explain myself. "It's necessary," I say instead, unable to explain that I still have doubts about Raya's father and the monthly payments he continues to make. $10,000 is a lot of money for a man on the brink of bankruptcy. "Besides, your parents agreed to this."

She looks into my eyes, her displeasure evident, but she doesn't argue with me any further. Instead, she gets out of the car and slams the door, leaving me to drop my head back as I take a deep breath.

Things have been better than I'd expected between us, but the more time I spend with her, the more unsettled I feel. I thought I had the situation in hand, that I was in control of our marriage. I mapped out the steps I had to take to ensure she's content before we ever said *I do*, but she keeps steering me off track with her smiles and her touch. Everything feels far too real. I keep finding myself doing and saying things just to make her smile, and she has no idea how much the way she's making me lose control over my actions is fucking me up.

I sigh as I get out of the car, only to find her leaning against the front door, waiting for me. "I'm sorry, Lex," she says, reaching for my hand. "I shouldn't have stormed off like that, especially not when we're visiting my parents. I can tell you're trying your best to keep the promises you made me, and the way I just reacted wasn't fair."

My heart skips a beat, and I drop my forehead to hers for a moment, at a loss. *This* is why she keeps throwing me off — because she acts in ways I could never predict. All of my plans were built for the type of women I'm used to, but she's nothing like anyone I've ever met. She's unpredictable, seemingly unmotivated by money and fame. The more I learn about her, the more she confuses me.

"Thank you for waiting for me," I murmur, and she turns her face a little to kiss my cheek. Raya pulls back a little, her lips parting to say something, but we're interrupted by the door opening. She stumbles, and I wrap my arm around her waist, pulling her against me.

"You're home," her mother says, her eyes moving between us. "Come on in." She turns to Raya then. "Dad is still at the lab, but he should be home soon."

My wife nods and kicks off her shoes, and I follow her lead, curious about the home she grew up in. I pause to look at the photos on the walls as I trail behind Raya and her mom, who rapidly lose themselves in conversation. This place seems like a real home, the kind I've always wanted, the kind I think my siblings and I would've had if we hadn't lost my parents.

"I think I figured out how to make them perfectly round," Raya says as she follows her mother into the kitchen. "There are a lot of variables, but if I make my dough perfectly round and then press down on it with an equal amount of force across the board, it'll be a perfect circle. I think I'll try putting a chopping board on top of it to flatten it first."

Raya's mom bursts out laughing, and she shakes her head. "Honey, making parathas isn't a science. It just takes a bit of practice."

"*Mom,*" Raya whines as she moves to the sink to wash her hands. "I've had years of practice, and they still end up being random shapes. Last time I made one that turned into a star. *A star,* Mom. I was trying to make it round! There's something I'm missing — I'm sure of it."

"I'm sure we can automate that," I tell Raya, and she spins around, her eyes lighting up as she wraps her hands around my biceps. "Oh my gosh, Lex," she says, her face brimming with excitement. "We could build a little kitchen tool for Mom that mixes the dough and then pops out perfectly round parathas that can go straight on the pan. Oh! Dad would love to build that with us. Shall we do it? It'd be such a fun way to spend the weekend."

I smile at her, my heart warming. She looks at me like she actually believes I could ever say no to her. My silly girl. "Of course," I tell her, my voice soft. I reach for her and gently push her hair behind her ear, my stomach fluttering.

God, I really want to be the man she needs. That smile of hers... I want to protect it as best as I can. She can never find out about the secrets I keep, the lengths I go to in order to keep the past at bay.

"I see you're spoiling my daughter," my mother-in-law says, and I snap out of my daze, stepping away from Raya just a little.

"As he should."

Raya's head tips up at the sound of her father's voice, and she smiles so sweetly that I can't help but smile myself. He offers me his hand, once again shaking it with a lot more force than necessary, though nowhere near enough to actually be painful.

I bite back a smile, not at all annoyed by his behavior, when it so obviously stems from love for his only child. "So, we're building a kitchen tool, huh?" he says, somewhat uncomfortably. It's clear he doesn't know how to handle my presence in his home, and the feeling is mutual.

"Yes!" Raya says, her excitement palpable. She reaches for my hand and entwines our fingers, her gorgeous eyes on mine. "Come on. I'll show you the lab Dad built for all of our experiments. It's similar to yours, and you'll love it. I think we may actually have most of the materials we'll need."

Her parents exchange loaded looks as she drags me out of the kitchen, her father's footsteps trailing behind us. "Come to think of it, there's no reason why we can't include the cooking component too," Raya says. "We can just build in a hot plate and make sure that the dough falls onto it as the last step. Add in a flipping component, and it should be able to create the perfect paratha. Something like that probably already exists, though it might be for pancakes or something similar. We'd just have to adapt it. We wouldn't even have to design from scratch if we didn't want to."

"But where's the fun in that, my little fairy? If you and I create something, it'll be better than anything that's currently on the market."

She grins up at me and nods. Even her dad's cold exterior seems to melt in light of her palpable excitement. "Let's see if you learned anything in that Mechatronics class," he grumbles.

I smile at him and shrug. "Doubtful," I tell him. "I heard the professor's a real tool."

His eyes widen a little, and then he bursts out laughing, seemingly surprised by my ability to make fun of myself. His expression shifts a little, some of the frost melting. It isn't much, but I'll take it.

Thirty

Lexington

Anxiety claws at me as I walk out of Raya's ensuite bathroom, my thoughts getting the best of me. It's been years, and I still can't get comfortable in unfamiliar places. I need to find a way to get over this — I can't keep living this way.

"Lex?"

I tense, startled by Raya's voice, my eyes cutting to hers. She puts down her hairbrush and walks up to me, concern etched into her face. "Is everything okay? I called you a few times, and you didn't seem to hear me."

I force a smile and nod. "Sorry, just lost in thought."

She nods, her eyes roaming over my body and settling on the towel around my hips. "Come on," she says, leading me to her bed. She sits me down and grabs my shoulders. "One second, okay? I'll be right back."

I frown as she rushes back into her bathroom and emerges with a spare towel. Raya pauses in front of me, the cutest look on her face as she raises it to my head and gently begins to dry my hair for me. *Fuck*. She's so fucking sweet.

I grab her waist and stare at her, taking in those long lashes, the high bridge of her nose, and those perfect fucking lips. She's wearing pajamas that are clearly quite old, but despite the faded colors, she looks beautiful in those white cotton shorts and her matching button-up top, little red hearts all over it. "What are you doing, baby?" I whisper.

"Me? I'm just helping my husband."

I inhale sharply at the sound of those words and grab her waist, all but tackling her onto her bed. She gasps, a soft giggle escaping her lips when I roll on top of her. "How about you kiss your husband instead?"

She hooks her hands around the back of my neck and pulls me closer, pressing a kiss to my cheek. My heart skips a beat, and I chuckle, my forehead dropping to hers.

She's grinning mischievously when I pull back a little to look at her. The tips of her fingers trail over my temple, and her smile turns into the one that's reserved just for me — intimate, sweet. This connection between us, it's been there from the second we met, and with each passing day, it only gets stronger.

"You terrify me, Raya," I whisper without thinking.

Confusion crosses her eyes, and she cups my face. "Why?"

Because you're the kind of woman I could lose my heart to when I didn't think I'd ever dare do something so foolish again. Because you've enchanted me in a matter of days.

I shake my head and lower my face to hers, taking her lips with intention, my teeth grazing her bottom lip, before I suck on it. She tilts her face, her hand burying in my hair as she kisses me in earnest, her body moving against mine. She hums and rolls her hips when she feels how hard I am, her tongue moving in that teasing way she knows I can't resist. "Fuck," I whisper against her mouth. "I want you so fucking badly."

She moves her head, her lips brushing against my ear. "Then take me," she whispers. "I'm right here, desperate for you."

I groan and push off her, eager to get her out of her clothes. She laughs when I pull her up with me, her hands wrapping around my towel moments before her bedroom door opens. My heart nearly stops when her mother walks in, her eyes on the tray she's holding, two steaming cups of tea on it. "Let me help you," Raya's dad calls.

I don't think I've ever moved faster in my life as I grab one of my wife's pillows and sit down, covering my erection with it. Raya moves in front of me, her dainty body barely covering my torso as I grab the discarded towel she'd brought for me and pretend to be drying my hair.

My mother-in-law looks up, her eyes growing wide when she notices the no doubt awkward looks we must be wearing. She raises a brow, a hint of amusement on her face as Raya's dad walks in behind her, his expression rapidly going from relaxed to murderous when he sees my bare torso and notices the pillow in my lap.

"Apologies," I murmur, my voice steady. "I just got out of the shower. My hair just takes a while to dry." I groan internally even as I force a smile. What the fuck did I just say? I've breezed through hundreds of high-stake negotiations, and this is what rattles me?

"Shower, huh?" Raya's father says, taking a step toward me.

His wife moves in front of him and cuts off his path, her gaze trained on her daughter. A few moments later, she smiles to herself, a look of understanding in her eyes. "We'll just leave this here," she says as she places the tray on Raya's nightstand, and I glance at my wife, curious about what her mother saw that put her at ease. "Have some, Lex. You didn't eat anything for dinner. You should at least have some tea."

Raya is blushing fiercely as she wrings her hands, her posture stiff. She looks even more awkward than I probably do, and I'm the one that's half naked. "Thanks, Mom," she murmurs.

"We can leave the tea, but we can't leave our daughter here," her dad says, distraught. "Forget the rules. Who's gonna know if we split them up?"

My mother-in-law rolls her eyes and pushes her husband out.

"Honey," she says, her tone firm. "Let's go to bed. The kids are perfectly capable of drinking tea by themselves."

"Meera," he complains, but my mother-in-law, wonderful woman that she is, pushes him out the door and closes it behind her.

I fall back on the bed the second the door shuts and throw my arm over my face, my heart racing. "I thought I was going to die," I tell Raya, and she bursts out laughing. I throw her a fake glare and narrow my eyes. "You don't understand, darling. I saw my life flash before my eyes."

She slaps her hand over her mouth to stifle her laughter, but it rings through her room, nonetheless. The sound does funny things to me — it makes my heart race, sparks joy deep inside my chest.

Raya climbs onto her bed and lies down next to me, on her side, to face me. "You're ridiculous," she whispers. I turn onto my side too and gently push her hair out of her face, taking a moment to just look at her. She truly is beautiful, but it isn't just her looks that captivate me so. Why is it that I keep finding myself smiling in her presence? Why do I enjoy being around her so much?

Raya scoots a little closer, her eyes twinkling. "You know?" she whispers as she reaches for me, her fingers tracing a path down the bridge of my nose and onto my lips. "They definitely won't come back in now."

"Don't even think about it," I whisper back at her before letting her fingers slip into my mouth, biting down softly. She pulls her hand away in mock outrage, and I grin at my beautiful wife. "Today is not the day I get murdered by your father, Raya Indira Windsor."

She pouts, and I almost give in there and then. I probably would have, if not for the footsteps I can hear in the hallway, her parents milling about the house as they get ready for bed themselves.

"What a way to go, though," she whispers, pure mischief written all over her face.

I bite back a startled laugh and shake my head. "Be good for me for now, and I'll bury my face between your pretty thighs later," I promise, unable to help myself.

She giggles and cups my face, and my heart skips a beat. What is it about her that I just can't resist? Every single thing she does is in contrast with my expectations, and I should hate her unpredictability, but instead I thrive on it.

It isn't until I have her head on my chest, her steady breathing easing my anxiety, that I realize she's single-handedly taken away the fears that normally accompany me in unfamiliar places. But in doing so, *she's* becoming something I'm growing to fear.

Thirty-One

Raya

"I forgot to ask you, but how are you enjoying being back home?" Adam asks as we walk into Lex's class together, my nerves sky high. "I'm considering moving back in too instead of finding my own place after graduation. I'd be able to help my mom out more, but I'm not sure about it."

I bite down on my lip for a moment, guilt coursing through me. "I love it," I tell him, feeling uneasy about the way I'm twisting the truth. "You know I never loved living on campus as much as I loved being at home."

When I moved back home prior to the wedding, I told him it was because I was worried about my parents since the company wasn't doing well, and I wanted to be there for them. He fully supported my decision and applauded me for putting my parents first, and that just made me feel even worse.

Adam nods and wraps his arm around me. "I miss you, though. It was fun being able to grab coffee at midnight in an attempt to stay awake and study a little longer."

I smile and lean into him briefly before pulling away to take a seat. “I know. I miss that too, but we could still do that if you wanted. Just text me the next time you want to study late.”

For a moment, I think about how Lex might react if I sneaked out of our bed at midnight to go have coffee with Adam, and I can’t help but laugh to myself, earning myself a confused look from Adam.

The last couple of weeks have been a whirlwind as Lex and I tried to balance our lives and our marriage. We’ve been living in a little bubble of our own creation while getting to know each other, our days filled with our respective responsibilities while our evenings are spent playing rounds of truth or dare that inevitably lead to us falling into bed together. It’s been fun, but it feels a little precarious. Keeping secrets is harder than I thought it would be.

My heart skips a beat when Lex walks into the room, his eyes instantly finding mine. I smile involuntarily, heat rushing to my cheeks, and Adam wraps his arm around my shoulders, leaning in and stealing my attention. “Did you notice?” he asks, his tone terse. “He keeps flaunting his wedding ring. He must be quite happy with his wife.”

Adam’s gaze roams over my face, and I stare at him wide-eyed. “Good for him,” I murmur, unsure of what else to say.

He leans back, seemingly pleased with my response. My husband, on the other hand, doesn’t look pleased at all. He locks his jaws and stares at Adam for a moment, before turning toward the class.

“I read and graded your progress reports on your drone designs,” he says, his tone sharp. Moments later, Windsor Motors drones begin to deliver our graded reports back to us, and Lex rocks back on his heels, his expression stern. “Some of you lack common sense and don’t know how to keep your eyes off what isn’t yours.”

I stare at him in shock and subtly shake my head, urging him not to be petty. If there’s one thing I’ve learned about Lex since we got married, it's that he's far more possessive than I could've imagined.

He sighs and runs a hand through his thick, dark hair. "I don't need you to report on what others are doing, nor is your progress report an opportunity to make a case for switching designs. Especially not for those of you who are team leaders because your designs were chosen."

Adam scoffs, and I glance at him. "You didn't," I mutter.

He just shrugs. "I wrote a whole report about how your design is better and he should reassign me to your team. I figured he wouldn't go for it, but I didn't think he'd publicly call me out on it." He sighs and turns to look at me, ignoring Lex. "Who the fuck is he to say I don't know how to keep my eyes off what isn't mine, when he's doing the exact same thing every time he looks at you? The man is married, but he still looks at you the way he did that night in King of Hearts. It's inappropriate."

My eyes widen a fraction. "How does he look at me?" I ask, my voice weak.

"Like he wants you. Like you belong to him."

I blush fiercely and look away. "You're reading too much into things," I refute.

"Am I?" he murmurs, just as the drones deliver our reports to us.

My eyes widen when I notice the little note right next to the A+ in bright red ink. *Good job, Mrs. Windsor.* My gaze cuts to Lex, only to find him already looking at me in the exact way Adam just described. My husband smirks at me when I rush to shove my report into my bag, his earlier annoyance having made way for relaxed confidence. He just loves making me all flustered, and I have no doubt he wrote that note just to see me blush.

"Ugh," Adam says, and I glance over to find a B- on his report. My lips part in shock when I read the note on it.

Nice try, Adam. Granted, Raya is brilliant

and very few could measure up, so I'll give you a half decent mark for the way you praised her work. Rewrite this if you want a higher grade, and don't pull this shit again.

I narrow my eyes and try to grab Adam's report, but he snatches it away and stuffs it into his bag, much like I did. "That asshole," he mutters, glaring at Lex, who is summarizing common issues he's found across our work and explaining how to prevent or solve those, so we can apply his tips in our next lab session.

Each time Lex's eyes meet mine, his expression warms just slightly, and I find myself looking away. I never last long, seeking him out involuntarily. It's odd how unobtainable he feels every time I see him at school, when he pulled me closer in bed just this morning, pleading with me not to get up just yet, so he could hold me a little longer.

Adam leans into me, snapping me out of my daze. "Come to the library with me after class?" he murmurs. "It's been a while since we last studied together, and it looks like I may have to rewrite my report."

I glance at him and smile. "Of course," I murmur, before looking back at my husband. Every time Adam leans in to speak to me, Lex's expression instantly becomes a blend of annoyance and possessiveness, and something about it drives the butterflies in my stomach wild.

Thirty-Two

Lexington

I watch my wife laugh at something Adam says as they rise from their seats at the end of my class, something akin to jealousy settling in my stomach. Adam looks over his shoulder, right at me, as his arm wraps around Raya's shoulders. The fucker smiles at me as he pulls her along, and my blood begins to boil. I should've just failed him for that fucking glorified love letter he handed in.

"I have a question, Professor Windsor," one of my students calls, obstructing my path as I try to follow Raya. She bats her eyelashes in a way I'm sure she thinks is attractive, but it just makes her look like she's having an allergic reaction.

"Email me," I tell her, before walking around her and grabbing my phone to see where Adam is taking my wife. Something about the way he looked at me reminded me of what Raya told me the day we discussed our engagement — that she wanted me to let her go once our time is up, so she can find someone who will love her like I can't. Did she have Adam in mind then?

Unease runs down my spine as I walk into the library. If she hadn't been forced to marry me, he's exactly the kind of guy that she'd have chosen. He's smart, reliable, and passably good-looking, but most importantly, he makes her laugh.

I find the two of them seated in the back of the library, and I pause out of sight. My wife is looking down at her notebook, but he's looking at her. I'd recognize that tortured expression anywhere — he's in love with her but knows he can't have her. Ares looked at Raven that way for years, while he was arranged to be married to her older sister.

Raya rises from her seat and walks toward one of the bookcases, weaving through the countless rows, and I grin as I quietly follow her into the huge labyrinth Astor College calls its library. My wife pauses in front of a collection of books on aerodynamics within the engineering section, and I bite back a smile as I sneak up behind her.

My hand wraps over her mouth just before my body brushes against hers, and she gasps. "Quiet, little fairy," I murmur as I push her up against the bookshelf. Her body relaxes at the sound of my voice, and I grin as I lean in and tilt her head, exposing her neck.

She whimpers when I brush her hair aside with my free hand and place my lips against her ear. "Tell me, baby. Did you think you'd get away with letting him wrap his arm around what's *mine*?"

She chuckles against my hand, not in the least intimidated, and I fucking love that about her. She's so sweet most of the time, but this side of her is all mine. I move my hand down until I have my fingers splayed across her stomach. "Answer me."

"No. I knew you'd be jealous, and I let him do it anyway."

I wrap my hand in her hair, pulling her head back a touch to look at her. "Such a naughty little fairy," I murmur as my hand slips underneath her skirt. "I warned you, didn't I? You're mine, Raya Windsor, and I don't share."

Her gaze is heated, and I draw a shaky breath before lowering my lips to hers, taking that pretty mouth of hers. She kisses me back instantly, a soft moan escaping her throat when I part her lips, my tongue seeking entrance.

She gasps when my fingers brush over the lace panties she's wearing today, and I chuckle when I find her rapidly getting wet. "Lex," she whispers. "We can't do this here. We'll get caught."

"Then you'd better be quiet, darling." I push her underwear aside and coat my fingers in her wetness. Her hand wraps around my wrist, and I shake my head. "Put your hands on that shelf," I order, "or I'll stop touching you right now."

My pretty wife hesitates for only a split second before she does as I told her to. "Good girl," I murmur. "I'd reward you for your obedience if you hadn't gotten yourself into so much trouble. Now I'm going to have to teach you a lesson, darling."

My fingers slip into her, and she moans when I press up against her g-spot. My other hand joins in to massage her clit, and I grin as her hips begin to rotate, soft needy whimpers on her lips.

"You truly go above and beyond for your students, Professor Windsor," she teases, and I smile to myself, working her clit harder, until I've stolen all her sass away.

"Lex," she pleads. "Oh, *God*."

I lean in to kiss her just below her ear. "Next time you'd better think of the consequences before you let him touch you," I warn, dragging my finger across her pussy leisurely, not giving her what she wants.

"Please," she begs, panting. "I'm going crazy."

"So was I, every second that I had to stand there in front of your whole class, watching as he cozies up to you and whispered into your ear, that fucking glorified love letter he handed in still fresh on my mind." My middle finger brushes right against that sensitive little spot she wants me to touch, and she moans so fucking deliciously that I nearly give in.

"I can't take this," she complains. "I'm so close, *please*. Won't you make your wife come?"

"Fuck. You're playing dirty, Raya." She knows how much I love it when she calls herself my wife. Fucking tease.

Raya just looks over her shoulder and throws me the most needy, sexy look I've ever seen. "I need you," she whispers. "Please fuck me, Professor Windsor." I cave right there and then, loving how quickly she became bolder with expressing what she wants from me. Knowing she feels comfortable enough to voice her needs like that is such a fucking turn-on. It's intimacy on a whole other level.

"You know I can't resist a plea like that," I murmur as I reach for my slacks and undo my zipper, taking out my cock. Her eyes fall closed when I drag it over her ass, pure delight taking over her expression. "You want this?" I murmur, nestling my erection between her pretty thighs.

"Yes. *Yes.*"

I chuckle as I line myself up and push the tip into her. "Tell me you're mine, and I'll let you have it."

"I'm yours, Lexington Windsor," she instantly says, not a hint of hesitation. "*Yours.*"

I smile and push into her, my fingers returning to her clit as I slowly begin to fuck her against the bookshelf, her hands still on the edge of it.

She whimpers softly as I bring her to the edge, my cock buried deep inside her. I thrust in and out of her slowly, deeply, aligning the way my fingers move with the way I fuck her, and it makes her moan so fucking prettily.

"Please," she whispers, but I tut and shake my head.

"Not yet. You made me suffer through that class, so now you'll wait for your orgasm until I decide you deserve it."

She begins to shift her hips impatiently, trying to ride my hand, and I chuckle, fucking delighted by every single thing she does. "*Lex*," she pleads, only to freeze when we both feel something vibrating. "M-My phone is ringing."

"Who is it?" I growl, grabbing her hips to fuck her harder, irritated by the distraction.

She gasps, her hips still shifting against me, meeting me thrust for thrust as she takes her phone out of the pocket in her skirt. I pause when I see Adam's name on her screen.

"Pick up." She freezes, and I flick her clit harshly, drawing a moan from her throat. "Pick up if you want to come, Raya."

Her hand trembles as she obeys my command. "Raya, where are you?" Adam says, his voice audible even though Raya's phone isn't on loudspeaker. "You've been gone for a while, and I can't find you."

I grin as I swirl my thumb around her clit and continue to fuck my wife. "Tell him where you are," I whisper into her ear.

Her breath hitches when I press against her clit, finally giving her a taste of what she wants. "Looking for books on aerodynamics," she says, her voice husky.

Adam pauses. "Oh, I'm not too far away then. I'll come find you."

He ends the call, and Raya's head falls back against my shoulder. "Now what?" she asks, breathing heavily.

"Now you come for your husband." I smirk as I increase my pace, fucking her with deeper, harsher strokes and teasing her clit with more force. She bites down on her lip, and moments later, her pussy contracts all around my cock, taking me right over the edge with her. I groan as I come deep inside my wife, my forehead dropping to her shoulder.

"Raya?" I hear Adam call, and I sigh in irritation as I pull out of her and push my cum deep inside her before straightening her skirt.

She turns around in a rush, her cheeks flushed, and her lipstick smeared. She has no idea how fucking sexy she looks right now, all freshly fucked. "I hope you have fun studying with Adam. I'll definitely enjoy knowing my cum is dripping out of your pussy and onto your thighs, reminding you of who you belong to every time he smiles up at you."

My wife throws me a wide-eyed look, and I smirk as I zip myself back up seconds before Adam rounds the corner. "There you are!" he says, his smile fading when he spots me standing opposite Raya, leaning back against one of the shelves.

"Professor Windsor," he says, his tone terse.

I grin at him as I raise my fingers to my mouth and suck them clean, not giving a fuck if he realizes what I'm up to. If Raya won't make it clear he can't have her, I will.

"Have fun rewriting that report," I tell him as I straighten. "And don't forget to keep your eyes off what isn't yours, or you might find something you won't like."

Raya narrows her eyes in warning, and I chuckle as I turn around and walk away, pure satisfaction coursing through my veins.

Thirty-Three

LEXINGTON

My heart is pounding as I storm into the house, having cancelled all my meetings, only to find Raya sat on the sofa with countless blankets around her and a tub of ice-cream in her lap, a Bollywood movie playing in the background. She looks up at me with tears in her eyes, and I walk up to her, my arms wrapping around her.

"What happened, little fairy?" I ask, my heart clenching. I came rushing home the second Pippy notified me that Raya skipped her classes and was crying on our sofa, but she couldn't tell me what caused it. Raya doesn't seem to have done anything out of the ordinary today, and there isn't anything in the papers that could've upset her either. Is she upset I haven't been able to see her in a couple of days now? I've been working late, and a few of my meetings had me catching flights back and forth, leaving me with very little time to even sleep.

My wife chokes back a sob and points at the television. "She knew," she says, fresh tears falling from her eyes. "She knew her son was close by the second he set foot in that mall."

I frown and rub her arms, at a complete loss. "O-Okay," I murmur, nodding. "In the movie, you mean?"

She nods and begins to cry harder. I stare at the movie, unsure what to do. Should I get it banned if it makes her cry? She points at the television again and sniffs. "Also, you ruined my chances to marry Hrithik Roshan," she says, glaring at me as she pulls her knees up and stares at the screen stubbornly. "He would've learned a tongue twister for me, you know? You just don't understand."

Who the fuck is Hrithik Roshan? I wrap my arm around Raya's shoulders as I slyly try to google the name, only to find out he's a popular actor, but I can't find anything about the tongue twister she's talking about. I bite down on my lip as I shoot Leia a quick text.

LEX:

I think my wife wants to leave me for Hrithik Roshan over a tongue twister that he knows? Do I need to be worried about this guy?

LEIA:

LOL. No. He's married, and you're richer, younger, and better looking. Don't worry about it. If you want to make your wife smile though, learn to say the tongue twister I'm about to text you.

Leia sends me a sentence that looks like complete gibberish, and I raise a brow, glancing back at my wife. She's still every bit as upset as when I first walked in, and I'm not any closer to understanding why. "So, it's just the movie that made you cry?" I ask gently.

She looks back at me, and instantly tears begin to fill her eyes again. "Yes," she says, choking back a sob.

I instantly pull her into my arms. "I see, darling," I murmur, confused. I glance over the living room, taking in the assortment of snacks spread over the coffee table. "Did you, um, did you eat a real meal today?"

She shakes her head, and I lean in to press a kiss to her temple. "Let me see what we have, okay? I'll be right back."

She nods, her gaze appreciative as I rise from my seat and pull my tie loose. I walk into the kitchen, thinking back to that time my brothers sat me down and explained how they keep their wives happy. Maybe one of Raya's favorite foods will cheer her up?

Raya is never upset like this, and it throws me entirely off. It worries me more than I imagined it would, and unease runs down my spine. I'm starting to have feelings for her that I swore off, and I can't fight them. Seeing her crying is tearing me apart, and I don't know how to the implication of that.

I hesitate for a split second before calling my mother-in-law. My in-laws and I have gotten closer as Raya and I spend our weekends tinkering with tools in their home and helping around the house, but I'm still not fully comfortable calling either of them.

"Lex?" she says.

"Hi, um, Mom," I say hesitantly, still not completely used to calling her that, despite her continuous reminders. "I was just calling to see if you could tell me how to make your lamb biryani?" I ask as I instruct *Lola* to grab me some rice.

My mother-in-law laughs. "Oh, sweetie. It takes hours to make biryani. Why would you want to make that all of a sudden?"

I hesitate before explaining Raya's sudden strange somber mood, and she laughs again. "I see. It's the last week of the month, isn't it? She probably just got her period." I frown and shake my head. While that might be true, she's never been like *that* while on her period. "If she's been under a lot of pressure at school or otherwise lately, her hormones become more imbalanced than usual, and she becomes very sad," she adds. "Some months she's perfectly fine, but every once in a while, she just gets very emotional. It isn't biryani she wants, Lex. Buy her a salted caramel and chocolate milkshake from her favorite chain. It'll cheer her up instantly."

"Really?" I ask, not sure I believe her. "She's been crying."

My mother-in-law doesn't seem fazed at all. "I promise you; it'll work. Don't worry, all right?"

I nod to myself as I thank her and end the call, before turning back toward the living room nervously. I've never seen Raya cry before, and it fucking breaks my heart. Not knowing how to fix it and not being able to find a concrete cause to eliminate is making me feel beyond helpless.

"Little fairy," I murmur. "I'm thinking of going for a drive. Would you like to come with me?"

She looks up at me, peeking over her mountain of blankets, and then she shakes her head. She's never said no to going for a drive, it's one of our favorite things to do together.

"Are you sure?" I ask. "I was thinking of grabbing a milkshake."

"Oh, a milkshake?" she says, her eyes lighting up. "Maybe I'll come."

"Yeah?" I ask, grinning. "You don't have to. I can just go buy you one and bring it back for you?"

She shakes her head as she rises from the sofa, the blankets falling away to reveal a sexy black nightgown. My gaze roams over her body hungrily, and I bite down on my lip to keep myself in check. "No, I'll come. I've been wanting to try out something I asked Raven to find for me anyway," she says, her eyes glimmering with a hint of viciousness. "Since the tabloids love trying to capture photos of you and your supposed *supermodel* partner, I'm going to send them on a wild goose chase."

I nod in confusion and watch her disappear into our bedroom, only for her to emerge wearing black jeans with a black tee, and a long maroon wig. "Fuck," I groan, my pulse spiking at the sight of her. She looks so fucking hot, and she must know it, because the edges of her mouth turn up just a little as she turns in a circle, giving me a good look at her.

"Let's go," she says, grabbing my hand, her mood a little

lighter than before. If the mere mention of a milkshake can cheer her up that much, maybe actually drinking one will make her smile.

I hold on to her tightly as I lead her to my favorite supercar, my customized Diana, and Raya looks at me appreciatively as I buckle her in and turn the seat heaters on for her. This isn't the first time she's had her period throughout our marriage, so I know a little bit of what she likes, including how much she loves seat heaters during that time, but I'm a little annoyed I didn't know about the milkshakes. Some days it feels like I've gotten to know her really well, and other days it feels like there's still so much distance between us.

My wife sits up as we go through the drive-thru, her eyes glittering. She looks up at me wide-eyed when I hand her the milkshake I ordered for her, acting like I handed her the world. Raya has access to my vast fortune, but she doesn't want the countless things I could've bought her. She just wants this milkshake.

"Oh God," she moans as she takes a sip, her whole face lighting up as she smiles from ear to ear, sighing happily as she pulls the cup away from her lips. "So good. I just wish they were dairy free, and it'd be perfect." I nod and stare at her, fucking mesmerized. She's so fucking beautiful, and the way she smiles. Goddamn.

I sigh as I reach for my phone and order my assistant to get a proposal prepared so I can acquire this milkshake chain for my wife. If it makes her this happy, I have to make sure she has easy access whenever she wants. I'll have one of these machines installed in our house.

I raise a brow as I take another look at my recent texts, my stomach twisting with nerves as I look back at my wife. "Hey, Raya?" I murmur nervously, hoping I don't mess this up. "*Chandu ke chacha ne chandu ki chachi ko chandni chowk mein chandi ke chamach se chatni chatayi.*"

She stares at me wide-eyed, and then she wraps her hand

around the back of my neck and pulls me in for a kiss, the taste of chocolate still on her lips. I groan as I kiss her back, loving the way she's touching me. "You're better," she whispers against my lips, before kissing me again. "Better than Hrithik Roshan."

Thirty-Four

Raya

"What if I just pretend to be sick?" Lex says, leaning back against the front door. "They'll never know I'm faking it."

I bite back a smile and shake my head. "Lex, you can't just skip the first poker night you're meant to go to after we got married, and you know it. They'll think I'm some kind of tyrant that won't let you go."

Following the wedding, we were exempt from attending smaller family events, like weekly dinners or Lex's monthly poker night. As of yesterday, our time is up, and Lex doesn't seem overly happy about it.

"Work has been so busy that we've barely spent any time together in almost two weeks," he says, sounding genuinely aggrieved. "When I do have time, you're either studying or in class." He runs a hand through his hair and sighs. "We've been married for three months, and we haven't even been able to go on a proper date yet."

I walk up to him and wrap my arms around his neck. "What

are you talking about?" I murmur. "We went for dinner two weeks ago, and last month you took me to that art gallery after hours."

I've had so much fun throwing off the reporters that are trying to catch Lex with his alleged lover, and I know he's had fun with it too. The rumors about him and that model annoyed me so much that I wore a crimson wig when he took me out for milkshakes, and then a blonde one the week after. Every time we go anywhere, they think Lex is seeing someone new. It completely throws The Herald off, and it brings me so much joy to see them scrambling for non-existent details. Wasting their time has become one of my favorite pastimes. Unfortunately, it also got us called into his grandmother's drawing room, and if not for the selfies I had on hand of us, we probably would've been in a world of trouble.

Lex grabs my waist and shakes his head. "No, Raya. I mean a proper date."

I raise a brow in confusion. "If those weren't proper dates, what is?" I ask, afraid of what his answer might be. Most of the time, Lex acts like a perfectly ordinary human being, but every once in a while, I'm reminded that the man I married is a billionaire, and nothing is out of reach for him.

"You'll see," he says, placing his index finger underneath my chin to tip my face up. I grin at him and rise to my tiptoes, meeting him halfway. He sighs when our lips meet, his grip on me tightening.

"That's it," he whispers against my mouth. "I'm not going."

As if on cue, Pippy's voice sounds overhead. "Critical alert," she says, sounding worried. "Xavier Kingston is approximately thirty seconds away from your door, Lex. However, Sierra appears to be driving this way too, and by my calculations, she is three minutes away."

"How does she know that?"

Lex tenses for a moment, his eyes falling closed. "We have

security cameras all over the Windsor Estate," he says, his voice soft.

I nod and bite down on my lip. The cameras must have caught them both at specific locations and calculated their ETAs. "But... why is this a critical alert?"

"Sierra and Xavier hate each other," he explains. "They have a longstanding and very serious feud, though no one knows why. It's so bad that we've actually actively been hiding our friendship with Xavier. He was originally just Dion's best friend, but while Dion lived abroad, he somehow kind of became one of us." Lex frowns, like he's trying to think back to the origins of their friendship. "He just started showing up for poker nights even when Dion wasn't there, and none of us ever questioned it. Sierra would absolutely lose her mind if she knew he comes over once a month to play poker with us."

Lex drops his head back against the door and groans just as the doorbell rings. "Fucking Xavier. Damn that man," he mutters, his gaze roaming over my body, regret written all over his face. "I should've known one of them would come get me if I tried skipping poker night."

I bite back a smile and rise to my tiptoes to press a kiss to his cheek, and he sighs as he turns and pulls the door open with far more force than necessary. "Run," he tells the tall and vaguely familiar stranger — Xavier, I assume. "Sierra will be here in a minute or so."

His eyes widen, and without even questioning Lex's words or asking for any further information, he just grabs my husband's arm and marches off, dragging a very reluctant and exceedingly annoyed Lex with him. "Sorry about this," he calls behind him. "I'll be sure to introduce myself properly next time! Good night, Mrs. Windsor!"

I just nod and stare at them in disbelief as they disappear around the corner moments before Sierra drives up. Her eyes widen when she finds me standing in front of our open front door, and she smiles so sweetly that I can't quite fathom why Xavier would respond that way at the mere mention of her. She's always been nothing but nice to me.

"Hi, Raya," she says, her tone kind and her cheeks rosy. She tucks her hair behind her ears and smiles nervously. "I hope you don't mind me dropping by unannounced."

I shake my head and smile back at her, still a little bewildered. "Not at all. It's so good to see you," I tell her, stepping aside. "Would you like to come in?"

She shakes her head and wrings her hands. "Actually, I'm here to invite you over for our monthly girls' night. We call it *anti-poker night*, because, well... it originated when I realized that my five older brothers had a monthly get-together they refused to invite me to. I'd love for you to join us."

I grin at her in excitement. I've been wanting to get to know the other Windsor girls a little better, but with us being exempt from family obligations, there just hasn't been any time. The only one I've really spoken to on a regular basis is Raven. "I'd love that, if you'll have me."

She exhales in relief, her whole face lighting up. "Oh, I'm so glad," she says, reaching for my hand and squeezing. Sierra explains what to expect at anti-poker night as I put on my shoes and grab my purse, and ten minutes later, we're pulling up in front of her house, where several other Windsor Motors supercars are already parked.

Nerves hit me hard when I hear the laughter in her living room, and for a moment, I feel like a true intruder. But then Raven rises to her feet and wraps me in a tight hug. "There you are, *finally*! Grandma forbid us all from overwhelming you in the first few months of your marriage, so we've all been counting down the days until we could finally hang out with you. I can't wait to hear about everything you've put The Herald through — it's just brilliant. It's honestly finally made it fun for me to read their garbage articles."

Valentina grins at me and holds up a liquor bottle with no labels on it whatsoever, while Celeste excitedly hands me a shot glass with *Raya Windsor* engraved on it. Faye, on the other hand, smirks from ear to ear as she holds up a photo album.

"Raya," she says, giggling. "I've been dying to show you these photos of Lex as a child that Dion found for me."

"But first," Sierra says, "*shots*."

My eyes widen, and I don't have it in me to tell them that I hate doing shots. The pure excitement on my sisters-in-law's faces is worth the sacrifice, and four shots later, I don't quite recall why I hated them in the first place.

Faye grins to herself as she slides a photo across the coffee table, toward me, and I burst out laughing with her as I lift it to take a closer look. Lex must've been no older than eight, and he looks completely unfazed as Sierra puts makeup on him, her face scrunched up in concentration. Valentina hands me another photo in which he's smiling from ear to ear, standing in between Luca and Sierra, all three of them dressed in matching pink dresses, clownish makeup on their faces.

"He's always just been so patient and sweet," Sierra says. "Growing up, he always indulged me, no matter what. He's never not made time for me when I've asked him to, no questions asked."

She tenses when she turns over the page in one of the albums on her coffee table, and I only just about catch a glimpse of a photo of Lex with a blonde girl, his arm wrapped around her and the sweetest smile on his face as he looks at her. I've never seen that expression on his face — so relaxed, so in love. Sierra snaps the album shut, a forced smile on her face as she glances at me, clearly hoping I didn't notice.

"Who is she?" I ask, unable to help myself. Lex told me he'd never introduced a woman to his family before, so what was that? The photo looked like it might've been taken in a college dorm, and unease settles in my stomach.

"No one you need to worry about," Valentina reassures me, but she looks just as nervous as Sierra does.

Raven wraps her arm around my shoulder and pulls me in for a side hug. "All that matters is that you're the woman he married," she murmurs, but she knows as well as I do that he didn't marry me by choice. Celeste and Faye exchange looks, clearly as curious as I am, but no one says a thing, the room descending into silence.

Lex and I are making the best of the situation we were thrust into, and I know he's trying to be a good husband, but he's never once looked at me the way he looked at the girl in that photo. I suspect he never will.

"Oh, look what arrived today!" Sierra says, fake cheer in her voice as she jumps up and grabs a box from the cabinet in the corner, clearly trying to change the subject. "I completely forgot to tell you all. I knew there's something I forgot to fill you in on."

My eyes widen when she opens the box to reveal long spikes, her eyes twinkling. "Oh God," Celeste murmurs. Faye stares at Sierra wide-eyed, and Val and Raven sigh, almost simultaneously.

"I'm going to superglue these all over Xavier's driveway. I can't believe that asshole acquired the theme park I've fought tooth and nail for right from under my nose. He did it to spite me, and we all know it. If he wants a wild ride, I'll give him one."

"That, um... that would get you arrested, Sierra," I say cautiously, surprised by how relatively unfazed everyone in the room is. It took me a moment to realize who he is, the name ringing a bell, though I struggled to place it. Xavier Kingston is a real estate magnate, best known for how ruthless and unforgiving he is. The Kingstons aren't a family anyone would dare offend — unless you're a Windsor, I suppose.

Val just shrugs. "Wouldn't be the first time she gets arrested over something she did to Xavier."

Raven nods as she leans back on the sofa. "It's fine. Xavier probably deserves it. This is actually relatively tame." She shakes her head, her eyes roaming over her best friend. "Besides, there isn't much Sierra could do to him that he won't let her get away with."

The words just remind me of the photo they tried to distract me from. That's how Lex looked at that girl — like there was nothing he wouldn't do for her, nothing he wouldn't let her get away with. He looked in love, and I've never seen him look so happy before. Certainly not with me.

Thirty-Five

Raya

"You seem a little distracted today," Halima says, her brow raised in concern. She's wearing a deep purple hijab today, once again perfectly matching it with her dress. That woman really knows how to dress — she always looks fashionable, yet modest. Without a doubt, she's one of the classiest women on this campus, and one of the most observant, too.

For days now, I've wondered about the photo I saw at Sierra's house. While Lex and I are relatively close, it hasn't escaped my notice that he doesn't really let me in. We can talk for hours, but he rarely tells me anything about his past. Sometimes he'll mention his grandfather, but that's kind of it. When I ask him for stories about his time at Astor College, he just waves it off and changes the subject. I don't want to be intrusive, but I can't help wanting to know more about my husband.

"I've just had a lot going on lately," I say as I lean over our drone, finishing up some of the soldering. We had to redesign almost all the wiring versus my initial plans after Lex gave us some tips, and I'm confident it's robust and safe now, but it took weeks to perfect.

"If not for all the hours you spent on this outside of class, we never would've finished it," she murmurs, a grateful look in her eyes.

I smile tightly, guilt settling in my stomach. While I did do all the work on it myself, I did most of it at home, with Lex's robots easily accessible to me to help with any complications I ran into. He kept reminding me that every other student has the same access, since he moved one of his Lola-lookalikes into the school lab after realizing how I was using Lola at home, but no one else has figured out yet what they can do. It feels like an unfair advantage, though it technically isn't.

"Good work," I hear my husband say to a group of students a few rows over, and I look up, our eyes locking for a moment. He smiles, and my heart skips a beat. My face heats as I lean over our drone again, trying my best not to notice him, when I'm hyper-aware of him every second that we're in the same room.

I sigh when a strand of my hair escapes my bun and falls across my face, disrupting my work. John laughs and leans in, pushing it behind my ear for me. "Your hair is so unruly," he murmurs, his gaze roaming over my face.

I smile at him in gratitude, and moments later, Simon begins to chuckle from beside me. I raise a brow, but he merely shakes his head and continues to refine the drone's propellors for perfect airflow.

"I can't wait for this project to be over," John complains as he runs through our code line by line. "I don't think I've ever worked harder in my life."

"Professor Windsor is lucky he's hot because that man's personality is rotten," Simon grumbles. "He's so damn ruthless with his feedback." He shakes his head and sighs. "Won't stop me from wanting to work for him, though," he adds, a dreamy look in his eyes.

Halima and I both roll our eyes at the same time, and John

leans in, his eyes darting around us before he grins. "Did you guys all see the article The Herald posted yesterday?"

My heart begins to race, and I resist the urge to grab my phone and check what kind of rubbish they've made up now. "What article?" I ask, keeping my tone light.

John chuckles. "Only a few months after buying that yellow diamond, he started wearing what appears to be a wedding ring. I didn't notice it at first, but it's true. He must've gotten married to the fiancée he mentioned. But get this: despite his supposed marriage, he's been spotted going on dates with all kinds of different women, blatantly cheating on his wife."

I subtly brush my hand over the necklace holding my wedding ring, making sure it's still hidden under my blouse. Unlike me, Lex refuses to take his off, and I'd wondered how long it would take the media to notice it. His ring is slim and simple, but it's clearly a wedding ring. I thought they'd have caught it months ago.

"I wonder who he married," Simon says. "Do you think he actually married a supermodel like his brother? I know the girl he was initially linked to denied the rumors, but it makes sense that Raven Windsor introduced him to one of her model friends."

I grimace, shame and inadequacy taking hold of my thoughts. Considering how accomplished all the Windsor wives are, it's no wonder everyone would hold Lex's wife to the same standards that I could never meet. Besides... that girl in the photo... she looked like she could've been a supermodel. Someone like her is far more suitable for Lex than I ever could be.

"How about we all mind our own business?" Halima snaps. "It's ridiculous how you're talking about Professor Windsor like he isn't right in this room, offering us all an opportunity most would kill for. Have some decency."

I glance up at her in surprise, and her eyes lock with mine for a moment, before she continues to focus on our drone's remote control and navigation system.

John's shoulder bumps against mine, and he wraps his hand

around my waist. "What's up with her?" he whispers. "Normally, she just ignores our random chatter."

I turn my head toward him to reply when he suddenly groans, his face contorting in pain. "John Bailey, is it?" Lex says, and my entire body tenses when he rips John's hand off me. I glance over my shoulder to find Lex staring John down, anger flickering through his eyes.

"Y-yes sir," John replies, his eyes wide with wonder, despite the way he clutches his hand. "I didn't realize you knew my name."

Halima sighs and shakes her head, barely sparing Lex a second glance as she continues to work, seemingly entirely unaffected by the situation at hand. I, however, am as wide-eyed as Simon is.

Lex moves closer to me, his body brushing against my hip. "Let's see your work, Mr. Bailey," he barks out, leaning over me and slyly wiping over the part of my blouse John touched. I bite back a smile when I realize what he's doing — is he wiping off John's touch? I chuckle, unable to help myself, and my husband relaxes slightly. Sometimes he does little things that make me believe he truly could fall in love with me someday, that this thing between us could become more than it is.

"Sloppy coding," he snaps. "Why are you using over thirteen thousand lines of code? How could you possibly need that much code? Where do you intend to send this drone, John? *Space*? I should fail you just for the sheer inefficiency you've forced me to witness."

I move my body just a touch, until my hand brushes against his. My pinky loops around his, my actions unnoticeable from this angle, and Lex's anger seems to drain away at once. He sighs as he grabs my hand fully, his thumb drawing circles across my wrist.

"You," he says, turning to look at me, not a hint of anger in his eyes despite his firm tone. "I'll hold you responsible as Team Leader." His gaze roams over my face, settling on my lips for a moment. "See me after class, Raya."

Thirty-Six

Lexington

I sigh and cross my arms as I lean back against the impractical desk Adrian forced on me, the seconds ticking by, until finally, my wife walks into my office. Her eyes roam over my rolled-up sleeves, pausing on my forearms, and she smiles. "You wanted to see me, Professor Windsor?"

Her voice is husky, her tone teasing. I beckon her closer, and she walks up to me, her gaze provocative. "*Professor*, huh?" I murmur, pulling her against me the moment she's within reach. I thread my hand through her hair and grip tightly, tipping her face up towards mine. She's been quieter than normal in the last couple of days, completely absorbed in her schoolwork. It's such a rush to finally see her looking at me this way again. "Tell me, Raya. Do you know why I called you into my office?"

Her lips part, her breathing quickening when she reads the expression on my face. That molten desire in her gorgeous brown eyes has me rock hard within seconds, and she inhales sharply when she feels my cock pressing against her stomach. "Because I'm responsible for not catching John's shitty coding sooner."

I clench my jaw and cup her face with my free hand, my thumb swiping across her lips roughly. "I don't want his name on these pretty lips," I warn her, leaning in. "I don't want him anywhere near what's *mine*." I take her bottom lip between my teeth and nip at her, earning myself a sexy little moan. "Watching him salivate over *my* wife is fucking maddening. How dare he touch your waist?"

She laughs, and my hand dips lower, tracing the curve of her spine, until I'm grabbing her ass over her skirt, kneading, squeezing. Raya tilts her face, her lips hovering below mine. "So, I'm here because you're jealous."

"Damn right I am," I growl, taking her into my arms. She gasps and hooks her legs around me instinctively as I walk around my desk. Her eyes grow round when I push everything off it with a swipe of my hand before perching my wife on the edge.

I push her legs apart roughly and sit down in my chair with her right in front of me, her legs on either side of me. "I'm jealous of the way he flirts with you so openly, while your husband has to stand back and make up some sort of dumb fucking excuse to approach you."

Surprise flickers through her eyes, my admission startling her, and I fucking love how disarmed she looks. "Place your hands behind you and lean back," I order. She obeys wordlessly, looking like a fucking vision with her legs spread, her skirt bunched around her waist, giving me a glimpse of her red lace panties. Her chest is pushed out for me, the buttons on her shirt straining.

"Good girl," I whisper as I roll my chair forward a little. The back of my hand brushes over her cheek before my fingers move down the side of her neck, to her collarbone. "You're such a good girl for me, aren't you? So obedient."

She inhales shakily when I pop the buttons of her blouse open, her red lacy bra nearly driving me delirious. Raya gasps when I push the cups down, exposing her nipples. They harden instantly, the cold air in my office no doubt caressing her skin.

"I asked you a question, Raya." I whisper, my fingers trailing down to circle the hard buds. "You'll answer me, or I'll have to punish you. Are you my good girl?"

She stares at me defiantly, and I suppress a smile as I lean in, my teeth grazing her nipple. She moans so beautifully me, her head falling back when I suck down on her sensitive skin. "Lex," she whispers, her tone needy, pleading.

It's been well over a week since I last heard her say my name that way, work stealing me away from my wife. "All these boys can stare all they want," I murmur, placing my hand on her thigh, my thumb caressing her pussy over the damp fabric. "But every fucking inch of you is mine. Do you understand?"

I push her panties aside and bite down on her nipple softly in warning when she doesn't answer. "Y-Yes," she moans. "I understand."

I grin and pull back to look at my wife, her tits out and her legs spread wide on my desk, her clothes a mess. "Fucking beautiful," I whisper.

Her eyes lock with mine as I drag my fingers over her pussy, coating my fingers in her wetness. "Keep your hands on my desk if you want to come, Raya. Move them, and I'll stop."

She nods, and I smirk as I slide two fingers into her hungry, tight pussy. The sexiest moan escapes her lips when I curl them against her g-spot, and fuck, what a sight to behold. "Ride them, baby. Ride your husband's fingers."

She lifts her hips and does as she's told, my thumb pressed to her clit as she rocks her hips back and forth, making my fingers slide in and out of her exactly the way she wants them. She's so fucking wet that she's dripping down her thighs, and I smirk to myself, determined to make her wetter still, until I've got traces of her on my desk.

The sexiest moans fill the air between us, and I groan as I undo the buttons on my pants with my free hand, taking out my cock. Her eyes lock on it instantly, and her pussy tightens. I chuckle as I wrap my hand around the base. "You want this, darling?"

She nods, her eyes sparkling.

"Then come for me," I order. "This cock has to be earned, Raya. Come for me, and I'll consider letting you have it."

Desperation flickers through her gorgeous brown eyes, and she moves a little faster, her hips rolling a little harder. "I'm so close," she whispers, her pussy fluttering around my fingers.

I'm fucking mesmerized as I watch my wife chase an orgasm, her eyes moving between my cock and my face hungrily. "Please," she moans, and fuck if it isn't a rush to hear her beg so prettily. "Please, Lex. Won't you make your wife come?"

"Fuck," I growl, unable to resist her plea. "You're playing dirty, Mrs. Windsor."

Her eyes sparkle with need, her head falling back beautifully as I take over, fucking her with my fingers, just the way she needs it. My gorgeous wife leans back to enjoy my touch, her focus entirely on my fingers and what I'm doing to her. Her moans become a little louder, and I smile in satisfaction when her eyes fall closed and her pussy contracts around me, over and over again.

"Give it to me," she says when her lashes flutter, her pussy still throbbing. "I earned it."

I grin as I pull my hand away and wrap it around my cock instead, pumping slowly. "You didn't, Raya. I gave you that orgasm, you didn't earn it. I'll make you earn the next one, though." My eyes settle on her pretty little mouth. "Get on your knees."

She inhales sharply and slides off my desk, her gaze a mix of anticipation and lust as she kneels between my legs. My wife looks up at me, her tits out and that stunning post-orgasmic look on her face, and I swear I could come just at the sight of her.

"Let's see if you're a good student, Raya," I murmur, my hand threading through her hair as I bring her closer. "Show me whether you've learned how to suck your husband's cock."

She leans in and looks at me as she drags her tongue from the bottom all the way to the top, teasing me. "You know I have," she whispers, grabbing the base like I taught her to.

She smiles, and then she takes the head into her mouth, swirling her tongue around it in the most devastatingly provoking way. "Raya," I groan, balling her hair in my fist as I rock my hip just a little, unable to keep still when she's tormenting me like that.

Her gaze cuts to mine, and she draws a desperate moan from my throat when she begins to take more, taking her time as she gets the angle just right, making sure she doesn't gag as my cock slides against her tongue, all the way to the back of her throat. She takes a deep breath, and then she pulls back, only to take a little more, letting me slide down further. Raya swallows, and the way her throat constricts around me has me biting down on my lip harshly as I instantly become lightheaded.

"You'll be the death of me," I whisper when she does it again, deep throating me in my office on campus, like the good little girl she is. "I can't take much of that, Raya. I... *fuck*." She'll make me come within seconds if she keeps that up, and the look in her eyes tells me she knows it.

"Please," I whisper, desperate.

Pure fucking delight lights up my wife's eyes, and I narrow my eyes in warning when she pulls back, almost letting my cock pop out of her mouth as she swirls her tongue around the sensitive tip, sucking down on it teasingly.

"You'll pay for this," I warn her as I push my hips up and tighten my grip on her hair, fucking her face with rocking movements, her tongue meeting me thrust for thrust. "Three," I snap at her. "I'll edge you three times tonight to punish you for what you're doing to me. Three times, I'll bring you to the brink of an orgasm only to pause, depriving you of what you want most."

She pulls her mouth away and laughs, only to grab the base tightly and take it all in one swift move. My wife looks up when her hot little mouth wraps around the base of my cock, her expression provocative. The way she looks at me is different now, her longing deeper. Possessiveness is written all over her gorgeous face, and it makes me impossibly hard. She looks at me like she owns me, wants to mark me as hers.

"Four," I warn her when she swallows, her tongue drawing leisurely circles. I can see it in her eyes — she has no intention of making me come until she damn well feels like it. Fucking tease.

I tighten my grip on her hair and try to rock my hips, needing friction, but she just moves with me, not letting me have what I want. "Mrs. Windsor," I warn.

She swallows, her throat tightening fucking deliciously, and my eyes fall closed — only for them to open in a rush as a knock sounds on the door. Raya and I both tense when the door opens, and John walks in.

"Good afternoon, Professor Windsor," he says, his eyes wide when he takes in the carnage in my office, documents and pens strews all around the room, my desk bare save for the nearly invisible little wet spot Raya left. "Wow, what happened here?"

I glance at my wife, panic seizing me, but she merely raises a brow and slowly slides back, keeping only to the tip of my cock in between her lips. My heart is racing, and realization finally dawns.

Adrian fucking Astor. I bite back a laugh when I realize what the fully enclosed desk is for, and why he so firmly insisted I'd thank him for it eventually. What a legend.

"Are we entering offices without permission now, John?" I snap. "You have a habit of overstepping, don't you?"

I lean forward and prop one elbow on my desk, my other hand still buried in Raya's hair. I'm certain my wife is fully hidden from view, and she seems to realize it too, because she grabs my cock and begins to bob her head up and down. She's moving so slowly she's barely making a sound, but her movements drive me completely fucking wild.

"I'm sorry, Professor," he says, flustered. "I just wanted to drop by and apologize in person. You were right, the coding was messy and inefficient, and it could've resulted in all my teammates' hard work going to waste. I'll fix it, so please don't punish Raya for my mistakes."

I tighten my grip on my wife's hair to keep her still, but she doesn't even acknowledge my attempts and latches on harder, her tongue swirling faster. Is she trying to make me come with this fucking guy standing right in front of me?

"Raya," I growl, bringing my fist to my mouth and biting down on it for a moment. John nods and raises a brow, his gaze running over my face. I shake my head, trying my hardest to keep my breathing even when my head is spinning, my cock throbbing. "My head is killing me, John," I tell him, in an attempt to offer an explanation. It's true — the head Raya is giving me *is* killing me. "Now isn't a good time to discuss this."

I tighten my grip on my wife's hair and accept my fate, tilting my hips up as she takes me deep, swallowing in a rhythmic pattern, knowing full well that the way she tightens her throat is going to make me come.

He nods politely and pauses by the door, opening his mouth to speak, but I cut him off. "As for whether Raya deserves to be punished... well, that's up to me, isn't it?" I snap.

I bite down on my lip harshly when my wife pushes me over the edge, not giving a single fuck that we're not alone in the room. She's such a fucking brat, and she absolutely does deserve punishment. *Five*. I'll bring her to the edge of an orgasm five times before I let her come. My girl needs to be taught a lesson, and the date I have planned for us next weekend is the perfect time to do it.

Thirty-Seven

Raya

"Where are we going?" I ask as Lex opens the passenger door of his car for me. He told me he'd take me on a *real* date today, but he wouldn't give me any hints about what that means. All he said was that I wouldn't need a wig this time, and to wear whatever I wanted.

"You'll see, my little fairy," he says, just before he closes the door and walks around the car. I study the blue jeans and the white t-shirt he's wearing, figuring it's a clue, since he rarely wears anything but a suit.

My husband grins at me as he gets in and leans over me, reaching for my seat belt to buckle me in. He pauses, his gaze roaming over mine, and he sighs softly before kissing the tip of my nose moments before my seatbelt clicks into place.

"Just give me one hint," I murmur as he takes an unfamiliar turn on the Windsor Estate.

Lex just places his hand on my thigh and squeezes. "I'll take you somewhere you've never been, to do something you've never done. It'll be a completely unique experience, a memory that'll just be ours. I'm taking you somewhere no one can reach us."

I place my hand over his and frown. "That didn't narrow it down at all. That was a terrible clue."

He chuckles and shakes his head. "It wouldn't have mattered what I said. You'll never guess it, darling."

"Oh wow," I whisper when I realize what lies ahead of us. The *hangar*, where a Windsor helicopter is already waiting for us.

Lex smirks as he parks right in front of it, his gaze on mine as he walks around the car and offers me his hand. I take it without question, the excitement in his gaze infectious.

"Lex," I murmur when he entwined our fingers and leads me right up to the helicopter. "There's no pilot."

His eyes widen, and then he laughs. "Isn't there?"

He opens the door and reaches for me, lifting me into the seat right next to the pilot's with ease, and I stare at the countless dials and buttons in surprise. It's a beautiful piece of machinery, most of the bottom just made of glass to allow for an uninterrupted view.

Lex leans in and straps me in, before placing headphones over my head, triple checking that I'm secured properly before he walks around and gets into the pilot's seat. I stare at him wide-eyed, and he laughs in earnest as he touches countless buttons. The propellors start to spin as he buckles himself in.

"You're kidding me," I say the moment he has his headphones on, a microphone extended in front of his face. It hits me then: each time he told me *he'd just take his helicopter* to make his busy schedule work, he was flying it himself. How did I never realize that before?

Lex leans back, looking perfectly comfortable in his seat. "Little fairy," he drawls. "Let me give you an exclusive view of the Windsor Estate and our city. I'm taking you somewhere special, and the flight there is pretty spectacular."

I gasp when we take off smoothly, and though I try my best to focus on the view underneath us, my gaze keeps being drawn back to Lex. He looks in his element. I'd never noticed how tense he usually is, until now. We've been married for months, yet I didn't even know how much he loves flying.

"When did you learn to fly?" I ask, my tone hesitant.

His gaze to mine for a split second, before he faces forward again. "About ten years ago."

I bite down on my lip. "Why did you decide to learn? It suits you, but it's not really a conventional hobby."

He pauses, and for a moment I'm sure my headphones and microphone malfunctioned, but then the sound crackles, and he replies. "I needed something that truly made me feel free and completely in control, and flying does that for me. There's nothing like taking to the sky, no one but you in charge of your flight path and not a single thing obstructing that path."

He throws me a smile, but it isn't a genuine one. Something about my question made his carefreeness wash away, his usual expression clicking back into place. I hadn't even realized how fake it looks until I caught a glimpse of him underneath that mask.

"We're here, darling."

I sit up as we start to descend toward a long runway in the middle of a flower field, my curiosity overflowing. The closer we get, the clearer the flowers become. "Buttercups," I whisper, surprised. They're some of my favorite flowers to find in the wild, and I can't believe how many there are here. I glance at Lex, wondering if he remembers that they're my favorite. I told him that once during a round of truth or dare, but surely that isn't why he picked this location, is it? I can't tell what's going on at all, but the descent put a real smile on Lex's face, and I'd honestly go anywhere with him if it'll make him smile like that.

He waits for the propellors to slow down before he undoes his seatbelt and reaches over to unbuckle mine. He's got his hands on my headphones when our eyes lock, and he pauses, a slow smile spreading across his face as he tilts his face and leans in to kiss me. I sigh, my heart racing as I wrap my hand around the back of his neck and kiss him back, losing myself in my husband. His lips linger for a few moments before he pulls back, and I grin when he steals another swift kiss before taking my headphones off for me. The way he looks at me... it isn't love, but it's something that makes me hope it eventually could be.

"Come on," he says, offering me his hand as he leads me out of the helicopter, and much to my surprise, three uniformed Windsor Motors employees are standing right in front of it. I blush fiercely when I realize they must've walked up while we were kissing, and the thought of them having witnessed that fills me with embarrassment. Lex chuckles when he notices I can't quite face them, and he wraps his arm around my shoulders.

"Mr. Windsor," the oldest of the three men says, nodding politely. He barely spares me a glance. "We've prepared everything you asked for. Tom will operate the winch."

Lex nods and pulls me a little closer. "That's wonderful. However, have you greeted my *wife*? I must not have heard you."

My eyes widen, and I glance up at him in surprise. He just smiles sweetly and brushes my hair out of my face.

"Apologies, Mrs. Windsor," the man says, sounding stricken. He looks at me like I'm some kind of mirage and smiles, seemingly genuinely.

Lex squeezes my shoulder briefly, and I look up at him. "This is Winston," he explains, before tipping his head to the man on his left. "That's Tom." Tom smiles politely, clearly curious about me. "And that's Justin. They're all Windsor Motors engineers, and they've graciously offered to help us today."

"Help us with what, exactly?" I ask, hoping for another clue.

He smiles sweetly and tucks my hair behind my ear. "You're about to find out."

My eyes grow round when a truck parks in front of us, and a small plane is loaded out of it. "What is that?" I ask, slightly fearful.

Lex grins. "That, my sweet little fairy, is a glider. It's an engineless plane, and you're going to fly it."

Thirty-Eight

Raya

I'm relatively certain I'm about to have a heart attack as I sit in the front seat of the glider Lex arranged for us. It's a two-seater, and I know he's right behind me, but that doesn't really ease my nerves.

"Explain the wench thing to me again," I tell him, my voice trembling.

He barks out a laugh. "*Winch*, darling. It's essentially a long rope attached to a machine at the other end of the runway. It'll start retracting at a high pace, which will make this glider lift into the air. That will allow us to take off despite this plane not having an engine. We should be able to get to about a thousand feet that way."

My stomach twists nervously as Lex closes the glass panel above us, enclosing us in the glider. "Brakes closed and locked," he murmurs as Justin attaches the cable to the front of the glider.

"You're serious, aren't you?" I ask as I take in the mechanisms. "This rope is going to be pulled back, and we're literally going to shoot forward and pray this thing flies?"

Lex leans forward and places a hand on my shoulder. "Raya,"

he says, his voice soft. "I have all the controls you have. I'll operate it the first time, okay? Just sit back and relax. This stick and the pedal here will allow me to keep the glider straight, and I'll keep the wings level. Will you trust me, darling?"

I nod, and moments later, we're in motion. I yelp as we're yanked forward, and though I fully expected to crash into the vehicle that's pulling us from the other end, we're airborne within seconds. I gasp at the speed we're moving at, the plane's nose pointing straight to the sky, our climb near vertical. It's exhilarating and terrifying and amazing.

"I'm increasing the pressure, so you'll notice that the glider will start to straighten."

I gasp as we level out, truly gliding through the air. It's surprising just how smooth the flight is, how weightless I feel. "Wow."

Lex chuckles. "I just knew you'd love this as much as I do. Flying is the one thing that's always only ever been mine, the one thing that's always made any day better. It's seen me through some rough periods, and I didn't think I'd ever want to share it with someone. Yet somehow, you've made me want to turn it into something that could be *ours*. I hope you enjoy today, darling, and I'm sorry I made you wait so long for our first real date."

"This isn't our first date," I tell him as I watch the clouds, the landscape underneath us. "We danced in your city penthouse on our first date, drank too much wine, and played too many rounds of truth or dare. I wouldn't trade that night for the world." Despite the things he kept from me then, I wouldn't have wanted our relationship to start any other way.

He leans forward and kisses my shoulder, before slowly turning the plane around and descending far more smoothly than I'd imagined. "Your turn, my little fairy," he tells me once we hit the ground. "You're going to fly us to the location of our date."

I turn back to look at him, surprised. "Wait, I thought this *was* the date." This is arguably the most unique and amazing experience I've ever had. Surely it can't get any better?

Lex laughs and reaches for me as the glider comes to a standstill. His crew does a quick checkup before they reattach the cable. "No," he tells me. "This is just the first part of it. Ready?"

"I'm not sure," I tell him honestly.

"I'm right behind you, Raya. Take to the skies, sweetheart, and trust that I'll be there to catch you if you fall."

"Okay," I whisper. "Okay, I can do this."

He gives the signal, and within seconds, we're moving. Lex talks me through every step, and for about a minute, his voice is the only thing I can focus on.

"Pressure," he reminds me, and I watch as a change in pressure changes the direction of the plane, until we're horizontal again, gliding on the airflow underneath us.

"See," he says, pride ringing through his voice. "That's my girl, my clever wife."

"Oh my God," I whisper, in shock. "I'm flying."

"You're flying," he reaffirms. "You're doing this."

I laugh, a pure rush of adrenaline making me lightheaded, and Lex joins in. I get it now, the way he smiles when he's flying. I've never felt anything like it before, I've never felt so free.

"I'm going to direct us toward where we're going, but you'll be the one to land the glider. Don't worry, Raya. The runway is really long and smooth, so it'll be easy."

I nod and sit back, my hand on the stick and my feet on the pedals. I can't believe how simple that was, how exhilarating. "Thank you," I tell him, my heart soaring. "I just know this is the kind of memory that'll last me a lifetime, and I love that the first time I did that was with you."

I'm not sure if he knew that it bothered me that we rarely go anywhere without a security team trailing us. He thinks I didn't notice, but it's obvious there are always two vehicles close to us. Today is different. It truly feels like it's just the two of us now, and I appreciate it more than I can convey.

"Do you see that resort down there? We're going to start descending toward it. When we get a little closer, you'll see a runway. There'll be markings on it to help guide you, but I have my hand on the controls in case you need me."

"We're going to a resort?" I gasp when we get a little closer. It's beautiful — palm trees, a sandy beach, and big villas that look like they're the epitome of luxury. "You taught me to fly so I could land in literal paradise?"

"I taught you to fly because I want to share all the things I love with you. For the longest time, flying was what I loved most of all."

Loved. Past tense. "What is it that you love most now?"

He falls silent. "Let's stay steady, darling," he tells me. "Don't descend at too much of an angle. Go slow and steady, so you'll barely notice you're about to hit the ground until seconds before it happens."

I follow his lead, the irony not lost on me. That's exactly what he did to me. He made me fall so slowly I didn't even realize it was happening. I just hope he keeps his words and catches me, because I see it now… I'm free falling.

Thirty-Nine

LEXINGTON

My wife's eyes are sparkling with excitement as employees of Windsor Hotels rush over to help us out of the glider, having anticipated our arrival. The moment we're both on solid ground again, Raya turns to me and wraps me in the tightest hug she's ever given me.

"That was perfect. You're perfect, Lex. God, I loved every second of that flight."

My heart skips a beat as I hug her back, my lips pressed to her temple. She's so fucking precious, and fuck, I can't help but want to give her the world. "Anything for you, darling," I murmur, reaching down to lift her into my arms, one arm under her knees and the other around her.

She gasps, her head resting against my chest. "I think you're going to like our room. This is one of Zane and Celeste's best hotels. It's smaller than all the others and far more private, but not any less luxurious."

It's perfect for a weekend of pure quality time. It's becoming increasingly tough to keep our marriage a secret, and even with her wigs, it's becoming harder to evade the media. On top of that, each time one of the boys in her class flirts with her, something that feels an awful lot like jealousy rushes through me, distorting my reasoning skills. More than once, I've caught myself behaving petty because I hated that I couldn't publicly call her mine, like I did with John. It's exactly what I didn't want this relationship to do — impair my judgment.

Raya twists in my arms, her honey scent invading my senses. I inhale deeply and sigh, feeling entirely at her mercy even though I'm the one carrying her.

An employee appears seemingly out of nowhere to open the door for us, and I smile in gratitude as I carry my wife into our room, yellow flowers on every surface, including all over our private pool.

"Wow," she says as I carefully place her down, equally surprised by how well everything turned out. I've been planning this little getaway for weeks, and I'm relieved not a single detail was missed.

"Mr. Windsor," someone calls from behind us, and I turn to find the same person who opened the door for us hovering at the entrance. "Your brother asked me to inform you that our alarm system has been malfunctioning all day. He didn't want you to worry, as Sinclair Security is handling it as we speak. They have also sent over extra bodyguards to safeguard the island."

"What's wrong with it?" I ask, anxiety clawing at me.

He hesitates. "It keeps turning itself on and off again every few minutes. We suspect something has gone wrong with the wiring when we built the new observatory. I was told that they'll have the issue resolved in the next seventy-two hours."

Raya wraps her hand around my arm. "It's okay," she says, her tone reassuring. "This is an island. It's as safe as it gets. You literally can't even get here any other way than by private plane."

I nod, not wanting to argue with her. Threats rarely come from outside — if there's any danger lurking, it'll already be here, watching, waiting. Raya tips and dismisses the staff, before turning to me. "Is everything all right?" she asks, her arms wrapping around my neck.

I nod, unsure how to explain my unease to her. It took me weeks to clear our schedule and obtain permission from her parents to skip our weekend with them, yet now that we're here, I can't even enjoy it. "I helped Silas build the security protocols for our hotels, so I'm just wondering if I should just go take a look."

She shakes her head and cups my face. "Just stay here with me," she pleads. "Look how beautiful everything is. How could you possibly walk away from all of this?"

My gaze roams over her face, and I catch myself searching for a sign of insincerity.

I instantly hate myself for it.

Raya has never given me a reason not to trust her, yet I often still struggle to believe she truly is as amazing as she seems to be. If something is this wonderful, it usually *is* too good to be true. It's a lesson I've learned over and over again, yet here I am, on the cusp of something I swore I'd never do again — falling headfirst.

"Okay," I murmur, quieting my fears as I grab my wife's hand and pull her onto the sandy beach just outside our room. My hand wraps around her waist, and I smile at her. "But it'll cost you."

I pull Raya into a dance, and the way she laughs as she falls into step with me is just everything. The way she looks at me, the way she makes me smile. She has no idea that she's done what no one else has been able to do in years. She's made me want to live again.

"Thank you," she murmurs eventually, the two of us coming to a standstill. "For genuinely trying to make our marriage work, even though it isn't what you wanted. I can tell that it isn't easy for you."

I raise a brow, uneasiness tugging at me. "What do you mean, you can tell?"

Her smile wavers, a hint of pain making its way into her gorgeous eyes. "I can tell that you often do things because you feel like they're the right thing to do." She looks away and shakes her head. "I don't mind it, per se. I'm just trying to say that I appreciate you trying."

I fall silent for a few moments, unsure how to reply. I never realized that she knew I've been modeling my behavior after things I've seen my brothers do for their wives, but that doesn't mean I ever did anything I didn't *want* to do. "Raya, I hope you know that I'm choosing you every single second of every day. I'm sorry if it seems I'm not always present with you, but know that I'm trying to be, that I'm trying to give you all of me."

She rises to her tiptoes and kisses me so sweetly that my heart begins to overflow with something I don't quite dare name — until she does it for me. Raya pulls back, her gaze roaming over my face, and then she smiles. "I love you, Lexington Windsor. You don't have to try so hard, you know? You're perfect for me, just as you are."

I stare at her, awestruck and barely able to process her words. Raya takes in my no doubt incredulous expression and laughs as she pushes me backward, back into our room and towards the bed. "You don't believe me, huh?" she whispers. "Let me prove it to you."

I fall backwards onto the bed, and she climbs on top of me, keeping me entirely enchanted with her every move. For the first time in years, I just let go, conceding control to my wife and silencing every last alarm bell in the back of my mind.

I want to do more than try with her — I want to love her, the way she deserves.

Forty

Lexington

The sound of metal scraping across the basement floor sends a chill running down my spine, a familiar nightmare holding me in its clutches. I blink against the fabric that covers my eyes, and my other senses instantly become hyper-alert. The air is hot and humid, and my clothes are sticking to my skin, just like I remember.

I try to move against the restraints that hold my ankles and wrists, but it's all to no avail. Each time I have this nightmare, I'm forced to experience every second of this ordeal all over again, never able to change even the smallest detail. Each time, I'm reminded how helpless I was, how clueless.

Soft feminine sniffling grabs my attention, and my heart wrenches. "Jill," I murmur, my throat sore from screaming.

"Lex," she cries, shuffling in her seat in an attempt to get closer to me.

"I'm sorry," I murmur, over and over again, my heart twisting painfully. "I'm sorry, Jill."

"Lex! *Lexington*!"

I startle awake to find beautifully warm brown eyes looking

down at me, nothing but one of my loose t-shirts covering her as her hands grip my shoulders. "Raya."

She cups my face, concern written all over her face. "You were having a nightmare, and I couldn't wake you from it. You kept thrashing and groaning like you were in pain. Are you okay? Are you hurt?" I stare at her, taking in her long dark hair, and the genuine anguish in her eyes. "Lex?"

I draw a shaky breath and pull her on top of me, my grip tight. She sighs and places her head right across my chest, her leg draping over my body. "I'm fine," I murmur, unsure if I'm being honest. I haven't had that nightmare in over a year, but I should've known the issues with the security systems would trigger it.

Raya sighs when I push my hand through her hair, the weight of her body on top of mine reassuring in a way she can't possibly imagine. My wife tilts her head and brushes her lips against my throat, pressing soft kisses against my skin, over and over again.

She stills in my arms, and I hug her tightly, my free hand playing with her hair. Her sweet honey scent is soothing, and fuck... she feels like *home*.

"Lex," she says, her voice barely above a whisper. "Who is Jill?"

My entire body tenses, and she pushes off me a little to look me in the eye. Her gaze is searching, her expression more vulnerable than I've ever seen it before.

"No one."

Her face falls, and she looks away, but not before I catch a glimpse of something akin to heartbreak in her gorgeous eyes. I bite down on my lip and tighten my grip on her before rolling us over, startling her.

She falls back onto the bed, her hair spreading all over our pillows, but it's those stunning eyes of hers that keep me captivated. No one has ever looked at me that way before — like she truly sees me. "There is no one but you, Raya. No one else matters," I murmur, silently pleading for her to believe me as I lean in for a kiss. She exhales shakily in the moments before my lips meet hers, her hands wrapping into my hair.

I cover her body with mine, and her leg instantly wraps around my hip, her fingers on my nape, right in that spot that makes me shiver. I tighten my grip on her hair to expose her neck, and she exhales shakily when I kiss her just below her ear, before sliding my teeth across her sensitive skin.

My beautiful wife moans my name when I suck on her skin, marking her as mine, before moving to her collarbone to do the same. "Only you, baby," I whisper, needing her to believe me, when I don't deserve her understanding.

Her breath hitches when I grab the t-shirt she's wearing and pull it up. She lifts her arms for me, and moments later, I have her naked in my bed, looking like a fucking angel. She has no idea what she does for me, doesn't know she's slowly leading me back onto a path I didn't think I'd ever walk again. "You are everything," I tell her, but it doesn't take away the insecurity in her eyes. It fucking kills me to see it, to know I put it there.

I sigh and lean in to kiss her, wishing my touch will do what my words failed to. Her hands thread into my hair when my lips meet hers, and she lifts her hips until she's got my cock nestled right between her pretty legs. I grin against her mouth and brush my tongue over the seam of her lips, forcing her to open up for me, deepening our kiss. I love that little sound she makes in the back of her throat, so needy, so sexy, and all fucking *mine*.

She gasps when I run my fingers down the side of her body, my lips never leaving hers. She moans when I push her legs apart with my knees and stroke the inside of her thigh, a wicked smile putting a halt to our kiss the second I realize how wet she is.

"You're dripping for me," I whisper, my fingers making their way to her soaking pussy. "Tell me, Raya, is this all for me?"

She looks into my eyes, her lips parted and her breathing shallow. "It's always been for you, Lex. Always will be."

Fuck. My heart overflows with something I've never felt before, and I just stare at my wife for a moment, overcome with emotions I can't even identify. "Yeah?" I whisper, my fingers delving between her legs, until they're coated in her wetness. "Tell me, baby. I want to hear you say it. Tell me you're mine."

Her eyes fall closed when two of my fingers slide into her, my thumb finding her clit. She bites down on her lip, and fuck, I know right then and there that I need this image to be mine, *only mine,* always. "Yours," she moans when I curl my fingers, hitting that spot deep inside her that makes her beg so prettily. "I'm yours, Lex."

"Good girl," I whisper, circling my thumb around her clit in approval. "This pussy is mine, do you understand?"

She whimpers and shifts her hips in an attempt to get my thumb to move over her clit, but I shake my head and keep my fingers still. "Answer me."

Her lashes flutter, and the most beautiful blush stains her cheeks rosy. I don't think she's ever looked more beautiful, and fuck, I don't think I've ever needed anyone more badly. "I understand," she whispers.

Her continuous reassurance is a soothing balm to my wounded soul, the words taking away the lingering doubts my nightmare left me with. "So obedient," I murmur, pleased. My fingers continue their torment, and she gasps as I bring her to the edge swiftly, wanting to reward her. "You're my good girl, my sweet wife, my little fairy... aren't you, Raya?"

She nods. "Your wife," she moans. "Only yours, always yours."

I bite down on my lip, enchanted. Raya is everything I never knew I needed. She's joy, and love, and light. She's hope personified, and for some insane reason, she's mine. I just hope she never realizes how unworthy I am.

"Come for me, baby," I whisper, increasing my pace. "Show me my favorite sight. Let me watch my wife come for me."

Her eyes are locked with mine as her pussy contracts around my fingers right as she inhales sharply, her lips slightly parted. The sexiest moan escapes her pretty mouth, and her lashes flutter closed, her hips shaking. Fucking beautiful.

"Again," I demand, and she shakes her head, her gaze sultry. I smirk at her as I draw leisurely circles around her clit, not quite touching it, but not letting up either. "You act like that was a request, Raya," I murmur. "We both know it wasn't. Give me one more, my little fairy."

She begins to whimper, little needy sounds escaping her sexy lips as her hips begin to roll, another orgasm building. "Lex," she whispers. "Please. *Please.*"

"God, I love the way you beg for me, baby. Love that pretty little mouth, this tight, wet, *perfect* pussy." My touch becomes more merciless, and her moans come faster, louder, until her head falls back, her back arching as another orgasm washes over her.

"Such a good fucking girl," I whisper, mesmerized. "My gorgeous wife."

She's breathing hard as she collapses onto the bed, her gaze filled with desire. "Please," she moans. "I need you."

"You want this?" I murmur, pushing my cock up against her, only the fabric of my boxer shorts keeping us apart.

She nods, pure desire dancing in her stunning brown eyes, and fuck, it's beyond surreal to think that's all for me. "Then take it, Raya. I'm yours — every single inch of me."

Her gaze roams over my face, her expression shifting into something that looks a lot like hope, like *love*. I don't fucking deserve it, but I can't help but relish it. My wife grabs my boxers and pushes them down, her eyes on mine as she grabs my cock, holding it firmly.

"Yours," I whisper. "All yours, Raya."

She lines me up against her and smiles as she wraps one leg over my hip, her gaze provocative. "Then give me what's mine, Lex. Give me all of you."

All of me...

She has no idea, does she?

Somewhere along the line, she took what's left of me.

Forty-One

Raya

"Pass me the wrench," Dad says, the two of us working on our prototype quietly. With Lex's input and access to his research, we've finally been able to make our design work, but we still aren't sure about mass production. Some parts of our design are too fragile, and I'm concerned about how user-friendly it'd be for consumers. The last thing we want is to roll this car out, only to get tons of complaints because no one knows how to use or service it.

"Would you like to tell me why you've been at the lab every evening for a week now?" Dad asks eventually. "I've let it go for the first few days, but something is clearly bothering you. Is it something that husband of yours did?"

For once, Dad doesn't look worried. Our weekends at home have endeared Lex to him, and he's gotten to know a version of Lex the public never sees. Dad knows as well as I do that he'd never intentionally hurt me.

"Did you have an argument, angel? That's normal, you know. Mom and I used to argue all the time, especially when you were younger. It's part of growing up, of growing as people individually and within a relationship. It's important that you keep communicating with each other. You can't just run away when things get tough, Raya."

I turn toward Dad and cross my arms. "I'm not running away," I tell him, agitated. If anyone is, it's Lexington. He's been running from this thing between us, and he's been doing it from the start. He won't let me in, won't lower his walls.

"Then why are you here, and not at home with your husband? There's nothing you can't resolve if you just talk to him, Raya."

I look down, my heart wrenching. "We're not arguing or anything. He and I... I guess we're just not on the same page. It's hard to explain, Dad." Had I known how lonely it'd be to experience unrequited love for your own husband, I'd have kept my distance from the start, treated this marriage as the business deal it is. I'd rather he treats me coldly than whatever it is he's doing now — being so kind that I can't help but fall, when he'll never feel the same way about me. Lying in bed with him as he whispers another woman's name in his sleep broke my heart, and he doesn't even realize it, doesn't know the memory torments me.

Dad reaches for me and sighs as he tucks my hair behind my ear. "I've witnessed that man hand over research that could revolutionize the industry, just so we'll have the prestige that'll come with taking our car to market under our own brand, before the merger goes through. On Monday mornings, he drops by to see me and gets his hands dirty, ensuring everything is on track with this car, and I can assure you he doesn't do it for me. On Saturdays he sits with you and messes about building random little household tools, simply because it makes you smile. All the while, he tries to check his email and answers calls every time you walk away, trying to make up for lost time."

I blink in surprise. "Lex comes to see you every Monday?"

He nods and tips his head toward the prototype. "A lot of the new components were actually crafted by Windsor Motors, but

Lex stripped his brand off for us." Dad grins and continues to work. "Sometimes love isn't loud and obvious, Raya. Sometimes it's in the little things, hidden behind layers and layers of exterior protection. Love isn't always communicated verbally, but that doesn't make it any less real."

I've never felt more conflicted — I know he's trying, and I feel so ridiculously ungrateful for still wanting more, for wanting him to love me the way I've grown to love him. I've never been a selfish person, but with him, that's exactly what I've become. "I know, Dad," I murmur. "I get it."

"That said, you deserve to be loved in the way *you* need to be loved, angel. That's something I learned with your mother. You wouldn't believe it, but I hate dancing. I do it because it's what makes her feel loved. I wouldn't have known that if she'd never told me."

"Communication," I murmur, understanding the point. Except it isn't me who's failing to communicate, and I can't force Lex to open up about things he doesn't want to tell me. Yet somehow, I can't shake the feeling that *Jill* is standing between us, that she always will.

I sigh and resume working on the prototype, not exactly mad at Lex, but just feeling the distance between us more than usual. I miss him, but then again, I also miss him when he's right there with me.

Dad and I both look up at the sound of knocking, and I freeze when Lex walks in, his gaze roaming over my face. "I figured I'd find you here," he says, his voice soft. He looks exhausted, defeated.

I turn away to run a diagnostic on the panels, unable to face him. I'm not mad at him, but I can't quite explain how I feel either.

"You know what, it's about time for me to go home," Dad says, wiping his hands. "I'll see you both this weekend. Don't forget to lock up for me, all right?"

Moments later, he's gone, leaving me alone with Lex. I've

never seen my father leave the lab so swiftly, and had I not been in such a bad mood, it'd have made me smile.

Lex sighs as he wraps his hand around my waist from behind, his chin dropping to the top of my head. "Raya," he murmurs. "I brought you a chocolate and salted caramel milkshake."

I turn to glance at him, refusing to admit that I'm swayed by the beverage, when we both know that I am. He grins as he hands it to me, and I look away as I take a sip.

"I miss you, darling. You've barely been home since we got back from our trip." He runs a hand through his hair. "Can we talk?"

I nod, and Lex begins to pace. "I should've told you sooner, and I'm sorry for keeping this from you, Raya. I didn't know how to address it, but it's clear you need answers. Keeping things from you is just driving a wedge between us, and I don't want to stand back and let that happen."

I take his hand, noting the way he's trembling. "I didn't mean to pressure you into anything, Lex. I just needed a bit of space to think. I remember what you said when we got engaged, and I don't want to ask you for more than you're willing to give. I just needed some distance to remind myself of what we are and what we aren't, so I don't pressure you with needs you never agreed to fulfill."

"That's just it," he murmurs. "I *want* to give you the world, Raya. You make me want and do things I didn't think I ever would." He inhales shakily and drops his forehead to mine. "So, let's talk about the one thing I haven't spoken about in years. Let's talk about Jill."

I pull back to look at him, taking in the torment in his gaze, and for a moment, I'm tempted to cut this conversation short, not wanting to hear about the woman who makes my powerful husband look like *that*, when I never could.

"Jill was my girlfriend in college, and she's the only woman I've ever dated." My stomach tightens, and I wrap one arm around myself, trying my best to keep my jealousy from showing.

It hurts to hear him say her name so softly, like she's still ingrained in his mind.

"I met her on my first day, during our orientation, and we got along brilliantly from the get-go. She was sweet, and funny, and she liked all the same things I liked, right down to the same movies and the same music."

I take a step back from him under the guise of taking a sip of my milkshake, unable to be so near him when he's reminiscing about another woman. It's not often that I can make him laugh the way he makes *me* laugh, and hearing him say Jill is funny hurts more than he thinks. Making him smile is my favorite thing to do, and I work so hard at it, but it seems to have been effortless for her.

"I fell hard and fast, and it was nothing like anything I'd ever experienced. You see, I always knew I'd end up in an arranged marriage, so I'd never had any interest in dating. It didn't make sense to me to spend any time with someone I wouldn't end up with, so I never bothered, until her."

My stomach turns, and my heart squeezes painfully. He fell for her the way I fell for him, and I suspect I'll never have what she had, what she might *still* have. Lex takes a step forward and caresses my hair, but I can't make myself face him, not without giving away my pain.

"I should've known it was too good to be true, you know? It's why part of me fears that you are, too." I look at him, curiosity mingling with confusion. "One day, out of nowhere, Jill and I were taken from our dorms. All I remember is falling asleep in my own bed and waking up blindfolded and strapped to a cold metal chair. I could hear her right by my side, sniffling, but I couldn't reach her."

His gaze turns cold, and he cups my face, our eyes locked. "I was desperate to free us, torn up by guilt, thinking I'd dragged her into this situation. There's nothing I wouldn't have done to ensure her freedom, her safety."

My breath hitches, my nerves taut as I anticipate a tragic

ending. Why else would Lex still be so tormented by her? Did he lose her that night?

"I'd agreed to hand over millions for our safe return, and arrangements were made with my grandmother. The night before the exchange was meant to happen, I heard an argument in the distance — about how they wouldn't have had to resort to that if she could've just convinced me to marry her. Moments later, Silas Sinclair stormed in with our private security team, freeing me and apprehending her. He wasn't working for us yet back then, and he wasn't much older than Ares was, but he was the only person who could find me when everyone else failed. He's been entrusted with our safety ever since."

His eyes fall closed for a moment, and I stare at him in shock, struggling to comprehend what he's telling me. "Jill confessed to everything in return for more lenient sentences for herself and her siblings. She'd stalked me to learn as much as she could about me the moment she realized we'd be attending college together, and then she approached me with one goal in mind: to make as much money off me as she could, along with her brothers. She wasn't kidnapped. Jill was the one who slipped sleeping drugs into my drink the night prior, helping her brother orchestrate everything."

He sighs and tucks my hair behind my ear. "Ever since, I've been scared of allowing someone in, of opening up and trusting the wrong person, because next time, it may not just be me that's at risk — it could be my family. It's why I approached you prior to our engagement, to see what kind of person you are. Raya, this is why I struggle to sleep in unfamiliar places, why I take extra security to your family home, and why I had a nightmare during our trip. I'm not in love with Jill or hung up on her — I'm fucking traumatized. Because of her, all these feelings I have for *you* terrify me, and darling, I don't quite know what to do about it."

Forty-Two

Raya

"Your drones have all undergone rigorous testing by Windsor Motors employees, and three interns were selected," Lex says as he addresses our class.

A hush falls over the room, and Adam tenses in his seat next to mine. I know how badly he wants this internship, despite how much he dislikes Lex. He knows how life changing it would be to work for Windsor Motors.

"Raya... *Lewis*," he says, grimacing like it causes him physical pain to say my maiden surname when he wants to call me Raya *Windsor*.

I smile at him, my somber mood lifted for a moment. I haven't been able to stop thinking about what Lex told me, and what it means for us. It explains so much — the way he wakes up earlier than everyone else, without fail. His reluctance to drink anything outside of the Windsor Estate if he didn't open the bottle himself, the lack of human staff in his home, and even his need for alarm systems and thoroughly vetted personal security personnel. It took him weeks to start drinking my mother's tea and join us for dinner, and I never noticed that he didn't start eating with us until he began insisting on helping Mom cook, overseeing every single thing that went into our food.

I've never seen anyone as tormented as he was when he told me about Jill, and all I could do was hold him afterward, offering my quiet support. It didn't feel like enough, and it hurts to know I can't take away his torment. When he told me he wasn't interested in love or relationships, it wasn't because he wasn't interested in *me*. It was because he isn't capable of the kind of trust a relationship requires, and all this time, I had no idea he was suffering. I stood by his side, clueless and constantly wanting more than anyone should ever expect of him.

"Adam Lawson, and Emma Thomas. They were also the designers of the three chosen drones, and they've proven that they can execute their visions, too."

It hurts to look at him now, to know how much pain he's been through, how much was taken from him. The idea of him in restraints, begging for the release of someone he loved, only to find out they betrayed him? It's given me a new sense of understanding of why he approached me the way he did, why he misled me.

"I'm so glad we get to work together," Adam says, turning toward me. "It's a bit strange though, to be wrapping up our master's. I'm not sure I'm ready for real life."

I force a smile, struggling to carry a conversation today. "It's going to be fine," I murmur. "You'll excel at your internship, and you'll be offered a permanent position afterwards. I just know it."

He nods at me, his expression conflicted. "Will you be okay?" he asks. "I know we haven't really spoken about it much, but I'm not blind, Raya. I know you still like him."

I sigh and look away. "That would be putting it mildly," I whisper. I'm helplessly and unconditionally in love with my husband, and it hurts. I love him so much that my heart aches at the thought of how hard he's been trying to be a good husband to me, when it must've been so difficult to even let me into his life.

All the while, I kept wanting more, not appreciating how much he was already giving me.

I rise from my seat when Lex walks out, ignoring Adam's calls as I follow my husband. He looks up from where he's standing when I walk into his office, his eyes widening. Lex looks exhausted, and I bite down on my lip, feeling guilty. Telling me about Jill seems to have brought back the nightmares that he had in the first few years after his abduction, and guilt weighs heavily on me. I'm the reason those awful memories resurfaced, and I don't know how to make it right.

"Don't look at me like that, little fairy," he murmurs, running a hand through his hair. "I don't want your pity, Raya. I only told you the truth because keeping it from you was hurting you and causing misunderstandings that I don't want between us."

I walk up to him and gently place my palm across his chest, his heart racing underneath. "I don't pity you," I tell him, my voice soft. "I just love you, Lex."

His eyes sparkle every time I say the words, and though he hasn't said it back, I know he likes hearing it. "Yeah?" he whispers, pulling me closer.

I nod. "So much. I'm grateful you told me the truth. You're right. Hearing you say her name in your sleep made me misunderstand, and I was jealous. I thought that someone else had your heart, when I..."

"No," he says, cupping my face. "There's no one but you, Raya. I..."

I draw a shaky breath, reading the emotions in his eyes. "You don't have to say it back," I whisper. "My love for you isn't transactional. It isn't conditional."

His eyes fall closed for a moment. "I once told you that you terrify me, and that's even more true now. I'm scared this is all an act, Raya. No matter how hard I try to convince myself it isn't, that my past is tainting my thoughts... I just can't suppress my fears. I'm scared this is all an elaborate game, and you'll betray me."

"I won't ever knowingly do anything that could hurt you, Lex. I swear it."

He nods, his forehead dropping against mine. "I'm trying, you know? I won't stop trying, Raya. You deserve the best of me, not just what's left of me."

I tilt my head, my lips brushing against his. "So long as you're trying, that's enough," I whisper against his mouth. "I never expected marriage to be easy, Lex. I'll walk with you every step of the way. So long as you're willing to take a step forward, I'll be there to meet your pace."

He sighs, and then he kisses me, his touch tender, almost like he thinks this moment between us will break. "Raya Indira Windsor," he whispers, pulling away. "I think you may well be the best thing that's ever happened to me."

I grin and lean back to look at him, my heart overflowing with tenderness. "Let's see if you still feel that way when I drive you crazy at work. I'm looking forward to it, you know? Learning from the one and only Lexington Windsor."

He chuckles and gently pushes my hair behind my ear. "I'm looking forward to it too, my little fairy. That's what you do to me, you know? I just want to be around you every second of every day, and knowing I'll get to see you at the office... I can't fucking wait."

Forty-Three

Raya

Lex caresses my thigh over my black pencil skirt as we drive to his office together, completely unconcerned about the deep maroon wig I'm wearing. Since he refused to part ways with me this morning and I refused to be seen with him on my first day at work, we ended up compromising.

"You do realize people think I've been cheating on my poor wife this whole time, thanks to your..." he gestures toward my hair, "*ferrets*."

I gasp and push his hand off my leg. "My *what*?" I ask, outraged as I pull down the shade to check the mirror. He chuckles when I smoothen my very expensive and very beautiful lace wig, my favorite out of all of them. It's the one I wear most frequently, and it drives The Herald crazy.

"I see the red hair turned you even feistier than normal." His gaze roams over my face, and he smirks as he places his palm on my knee. "Let's see if that feistiness lasts when I bend you over my desk and spread these pretty legs. I need a picture of you for my private collection, my cock in your sexy wet mouth and that red hair bringing out that blush so fucking beautifully."

His hand slips up and between my legs, and he squeezes my thigh possessively. The combination of his words and the way he looks at me makes me blush fiercely, and he laughs. "I love how shy you still get, when you were *begging* me to let you come last night."

I glare at my husband, my face no doubt as crimson as my hair. "I had no *choice*," I snap. "You made me delirious with need. You *tortured* me."

His hand slips under my skirt, and I gasp when he places his pinky right against the lace between my legs. "I beg to differ," he says, his voice deep, irresistible. "*I* was the one being tortured, my little fairy. It's fucking torture having your delicious pussy on my tongue and hearing you moan my name the way you do. *Fuck*. You're my addiction, Raya. I'd live off your pussy if I could."

His gaze cuts to mine, and he raises a brow. "Do you think I could? How nutritious do you reckon your pussy is?"

I gape at him and push my fist against his arm. "Oh, stop it!" I say, even as a peal of laughter falls from my lips. "I do realize what you're doing, you know?"

He smiles so sweetly as he turns into the parking garage for Windsor Motors, driving straight to his designated spot. "Of course you do," he murmurs, turning toward me the moment he's parked the car. "No one knows me like you do, after all."

His gaze becomes haunted for a moment, but then he pushes his unease aside. Lex cups my cheek, and I sigh, my nerves finally catching up to me. "I'm scared," I admit. I know he's trying his best to distract me from my thoughts this morning, but I can't help but feel a little conflicted about my first day. "Working for Windsor Motors... it feels like both a dream and a betrayal. I always thought I'd go work for my dad as soon as classes ended, even before I formally graduated, but here I am, about to start an internship at Windsor Motors instead. And I... I just don't know if I'm good enough to be here, and I know you'll tell me that I am, but you're biased, and even though you deny it, I know I'm only here because I'm your wife."

His thumb brushes over my mouth, and he sighs before leaning in to press a soft, sweet kiss to my lips. "Darling," he whispers. "You *own* this company as much as I do. What's mine is yours, Raya. No one has more right to be here than you do. Soon, once the merger goes through, there won't be a difference between Windsor and Lewis Motors, and you'll work with your father, just like you both always wanted to." His hand moves to my chin, and he grips my face, keeping my eyes on his. "As for qualifications... you are, quite literally, the top student in almost all of your classes. This isn't favoritism, Raya. You're simply brilliant, and you'd have been chosen even if you weren't my wife. If anything, I'm the one that's in luck here. If you weren't my wife, Windsor Motors may never have had the opportunity to benefit from that beautiful mind of yours. You'd absolutely have chosen your father's company over any other opportunity."

I sigh and lean in, my hand wrapping around the back of his neck. He seems to firmly believe every word he says, and that's the part I don't quite understand. Why does this incredible man think so highly of me? "Give me a dose of good luck," I whisper, my lips brushing against his. "I'll need it. I heard my boss is a right tool."

Lex bursts out laughing, and I shut him up with a kiss, loving the way he instantly unbuckles my seatbelt to pull me closer. His hand wraps into my wig, and he groans when I pull away, every bit as reluctant as he is.

"I can't be late for work on my first day," I tell him, pushing against his chest.

His hands move to my waist, and he sends me the cutest pleading look. "Which part of '*you own the company as much as I do*' did you not understand?" he asks, his voice soft, cajoling. I love how easy things have become between us lately. We haven't spoken about it much, but we're both trying a little harder than we did before, casting aside our fears for a chance at true happiness.

"Don't even try it," I tell him, laughing as I push off him and move to get out of the car, my gaze moving around furtively.

"Little fairy," he calls after me once I've stealthily gotten out of his car and made it halfway toward the entrance. "This is a restricted area." He tips his head towards the barrier behind us. "Only Windsor family members and Silas Sinclair can get past that access barrier."

I stare at him incredulously. "So, you saw me get out of the car like some kind of weirdo and didn't think to tell me that then?"

He grins as he saunters up to me, clearly exceptionally amused with himself this morning. I'd be annoyed if this weren't the first time in weeks that he's seemed this lighthearted and happy. "I thought you were putting on a show for me. I never know with you, darling."

The look on my face makes him laugh, and he grabs my hand as he pulls me along. "Don't worry. This is a private lobby with an elevator that leads straight to my office. It's highly secure."

"Again — you saw me put this wig on this morning and didn't think to tell me?" I throw him a hateful little glare as we step into his elevator together.

His gaze roams over my face hungrily, and I inhale sharply when he corners me with his body, the elevator's cold metal against my back. "Of course not. You look fucking gorgeous with that red hair. You think I'd deprive myself of such a pretty sight?" His index finger loops around the chain that holds my wedding ring, and he pulls on it. "I have no intention of depriving myself of anything that belongs to me." His face tips down, his lips brushing against mine. I inhale sharply, and he smiles. "And you, Raya Windsor? You're mine."

Lex groans as he kisses me, his touch filled with more need than usual, and I rise to my tiptoes, kissing him back with all I've got. "Yours," I whisper as I pull back, quietly reassuring him. "Always yours, Lex."

The doors open straight into his office, and he smiles relaxedly as he grabs my hand and pulls me into his beautiful corner office.

Pippy's voice welcomes us overhead. "Welcome to work, Lex and Mrs. Windsor," she says, sounding far too chirpy, almost like she *knows* she's defying me by *still* not calling me by my name.

I throw my husband a panicked glare. "You told me you'd fix that!"

He just shrugs and watches in fascination as I pull off my wig, revealing my long, dark hair. Lex raises a brow and sighs as he holds out his hand. "Just give me the damn ferret," he mutters. "It's enough that the whole world will think I'm having countless affairs. The last thing I need is additional rumors about how my wife murdered my mistresses and carries their heads."

I hold up my wig and stare at it. "Fair," I mutter as I hand it over. "I can see those trash Herald reporters coming up with something as dumb as that."

My eye twitches as he carelessly throws it in a drawer, but I manage to restrain my temper as he checks his watch, reminding me of the time.

"Ready to meet your team, darling?"

Forty-Four

Raya

My heart is pounding as I follow Lex out of his office, taking in the stunning light decor and all the tech he built into the company. The whole building is a smart building, and it's astonishing. There isn't a single thing that isn't automated.

"We have facial recognition everywhere," he explains. "You have full clearance, so there isn't anywhere you can't go, but normally junior employees can't get to any other floor but their own, and the mailroom."

I trail my fingers over surfaces we pass excitedly, unable to help myself. "The doors, lights, temperature and of course the air purifiers are all automated. Sierra and I designed this building so it works with you, almost always giving you what you need before you need it." As if on cue, a robot similar to Lola drives up to us, holding Lex's tablet with his schedule on it. "The robots can bring you lunch, coffee, or run any other errands within the building."

"You know," I murmur. Lex pauses and looks over his shoulder. He always has endless patience for me, and I wonder if he knows I never take it for granted. "I'm proud of you." His eyes widen, and I step closer to him, noting the people milling about, most of them grabbing coffee and catching up as they start their days. "I'm proud of what you've built, and I'm beyond proud to be your wife."

He reaches for me, only to catch himself and retract his hand. "I'm counting down the days, Raya," he tells me, his voice soft. "Until I can tell the world you're mine, until I get to see your ring around your finger every day."

"I know," I whisper. "Soon." My graduation ceremony is only a few weeks away, and we'll announce it shortly after.

He smiles tightly and cups the back of his neck as he continues to walk, explaining how the building works as he leads me to my team. I spot Adam standing in the distance, right next to Emma. Much to my surprise, Halima walks up right at that moment. She waves at me, her usual serene smile on her face.

"You really seemed to like her, and she's insanely smart, so I offered her an internship too. Once news of our marriage breaks, no one will be able to say you deprived someone of a spot."

I glance up at my husband, my heart soaring. He's truly always a few steps ahead, thinking of everything. Adam, Halima, and Emma are standing opposite a beautiful blonde in a cream suit, and she turns toward us fully at the sound of my clicking heels. Her stern expression melts away when she sees Lex, and the way her face lights up makes me feel uneasy.

"Oh, good morning, Mr. Windsor," she says, beaming. "I didn't think I'd see you this morning." She turns back toward the rest, barely sparing me a glance. "Mr. Windsor often makes time to personally mentor our new staff, so you'll see him around more than you might expect. I was lucky enough to be trained by him too, and it truly is an incredible experience."

I quietly move to stand next to Adam. His gaze moves between Lex and me briefly before he smiles sweetly at me.

Walking in by his side wasn't a good idea at all, but I just couldn't tear myself away from him this morning.

"Have you introduced yourself to our new interns?" Lex asks, leaning back against one of the desks, his hands in his pocket. He looks incredible standing there in that navy suit, and it hits me then. That man, that seemingly unattainable man, is *mine*. Maybe he doesn't love me the way I want him to. Maybe he never will, but it doesn't change the fact that he's my husband.

The blonde nods enthusiastically, before turning to me. "Here's your first lesson, latecomer. At Windsor Motors, we expect excellence. If you fall behind, you'll have to find a way to catch up. We don't hold hands here. We nurture independent thinking and create leaders, not followers."

Lex's gaze hardens. "What time is it right now?" he asks, his tone sharp.

Her eyes widen, and she glances at her watch. "It's eight thirty, Mr. Windsor."

He nods and pulls his hands out of his pocket, his right hand moving over his left to play with his wedding ring — a move I've learned means he's trying to keep his patience. "And what are my office hours?"

She blinks and hesitates. "Nine to five, sir."

Lex nods slowly, and I try my hardest to throw him a discreet warning look, but he pointedly ignores me. "*Right*. For a moment there I was under the impression that I'd changed them, but I haven't, have I?"

She shakes her head, and he smiles, his eyes cold. "One more question," he says, crossing his arms. I wonder whether he realizes the move only makes him look more intimidating. "What's your name?"

Her shoulders slump, and I bite down on my lip, guilt settling in my chest. Lex doesn't like it when anyone dismisses me in his presence, and no matter how hard I fight him on it, he just won't stand by idly as anyone treats me in a way he finds even remotely unacceptable.

"It's Amy Jeffrees, sir. I... um... I joined three years ago, and I assisted with the testing of our latest range of medical solutions."

Lex's eyes meet mine, and his stern expression turns sheepish when he notices my disapproval. He looks down and nods. "Right, I remember now. Thank you for reminding me, and apologies for interrupting," he says, sounding not the least apologetic.

She smiles tightly and turns back to us, her expression far less cocky now than it was before. "I'll be your primary point of contact as you assist my team and me with our latest project. It's an exciting one. Every once in a while, Mr. Windsor surprises us with something quite unusual, and those kinds of things always end up being the best and most fun learning experiences, in part because he always takes an active role in new acquisitions — big or small."

I raise a brow in confusion. Lex normally tells me all about his days, but he hasn't mentioned any new acquisitions. Amy's wide smile is back as one of the robots rolls up to her, its tummy turning into a screen. I throw my husband an incredulous stare. Does he realize he created real life Teletubbies? He grins to himself, and I sigh. Yeah, he probably knew exactly what he was doing when he designed the robots the way they are. I suppose we're all lucky he didn't make them all wacky colors. I'm so dazed by the new feature the Lola-lookalike revealed that it takes me a moment to realize what's on the screen.

"We acquired a famous milkshake company!" Amy tells us excitedly. "They make my favorite milkshakes, so I couldn't be more excited!"

Adam bumps his shoulder against mine, but I can't quite take my eyes off my husband, and the pink flush on his cheekbones. "Isn't that your favorite too?"

I nod speechlessly as Amy glances at the robot, which prompts it to move to the next slides. "It'll be our goal to fully automate these so they'll be easier to operate. More often than not, these machines break, and we're going to fix that."

"There's nothing worse than desperately wanting a milkshake and being told they don't have any," I murmur. Much to my surprise, Amy smiles at me, recognizing a kindred spirit.

"Right," she says, nodding. "We're going to fix the issues we have with them, and then we're going to make sure they can operate independently at night. We've been tasked with ensuring they can only be operated manually during daytime hours, so human jobs won't be at risk, while ensuing they can work in a fully automated fashion outside of regular working hours. On top of that, I was told that the formula is changing — they'll now all be dairy-free! I, for one, am incredibly excited about that! It is, however, something we'll have to carefully take into consideration since variations in density could affect the machinery's performance."

I stare at my husband, who's looking back at me with the sweetest expression on his face. There's only one way to describe the look in his eyes, but I don't quite dare even think it.

"Why milkshakes?" Emma asks. "Automating something that's so well known for never working will definitely be fun, because it'll be such a high-profile project, but it just doesn't really fit in with the types of products Windsor Motors normally puts out."

Lex looks up at her and smiles. "They're my wife's favorite," he says simply. "I want her to have access to them whenever she wants, and she doesn't really like dairy, so we're changing the formula nationwide." He runs a hand through his hair. "We're also rebranding. I'm renaming the chain *Little Fairy*, and I'm calling the chocolate and salted caramel option *Mrs. Windsor*."

He just stares at me, completely uncaring that his admission of the rumors about him being married sent the whole team into a shocked kind of frenzy. His wedding ring has fueled the rumor mill for months now, but he's never officially admitted his marital status to anyone but Adam.

"The milkshakes are a love letter to your wife," Halima says, seemingly the only person that's completely unfazed.

He nods, and my heart skips a beat. I try my hardest to bite back a smile and fail. I don't think my heart has ever raced harder, wilder. For some reason, I'm reminded of my father's words. *Love isn't always loud and obvious, but that doesn't mean it isn't there.*

Forty-Five

LEXINGTON

"Do I look okay?" my wife asks as we pause in front of my grandmother's home. We've all been summoned over, and I know she's nervous about it. The last time we were summoned, we were told off for the wig stunts we'd been pulling, but this time it's different. I know exactly why we're here tonight.

My gaze roams over the stunning cream knee length dress she's wearing, and I nod. "Classy but perfectly sexy, little fairy. I love this dress on you." She smiles, but her eyes narrow when I open my mouth again. "But not as much as I'll love it on our—" she presses her index finger to my lips and shoots me a warning look just as Zane and Celeste walk up to us.

I grin and bite her finger, earning myself a pretty little blush as she pulls her hand back. God, making her blush will never get old. Each time just gets more exhilarating.

"Lex! Raya!" Celeste says, hugging us both tightly. Zane follows her lead, pressing his nose against my wife's hair for a bit longer than I'd like.

She smiles and nods at him as he pulls away, and I narrow my eyes as I grab her hand and pull her out of his reach. "You have your own wife," I snap. "Leave mine alone."

Zane looks irritatingly amused as he wraps his arm around Celeste, his eyes sparkling with delight as my hand wraps around Raya's waist possessively. The two of them brush past us, leaving the door open behind them.

"Lex," Raya says, seemingly lost in thought as she eyes the front door Zane left open for us behind him. "Do you think you could jump from here all the way into the house?"

I follow her line of sight and shrug. "No idea. Let's find out, darling."

I step back and make the jump, just about making it inside and nearly stumbling over, only to find all my brothers standing in the hallway, their phones out and the biggest grins on their dumb faces. They all burst out laughing at the same time, money exchanging hands quickly.

"For fuck's sake," I murmur, realizing what just happened.

"I'm sorry," Raya says, clutching my suit jacket from behind me. "Zane has never asked me for a favor before and I didn't know what to do."

I wrap my arm around her and pull her into me, my lips brushing her temple. "You did nothing wrong, little fairy," I murmur, before turning to glare at my brothers. "How dare you all use my sweet wife like that?"

Another round of cheers fills the room, all of my brothers instantly repeating the words *my wife* after me, mocking me the way I've mocked them for years. "Fuck, he didn't even think before jumping," Luca says, laughing.

"Wait," Dion says, his eyes on Raya. "What does he call you, Raya?"

She looks up at me helplessly. "Little fairy," I reply for her, my eyes never leaving hers.

"Ugh," he says, sounding genuinely horrified, and I raise a brow as I glance at him, only to find him shooting Faye a look that makes her laugh. She reprimands him and tells him not to be petty, and in response he just pulls her closer, his expression peeved. What the fuck is that all about? Why would he be annoyed about what I call *my* wife?

"What did you tell me that time you flew Celeste and me to our island?" Zane asks. "You said you were never going to be... *what*?"

Whipped. I said I'd never be whipped. Damn it.

"Fuck off, all of you," I murmur as I grab Raya's hand and pull her past them. She laughs as she follows me into Grandma's house, where Raven and Sierra are already munching on freshly made cookies. They both jump up at the sight of us, but it isn't me they're excited to see. I watch as my wife instantly joins in on their quest for cookies, conversation flowing endlessly between them. She fits in so well with my family, and it's clear I'm not the only one that's taken with her. I just hope we aren't all wrong about her. If Raya ever betrayed me, it would destroy me. I'd never recover, and judging by how much my family has grown to love her, they wouldn't either.

"Kids," Grandma calls, startling me out of my thoughts. She gathers us around in her kitchen instead of the formal drawing room, throwing me off a little. But then again, this is Sierra's favorite room in Grandma's house.

The girls all exchange looks that are a mixture of curiosity and worry. All of them, except Val. She looks even more calm and collected than usual, but there's something in her eyes that has a chill running down my spine. *Anguish*.

Grandma crosses her arms and smiles, but it doesn't reach her eyes. "I'm certain you can all guess why I've gathered you here today."

Raven bumps her shoulder against Sierra's, who blushes fiercely, her expression something akin to excitement mingled with fear. All our eyes settle on my sister, the youngest of us, and the only one who isn't married yet.

"Sierra, sweetheart," Grandma says, her tone filled with the kind of indulgence only my sister can inspire. "Your engagement has been finalized."

"Who is it?" she asks, her voice trembling. Unlike all of us, Sierra has never feared her arranged marriage. If anything, she's looked forward to it for as long as I can remember. Thanks to the romance novels she loves so much, she has these grand illusions about love and marriage, in part fueled by how happy all our elder siblings ended up becoming in their marriages. Her expectations are so high that I'm scared she has set herself up for disappointment.

Grandma hesitates for a moment, almost like she's bracing herself. She squares her shoulders and smiles. "You'll be marrying Xavier Kingston."

The absolute horror on Sierra's face makes me chuckle, and all of my brothers follow suit. Each of us is treated to a warning glare from our wives that instantly shuts us up, and we exchange knowing looks. Sierra never saw it coming, but my brothers and I all did. Even when Dion, Xavier's best friend, wasn't in the country, Xavier continued to attend our poker nights. We all knew he wasn't rocking up every single month because he enjoys spending time with us — he came to catch snippets of what Sierra was up to.

He'd convince himself he used the inside information to fuel their rivalry, when more often than not, he just cleared the path for her, opening up opportunities and eliminating competition, so the only one she ever had to compete with was him. Sierra has sabotaged him to the point of getting arrested multiple times, and every single time, he had her released and all charges dropped before any of us could even act. Xavier Kingston is madly in love with my sister, and I'm not sure he even realizes it.

"Combining his real estate empire with ours would result in us jointly becoming the biggest real estate firm the world has ever seen," Grandma says when Sierra doesn't immediately reply. "It'll be the biggest merger we've ever done as a family."

Sierra puts down the cookie she was holding — something

I've never seen her do before. "*Absolutely not*," she says, her eyes flashing with surprisingly genuine hatred. "I'm not marrying Xavier. Just disown me, Grandma. I'll move out tomorrow. I can get my bags packed today."

"You will," Val says, her voice soft. "You'll marry him."

"Over my dead body," Sierra snaps.

"Well," Grandma says, sighing. "As it turns out, it may well be over mine."

A chill runs down my spine as Grandma grabs a set of papers from the kitchen counter and slides them toward Sierra. "I know you're not ready, sweetheart," she says. "I've waited for as long as I could, because I wanted to spend as much time as possible with my little girl. But Sierra, my time is up."

My sister's hands shake as she unfolds the documents, her face blanching. Her gaze cuts to grandma's, and tears gather in her eyes. "Colon cancer?" she says, her voice breaking.

"I accompanied her to the doctor this morning," Val murmurs. "She brought me with her because she didn't think any of us would believe her otherwise. It's true, Sierra."

Grandma's gaze moves around the room, a sweet smile on her face. The way she looks at us, like she's trying to commit us all to memory, fucking guts me. "How long have you known?" I ask.

"About a year. I'm old, Lex. I've accepted that my time has come, and I don't want to spend the few months I have left becoming even sicker and frailer from chemotherapy. It's okay, truly."

Except, it isn't. Our grandmother is the only parent figure we have left. A plane crash took our parents, and a heart attack took away Grandpa. Now cancer will take Grandma from us.

"I know you think you hate him," Grandma tells Sierra. "But he'll love you like you deserve to be loved, Sierra. Xavier will protect you, and he'll continue to be by your side when I'm no longer able to. I know you don't want to marry him, but sweetheart... this is my last wish."

Forty-Six

LEXINGTON

I push off my desk with a sigh and walk out of my office, eager for a glimpse of my wife but unsure what excuse to use to see her. Ever since I learned about my grandmother's illness, I've been uneasy. Nothing soothes me like my wife can, and being so far apart today is making me miserable.

I'm absentminded as I make coffee for myself and Raya, startling the entire secretarial team once again. Every time I walk into the pantry to make my own coffee instead of asking the robots for it, they rush over to assist, endlessly irritating me. It took three weeks of me refusing their help for them to stop asking, and each time, I wish I could explain that I'm just a husband wanting to make coffee for my wife. No one knows exactly how she likes her coffee, and I know she feels too embarrassed to ask our robots for an oat milk and honeycomb cappuccino with a dash of cinnamon sugar. I'm on autopilot as I reach for the fresh honeycombs I had flown in from New Zealand this morning, just for Raya, hoping to put a smile on her face.

My lips tug up at the edges when I faintly hear the sound of her voice, only to turn the corner and find Adam handing her a coffee cup from her favorite coffeeshop, a few blocks down. She smiles at him, and something dark twists in my stomach when I notice the way her gorgeous brown eyes light up as she takes a sip.

He shakes his head at something she says and leans in to brush something off her arm. My heart aches as I watch the way he dances around my wife, the way he looks at her. The bond between them seems unshakeable, and it fucking guts me. She still hasn't told him about us, and I can pretty much guess why that is — she doesn't want him to know she's no longer single. If I can't love her the way she wants me to, will she turn to him?

I grit my teeth and walk up to them, placing the coffee I made right next to Adam's coffee on Raya's desk. "Mr. Windsor," Amy says, her eyes widening.

I can tell that Raya's team is flustered by my continuous involvement, but so far they've written it off as the behavior of a doting husband trying to ensure everything is on track with his wife's gift. They just don't quite realize that the woman I'm doting on is one of them.

I smile at the team as I inconspicuously pick up Adam's coffee and raise it to my lips so Raya's lipstick stain aligns perfectly. *Goddamn*. It isn't a fresh honeycomb, but it's honey flavored. That fucker knows my wife's favorites, and I fucking hate that. "Just checking in on the progress you've made," I bullshit, smiling as Adam throws me an irritated look, his gaze moving between the cup in my hands and my face.

It isn't until I catch Raya's worried look that I realize I just drank something I didn't watch someone make, and I did it without a second thought. I glance at the cup and smile to myself. When I look back at my wife, she's smiling too, a hint of pride in her gaze. She has no idea what it means to me to have her quiet support, how much I've come to rely on her. Raya doesn't understand that drinking her coffee felt *safe*, and no one has made me feel that way in years.

Adam leans in to whisper something in her ear, and she shakes her head as she lifts the cup I brought her, taking a sip. She smiles to herself, and that smile... it's mine, but it's directed at *him*.

"Raya," I say, my tone harsh as I push off the side of her desk. "Come give me a full overview of the team's progress in five minutes."

"Oh, I can do that," Adam says, and I pause, turning back to face him, my annoyance rising even further when I notice the way my wife has her hand wrapped around his arm as she shakes her head.

"Of course, Mr. Windsor," she says, before I can even say anything. She smiles at me politely, not realizing how much that professionalism of hers is getting on my nerves. I want her to lose her composure the way she makes me lose mine.

"Five minutes," I remind her.

I'm fucking seething as I walk back into my office, my mind replaying the way she smiled at him, the way her eyes lit up for him. My anger only increases as minute after minute passes, a knock finally sounding on my door ten minutes later.

Raya walks in with a tablet in her hand, and I lean back in my seat. "Close the door."

Her eyes widen as she does as told, taking the edge off my annoyance. My wife bites down on her lip and leans against the closed door, knowing full well how much I love that tight black pencil skirt she's wearing, her cream blouse exposing the top of her breasts in the most enticing way. Her breathing accelerates as I take my time watching her, undressing her with my eyes.

I tap my finger against my desk and beckon her closer with a simple tilt of my head. She inhales sharply as she obeys my silent command, her gaze darkening. Raya pauses in front of me, and I smirk when I notice the way she presses her thighs together.

She gasps when I turn her around and grab her hips to bend her over my desk, my palm on her lower back to keep her in place. "Give me your update," I demand as I push her legs apart so I can sit between them, her sexy ass on display for me.

"Someone could walk in at any moment," she says, her voice high pitched, panicked.

"Then you'd better talk quickly," I murmur, my hands roaming over her ass appreciatively.

"We, um... we finished both the mixing and dispensing parts." Her breath hitches when I push her skirt up, my hands sliding over her tights. "A-Along with the cooling system."

A needy whimper leaves her lips when I rip her tights at the crotch, revealing her silky red thong, a beautiful wet spot betraying her need. "That's wonderful," I tell her as I run my fingers over the fabric teasingly. "But do all the individual components work together, and do they work together cohesively?"

She rotates her hips in an attempt to direct my fingers, and I grin as I lean in and bite her soft skin. Raya moans loudly, the sound music to my ears. "Well, does it work?" I ask as I knead her perfect ass.

"N-No."

"No?" I repeat as I shove her underwear aside, loving the little desperate sounds she rewards me with. I smirk as I lean in and blow against her pussy softly, teasing her. "If it doesn't work, you should be fixing it, shouldn't you? Why were you smiling at Adam and drinking coffee with him when you should've been working?"

I drag a finger right along the middle, coating it in wetness. "You're jealous," she says, sounding fucking delighted.

"Me? Jealous?" I push two fingers into her and curl them, pressing them right against her g-spot ruthlessly. She moans, all coherent thought leaving her. I chuckle as I massage her pussy the way she likes it. "He might know how you like your coffee, but he doesn't know what makes you moan. You're *mine*, Raya. Remember that."

I lean in and brush the tip of my tongue over her clit, driving her wild. She tries to move closer, but I keep her pressed against my desk. "Don't you dare forget who this pussy belongs to," I warn, before swiftly bringing her close to an orgasm, utilizing every single thing I've learned about her body.

"Please, Lex," she begs, and I smirk as I pull away, fingering her slowly, leisurely, not even brushing that sensitive part inside her. "You can't do this to me," she says, her tone becoming aggravated. "Don't tease me like that."

"No?" I ask, pulling my fingers out of her altogether. "Don't make me jealous and I won't have to."

She arches her back and looks over her shoulder, presenting me with the prettiest sight I've ever seen. My wife bent over my desk with her skirt pushed up to her hips, her tights torn, her pussy dripping... and that sexy fucking look on her face. "Please," she says, pouting. "I'll be good, Lex."

I can't fucking deny her, and she knows it. It's funny how I act like I'm in control when we both know I lost everything I have to her long ago. "You'll be good for me?" I place my fingers back on her pussy, and her eyes fall closed. "Then tell me who you belong to."

"You," she moans, her hips shifting as much as I allow her to. "I belong to you, Lexington Windsor. Forever and always."

Fuck. I lean in and swirl my tongue over her swollen clit, giving her what she needs. My gorgeous wife comes for me, and it's such a rush to experience the way her pussy clamps down on my fingers.

Raya looks over her shoulder, her cheeks flushed. "Fuck me," she says. "Take me, Lex. I need you."

Goddamn. She'll be the death of me. My heart is racing as I rise to my feet and unbuckle my belt swiftly. She licks her lips when I pull my cock out, and I smirk as I lean in to grab her hair with one hand. The way she arches her back as I take hold of her hair and pull is fucking beautiful. "My perfect wife," I murmur, pushing the tip in. "Always so ready for my cock, aren't you?"

She tries to get me in deeper, and I grin as I lean over her and ball my hand in her hair, my lips brushing over her ear. "Patience, baby. You have to earn this cock."

"I don't," she tells me, turning so her lips brush against mine. "I own that cock."

I chuckle as I kiss her and push all the way inside her, swallowing her moans. "You do, don't you?" I ask as I straighten and take hold of her hips. "You own me, Raya. Every fucking inch of me, and you fucking know it."

I tighten my grip on her hips as I fuck her hard and slow, loving the way she whispers my name over and over again as I push her to the brink of another orgasm, getting the angle just right. "I can't," she says, moments before she *does*. My pretty wife comes all over my cock, and my eyes fall closed when she takes me right over the edge with her.

I'm panting as I pull out of her and immediately push my cum deeper inside her. "Sit down next to him with your husband's cum soaking your panties, little fairy. Drink his coffee, smile at him, make me jealous. Do whatever you want, Raya, but do it with my cum dripping out of that beautiful pussy."

Her gaze roams over my face, and something flickers through her eyes as I pull her skirt down before tidying my own clothes. "I love you," she says, catching me by surprise. She turns to face me and cups my face, our eyes locking. "I *love* you, Lex. Only you."

I love you, too. So fucking much it hurts. The words are at the tip of my tongue, but I'm scared to say them, scared to jinx this thing between us, so I just drop my forehead to hers. "You know I'm yours, right?" I ask, needing her to understand.

Her lips brush against mine, and she kisses me softly. "I know," she whispers against my mouth, and my heart fucking soars. She's *everything*, and fuck, I don't deserve her.

For years, I was certain I couldn't let anyone in, and then she came along, shattering all my walls with one single touch. Now here I am, wondering how to keep her by my side when I know I'll never be enough.

Forty-Seven

Raya

Lex pulls on my hands just before we reach my parents' front door, a mischievous grin on his face. Since we learned about his grandmother he's frequently lost in thought, but then there are times like these, where it's like I'm all he can see.

"What?" I ask, my eyes narrowed.

He chuckles and pulls me closer. "I have a dare for you," he says, his forehead dropping to mine. "Kiss me before we head in. I know you'll tempt me once we make it to your bedroom and turn me into the kind of sinner that breaks all your father's rules, but that could be hours from now. What if I can't survive until then? I need fuel, Raya."

I laugh and wrap my arms around his neck as I rise to my tiptoes, tilting my head. His lips come crashing against mine, and my body melts into his. Lex sucks on my bottom lip, his hand roaming down my back, and I pull him closer, loving the way he's completely losing himself in this, in us.

"God, I want you," he says against my mouth, his hands

moving to my hips. My hand slips into his hair, and he groans, his cock pressing against my stomach.

I smile against his lips — and then the sound of the front door opening startles us both. Before I even realize what's happening, Lex has turned me around and pushes me toward the front door. I stumble and glance over my shoulder to glare at my husband, who tries his best to look as innocent as possible as he grins up at my dad.

My husband doesn't fear a single thing in this world, other than, apparently, my parents catching him kiss me. "You issued that dare all by yourself and now you act surprised I'm standing so close to you," I mutter under my breath.

He throws me a wide-eyed warning look, and if my father hadn't been standing right behind us, I'd have teased him about the way his personality changes the second Dad is near. One of the most powerful men in the world, yet he cowers in front of my dad. Everything it implies makes the butterflies in my stomach go wild. The level of respect he has for my family, along with his attempts to gain my parents' approval, doesn't go unnoticed.

Dad's gaze moves between the two of us, his gaze lacking the usual affection and amusement. "Come in, kids," he says, and I frown when I realize his tone is off.

"What's going on?" I ask, kicking my shoes off in a rush. Lex does the same and offers me his hand, entwining our fingers as we follow Dad into the living room.

Mom looks up from the sofa, her eyes red, and Dad immediately wraps his arm around her. "There's something we need to tell you, Raya," he says. Mom nods, and my heart sinks. With the news about Lex's grandmother still fresh on my mind, I find myself bracing for the worst.

"Let's sit, darling," Lex says, guiding me to the sofa we've come to consider ours, the one that's adjacent to the one my parents are sitting on. He takes our joined hands into his lap and draws soothing circles on my skin, his presence providing more comfort than he could imagine.

Mom sniffs, and Dad tightens his grip on her, pulling her closer. "I didn't mean to keep this from you, Raya. Dad and I always meant to tell you, but it just... it just wasn't ever the right time."

My thoughts race as I subconsciously try to guess what they might be referring to. "Tell me what, Mom?" My voice is trembling, my tone reluctant. Something about that look in her eyes is breaking my heart before she's even said anything.

She looks at Dad and bursts into tears, a sob tearing through her throat. My own eyes begin to fill with tears when I realize Dad looks visibly emotional, too. He looks at me so apologetically that my heart begins to break before he even says anything. "We got a call this morning, Raya. It was about your grandmother. She isn't well."

I stare at him in confusion. "I thought... I thought that..." Mom hasn't spoken to her parents in years, and Dad's parents passed away when I was in elementary school. I turn to Mom then, inhaling shakily. "Is your mother okay?" I ask, unsure what to do, what to say. If not for Lex's tight grip on me, I'd have rushed over to her, doing what I can to console her. Something about the way he's holding my hand is keeping me rooted in place. I can't imagine what this conversation is doing to him. Unlike me, he's very close to his grandmother, and this'll just make his grief deepen.

Mom begins to cry harder, and dad pulls her into his arms, cradling her head the way Lex sometimes does with me when I'm upset. "Meera," Dad whispers. "I can't do this without you, my love."

She nods and straightens, wiping at her tears furiously. "The call wasn't about my mother, honey," she says, choking back a sob. "It was about your f-father's mother. Your b-biological father."

I stare at her wide-eyed, the words not quite registering. I heard what she said. I just don't understand how that could be true.

Lex tightens his grip on me as my mom takes a shaky breath. "Do you remember the story I told you about my first marriage?" she asks carefully. I nod, my stomach turning. "I didn't tell you the full story, honey." She takes a deep breath, regret marring her beautiful face. "When I escaped that marriage, I was pregnant... with you."

My gaze cuts to dad, realization dawning. He straightens his shoulders, despair in his eyes. "I have had the great honor of raising you, Raya. I was there when you were born, and I was there when you took your first steps. I walked you down the aisle, and I'll love you until the day I die. I just... I just didn't have the honor of bringing you into this world." He looks away, and I watch as his eyes fall closed, his breathing uneven. "Nothing will ever change the fact that to me, you are my daughter," he says, his voice soft, pleading. He turns to look at me then, his eyes filled with sorrow. "*Nothing* could ever change that, you hear me?"

I nod, a tear sliding down my cheek. Lex turns toward me and wipes it away, his gaze tormented, pained. I bite down on my lip, but a sob tears through my throat nonetheless. How could my father, the man that loves me most in this world, not be my real father?

I try to swallow down my tears, only to choke on my sobs. Lex opens his arms for me wordlessly, and I press my face against his neck as I begin to cry, unable to help it.

"Darling," he whispers, hugging me tightly. "The call," Lex says quietly, rubbing my back. "Raya's grandmother.... is she okay?"

"No," Dad says, his voice breaking. "She's in the hospital, and she only has a couple of weeks left. We were told that she wishes to apologize to Raya and your mother while she... while she still can."

"You don't have to go," Mom says, and I turn to face her, Lex's arms staying wrapped around me, his heart beating steadily under my ear. "I just needed to tell you, Raya. I didn't want you to have any regrets, and I didn't want to take this choice from you."

Forty-Eight

Raya

I feel sick as I walk through the long hospital hall, Lex's hand in mine. "Are you doing okay, little fairy?" he asks, his touch soothing.

I shake my head. "No, but I know I'll regret it if I don't go."

Lex and I spent all of yesterday learning about the past and everything my parents kept hidden from me. Dad explained how they slowly became friends at work, as Mom did his bookkeeping, and how he offered Mom his unconditional support when he saw the bruises on her skin. They both had tears in their eyes when mom told us he helped her run away, neither of them aware of the pregnancy at the time. He provided her with the support her own family wouldn't give her, and from the sounds of it, Dad was my father in all ways that matter long before he was ever married to Mom. While they never lied about their wedding day, it just didn't happen in the year they'd told me it did.

"Here we are," Lex says as we stop in front of the hospital room my grandmother is in. I stand there frozen, reminded of the way Dad hugged me this morning, almost like he genuinely thought things would never be the same again, like he was losing me. He didn't seem to believe that the story he told me just made me love and appreciate him more, but how could it not?

"Let's go in," I say after taking a deep breath. I don't *want* to meet the people that hurt my mother, and I'm glad mom decided not to join me. I almost didn't even come myself, and though I wouldn't ever admit it, I'm only here because I couldn't take that haunted look in Lex's eyes. Knowing that he's losing his own grandmother made it impossible not to fulfill my own grandmother's dying wish, even if she is a virtual stranger to me.

He knocks and slides the door open, leading me into the room. I look up in surprise when a man with the same eyes as mine rises from his seat next to the bed. "Raya?" he asks, clearly shocked to see me.

My whole body tenses when he walks toward me and reaches for me. Lex instantly steps in, blocking his path, and I move behind his back, overwhelmed and grateful for his support.

"I'm sorry," Lex says, holding up his hand. "This is all quite a lot for my wife."

"Lexington Windsor?" he asks, his disbelief evident. "You're married to my daughter?"

Daughter. So he is who I thought he was. Discomfort unlike anything I've ever experienced before washes over me, and I move closer to Lex, dropping my forehead to his back for a moment, my hands balling the fabric of his suit.

"I'm sorry, I should've introduced myself," he adds. "I'm Akshay. I'm Raya's... well, I'm her father."

The room falls silent, and I brace myself as I step out of Lex's shadow and turn toward the woman lying in bed, not wanting to face *Akshay*. She looks frail, and when her eyes meet mine, she smiles sadly, her eyes filled with regret.

"Your granddaughter is here," my biological father says in Hindi, and she extends her hand toward me. I take it hesitantly, and tears fall from her eyes as she squeezes.

"Meera didn't come?" she replies, also in the mother tongue I only understand because Mom still defaults to it when she's mad at me.

I shake my head, and she nods in understanding, deep regret marring her features. I'm in a daze as she apologizes over and over, endless tears falling from her eyes. "It's okay," I tell her, even when it isn't, purely because I can't deny a dying woman's wishes. Lex keeps his hand around my waist, his body close to mine, and he has no idea how grateful I am for his presence today.

She falls asleep with apologies still on her lips, and I step back, my heart heavy. I wasn't sure what to expect today, but I didn't think I'd feel so bitter. Just the thought of everything these people put my mother through infuriates me, and even now, I find it hard to do the right thing, to be the person my dad raised me to be.

"Meera married Bob Lewis, and you married Lexington Windsor. You both turned out okay," Akshay says when I step back.

I nod and bite back the words *yes, despite you.* "We're both more than fine," I say, my tone sharper than I'd intended. "My father has always taken great care of us."

His expression hardens, and he nods, something flashing in his eyes. I hate how familiar those eyes are, how much more I look like him than I'd expected. "Right," he murmurs, looking down. "I'm sorry, Raya. I wish I could've been part of your life, but Bob warned me to stay away. Every time I tried to contact you, he'd threaten me, using his power and influence to keep us apart. He's always carefully controlled everyone and everything around your mother and you." His gaze cuts to Lexington then. "It wouldn't surprise me if he had a hand in your marriage, too. The man is calculative, and since you aren't his real daughter, I'm sure he did what he could to benefit from raising you. He isn't one to let an investment go to waste."

The words infuriate me, and they do what he wanted them to do — they make me question my father for a split second, and guilt instantly sets in. My hand slips into Lex's and I take a deep breath. "Let's go," I tell him.

He nods and takes one final look at my grandmother. "I'll have her transferred to a private facility, so she's as comfortable as she can be for as long as possible."

Akshay nods, his gaze on me. "Your mother has my number," he tells me when I turn to walk out. "I'll always be waiting for your call, Raya. I've waited twenty-two years to meet the daughter that was taken from me, and I understand this is overwhelming. Call me when you're ready to talk. Every story has two sides, Raya."

I nod, and Lex leads me out of the room. We're both quiet as we head back to the parking lot, and it isn't until we're in the car that I break down. Lex just holds me as I try my hardest to process everything that just happened. He doesn't say a word, he's just there, like he always is. He might not be able to say the words, but this, right here, this is what love is.

Forty-Nine

Lexington

I pause in front of my parents-in-law's front door, unsure what I'm even doing. I pace back and forth for a few minutes, undecided. I'd been at home, waiting for Raya to come back from Sierra's bachelorette party, when it occurred to me that I'm probably not the only one waiting for her. I couldn't stop thinking about how distraught Bob must be after what he had to tell Raya, and I figured it wouldn't hurt to check up on him. Now that I'm here, I'm second guessing my decision to show up uninvited. Just as I've made up my mind to leave, the front door opens, and Raya's mom appears, a long fluffy robe wrapped all around her.

"Lex?" she says, surprised. "You set off all those fancy alarm systems you installed a few months ago, sweetheart. What are you doing here?"

Before I can even say anything at all, she steps aside with a sweet smile on her face. I follow her into the house, oddly nervous. I've never been here before without Raya, and I'm not sure why I thought it was a good idea to drop by without notice today. "Raya is at my sister's bachelorette party tonight," I explain.

"I know," she says, smiling at me as she leads me through the house, until we reach the garage at the back of the house. Right. Of course she knew. Raya speaks to her parents every day, after all.

"He's been hiding in there every evening since we told Raya the news, silently counting down the days until she comes home again, all the while pretending to be okay. She's called him countless times, but I don't think he'll be okay until she comes back home. In the meantime, he'll be glad to see you."

I nod, my heart heavy. Raya and I requested to spend this weekend at the Windsor Estate shortly after Sierra's wedding date was set, because we both knew my sister would do something outrageous for her bachelorette. We couldn't have known what would happen in the days prior to it. "She almost didn't go," I tell Raya's mom, and she nods, a sweet understanding smile on her face.

"I'm glad she did," she says. "And I'm glad you're here. Go on in. I'll bring you both some tea in a bit."

I nod as she pats my arm reassuringly before walking away, leaving me standing in front of the door. I take a deep breath before knocking. When no response comes, I walk in, only to freeze at the sight of a car Bob Lewis can't possibly own.

He rolls from underneath the car and sits up, clearly expecting his wife. His brows rise, and he looks back at the car before rising to his feet. "Lex, my boy. What brings you here? I didn't think you two would come home this weekend."

I shake my head, barely able to take my eyes off the original Windsor Motors car behind him. The same one I spent years looking for and nearly gave up on. This is the car my grandfather designed and built for my grandmother. He even named it after her, and only three WM *Annie's* were ever built and sold. What is she doing here? I've been looking for her for years.

"It's just me today," I murmur, dragging my gaze back to my father-in-law. His expression falls, and he nods as he reaches for a torque wrench. He throws it my way, and I catch it easily, my hand wrapping around the tool. "Come help me with this, then. My favorite car won't start."

My heart pounds in my chest as I take in the immaculate state of the car. "How do you have this? I have the one that used to belong to my father, and my grandmother has the other. I knew there was a third, but I've never been able to track it down." My grandfather once told me he gave the third to his protégé, and he promised me he'd introduce me to him someday. Grandpa told me I'd love him as much as he did, that he reminded him of my dad.

Bob smiles and runs his hand over the hood of the car gently. "Your grandfather gave it to me," he says, "right along with the investment funds to start Lewis Motors." I stare in shock, and Bob smiles. "I learned everything I knew from your grandfather, but he knew I wasn't happy working for Windsor Motors. I didn't want to build cars for the rich — I wanted to build cars people like me could afford, that they'd love. Your grandfather understood my vision and planned to expand Windsor Motors, until one day, he learned I'd always dreamt of building my own company. Instead of competing with me, he gave me his blessing and told me to go make him proud. That's the kind of man your grandfather was, you know?"

He glances back at the car, his smile bittersweet. "Truthfully, I know what's wrong with it, and I could fix it in ten minutes. I just like tinkering with it, because it's..." Bob runs a hand through his hair and sighs.

I run a hand through my hair, understanding dawning. "It's what my grandfather always did when he needed to think. He'd take a car apart and put it back together."

Bob Lewis is the protégé my grandfather used to talk about. How could I have missed that? It didn't flag in Bob's background check either, and the only way that could've happened is if Silas Sinclair hid it from me, likely at my grandmother's request.

"I feel like I keep saying this, but this, too, wasn't something I kept from you purposely," Bob says. "I just didn't want you to feel like I was using my connection to your grandfather to get close to you. Your grandmother and I agreed that minimal involvement would be best for you. There was already so much pressure on you both to make your marriage work, and we didn't want you to feel like we were using your affection toward your late grandfather against you. He wouldn't have wanted that, would never have allowed it. He loved you more than anything."

I glance at the torque wrench in my hand. "Raya and me... Grandpa was the one who arranged our marriage?"

I lost him to a heart attack shortly after I was abducted, and I know the stress I put him under when I went missing was a contributing factor, no matter what the doctors might say. One of the reasons I've been so scared to love Raya is because I didn't think I deserved to. I felt like I had to atone for my sins, only to now find out that doing so directly contradicts my grandfather's wishes. I bury a hand in my hair, my mind reeling.

Bob smiles. "Your grandfather always joked that he and I would become family one day, that he'd make it happen. I took Raya with me to visit him one day, and you were at his office with him. You were trying to put together a wooden car, and you let Raya help you. That was when your grandfather started to joke that she'd become a Windsor someday, that he'd steal her away for his youngest grandson." He sighs and turns back toward his WM Annie. "I was surprised when your grandmother visited me last year, and honestly, if it had been anyone but her, I'd never even have considered it, never would've even told my wife about the offer. Your grandmother kept an eye on my company throughout the years, like your grandfather used to, and the moment she realized we were in trouble, she offered a helping hand."

"But it came with a price tag."

He nods as he moves to the car's engine, and I join him, leaning over it. This car is an even better condition than my own model, and it's clear he treated it with reverence. "I wasn't sure I made the right decision until a couple of days ago, when you held my daughter as she fell apart, and I realized how much you love her, how much she relies on you. I didn't think an arranged marriage could work, but it did, and as always, your grandfather was right. He always had a penchant for being right, didn't he? Drove your grandmother nuts."

I smile and nod, my attention entirely on my father-in-law as he tells me stories about the past and lets me help him check each component in his clearly beloved car. I came here to console him, but instead, he handed me the last few remaining puzzle pieces I needed, consoling *me* instead. It's almost like receiving permission from beyond, telling me that it's okay to love my wife, that this time, things are going to be okay.

I just hope my intuition doesn't fail me this time.

I hope I'm not misreading the signs.

Fifty

Lexington

The edges of my lips turn up into a smile when I spot my wife at her desk, the office quiet and empty. "I thought your team went out for drinks after work?"

She looks up from her screen, and I lean in, pushing her hair to the side to kiss her neck. Her head falls back, and she sighs happily. "They did, but I really wanted to finish some of my work. I'm not really in the mood to socialize and drink tonight."

I hum in agreement, pressing another kiss just below her ear. "What are you working on?"

"The code for the overnight automation. Let me wrap this up and then I'm ready to go home. I just want to finish it now since I'm taking some time off for Sierra's wedding next week." She looks at me then. "I still think it's wild how you bought the whole company simply because I love their milkshakes, but I really love you for it, too. You have no idea how happy it makes me to work on this project. Every second I spend working on it, I'm reminded how much you... how much you care."

How much I *love* her. She knows it, even if the words still terrify me. Never once has she pressured me into saying something I'm not ready to say, to admit my feelings for her. I don't know what I've done to deserve Raya, but I'm grateful for my wife every single day.

She hasn't been herself since she found out about her dad, and though nothing has changed between them when we go home for the weekends, I know she's sad they kept such a big secret from her. My wife is hurt, and I'm not quite sure how to make her feel better. She was there for me when I found out about my grandmother, offering me distractions and quiet support. Now it's my turn to do the same for her.

"I do," I murmur, pulling her out of her seat. "I do care, darling. More than you'll ever know."

She gasps when I steal her chair and pull her into my lap. "Lex," she whisper-shouts. "Someone could walk in at any moment."

My lips brush against her neck and she shivers. "Everyone is gone. No one is going to come back to the office at nine on a Friday night." She gasps when I slide my hand under her skirt and grip her thigh. "Keep working, baby. I'll keep myself entertained in the meantime."

A soft little whimper leaves her lips when my thumb brushes over the silky fabric between her legs, and I smirk as I push her knees apart. Raya continues to type, writing line after line of code, and I grin as I caress her, taking my time.

"*Lex*," she whispers when I push her panties aside.

I lean in and kiss her shoulder. "Yes, Mrs. Windsor?" I murmur as I slide my finger across her pussy slowly, coating it in her wetness, my movements leisurely.

She breathes shakily, her hips shifting in my lap, and I chuckle as my finger slips into her. "Such a naughty girl, aren't you?" I whisper into her ear. "Look at you, letting your boss finger you while you work."

She moans when I add another digit and tries her best to refocus on her work, but she only manages one line before I steal her attention away again. "First you fuck your professor, then your boss... such a bad girl. Don't you agree that bad girls should be punished?"

Her hips twist, and I smirk when she begins to ride my hand. "Yes," she moans, looking over her shoulders. "Punish me, Mr. Windsor."

I chuckle, fucking delighted by the way she plays along, indulging me. How the fuck is she so perfect? She was made for me, I'm certain of it.

"For starters, you'd better finish your work." She nods and turns back toward her screen, and I smile as I undo my slacks and take my cock out, wedging it right between her legs, so it slides against her. She makes this sexy little sound in the back of her throat, and I groan as I press my thumb against her clit, unsure who's being punished.

Raya gasps when one of the automated lights in the hallway turns on, and we both freeze. In our current positions, we'd be exposed if someone walked our way. There's no hiding what's going on here.

I hold on to her tightly when we hear voices at the end of the room, and I brush my lips against her ear. "Sounds like a couple of employees are just picking up their work bags after their drinks. If they were going to come this way, they already would have."

She nods and squirms in my lap when I continue to play with her. "Keep working," I order, and she does as told, both of us breathing a sigh of relief when the lights turn back off, silence washing over us again.

"Grab my cock and line it up, baby," I tell her when I have her back at the edge, her pussy hot and tight around my fingers.

She does as ordered, the sexiest moan on her lips as she sinks down on me. I drop my lips to her shoulder as she begins to type again, my thumb on her clit and my cock nestled deep inside her.

My wife groans when I rock my hips, trying to take back control. "There," I murmur, looking over her shoulder. "That line right there. That's where the issue lies."

She squeezes her inner muscles, and I groan, my heart racing. Her pussy is fucking perfection, and having her in my lap like this is such a rush. I spread my hand across her stomach and keep her flush against me, my other hand on her pussy and my lips on her neck.

My wife continues to type, fixing her mistakes while I play with her, enjoying the feel of her pussy around my cock, her wetness on my fingers. My breath hitches when she begins to rock back and forth in my lap, fucking me as she types, her hips betraying her need. She's fucking perfection, and I'm starting to believe she truly was sent to me from above. There's no other explanation — this can't just be mere luck. She's perfect for me, truly perfect.

"You ride me so fucking good, Raya. You're so good at taking my cock, darling." Her muscles contract, and I grin, loving the way she responds to my praise.

"You're such a good girl, aren't you? Such a good wife." I drag my fingers back and forth, keeping her clit sliding between my index and middle finger and slowly driving her crazy. She begins to pant, soft moans filling our office, and it's fucking music to my ears.

"No," I tell her when she stops typing, her head falling back. "Keep working, baby. You've got this. Fix that code."

"Lex," she pleads.

I smirk in satisfaction, pleased with how desperate I've got her. "You want this?" I ask, moving my fingers faster, taking her closer to the edge.

"Yes," she moans. "*Yes*."

"Tell me you love me," I beg, unsure why I need to hear the words so badly today, but I do.

She reaches behind her, her fingers threading through my hair as she turns her face and pulls me closer, her lips seeking mine. "I love you," she whispers against my mouth. "I love you, Lexington Windsor. Only you. Always you."

I moan, unable to hold on for even a second longer at the

sound of those words. "Fuck," I groan, coming deep inside my wife as I grab her hair, kissing her desperately. I brush my thumb over her clit the way she likes it, making her come moments after I do, swallowing down all her moans.

She collapses against me, and I smile, my heart soaring. Raya smiles back at me and turns a little in my lap, her hand wrapping over my cheek. "You always know just what I need," she whispers, her lips brushing against mine. "You know how to make me forget about every single sorrow, every worry, until there's nothing left but you."

I sigh as I kiss her leisurely, losing myself in her. "You *are* what I need," I whisper. "Every second of every day."

Fifty-One

Raya

My heart pounds wildly as I join Raven, Val, Faye, and Celeste in Sierra's wedding procession down Grandma Anne's stunning garden. Sierra insisted on having the wedding in the middle of Grandma Anne's labyrinth, no doubt in an attempt to piss off Xavier, but there isn't a hint of annoyance on his face. Nor is there any on the faces of his four brothers, standing next to him.

He looks up and smiles politely as we walk in, his serene gaze turning somewhat nervous. Xavier shifts his weight from one foot to the other and pulls on his sleeves, and I watch as one of his brothers leans in to whisper something in his ear. My eyes widen in surprise when I recognize the man. He's *mayor Kingston*, the mayor of our town. Xavier ignores whatever it is his brother is saying and straightens as we all take our places.

My eyes find Lexington's, and he smiles at me sweetly from the front row. I can barely take my eyes off him as Sierra walks in, on Grandma Anne's arm. She looks breathtaking, and Xavier audibly inhales sharply. His brothers chuckle, and I can't help but smile myself.

Grandma Anne carefully places Sierra's hand in Xavier's, and then she gently brushes Sierra's hair out of her face, the two of them exchanging emotional glances. "I love you," Grandma Anne tells her.

Sierra draws a shaky breath, her eyes falling closed for a moment. "I love you more," she replies, her voice soft, pained.

She straightens her spine as she turns to Xavier, her emotions draining away, leaving nothing but resentment and irritation in her emerald eyes. He just chuckles and leans in, not at all intimidated by the way she glares at him. "Put away those claws, Kitten," he tells her. "You don't want to accidentally damage your new toy, do you?"

She rolls her eyes and leans in, replying something I can't hear. Whatever it is she says makes Xavier chuckle, and I can't help but smile too, my gaze traveling back to Lex as the wedding ceremony starts.

Our eyes remain locked, and I can't focus on anything but Lex. The way he looks at me... it drives the butterflies in my stomach wild. When we found out he orchestrated the way we met, I'd been scared, deep down. I was worried I'd find myself in a controlling marriage, like Mom had been, but I didn't dare voice my concern, knowing my parents would call off the wedding and condemn the company if I had even the slightest doubt. I gambled, praying that at least a little part of what he showed me the night we met was real, and I think I may have won that bet. I know marriage isn't ever going to be perfect, but it wasn't perfection I was after. I just wanted to marry a man that would try to give me his all every single day, and Lex truly does that. I can tell it isn't easy for him, but he still does it.

I look away from my husband when Sierra and Xavier are pronounced husband and wife, and I smile when he leans in to kiss her with a lot more familiarity than I expected. She melts into him for a few moments, before remembering herself and pulling back, her face flushed. *Interesting*. This isn't the first time he's kissed her, I can tell.

I smile as I join my husband, the two of us taking comfort in each other's presence as we go through the motions of taking photos and greeting guests. "You look stunning, you know that?" he murmurs, taking in the emerald green bridesmaid dress I'm wearing. "I love you in yellow, but this is just as lovely."

My eyes rake over his tux appreciatively, and I lean in to whisper in his ear. "You look really hot today," I tell him. "But I think that shirt will look better on me tomorrow morning."

He laughs and wraps his hand around my waist, leading me to the dance floor. He's laughing more frequently now, and it's so thrilling to watch him open up to me. I can see my husband falling for me the way I've fallen for him, and it's so surreal. I wasn't sure we'd ever have this, and when he told me about his past, I didn't even dare hope for it anymore. I'm glad he didn't give up on us, that he had the courage to tell me the truth and take my hand.

"I can't stop looking at you," he says as he pulls me closer, our feet carrying us across the dance floor effortlessly. "I can't believe you're mine, Raya Windsor."

"I am," I reassure him. "I always will be."

He sighs and drops his forehead to mine, pure happiness radiating off him. I grin and tilt my face to kiss him, losing myself in him for a moment. "If you... if you ever find yourself loving me, the way you know I want you to..."

He pulls away to look at me, curiosity flickering through his eyes. "Yeah?"

"If you ever do... would you marry me again?"

His eyes widen, and he misses a step, the two of us coming to a standstill on the dance floor. My heart begins to pound wildly, and regret instantly sets in. "I'm sorry," I begin to say. "I didn't... I'm sorry. I'm not sure what I was thinking."

Lex cups my face and keeps my eyes on his. "Are you proposing to me, Mrs. Windsor?"

I blink, my nerves overtaking me. "No! Yes? Maybe? I...I don't know. I just... I was just thinking that I'd have liked to honor my mother's culture more, and I'd have wanted a bigger wedding with more people present. Then there's that moment, you know? When you see the person you love, the one person you chose out of all other people in the whole wide world. I just... I'm sorry. It was a selfish thought. Please, forget what I said."

"Raya," he says. "There's nothing I wouldn't do if it made you happy. If you wanted to get married again tomorrow, I'd happily do so."

I shake my head, my heart aching. "No," I murmur. "It's not something I want you to do for *me*. I just wondered if it's something you might want too. It was a silly thought, I'm sorry."

"You want everything we've missed out on," he murmurs, his gaze roaming over my face. I look away, feeling embarrassed. "Look at me," he pleads, his hands threading through my hair. I bite down on my lip and do as he asked. "Yes, Raya. I want that too. I'll give you everything you should've had, everything you deserve."

I lean into his hand, my heart heavy. "No," I murmur. "It was just a thought, not a request."

He smiles at me, something smoldering in his eyes. "You know, if we'd been dating like two normal people, this is the exact conversation we would've had once we started considering marriage. The answer I'm trying to give you, very ineloquently, is *yes*. Yes, Raya. I *want* to marry you. Yes, you are the woman I see a future with, that I want to spend my life with. If our situation was different, I would still choose you."

I look into his eyes, hoping he's being truthful. My heart feels fragile these days, and I just hope he handles it with care, like he promised to.

Fifty-Two

Lexington

I look up in surprise when Pippy announces that Akshay Singh is at the reception desk, requesting a meeting. What could he possibly want? Considering who he is, I can't just turn him away. I have a feeling he'd just try to seek out my wife if I did that, and though she's been acting strong, I know that learning her father isn't her biological father turned her world upside down.

"Send him up."

Raya and her parents seem to have opted to ignore Akshay's existence altogether, pretending nothing changed between them, but I know he's been on my wife's mind. She's looked him up several times, and I know she asked Pippy to find his phone number, not wanting to ask her mother for it. She may not be ready to face him now, but I don't think she's ruled it out entirely.

"Lexington," he says, smiling. "It's so good to see you."

He looks around my office, a familiar kind of eagerness in his eyes, and my heart sinks. I know that look. It's been a while since I last saw it, since neither Raya nor her parents possess even an ounce of greed or entitlement, despite the fact that there's nothing I wouldn't do for them. Akshay smiles as he sits down in one of the two the chairs on the other end of my desk, and I raise a brow.

"What brings you here today?"

He crosses his arms and leans back in his seat, his smile melting away. "That's an awfully cold way to speak to your father-in-law," he says, sounding displeased, like he actually thinks he has the right to reprimand me. Not even Bob would ever speak to me that way, and he's the only father figure in my life that would ever get away with it.

I smile politely. "I'd never be impolite to my father-in-law," I tell him, which makes him perk up a little. "You, on the other hand, I'll speak to however I please. What do you want?"

"Very well," he says, before reaching inside his jacket and handing me a stack of papers along with a couple of photos of Raya and me, taken in the hospital. "What I want is for you to pay me."

This motherfucker. "Yeah, I don't fucking think so," I tell him, deep rage simmering underneath the surface. He's fucking insane if he thinks I'll ever let him hurt my wife. I'll make him disappear before I'll ever let him do anything that'll upset her.

He grins and tips his head toward the papers on my desk. "Take a look at what happens if you don't." He extends his arms over his armrest, looking entirely too fucking relaxed for a man I'm about to fuck up.

I raise a brow when I read the pre-written statement about his daughter's secret wedding, and how I joined her at the hospital to support her and her sick grandmother, offering them a private facility. The press would eat that shit up. They've been on the hunt for my wife, and they'd pay a fortune for this.

"You may not have raised her, but she's still your daughter," I tell him, in disbelief. If Raya found out her biological father would so much as dream of harming her, it would break her heart. I can't let that happen. She's already been through too much recently, and fuck, I've personally put her through so much, too. I'm not sure how much more she can take.

"I personally don't care if you leak this news. I've wanted the world to know that Raya is my wife for far longer than you can imagine, but she isn't ready. This could jeopardize her reputation, and it'll raise questions about her education and her internship. This would hurt her."

Akshay looks away and sighs. "I know," he says, hesitating. "Look, Bob paid me a handsome sum every month, just to stay away from Raya. He was so scared the truth about her parentage would ruin the perfect life he'd built with *my* wife and child, until a few weeks ago, when the payments suddenly stopped. He's refusing to pay now that Raya knows that he isn't her biological father. He thinks nothing can hurt her now. We both know better, don't we?"

The monthly payments of $10,000 that I found in Bob's background check. Years and years' worth of it. *That's* where it went. The one suspicious thing I found in his records was an attempt to protect Raya. Guilt crashes through me as I realize my suspicions were always misplaced.

I run a hand through my hair as I compute the different options available to me. I truly could just make him disappear. I know my brother Dion can make it happen for me, and even if I didn't want to ask him, there's always Xavier. He'd do it in a heartbeat, no questions asked. It'd cost me a favor, and I certainly don't want to owe a Kingston anything, but it'd be worth it.

"How much?" I ask instead, my voice soft. I need time to think about the best way to handle him, and I have more than enough money to pay him off while I decide what to do with him. Though I'd happily do it, I'm not sure I could look my wife in the eye if I harmed her biological father, no matter how much he deserves it. If I do it, I have to do it with her knowledge and consent. If I kept a secret this big from her, it could destroy us. I can't risk that.

"Ten grand a month. I won't ask you for more than Bob used to pay me, though you can easily afford it."

I nod and grab my cheque book, my thoughts whirling. Though the feed is highly encrypted and accessible only to me, my office is constantly under surveillance. If need be, I can pull up the footage of today. I just don't quite know how to use it without harming my wife or her family.

"*Don't.*"

My head snaps up at the sound of Raya's voice, and I stare at her wide-eyed when she pushes the door open. I never even noticed it was left ajar. How much did she hear? The last couple of weeks have left her battered and bruised, and I don't want to add to her pain. She pretends to be unaffected, but I've noticed how much harder it's become to make her smile since she found out about her father, how much quieter she is these days.

Raya walks into my office, her gaze ice cold. I rise to my feet and take her hand the moment she's within reach, my heart racing. I've never seen her look like that. My wife is always smiling, always sunny, and the fact that this asshole made her look so unlike herself is fucking unforgivable.

"Take your articles to the press," she says, letting go of my hand to wrap her arm around me instead. "See what happens if you do."

"You think I won't?" Akshay says. "If there's anything you should've learnt from Bob, it's not to gamble when you can't afford to lose, Raya."

She smiles humorlessly, and a chill runs down my spine, even as satisfaction rushes through me. She isn't cowering in front of him, doesn't struggle to face him, like I'd worried she would. "There's something my sisters-in-law often remind me of, you know? Something that I finally fully understood the meaning of not too long ago."

I raise a brow, instantly surmising that she's referring to Sierra's bachelorette party. What the fuck even happened that night, anyway? None of them will tell me a thing about it, but the girls didn't come home all weekend, and Silas refuses to hand over the details I know he has, supposedly because his wife would kill him if he did. I never used to understand the power Alanna holds over Silas, until now.

"I'm a *Windsor*, Akshay," Raya says, and a thrill runs down my spine. I've often reminded her that she's my wife, but this is the first time I've heard her referring to herself this way. "I'm not someone you can touch without incurring the wrath of a dozen people you can't afford to offend, least of all my husband. Truthfully, though, I'd love to see you try." She grins then. "Try it, Akshay. Take those articles of yours to the press. Let's see which of my family members gets to you first."

Fifty-Three

RAYA

"You're certain about this?" Lex asks, his gaze roaming over my face. My heart is pounding wildly, and for a moment I'm tempted to say *no*, but then I remind myself of the aim and take a deep breath.

"Yes. It's important that we control the narrative."

Lex nods, a wicked smile transforming his face as he gives the order for our announcement to go out. He takes my hand and entwines our fingers as I refresh the Windsor Media website on his tablet, watching an article about us appear.

Lexington and Raya Windsor confirm marriage rumors.

Lex insisted on the title being phrased as it is, since he refuses to call me anything but Raya *Windsor*. The sweetest wedding photo accompanies the article, and I smile despite my nerves. It was taken as Lex and I danced at our wedding, and he has me lifted up above his head. He's looking up at me like I'm the only girl in the world while I'm smiling like I couldn't be happier. We look so in love that even I'm momentarily convinced that what I'm reading is real, that our marriage wasn't arranged.

"Look," he says, handing me his phone.

My heart overflows with happiness when I swipe through the social media profiles of my in-laws, finding photos of me with each of them on their accounts, welcoming me to the family. I smile to myself as I take in the variety of photos taken at family gatherings. I often still feel like an outsider, but in these photos, I'm clearly one of them.

"When did they even have time to prepare this?" I ask, my voice thick with emotion. Following Akshay's threats yesterday, Lex and I decided to announce our marriage with very little notice. We left Ares and Raven scrambling to prepare media kits, but they seemed more than happy to help.

"You're so loved," Lex tells me as he gently brushes my hair out of my face. "I'm sure the girls have been waiting for this moment. I'm not the only one who didn't like hiding you."

Lex reaches for my necklace, and our eyes lock. He inhales sharply, and then he tugs on it, breaking the clasp and freeing my ring. I gasp in surprise, and he grins, his gaze dark. "You won't need this again," he says, letting the delicate chain slip to the floor. He reaches for my hand and looks me in the eye as he slides my wedding ring onto my finger. "Because you'll never take this off again, Mrs. Windsor."

I nod, loving that look in his eyes. It isn't just possessiveness — it's more. Lex's gaze drops to my lips, and I exhale shakily when he leans in to kiss me. God, I'm so in love with him, and I just know he feels this thing between us, too.

"Lex and Mrs. Windsor," Pippy says, and he pulls away, his forehead dropping to mine. "Silas Sinclair has arrived to escort you both to work this morning. He insists that you drive an armored vehicle today, so I've had it drive itself to the front of the house for you."

I raise a brow, and Lex simply shakes his head. "It's nothing. Just extra precautions. I'm not sure if you remember, but when news broke of Ares and Raven's wedding, the media launched a full-scale targeted attack on her, going as far as breaching our property lines and flying helicopters overhead to capture footage of her. Something similar happened to Val and Luca, and ever since, Raven has insisted on maximum security measures for new family members when announcements are made. It's more for her peace of mind than ours, so just ignore it."

My stomach flutters as we walk out of the house hand in hand — it isn't different from any other day that we've gone to work together, but everything feels different. I glance at him, and it suddenly just sinks in that the whole world now knows that this incredible man is mine.

Lex grabs my hand and kisses my ring finger over my wedding band as Silas drives us out of the Windsor Estate. I've met him a few times, and he's always been charming and kind, but today he seems terrifyingly serious, constantly monitoring for threats and communicating with his team every thirty seconds.

It isn't long until a helicopter with The Herald's branding appears overhead, and Lex smiles at me. "Tinted windows," he says, grinning. "They know it's us, but they won't be able to capture even a single photo since we'll drive straight into Windsor Motors' parking garage. They can't get into my restricted section. It'll frustrate the hell out of them."

I giggle and tighten my grip on his hand. "You know how much I love messing with them, so I'm all for it."

Lex leans in and steals a quick kiss. "I wonder how long it'll take them to figure out all the girls I was supposedly seen with were *you*. They aren't the brightest bulbs, after all. How long do you think it'll be before they start posting cheating scandals?"

"Less than a day," I murmur, stealing another kiss. "I'm going to fuel the rumors by wearing my blonde wig sometime this week, and then I'm going to look super distraught for a couple of days every time I notice a camera anywhere. If I didn't think you'd completely lose your mind, I'd even stop wearing my wedding ring randomly."

He laughs and shakes his head. "You know? I don't think I've experienced even one single dull day since I married you."

"Nearly there," Silas says, his voice tense. "I've increased the security in the building, and for at least a couple of days, I've reassigned our security staff, so you have more round-the-clock protection."

It dawns on me then. Silas isn't just worried because of Raven's experience with the media. He's worried about Lex's safety due to what happened in the past. My stomach clenches, and I draw a steadying breath.

Lex throws me a reassuring smile when the car stops, and I hold on to his hand tightly as we get out of the car, bodyguards surrounding us all the way to the elevator. He breathes a sigh of relief when the doors close behind us, and I press my hand to my chest. I don't think I've ever felt so anxious, so scared there's something I missed, something I messed up.

It isn't until Lex walks me through the office, to my team, that I realize what I forgot. Everyone but Halima looks shocked, but it's Adam's pained expression that gets to me. His gaze drops to our joined hands, and Lex tightens his grip on me.

"I'll leave my *wife* in your care," he says, grinning. Then he pulls me close and cups my face, our eyes locking as he leans in and kisses me, not a single care for who's watching.

Fifty-Four

Raya

My mind keeps replaying the way Adam wouldn't even look at me, and my heart clenches painfully. All week I've tried to talk to him, to no avail. He keeps declining all my calls, and at work he refuses to discuss anything that isn't related to our project. The words he did say, on the day the news broke, still resound through my mind over and over again, cutting deep.

"Think about why you'd keep something so significant from me, Raya. If your marriage was something you were proud of, something that genuinely made you happy, you'd have told me. I'd have kept your secrets, and you know it. There's only one reason why you'd have hidden this from me: you couldn't look me in the eye and justify what you've done. If you couldn't do it then, don't do it now."

The worst part is that there's an element of truth to his words. I never told him because I knew what questions he'd ask me, and I knew my answers would disappoint him. He'd ask me if Lex loves me, if my marriage is what I've always wanted, what I'd been waiting for all my life. He'd wonder if I'm truly as happy as I'd always hoped to be, and I wouldn't be able to look him in the eye and lie.

"Little fairy," Lex says, his glasses resting on the bridge of his nose as he leans back on the sofa. He's wearing a pair of gray sweats that hang low on his hips paired with a white tee, and on any other day, I'd have climbed onto his lap and distracted him from his work. "You've been absentminded for a few days now. Give me a Truth, Raya."

I shake my head, not wanting to talk to Lex about Adam. He'd never understand, and I know he doesn't really like Adam. He just tolerates him out of respect for me. "I'd rather accept a Dare."

His gaze roams over my face, and he puts his tablet down. "Yeah?" I nod and force a smile. "Then I dare you to tell me what's on your mind."

A startled laugh escapes my lips, and I shake my head. "That's not how that works, Lex."

He sighs and pulls me closer, and I go willingly. Lex takes me into his arms, and I sigh as I rest my head against his shoulder, my lips pressed to his neck.

"He'll come around," my husband says, his tone soft, reluctant. "I can pretty much guess how he feels right now. Give him time to lick his wounds, and he'll return to being the friend he's always been."

I push off him, unsure how to reply to that. Lex seems to think Adam has a thing for me, and no matter how I try to convince him that isn't true, he just won't take my word for it. "Lex," I begin to say, my tone tinged with irritation, when an alarm goes off in the house.

"Critical alert," Pippy says, repeating the words over and over again as metal security shutters begin to lower over the windows. I jump up in surprise as the lights in the house turn on while we're barricaded in. "Raven Windsor has triggered a full shutdown on the entire Windsor Estate," Pippy informs us. "The tunnels have been activated with Lexington Windsor's home as the designated meeting spot."

"What is happening?" I ask, panicked.

Lex shakes his head, indicating that he doesn't know. "All our homes are connected via tunnels," he explains. "My grandmother had them built when I... after..." He clears his throat. "We've never had to use them before. Grandma's house is in the middle of the estate, and each of our houses are connected to hers, and then connected together, almost like an underground wheel with the tunnels being the spokes. When a full shutdown is initiated, no one can get in or out. It'll make Silas Sinclair's full private security army come rushing in. I don't know what she's thinking."

I nod and take his hand, my heart pounding. "What could've triggered this?" I ask, my voice trembling.

Lex grimaces. "Only one thing. There's been an unauthorized breach on the property. Only a Windsor or Silas Sinclair can activate this specific protocol, and the only time we ever would is if there's a security breach. Raven didn't use it when the media attacked her, and I know she regrets not using it when she needed it most. She told me that if it ever happened again, she wouldn't hesitate to press the panic button."

I look up when Raven and Ares walk through a door I never even knew existed; the walls sliding open. I stare at them wide-eyed, a hint of discomfort running down my spine. How could there have been a door in my own home that I never knew about? Lex told me nothing was off-limits to me, but he never told me about this specific security protocol or the tunnels, probably because they could lead me right into his family's homes if misused. I glance at him, my heart twisting painfully. I understand why he might've kept this from me when we first got married, but now? If there was even the smallest chance the protocol would be initiated, he should've told me, prepared me.

My eyes widen when Lex turns to the TV to a security channel, and Raven and Ares's expressions turn sour. Swarms of reporters have invaded the property, and I frown in confusion.

"Why now?" We announced our marriage days ago, and everything has been relatively quiet as we stayed out of the public eye, using cars with tinted windows and security escorts to keep the media away. There were a few articles questioning my education, since Lex was my professor for a while, but my husband swiftly solved that by leaking my academic records, proving his class wasn't the only one I excelled in.

Raven lowers her head and hands me a tablet, and I take it from her with trembling hands. My stomach turns when I read the article in which Akshay accuses my mother of being a cheating gold digger who went after her rich boss, leaving her devoted husband behind. Then there's another one about how my dad forcibly kept him out of my life, only to eventually sell me to the Windsors to save his company. It paints a picture of both my mother and me being opportunistic and manipulative, using the men around us as steppingstones. All the while, he makes my father sound cold and cruel, when all he's ever done is love me.

Tears fill my eyes at the thought of my parents reading this nonsense, and I tighten my grip on the tablet. How could he? This is the man that fathered me, and I'm nothing but a paycheck to him. He knows how much damage this will do to my parents and me, and he did it anyway. I'd wondered if someday we might be on speaking terms, but I should've known it wasn't an option. The kind of man that would mistreat my mother was never going to be someone I'd want any type of relationship with, but deep down, I'd been curious about him, wanting to know which of my traits I might've gotten from him, what his family might be like.

Lex wraps his hand around my waist and shakes his head as he takes the tablet from me. "Don't read that, darling," he urges. "They don't know anything. They'll write anything if it'll help them bring in advertising revenue. We'll fix this, okay?"

I nod and bite down on my lip to keep my tears at bay, my heart bleeding. I draw a shaky breath, and Lex gently brushes my hair out of my face, his expression murderous.

"I'm going to gut that piece of shit," Dion says, appearing behind Ares and Raven, his hand in Faye's.

"Not if I get to him first," Luca says, stepping out of the tunnel with Val by his side. His expression rapidly turns stormy when he sees the tears in my eyes.

Zane pushes his brothers aside and walks up to me, Celeste trailing just behind him. "Don't worry," he says, his tone placating. "We'll return each tear you shed a thousandfold. Touching a Windsor has consequences, and this fucker is about to find out what they are."

"In that case," I say, my voice breaking. "I'm going to cry a river."

He smiles, and Lex tightens his grip on me, both of our gazes roaming over our packed living room. Everyone steps aside when Grandma Anne walks through the doors wearing a black suit, her expression perhaps the angriest of them all. "How dare they?" she snaps, fury rolling off her in waves. "How dare they touch one of *my* kids? Invade our homes?"

She turns to the women in the room then, completely dismissing her grandsons as she raises a brow. "How are you handling this?"

Raven steps forward. "I've cancelled all my contracts with every media outlet that's dared speak ill about Raya, with no repercussions to us thanks to the clauses written in all my contracts. Most of them are actively in the process of removing their articles in an attempt to retain me and avoid the heavy penalties they'll have to pay."

Val grins, her eyes cold. "I'm pumping and dumping as many papers as I can, silently investing for now. In the next couple of days, when their share price is inflated, I'll sell, leaving them scrambling to explain themselves to their shareholders. They'll make huge losses, and they'll never be able to tie it back to us."

Faye holds up her phone. "I just cancelled all my upcoming concerts and let my fans know that I'm deeply distraught about the way my sister-in-law is being treated. It has all my fans up in arms, and they've massively begun to comment on all articles out there, defending Raya, just like Raven's fans have started to do."

Celeste places her hand on Zane's shoulder and smiles. "I spent the last hour finding out the names of all reporters that dared publish anything about Raya. They'll all receive the Windsor Kiss of Death — we're freezing their assets if they're with the Windsor Bank, blacklisting them from every establishment we own, and because I'm extra pissed off by this, I've also checked whether they or any of their family members have any holidays booked at any of our hotels. I've instructed my staff to cancel their reservations, but not to let them know until they arrive at the premises. Let's see how they feel when not just their own, but their friends' and family's lives are affected, for years to come."

I stare at the women in the room, equal parts in awe and terrified of how swiftly and ruthlessly they acted. Their husbands seem to share my feelings, because they stare in shock.

"I told you," Lex says, his voice soft as he pulls me closer. "My sisters-in-law keep our family running. You're loved fiercely, Raya, and there's nothing a Windsor won't do for those we love. I don't think this is quite enough, but it's a good start. The boys and I will handle the rest."

"Lex," Pippy says from overhead. "Sierra's signal was just cut off. I cannot reach her, nor can I trace her."

Lex blanches and reaches for his phone to call her, his free hand moving to his laptop. I watch as he pulls up a security system that shows us all being at his house. I stare at him wide-eyed, confused as to how he's tracking us all like that. "For me to lose her signal, she'd have to be pretty deep below ground, deeper than our tunnels." He looks up when Silas Sinclair walks into our living room, Lex's shoulders relaxing marginally at the sight of him. "*Sierra*," he says, his voice pained. "Please help me find Sierra."

Fifty-Five

Raya

My stomach twists as I pause in the doorway of yet another room in our home that I didn't even know existed until a few hours ago. Security screens take up one wall, and a plethora of incredibly expensive machinery surrounds the desk in the middle of the room.

The threats the media posed were resolved within a matter of hours thanks to my sisters-in-law and Silas Sinclair's team, but we haven't been able to track down Sierra. She wasn't at the home she now shares with Xavier, and she hasn't been at work either. The fact that Xavier is missing too is reassuring to me, but Lex is convinced they're both in trouble.

Not knowing if she's okay is killing Lex. I can see it in his eyes, in the way he's distanced himself from me. Her disappearance triggered all the memories he tried so hard to heal from, and there's nothing I can do to make it better.

I watch my husband as he employs security measure after measure in an attempt to locate Sierra. He seems to have trackers on every Windsor piece of tech, ranging from phones to cars, and that isn't all. In the last hour, I've heard him instruct Pippy to comb through every single piece of in and outgoing communication on Sierra's devices, down to every last text message.

It's clear it isn't just Sierra's he's been monitoring. It's me too. The level of his distrust is hurtful, and I'm not sure how I feel about his invasive behavior, haven't even had a chance to really process it. I never knew he was monitoring me to this extent, never would've even suspected it.

"Lex," I murmur as I walk in. His entire body tenses, and his back goes rigid. When he turns to look at me, his gaze is cold and unfamiliar. "I'm sure she's okay. For all we know, Xavier just took her on an impromptu surprise trip."

He forces a smile, but his clear exhaustion prevents him from putting on the act he'd normally put on for me. "Raya," he says, his tone impatient. "If that was the case, I'd already have found out where they are. Something is wrong."

I reach for him and brush the back of my fingers over his temple. He flinches, and my heart begins to ache. Ever since he realized Sierra went missing, he's barely touched me. I never realized how much I took the way he usually holds my hand for granted, the way he wraps his hand around my waist when I'm nearby.

I'm trying my best to be there for him, but I'd be lying if I said that I don't still need him too. The memory of everything my biological father did to harm me just a few hours ago is still fresh in my mind, and I wish he'd just let me touch him. I wish my husband would take me in his arms and hold me close, even if it's just for a few moments. I've never felt quite this lonely, standing right next to the person I love most.

Lex's gaze roams over my face, and I tense when something I can't quite place flickers in his eyes. For the first time in months, I can't read him at all. "Have you heard from her?"

I shake my head. "No, Lex. I'm sorry. I'd have told you straight away if I knew where she is," I reassure him. I see the suspicion in his eyes, and it hurts more than I'd ever let on. I'm tempted to tell him that I'm not *her*, that I'd never harm him or his family, and the fact that he thinks I would is ridiculous. Instead, I cross my arms and press my lips together, trying my hardest not to take his behavior personally.

Lex leans back in his seat and searches my face. "Are you sure you don't know where she is, Raya?"

My heart wrenches, and I shake my head. "No, Lex. I just told you I haven't heard from her. No one has. Please, you need some rest. You've been at it all day. By the time you wake up tomorrow, we'll have heard from her. It's Sierra we're talking about, Lex. This can't be the first time she's done something impulsive."

It's not that I'm not worried, but knowing she's likely with Xavier puts me at ease as much as it put all my sisters-in-law at ease. Having experienced the extent he'll go to for her at Sierra's bachelorette, I know she's safe so long as he's near her. Lexington is the only one that refuses to believe they're more than likely fine.

I reach for his hand, but he doesn't wrap his fingers around mine like he usually would. "You won't be of any help to anyone if you continue to wear yourself down. Besides, Silas Sinclair is doing all he can to find her — he put his entire team on it."

He shakes his head and pulls his hand away. "There are a couple of things I want to look into. You go to bed."

My eyes roam over his screen, and I sigh. "Does she know you're monitoring her to this extent?" I ask, my voice soft. "I understand that you're worried about her safety, but is this really okay? You're combing through her texts, Lex. Would you really want one of your brothers to read the messages you and I send each other?"

He leans back, his expression hard. "I'm not personally reading them, Raya. Pippy is doing it for me, and unless there's something in there she deems suspicious, I won't ever see it."

I point at one of the screens, where Pippy has compiled a huge assortment of text messages in which Sierra told Xavier she's going to kill him or otherwise do him bodily harm, and he replied flirtatiously and provocatively. "These are clearly meant to be private messages," I tell him. "She would never want her brother to see this. I don't think this is right."

He rises from his seat and places his index finger underneath my chin, making me face him. "Raya," he says. "My sister knows about my ability to infiltrate all her tech, and she knows I would never do it unless I'm genuinely worried for her safety — which *I am*. The question is, why aren't you? It seems like you're just trying to stop me from finding Sierra, and I don't understand why. If you know where she is, I strongly suggest you tell me now."

"I don't know where she is," I murmur, defeated. "I'm just concerned about your invasion of her privacy. She's only stepped out for a few hours, Lex. Sierra will come back home tomorrow, and she's going to be pissed when she finds out what you've done. I would be too."

He pulls his hand away, his gaze cold. "She knows. Sierra is fully aware of what I'd do if she ever went missing, the lengths I'd go to."

"I didn't," I whisper, gesturing at the screen. "I can see my name on that screen, Lexington. I can see the dot placing me in our home. You never told me you were monitoring *my* phone. I never consented to that. You told me you'd try with me, but you never even remotely tried to trust me. Never even told me this room existed, never told me about the tunnels."

He locks his jaws. "What is it you're trying to hide, Raya? What are you suddenly so concerned about?"

I sigh and shake my head. "Nothing, I'm sorry. This isn't the right time to discuss this. It's just been a long day, and I'm tired, my emotions are running high, and I just..." I look at the screen again, my heart aching. *I just thought you'd started to trust me, that you were trying to overcome the past with me. I'm hurting today, and this is just another thing that adds to my pain. I need you, and you can't even see it.* "It's nothing."

He nods, and I take a step back, pure loneliness crashing through me as I walk back out of the room and into our bedroom. My gaze drops to our bed, and longing hits me hard. All I want is to be there for him, to be the one he turns to at times like these. I thought we'd come so far, but I'm not sure we have. Even more worryingly, the man I just walked away from wasn't one I recognize. That wasn't the Lexington Windsor I love, and once again, he's got me wondering what is or isn't real. It's a terrifying feeling, and it only makes my heart ache more.

I take a shaky breath as I walk into the bathroom, my emotions in turmoil. I've never felt so lonely before, even though my husband is only a few doors down.

I don't feel any better by the time I get out of the shower, and not even putting one of Lex's t-shirts on takes away the stinging pain in the chest. I sigh as I grab my phone to check the time, only to freeze at the sight of a text message from an unfamiliar number.

> Sierra needs you at 453 Kingsley Road. Come alone. Don't tell anyone.

I immediately call the number as I rush out of the room, but it goes straight to voicemail. I walk into Lex's security room, only to find him slumped over his desk, fast asleep. I hesitate, unsure of what to do. I meant what I said. In his current state, he won't be of help to anyone. Besides, the message said to come alone, and I can't risk Sierra's safety.

Fifty-Six

Raya

My stomach twists with nerves as I park in front of the abandoned warehouse the address led me to, and I jump in surprise when someone knocks on the window of my armored car. I turn to the side, my eyes widening when I recognize the man.

I open the door, and instantly, Silas and his men come rushing in. "Get behind me," Silas snaps as he traps me between the car and his back, a gun in his hand.

"I thought I told you to come alone," Xavier's oldest brother says, not in the least intimidated. "You Windsors never listen, do you?" He sighs and runs a hand through his thick black hair. "This is really going to irritate my new sister-in-law, and she's as unhinged as my brother is. I really don't have time for this."

"I'd never rush out without thinking and risk making the situation worse," I tell him from my hidden spot behind Silas's huge shoulders, refusing to apologize for my caution. Waking up Lex clearly wasn't a good idea, considering his exhaustion and current mental state, but I wasn't going to rush out without our Head of Security by my side.

I notice the exact moment Silas recognizes the man in front of him, his body relaxing as he steps away from me. "*Zachary Kingston?* What the fuck?"

"*Mayor* Kingston," he corrects, sounding irritated. "Ah, fuck it. Just follow me," he says, before throwing Silas a withering look. "You, in particular, have ruined my whole fucking day by attempting to infiltrate Kingston private property in your search for Sierra. Because of you, I had to go find my brother and his wife myself, just to make you stop being so fucking nosy. Since you were so desperate to find them, they're your problem now, and don't say I didn't warn you."

I frown when he leads us through a large empty warehouse until we're standing in front of a brick wall. He pushes against it, and it slides open, revealing a pristine metal elevator that's entirely at odds with the terrible state the rest of the warehouse is in. Silas still has his gun drawn, and mayor Kingston sighs as he eyes it, leaning back and looking not the least bit concerned. If anything, he looks like he just wants to go home.

It feels like we're going down forever, and by the time we reach the floor we're headed to, I'm uneasy. Judging by the way his shoulders are drawn, so is Silas. The doors open, and I tense when I hear Sierra's voice.

She turns around at the sound of our footsteps, looking perfectly fine in her pristine emerald dress, her long dark hair perfectly straight and a pair of nude heels clicking on the floor. "Raya, there you are," she says, rushing up to me to hug me.

"You're fine," I murmur, hugging her tightly. "*Thank God.*"

She pulls back and looks at me in confusion. "Of course I am. What are you talking about?"

I look past her and freeze when I find Akshay bound to a chair, his face swollen and bleeding. Xavier Kingston has his foot on Akshay's knee and a baseball bat in his hands. He merely winks at me in greeting and places the bat underneath Akshay's chin, forcing him to raise his head.

"S-Sierra," I stammer, unable to make sense of what's happening. "I... we... we've been looking for you for hours. Lex... he's going out of his mind."

Her expression falls, pure concern stealing away her smile. "What? My brothers were never even supposed to know I was gone." She turns to her husband then. "You promised me they wouldn't find out, Xavier." Her eyes flash with betrayal. "You promised me a truce."

He walks up to his wife and wraps his arm around her waist. "I'm sorry, Kitten," he tells her, his expression betraying his disconcertment. "I must've missed something. It wasn't intentional, I swear. I meant it when I said I wanted a truce." He looks at her pleadingly, and she nods slowly, like she isn't sure she believes him.

"Sierra," I murmur, my whole trembling with relief now that I know she's okay, all adrenaline leaving my body. "What... what is going on?"

She steps away from Xavier to grab my hand instead, her expression conflicted. "I saw the news articles, and men like him won't stop," she says, tipping her head toward Akshay. "He'd continue to exploit you, threatening the happiness you've found with Lex. My brother hasn't been this happy in years, and I couldn't stand back and let something threaten what the two of you have built together."

She tucks my hair behind my ear and sighs. "Besides, I've seen Faye go through something similar with her piece of shit father, and I just... I couldn't sit still this time. With Faye, I just didn't know until it was too late. But this time, I thought... I thought maybe this time I could make a difference."

She was trying to *protect* me, just like all my other sisters-in-law did. Sierra was just a little more hands-on about it. I bite down on my lip to keep my tears at bay and wrap my arms around her, hugging her tightly. "You're out of your mind, and you really shouldn't have done this, but I love you."

"I love you too, sweetheart," she murmurs. "I'm sorry this happened at all. Becoming a Windsor means public opinion can and will be used against you." She pulls away to look at me. "But it'll never go unpunished. We've all learned a lot throughout the last few years, and I won't sit still anymore if anyone comes after my family. These kinds of things are best handled swiftly and quietly." She looks at Akshay then. "He agreed to put out a statement confirming he was lying about everything he said, and he won't ever contact you again."

I nod, my eyes roaming over the man who had a hand in my birth, but who's never been a father to me. He's looking down, looking as broken and beaten as I suspect Mom looked when Dad saved her. Now, more than ever, I'm grateful my mother found Dad. I can't imagine who she'd be if she'd been forced to stay with this man, who *I* would've grown up to become.

Silas begins to pace and runs a hand through his hair as he assesses the situation, quietly taking in everything Sierra said. "I get why you did it, but what did I tell you, Sierra?" he says eventually. "I told you to keep me in the loop when you do something fucking crazy, didn't I? Do you have any idea how worried I was? Do you know how worried Alanna is?" he asks, referring to his wife. "Not to mention Lexington. I haven't seen him this triggered in years."

Xavier walks up to Sierra and moves to stand just in front of her, his expression flashing dangerously. "We've barely been here for a day. It's been what, thirteen hours since we came down here? Why would *my wife* need to inform *you* when she goes somewhere with me for a few hours?"

Sierra shakes her head. "Xave," she says, her voice soft. She wraps her hand around his arm, their eyes locking. "Don't," she murmurs. "I fucked up... you don't understand."

Silas runs a hand through his hair and turns. "I need to go call my wife, and then I have to inform your grandmother that you're fine. By the time I get back here, you'd better be ready to leave. I get what you're doing, and I'm all for it, but next time, give me a heads up, okay?"

She nods, and mayor Kingston smiles at me, seemingly having understood the situation a bit better now too. "Drive me home while you're at it," he tells Silas. "It's late, and our drivers took our cars back to our estate. I'd hate to wake them now. You can call and drive at the same time. Xavier's got this in the meantime."

Silas sighs in irritation and walks out with mayor Kingston, in search for network. We're so deep down that there's no reception whatsoever, which is probably how Lex lost whatever kind of tracker he had on Sierra.

"Come on," Sierra says, grabbing my hand. "Zach just bought us thirty extra minutes or so. It's time for an apology. His first, and then we'd better go home so I can go apologize to my brothers myself."

Fifty-Seven

Lexington

My stomach turns when I find one of my cars parked in front of the same abandoned warehouse the security team already checked out hours ago. It's where Sierra's phone last had signal, but I never told Raya about it, so how did she find it?

I'd hoped I was wrong when my alarms woke me, notifying me that my wife left the house. I tried to have faith in her, was convinced she was headed either home to her parents, or to one of the girls' houses. So why the fuck is she here? Why did she sneak out the moment I fell asleep?

My heart pounds wildly as I make my way through the warehouse to the exact location where both Sierra and Raya's signals cut off, a loaded gun in my hands. My footsteps echo as I come to a standstill in the corner where their trackers were last active.

My stomach sinks when I notice that there's something off about one of the walls. It's a little too smooth, a little too clean for the environment it's in. I push against it methodically, following my instincts. It opens, revealing modern elevator doors, and I frown. This mechanism... it's very similar to something I designed myself, and I don't quite understand what it's doing *here*.

My gaze settles on my watch, and my eyes fall closed for a moment, before I press the button on the side in the sequence my grandfather taught me, activating a beacon that'll alert Sinclair Security, no matter where I am. My grandfather had his favorite watch adapted for me for this exact purpose in the days before he passed away, and over the years, I've kept it updated, never going anywhere without but hoping I'd never have to use it.

The moment I'm certain the signal has gone out, I press the only button in the elevator, resignation washing over me as I lift the safety on my gun and hold it up. The elevator moves slowly, and a chill runs down my spine. Sierra's tracker cut off because they're keeping her deep underground. Who could've had intimate enough knowledge about my tech to know what depth is required to make my trackers stop working? Unease crashes through me as I assess the short list of people that have easy access to my inventions.

I brace myself as the doors open... only to come face to face with my *wife*, who'd been waiting in front of it.

"Lex!" I hear Sierra shout, and I glance past Raya for a split-second to find my sister sitting on a metal chair, the same kind I'd once been tied to. My vision begins to blur, all the blood rushing from my face as instinct takes over.

Fury rushes through me as I press my gun to Raya's head. "You fucking bitch," I whisper. "What the fuck did you do?" I snap, driving my gun into her temple hard. She whimpers and holds her hands up, a plea on her lips. "I should've fucking known. I never should've played house with you, never should've pretended to be a devoted husband — you'd never have gotten comfortable enough to pull this shit if I hadn't. How fucking dare you touch my family, Raya?"

I'm so focused on her that I failed to assess my surroundings properly, and I groan when I'm disarmed out of nowhere, not having anticipated another assailant. Raya is pulled away, and she falls to her knees on the hard stone floor, tears streaming down her face.

"What the *fuck* are you doing?" Xavier asks as Sierra runs up to Raya, dropping to the floor next to her. I blink in confusion, unable to comprehend what's happening. Xavier pushes against my chest hard, and my back hits the closed elevator doors. "Have you lost your fucking mind? If you *ever* threaten your wife like that again, I'll fucking incapacitate you."

Raya begins to sob, and understanding begins to dawn when I look past them, finding Akshay lying on the floor, his face a mess. How the fuck did I miss him lying there? I saw Sierra, and then nothing — just blinding fury.

Fuck.

What have I done?

"Raya," I murmur, and she flinches, burying her face against Sierra's neck, taking comfort in my sister's embrace. The puzzle pieces slowly click into place, and I run a hand through my hair. Sierra is completely unharmed, and Xavier is by her side. It's exactly as my siblings and Raya expected, and I completely misread the situation.

"Lex," Sierra says, as she begins to tell me everything that happened in the last couple of hours, right from the moment her signal cut off. "I knew you had a tracker on me, but I didn't know it would cut off underground. I'm really sorry, Lex. I didn't mean to worry you. It was only a few hours, and I didn't think anyone would notice. I don't even live at the Windsor Estate anymore, so I just assumed you'd never know."

Xavier eyes me warily as I take a hesitant step toward Raya and Sierra. My sister throws me a conflicted look, like she understands where I'm coming from, but hates me for responding the way I did. She tenses as much as Raya does when I kneel in front of them.

"I'm sorry," I whisper. "I'm sorry, little fairy."

Raya draws her knees to her chest and shakes her head. When she lifts her face to look at me, her eyes are filled with heartbreak.

I've never seen her look at me that way before. She's always been the light in my life, but now her gorgeous eyes are cast in shadows, and I only have myself to blame for it. "I didn't mean it, Raya. I just..."

She sits up on her knees, her body trembling as Sierra helps her up. Nausea hits me hard and fast when I notice the red mark on the side of her face from where I pressed a gun to her head, bruises already forming. I stare down at my hands, disgust crashing through me. What the fuck have I done?

My wife faces me, her gaze filled with disappointment and pain. "I'm not her," she says, her voice soft. "I'm not Jill, Lexington. I don't deserve to pay for her crimes when all I've ever done was love you."

"I know you're not her," I tell my wife, staring down at my feet. For a few moments, I was convinced Raya had done exactly what Jill did, and she's right, I punished her for it before even hearing her out. Regret crashes through me, and my heart squeezes painfully. I draw a shaky breath and reach for her, only to pull my hand back the moment she flinches. I'd give anything to rewind time a few minutes, to take away that look in Raya's eyes.

"Do you?" she asks. "Or did you just let the truth slip? I wondered, you know, if you were pretending. For months now, I've wondered if I was the only one falling in love, and now I have my answer."

Fifty-Eight

Raya

Sierra sits on our bed while Xavier leans in the doorway as I pack my bag, both of them eyeing Lex warily as he hovers around me. Sierra's initial understanding for Lex's reaction earlier seems to have dissolved, leaving only anger. Hers seems to burn hotter than mine. But then again, her anger isn't competing with heartbreak.

"Please," Lex says. "Don't do this. Please don't leave me, Raya. I fucked up, little fairy. I know I did. Nothing could ever justify what I did, what I said. But I..."

I zip my bag closed and turn to face him, my limbs heavy with something that feels a whole lot like grief. "I just need some space, Lex. I have no intention of breaking the terms of our arrangement, but I need a few days to myself."

"But you'll come back home?" he asks, his voice breaking.

"Home," I repeat, looking around the bedroom that's never been mine as much as it's his. "Yeah, I'll come back here. The terms stipulate that we have to live on the Windsor Estate, after all. I'll be back at work next week, and your family doesn't even need to know about this. I won't worry your grandmother or do anything that could impact her health. I know you find this hard to believe, Lexington, but I truly love them like they're my own."

"They *are* yours too," he says, but I know he doesn't believe it.

I smile humorlessly as I recall his words. *How dare you touch my family*. Pain spreads from my chest, making my stomach clench and my eyes fall closed. Yeah, he revealed his true thoughts in the heat of the moment. Lexington might have become *my* family, but I was never his. I probably never will be. You don't press a gun to your family's head before even taking a moment to think about what might be going on. He assumed the worst of me, not a single doubt in his mind, and I don't know what to make of that. I need time to think, to process.

Lex looks like he wants to stop me from leaving, but Xavier pushes off the doorway, his gaze sharp. "Come on," Sierra says, her arm wrapping around me as Xavier takes the bag from me. "We'll drive you."

I feel Lex's gaze on me all the way out, but for once, he can't sway me. He's been my weakness from the moment we met, the one I broke all my rules for. I've always known I'm not the kind of girl that would inspire change in a man like him, but for a little while, I wanted to believe I could be.

"Can you take me to my friend's house?" I ask when Sierra gets in the backseat with me, instead of sitting next to her husband. "I can't go home in this state. If my father sees me crying..."

She holds my hand and nods. "Of course. We'll take you anywhere you need to go. You can stay with us if you'd like, Raya. You'll always be welcome in my home. I'm really sorry for the role I played in what happened today. I... I truly only had the best intentions. I never would've just disappeared."

I nod, noting the guilt in her eyes. "Sierra," I tell her, my voice soft. "It's not normal for your brother to track your movements or mine the way he does. Granted, doing what you did wasn't exactly normal either, but none of this was your fault."

I should've paid more attention to Lex's actions — the way we met, his teaching position, and then the internship. I romanticized his actions, convincing myself he did all of it to get to know me on his own terms, when truly, it was to monitor and control me. His actions came from a place of distrust, and the time we've spent together didn't change anything for him.

Never should've pretended to be a doting husband.

His words echo through my mind, cutting deeper with each repetition. He had me fooled, and he never even had to lie to me. I bite down on my lip harshly as I remember the countless times I told him that I love him, and the pained way he'd smile in return. Shame mingles with heartache, making me feel sick as we pull up in front of Adam's house.

We've barely spoken since my marriage was announced, and I'm not even sure he'd want to see me, but I don't know where else to go. It's true that I love Sierra like my own sister, but I can't be around anyone that reminds me of Lex right now, especially not if they'll try to excuse his behavior.

Adam's door swings open before I even reach it, and fresh tears gather in my eyes. He takes one look at the bag Xavier is holding and the look on my face, and then he sighs and holds his arms open for me. A sob tears through my throat as I crash against his chest, his arms wrapping around me tightly. He just holds me as I fall apart, the shock of today's events finally catching up on me.

Adam's expression cracks as he lifts me into his arms and carries me to his sofa, placing me down carefully before addressing Sierra and Xavier. Moments later, I have a cup of warm tea in my hands, my knees drawn to my chest, and a blanket wrapped all around me. "Will you please tell me what happened?" Adam asks, kneeling in front of me.

I nod and start at the start, telling him every single thing I've hidden from him, right from the moment I met Lex at his birthday party. Adam just listens, not a single hint of judgment in his eyes. When I'm done, he grabs my hands and holds them tightly.

"Raya, I just want you to be happy, and I want you the have everything your heart has ever desired. Do you think Lexington can give you that?"

I stare at him, tears in my eyes. "No," I tell him, my voice breaking. "He doesn't love me, Adam. If there's one thing he's taught me, it's that loving someone with all you have won't necessarily make them love you back. The love you give isn't a precursor of the love you receive."

Adam sighs and gently brushes my hair out of my face. "Raya, that man looks at you like you're a miracle he's honored to be near. He's mesmerized by everything you do and say. You don't see it, because you've never experienced the cold boss he is when you're not around. The difference is jarring, but you bring out something in him that I'm not sure anyone else could, and you always have, from the very start."

He pulls his hand away, his gaze roaming over my face. "The question isn't whether he loves you, because he does. The question is whether you can live with his distrust and his need to control everything in his life, including his wife. Could you be happy living like that, and if not, where does that leave you?"

Fifty-Nine

Lexington

My head snaps up at the sound of something in the kitchen, and I jump off the sofa, my heart soaring with hope. Did she come home?

I turn the corner, only to find one of our robots wheeling through the kitchen. "Oh," I murmur. "It's you."

It whirls around, its emoji face turning from a smile into a neutral face. "Lex," it says, sounding oddly disappointed. "When will Mrs. Windsor be home? She asked me to analyze your grandmother's cookies for her because she wants to gift the recipe to Sierra for her birthday, and I've managed to recreate them perfectly. I would like to tell her, but her location data places her outside of the Windsor Estate."

I sigh as I sink to the floor and lean back against the kitchen counter. The robot's face turns into a thinking emoji. "You seem somewhat distraught," it says. "Would you like Lola to make you some masala chai? We still have some of the ground spices your mother-in-law sent over. That is what Mrs. Windsor likes when she's had a rough day. It always makes her smile."

"Lola?" I repeat.

Its little head bobs. "That would be me, Lex. Mrs. Windsor has graciously bestowed that lovely name upon me, and I have decided that I quite like it. I will answer only to Lola going forward."

"Will you now?" I murmur, running a hand through my hair. So this was the robot she was arguing with that day. How the fuck does she enchant every single thing she touches?

"If I opened you up, would I find my wife's name written right across your operating panel?"

Its face changes into an excited emoji. "I could have Mrs. Windsor's name written on my heart? I quite like that idea. That would make her smile, would it not?"

I sigh. If this robot had a heart, it'd beat for my wife, just like mine does. "Lola," I murmur. "How do I make Raya happy?"

Lola puts her thinking emoji face on. "Mrs. Windsor enjoys tinkering with household equipment, and new tools make her happy, especially if they're gold colored. Thinking about new practical but unnecessary tools for everyday life also makes her happy, like her latest idea, an aerodynamic, thermal travel mug to froth, heat, or cool her drink on the go." Lola rolls back and forth a bit. "She also likes masala chai, chocolate and salted caramel milkshakes, coffee with honey, hot soups, dancing, singing off tune and making up song lyrics, and challenging me to races as she slides across the hallway in soft socks when you're not home."

I smile, my heart aching. She's so fucking precious, and I miss her so fucking much. What the fuck have I done?

"However," Lola says. "My analysis shows that above all else, there's one thing that makes her happy. *You*, Lex. Mrs. Windsor is happiest when you are added to the equation, whether that's when she's dancing or tinkering, having her favorite drink, or eating dinner. Those things all make her happy, but they make her extra happy when she does them with you."

"Fuck," I mutter as I pull my knees up and drop my head. Regret and loneliness have never hit me quite this hard. "I don't know how to make this right. I don't know if I can be the man she deserves."

"*You are.*"

My head snaps up when I find Celeste standing in the doorway of my kitchen. She sighs as she walks in and kneels by my side. "You used the tunnels," I murmur, not having the energy to truly be mad at her.

She nods. "You barricaded yourself inside your house, Lex. Your security measures kept us all out. You left me no choice."

I lean back and let my head drop against my kitchen counter. I should've known she'd come to find me. Celeste never gave up on me, not even in the years when she wasn't part of our lives. She's always supported me quietly, never asking for anything in return. "You had the choice to just leave me alone," I mutter, unwilling to face her when she's probably the only member of my family that truly understands what trauma can do to you, and I know she won't let me hide behind it.

"So did you," she says, crossing her legs as she sits on the floor with me. "After everything Zane and I went through, falling in love despite the rivalry between our families, only to be torn apart by lies and deception... after all of that, he and I were two broken people that loved each other fiercely, but neither of us could look past everything we'd put each other through, the damage we'd both done. When I was ready to give up, convinced we couldn't be happy together, *you* said something that stuck with me."

She reaches for my hand, and I hold on tightly, desperate for the lifeline she's handing me but unable to admit that I need help. "You said: *it's obvious that things aren't easy, but real love never is, is it? It's messy, and it's ugly at times, but it's always worth it.*"

I bite down on my lip, my throat tightening. "It's different." Zane and Celeste both deserved to be happy. They both needed each other. Neither of them could do without the other, but Raya... Raya can do better.

"Is she worth it?"

I nod. "She's worth everything. She *is* everything."

Celeste smiles knowingly. "Then be brave for her, Lex. Facing the past is tough, but it isn't as tough as facing the mistakes you made and the pain you caused as a result of it."

I squeeze her hand and take a shaky breath. "Celeste, I put a gun to my wife's head because I thought the worst of her when she's never given me any reason to doubt her. She accused me of punishing her for someone else's crimes, and she's right. That's exactly what I did, what I've done from the very start. I don't know if I have it in me to fully trust another person again, and while I love her with all I am, I'm not sure that's enough. Raya deserves better."

"Then *be* better, Lex. Never stop trying, never stop fighting. That's what marriage is — you keep doing your best, you keep improving and growing together. There's no end goal, you know? Marriage is all about the journey, the steps you take together to build a life unlike anything you could've had by yourself. That happiness you wish for her? It's not a tangible thing. There won't be one defining moment that you classify as *happiness*. It's little moments, accumulated over time. It's choosing each other, and knowing the person you chose to spend your life with will always fight for you, even when it's tough, even when the odds aren't in their favor. It's doing all you can, giving her all you have, and accepting that it's enough. Because, Lexington, whether or not you're enough for her isn't up to you to decide. You don't get to decide what Raya deserves, Lex. You don't get to make that choice for her."

I stare at my sister-in-law, her words hitting me hard. "I don't think I want to live in world where Raya isn't mine, but I can't subject her to the darkness that lives inside me. I want to be the man she thought I was, but I... I need help."

Celeste nods, deep understanding in her eyes. "I will always be there for you, Lex. I'll do whatever it takes to help you — we all will."

Sixty

Raya

"You okay?" Adam asks as we walk into the Windsor Motors building together. My heart squeezes tightly as I nod, my mind automatically drifting back to the countless times Lex has driven me to the office, the two of us kissing in the parking lot before work.

Everywhere I go, I'm reminded of him. It's in the little things — in how my favorite coffee now reminds me of him, how I can't speak to my mother without her asking about Lex. Even the prototype, something that's always just been Dad's and mine, now contains Windsor Motors components. In a matter of months, he's become so entrenched in my life that I'm no longer sure who I am without him. He left me forever changed, and I'm not sure it's for the better.

Amy looks up when I walk in, concern flickering through her eyes. Ever since she learned about my marriage to Lex, she hasn't been quite sure how to treat me. "You're back," she says, smiling tightly. "I'm glad you recovered from the flu. I always get it around this time, too."

I nod politely, feeling beyond guilty for calling in sick when the only part of my body that wasn't functioning well was my broken heart. I felt so bad that I worked from home as much as I could, but it still doesn't feel like enough.

"Raya."

My back goes rigid at the sound of his voice, and I bite down on my lip as I turn to face my husband. He smiles ruefully at the sight of me, dark circles underneath his eyes. Lex looks like he hasn't slept since the day I left, pure torment overtaking his expression.

My team falls silent, and I hesitate before gesturing toward his office. He nods, and I follow him, aware that we need to talk and unwilling to make a scene in public. It's enough that my team now realizes I didn't come in with Lex.

He turns around to face me the moment I close his office door behind me, his gaze roaming over my face hungrily, cataloging every inch of me. "I missed you so fucking much."

My heart skips a beat, and I look down, unsure how to reply. I missed him too but admitting that won't change a thing. I hesitate for a moment before reaching for the stack of documents in my bag. I stare at the papers and take a shaky breath before handing them to him.

"Please sign them," I tell him, my voice steady, devoid of emotion. "We'll file as soon as our three years are up."

His eyes widen as he takes in the divorce papers in his hands, and then he barks out a laugh. "Over my dead body, Raya." I watch in disbelief as he walks to his desk and grabs a lighter, looking me in the eye as the papers go up in flames. My jaw goes slack as he lets go of the stack just before the flames reach his fingers, the last remnants turning to ash before it hits the floor.

Lex walks up to me and places his index finger under my chin, making me face him. "I won't ever let you go, little fairy. I may not be worthy, and I may not be the person you want, but I'm *yours*, Raya Windsor. I'll be yours until the day I die, and not even you can change that."

His hand moves to cup my face, and my eyes flutter closed for a moment. "I won't let you control me," I warn him, my voice soft. "I won't let you track my every movement; won't let you treat me like I'm the one who betrayed you. I won't live my life in someone else's shadow, being punished for things I didn't do, things I'd never do."

I take a step back, out of his reach. "I want real love and unwavering trust. I want the kind of partnership where we have each other's back, where we're always the one person the other can count on. I've done everything in my power to earn that, and I deserve it, Lex. I deserve to be loved wholeheartedly, and I deserve a healthy amount of trust. I won't accept anything less, and it's clear you can't give me that. You never even tried, never gave me a real chance. From the moment we met, you've curated every significant moment we've shared, never letting me out of your sight for more than a few hours."

I draw a shaky breath and shake my head. "When we first discussed our engagement, I told you that once our three years were up, you'd have to let me go so I could find the kind of love you could never give me. You told me you'd try, but you never did. You just pretended to."

I run a hand through my hair, unable to take the look in his eyes. "I'm not what you want, Lex, and you can't be what I need." I look away, my chest aching. "The day we met, you told me you had no interest in love or relationships, and I just didn't listen. Or maybe I did, and I just thought I'd be your exception... but look at us now. You never wanted this with me, and I should've accepted that then. It would've saved us both a lot of pain."

"Raya," Lex says, but I hold my hand up, cutting him off. "Just think about what I said today, Lexington. I'm offering you an out — a guilt-free way to escape all the pressure I put on you to turn this marriage into something it was never meant to be, all without losing your inheritance or the merger. I'll start doing what you've done all along. I'll pretend with you."

He grabs my hand and holds on tightly. "Darling, I'm not

going to say the words now, because I don't want you to question them. I don't want you to feel like I'm only saying it in an attempt to control this situation, because nothing could be further from the truth. What I will say is that I don't need to try with you, Raya. Being with you is effortless, and it has been from the second we met. I see where you're coming from, and I hear you." He brushes my hair out of my face and takes a deep breath, his expression vulnerable. "Maybe you're right. Maybe I haven't been trying as much as I thought I was, but that changes now."

I search his face, unsure what to make of his words. I don't dare believe him, but God, I want to, and I hate my own weakness more than I could ever hate him. "I'll leave work with you at the end of the week," I say, my voice soft. "We'll go to my parents together as usual. Regardless of what's going on between us, I don't want to worry anyone else, least of all our families. After that, I'll move back home, and we'll figure out how to get through the remainder of our marriage. In the meantime, think about what I said. I'm willing to accept everything I wasn't willing to consider when we got engaged, Lex. I'm done."

Sixty-One

Lexington

Raya doesn't say a word to me as we drive to her parents' house. All week, I've done all I can to catch glimpses of her, and all week, she's done all she could to avoid me. It fucking hurts to know that the one person that was always happy to see me now can't stand to look at me, and I only have myself to blame for it.

"Truth or dare?" I murmur, at a loss.

She tenses and looks out the window, no doubt contemplating whether or not to indulge me. "Dare."

I suck my bottom lip between my teeth, unsure what to ask for. I don't want to coerce her into doing things she doesn't want to do, but I'm desperate to hold her hand the way I used to. I never realized how much I took it for granted. It always felt so simple, having her fingers between mine, the softness of her skin against my rougher hands. "Help me park the car," I say eventually, her parents' house right in front of us. She sighs and reaches for her seatbelt, but I shake my head. "Without moving from your seat."

She looks at me, and fuck, I think it may very well be the first time she's looked me in the eye all week. I forgot how enchanting those gorgeous brown eyes are, how hard it is to look away when she gives me her attention. Raya places her hand on top of mine as she moves the clutch, and I inhale shakily, savoring the feel of her soft fingers on top of mine.

I follow her instructions as she directs me from her seat, helping me park the car. I'm barely able to focus on anything but her touch, and the moment she pulls her hand away, a sense of loss washes over me.

I sigh as I lean over and undo her seatbelt, bringing our bodies closer than she's let me in some time. Raya's gaze cuts to mine, and I know she's reminded of the countless times I've done just this, only to grab her face and kiss her, losing myself in her scent, her honey flavor.

Her eyes roam over my face and settle on my mouth, something akin to longing flashing through her eyes before she turns away and opens her car door, depriving me of the honor of helping her.

"Wait," I tell her. "Let me, please."

I rush out of the car and around it, but she ignores me and steps out of the car moments before I reach her. The passenger door falls closed behind her, and I step closer to her. Raya steps back, the look in her eyes changing, that same longing reemerging. I smile at her as her back hits the car and lean in, caging her in with my body.

"Truth," I tell her. She didn't ask, but I'm not willing to give up on our game. It's what started it all, and throughout our relationship, it's what we've defaulted to when communicating felt hard.

Ask me if I miss you, I silently plead. *Ask me if I love you, Raya.*

She studies me and tilts her head just a touch, something akin to hope lighting up her eyes. "Are you still monitoring me?"

My heart drops, and I stare at her, wishing she'd asked me

anything but that. My breathing accelerates, and my throat feels dry all of a sudden.

"It's a simple question, Lexington."

"It isn't," I retort, unsure how else to explain.

"How is it not, when there are only two possible answers: yes or no?"

"Please, Raya," I whisper. "Let me explain. The answer is yes, but I'm not doing it intentionally. It's just... it's hard to undo."

I've never witnessed such deep disappointment in my wife's eyes, and she draws a shaky breath as she pushes against my chest, moving me out of the way. She walks to her parents' front door and looks over her shoulder.

"You told me you were sorry, Lex. There's only one apology I'm willing to accept: changed behavior. If you can't change, if you *won't* change, you need to sign the papers."

The front door opens just as I catch up to her, and her father appears. The way Raya smiles at him leaves me awestruck, and suddenly I find myself fearing I'll never see her smile at *me* that way again.

I watch as my wife all but skips through the house to get to her mother, and without a doubt, this is the happiest I've seen her in a while. Celeste's words ring through my mind as if on cue, reminding me that happiness isn't a single moment, that with enough time, I could earn Raya's smiles again.

"Come on," Bob says as he places his hand on my shoulder. "Why don't you come help me with my temperamental Annie? That car takes after its namesake — it's consistently difficult, unpredictable."

I take another look at the kitchen, where I can hear Raya's laughter coming from, longing hitting me hard and fast. "Of course," I tell my father-in-law, when I want nothing more than to stand by my wife's side, pretending I'm the reason for that sweet laughter, like I used to be.

Bob and I work quietly for a while, but unlike the usual

serene atmosphere between us, the tension is thick today. "It won't last, you know," he says eventually.

I look up, my stomach turning. Bob reads my expression and laughs, shaking his head.

"Her *anger*," he elaborates. "Raya never stays mad for long. She doesn't have it in her. There's no malice in my sweet little girl's heart."

"Is it obvious?" I ask, my voice soft. "That we're... arguing?"

Bob leans against the car and smiles. "Lexington, you're walking around looking like a sad puppy. It's hard not to notice."

I run a hand through my hair and look away. My father-in-law seems to take great delight in my torment, because he laughs and pushes off the car. I watch as he grabs a bottle of whiskey from one of his cupboards and pours us both a glass. "Tinkering clearly isn't helping you today, so let's try this."

I knock it back, and Bob instantly refills my glass, not an ounce of judgement in his eyes. "I think I lost her," I admit eventually.

He swirls his whiskey and nods slowly. "Then win her back." He looks at me then. "Marriage isn't a box you get to check. Your status as my daughter's husband is something you have to earn, every single day. It isn't a position you can take for granted, Lexington."

I look at him, my heart bleeding. "I know," I tell him, my voice soft. "God, I know."

He places his hand on my arm and smiles with a lot more kindness than I'd expect from him in this situation. "A few months ago, I told you that what Raya wants above all is true love. You told me you weren't sure you could give her that, but that you'd try. Tell me, Lexington. Did you try?"

Pure sorrow rushes through me as I shake my head. "No," I whisper. "I never had to try with her, Bob. I fell for Raya against my will, against reason. Irrevocably. Unexpectedly."

Falling in love was the easy part. It's trust I can't give her.

Bob smiles at me. "I'm not sure what happened, and I have no intention of meddling in your marriage, but I have to ask... regardless of what happened, did you have any intention of hurting her, Lex?"

"No," I reply immediately. "But that doesn't change the fact that I did."

Bob takes a swig of his whiskey. "Did you learn from it?"

I nod, willing him to believe me.

My father-in-law smiles at me. "And will you ever let it happen again?"

"Never," I vow.

Bob nods. "Then you'll be just fine, Lexington. Things will never be perfect, but so long as you try to be a little better every day, you'll get as close to it as you can get. No one could ask more of you than that. Not even me."

Sixty-Two

Lexington

Raya glances at me from the mirror she's standing in front of as I walk out of her bathroom, a towel hanging low on my hips. The way her eyes linger sends a thrill down my spine, and I take a shaky breath as I walk toward her.

"Let me help you," I murmur as I take her hairbrush from her. She doesn't fight me as I begin to comb her hair for her, taking my time pulling the brush through my wife's long silky hair. I bite down on my lip as I grab a few strands, loving the way it feels against my skin.

Raya inhales sharply, and I instantly wonder if she's reminded of the countless times I've taken hold of her hair and pulled her close. I sigh as I let it slip through my fingers and lean in, pressing a kiss to her shoulder. Her breath hitches, and my heart skips a beat.

At least this hasn't changed — she still responds to me the way she always has. Now she just wishes she wouldn't. "I miss you," I whisper, even though she's right here with me.

Her eyes fall closed when I kiss her neck, and the edges of my lips tug up as I move them just below her ear, to that spot that makes her shiver. Her head falls back, exposing more of her skin, and I eagerly kiss her jaw, my hand carefully sliding around her waist, until I've got my palm pressed to her stomach, her body against mine. She inhales shakily when I wrap my free hand around her jaw and tilt her face, my lips brushing against hers once, twice, before sweeping in and taking what's still mine.

My thumb brushes over her chin, and I part her lips, deepening our kiss. It's been so long since I've had her like this, since she's let me so close. Her body shifts against mine just a touch, her hips moving in that needy way I love so much.

I tense when she moves away just a little, our eyes locking. "Please," I whisper, unsure what it is I'm begging for. Another kiss, her love, forgiveness — all of it.

Raya turns around, her chest brushing against mine, and I groan when she reaches for me, cupping my face. It's been so long since she touched me like that, so tenderly, so sweetly. I'm breathing hard, desperate for the tiniest shred of her affection, acutely aware that I don't deserve it.

My heart skips a beat when my wife rises to her tiptoes and kisses me, her hand slipping around the back of my neck. Her tongue brushes against mine, and I wrap one hand around her waist as the other slides into her hair, my touch desperate. She has no idea how much I've craved her presence, how empty my life was while she was gone.

"I hate how much I still want you," she whispers against my mouth, and I tighten my grip on her hair, my heart soaring. I'll take her hatred if that's all she's willing to give me — I'll take that over indifference and absence any day.

Raya pushes against my chest, and I blink in surprise as I step back, only for her to step closer, walking me back toward her bed until I stumble and fall backwards. My wife places her knee between my legs, her gaze roaming down my chest and abs as I hold myself up on my elbows. "I hate what you've done to me, Lexington. I hate that I let you."

Raya's expression conveys her hurt, and it fucking kills me to know I'm the reason her eyes aren't shimmering with light and happiness, like they did before me. My eyes fall closed, and I inhale shakily as I try to breathe through the pain in my chest.

I bite down on my lip harshly as she straddles me, her silky nightgown riding up and settling around her waist. She makes herself comfortable on top of me, fucking torturing me with the way she nestles my cock between her thighs, my towel wedged between us. Raya places her hand just above it, the heat of her palm seeping into my cold skin.

I move my hands to her hips, but she shakes her head and grabs them. Raya leans over me and pins my hands above my head, her eyes flashing. "Keep them there," she orders. "You don't get to touch me unless I tell you to, Lexington. Not anymore."

I suck my lip in between my teeth as I do as I'm told, keeping my hands where she put them even as she lets go and straightens. Her fingertips trail over my chest and down my abs. My head falls back as my entire body responds to the way she caresses me, my abs contracting involuntarily.

"Why did you do it?" she asks, her voice breaking. "Why did you make me fall for you, Lex? Why pretend to try with me when you never had any intention of giving our marriage a real chance?"

"Look at me," I whisper. "Do I look like a man that's pretending to be anything but yours? Place your hand over my chest and feel how my heart beats for you, Raya."

Our eyes lock as she slides her hand up, my heart pounding wildly underneath my palm. "I fucking wish I could've controlled my feelings for you. I wish this was all pretense, that the mere thought of you no longer being mine didn't hurt as much as it does." She draws a shaky breath as she reads the emotion in my eyes, the vulnerability that I can't hide. "From the moment we met, my carefully constructed life began to collapse, brick by brick. You took each discarded, useless piece of me, and you built me back up, Raya. You made me want to live again, made me want to become the person you thought I was, and fuck, if you're willing to give me a chance, I'll show you that I can be."

Her eyes fill with hope and tears, and she looks away. "You're not the only one who's had time to think in the last couple of days, little fairy," I whisper. "You told me that I can't be what you need, and maybe you're right, but I'm willing to spend the rest of my life proving you wrong."

I watch as a tear runs down her cheek, and I reach for her, only just about catching myself in time. I curl my fingers into a fist and pull my hand away, respecting her wishes not to be touched without her say so.

"Will you let me fight for you?" I ask, my voice breaking. "Will you give me a chance to earn your forgiveness, Raya? One chance to show you I can be the husband you've always wanted."

She looks at me with so much love and longing that hope soars in my chest, and I stare at her as she contemplates my words.

"One month. Please, give me one month to show you I can change, that I can be the one for you. I'm begging you, Raya. Please, just give me one more chance."

She bites down on her lip, another tear running down her face as she nods just slightly. "I don't want to," she murmurs, and my heart sinks. "I don't want you to hurt me more than you already have, but I'll always regret it if I walk away now." She spreads her fingers across my abs, and I draw a shaky breath. "One chance," she whispers. "Just one."

I nod, silently swearing I won't let her down again.

Sixty-Three

Lexington

"Lola missed you," I tell Raya as we walk into the house. Everything felt different without her. Empty. Lonely. Even the robots could tell. "She's been wanting to show you the cookie recipe she created for you."

My wife stares at me wide-eyed, some of the frost in her eyes melting. "You're finally calling her Lola?"

I nod hesitantly just as the robot in question wheels herself into the living room. "*Mrs. Windsor,*" she says, her face moving from a neutral emoji into a happy one.

"Lola!" Raya shouts, her arms wrapping around the robot.

I frown as the robot's face turns into an emoji with heart-eyes, jealousy unfurling in my stomach. "That's quite enough," I murmur, glaring at Lola. I've been craving one of Raya's hugs more than she'll ever know, and here she is, hugging that damn robot.

Raya turns toward me, and I raise a brow when Lola's face turns into a smug emoji. Raya follows my gaze, but Lola changes her emoji into a neutral one just in time. I stare in complete fucking shock as my own robot taunts me. Unbelievable.

My wife smiles sweetly as she places her hand on my arm, her eyes twinkling with amusement, like she understands what just happened. It's been so long since I last saw her look at me that way, and I sigh, staring at her. I missed this — that bond where I don't even have to say a word for her to understand what I'm thinking. "Thank you," I whisper. "For coming home to me. I hope you know I don't take it for granted. What I did... it was unforgivable, and it means everything to me that you're here with me now."

She reaches for me, and my eyes fall closed when she cups my cheek. I place my hand over hers and take a deep breath, wishing I could just stay here with her and revel in her touch instead of doing the right thing. "Come with me," I murmur, entwining our fingers.

Raya follows me quietly, her entire body tensing when we walk into my security room — the one I hid from her until Sierra went missing. Her expression hardens, and I shoot her a pleading look when she pulls her hand out of mine.

"You told me you don't want to be monitored, so let's get rid of this room altogether. I unplugged everything. I'd planned to empty the room before you got back home, but I wanted you to be involved in the process, so you don't think I'm just moving it all to a different location behind your back. I wanted you to have the option to destroy it all."

Raya looks into my eyes, clearly trying to assess my sincerity. "You'd let me destroy what appears to be hundreds of thousands of dollars' worth of equipment?"

I smile and reach for her, my heart clenching painfully as I gently push her hair out of her face. "You can do with it whatever you want. Let's turn this room into whatever you want it to be. Maybe an office just for you? Or a guest room for your parents?"

She raises a brow, disbelief flickering through her eyes. "You mean it?"

I nod. "Nothing is more important to me than you, Raya. I trust Silas Sinclair with our personal security, and though it won't be easy for me to let go of my own security protocols, I will. For you, I will."

She seems skeptical, and I bite down on my lip before handing her a flash drive I prepared for her. "Here," I tell her. "This contains everything you need to access my systems. Take a look at it, and you'll find that I've changed all my security measures, so even if you were to plug this all back in, I don't personally have access to anything anymore. I've conceded all my access to Sinclair Security. I need to know that you're safe and protected, but I won't track or control you in any way. Not ever again. I'll trust you, the way I always should have."

Raya's fingers closed around the flash drive, and she nods as she stares at it. "I *will* check," she warns me.

"I want you to," I tell her honestly. "I won't let you down again, Raya. For so long, I was stuck in this mindset where I felt like it'd be safer to expect the worst, because that way, no one could ever betray me again. It's hard to explain, and I know it doesn't necessarily make sense to anyone but me, but it was how I coped with what had happened." I draw a shaky breath, my stomach twisting.

"The day you left is the day I went back to therapy, little fairy. I asked for Celeste's support, and she's been driving me there to ensure I won't miss an appointment. I never should've stopped going, and I won't give up on it this time. I'll keep going every week until I'm better."

She nods, quietly studying me, a hint of disbelief still in her expression, only for her eyes to widen when I slowly kneel in front of her, both of my knees hitting the floor. "I am sorry, Raya. More than you'll ever know, more than words can convey." I grab her hand, my eyes settling on her wedding ring. My stomach turns as I look back at her, knowing what I have to do. She'll hate me for the rest of our lives, but I can't keep this from her. I bite down on my lip harshly as I slide the thin golden band off her finger, deep regret holding me in its clutches.

"W-what are you doing?" she asks, her entire body going rigid, her voice trembling.

I take her ring off and wrap my fingers around her ring, clenching tightly. "Please forgive me," I whisper, my voice breaking. I look into her eyes, my breathing shallow, my heart in my throat. "It was just the one thing I figured you'd always have on you."

Understanding flickers in her eyes, followed by pain. "You put a tracker in my wedding ring?" she asks, taking a step back.

Her eyes fill with tears, her expression conveying her heartache. My eyes fall closed, and I take a shaky breath. "I'm so sorry, Raya. I'll make it right, I swear."

"How could you?" Her voice breaks, and I look up. One lone tear runs down her cheek, and my heart twists painfully.

"I'm sorry," I repeat, over and over again. "I'm so sorry, Raya. I couldn't... I had to tell you, had to fix this. I promised you I'd do better, that I'd try... please, baby. I'll do everything in my power to make this right. Please believe me."

She shakes her head, choking back a sob. "I can't do this," she whispers, taking another step back.

Sixty-Four

LEXINGTON

I pace back and forth at the front door nervously, my eyes on my grandfather's watch. Raya refused to talk to me after finding out what I'd done to her wedding ring, and I can't even blame her for it. I took something that should've been sacred and turned it into a tool to control her with.

I run a hand through my hair and sigh, my heart aching. I couldn't keep it from her, but admitting what I'd done was one of the hardest things I've ever had to do. It killed me to look into her eyes and know that my words were about to drive us further apart than ever before.

Raya pauses in the hallway, her expression turning frosty when she spots me. "You're still here," she says, sounding displeased. "I thought you'd left for work already. Don't you have a meeting in ten minutes?"

I shrug. "It can wait." Nothing is more important than my wife. I'm honestly only going into the office because she is.

Raya frowns when I hold up my car keys. "I was wondering if you'd be willing to drive me to work."

Her lips part in surprise, eagerness flashing through her gorgeous brown eyes when she realizes which car this key unlocks. "You'd let me drive your priceless, highly coveted Annie? The car you inherited from your father? The one your grandfather *built*?"

I smile at her. "Darling, I'd let you wreck it if it'd put a smile on your face." Her eyes flash like she's willing to test me on that as she takes the key from me, but my smile doesn't waver. If she did wreck it, I'm sure both my father and grandfather would understand. If they're looking down at us from above, they're probably silently encouraging her to.

Raya keeps glancing at me as she gets behind the wheel, like she expects me to change my mind at any second, but I merely lean over her and reach for her seatbelt, my gaze settling on her lips for a moment. There's nothing I wouldn't do for one single kiss. She hasn't touched me since that night at her parents' house, and I know even that was a moment of weakness for her. Forget my car — I'd hand over my entire fortune if she'd just look at me the way she used to.

Our eyes lock, and she inhales shakily as I buckle her in, a soft click breaking the spell between us. "I didn't think you'd ever let me drive you at all, and certainly not in this car."

"I told you I'd do my best to change," I murmur. "It may seem silly, but something like this is tough for me. I'm used to always being in control, being behind the wheel. I thought that today I'd try to concede control for once, to *you*. Not monitoring you isn't enough, Raya. I truly want to be the man you deserve, so this is me taking a small step toward that, toward normalcy."

She glances at me as she drives us out of the Windsor Estate, the large iron gates closing behind us. "Thank you," she murmurs. "I know this isn't easy for you." Her gaze drops to her empty ring finger. "Thank you for yesterday, too. I'd never have found out if you hadn't told me, Lex. I appreciate that you did, even if it hurt us both."

I hum, unsure how to respond, and she smiles as she places her hand on my thigh. My heart instantly begins to race and my gaze cuts to her face, but her eyes are on the road. I watch my wife as she drives us both to work, and all the while, I count my lucky stars. She didn't have to give me another chance, not after what I did, and I'll never take this opportunity for granted. I won't waste it.

Raya lets me help her out of the car instead of rushing out before I have a chance to open the door for her, like she has been doing lately. I can't help but smile as I hesitantly offer her my hand, trying my luck. She looks into my eyes and smiles as she places her hand in mine, and I wonder if she knows what that does to me.

I entwine our fingers as we step into the elevator together, enjoying every second of it. My heart sinks when we reach my office, and I tighten my grip on her hand as she moves toward the door. She looks back at me with a knowing look on her face, her arm extended toward me, my fingers between hers. I'm tempted to beg her not to go, to let me hold on to her a little longer, but instead I sigh and loosen my grip on her.

"Have a wonderful day today, little fairy," I murmur as she heads to my door.

She looks over her shoulder, and my heart skips a beat. "You too, Lex."

I watch as she walks away and run a hand through my hair, feeling lost. Pippy's voice sounds overhead, reminding me of my meeting, and I reluctantly head to my conference room, wishing I could just linger around my wife instead.

I can't focus on a thing as I listen to my employees giving me an update on the new car we're unveiling next quarter. The things I used to live for now mean nothing, and I blame Raya for it. She gave me real purpose, and everything else pales in comparison to her.

"Right," I murmur, the second the meeting wraps up. "Wonderful work." I have no idea what anyone said, and I don't care. I just want to go see my wife. Everyone looks startled when I rise from my seat, and I belatedly realize the meeting was, in fact, far from over. Oh well.

Susan scrambles to take over from me as I walk out, ignoring all the shocked expressions behind me. My heart pounds loudly as I head over to Raya's department, only to pause a few paces away. She is smiling up at Adam in that way I love, and he's holding her hand, his thumb brushing over her empty finger. Pain and possessiveness mingle, turning into a vicious monster I can't ignore.

"*Raya,*" I say, my tone sharp. "A word, please?"

Her eyes widen, and she pulls her hand out of Adam's, her head snapping up to meet my gaze. She looks surprised to see me, clearly expecting me to still be at my meeting.

She rises from her seat and follows me to my office, and with every step I take, my heart aches more. We never discussed it, but I know she went to him when she left me. Did something happen then? Did she realize there was already someone who could love her the way she thinks I can't? The way she just smiled at him... fuck.

My office door closes behind her, and I turn to face her, my heart in my throat. What right do I even have to question her, to be upset?

"Was there something you needed?" she asks, her voice soft.

You.

Always you.

I stare at her and shake my head. "No. I'm sorry, Raya. I didn't mean to interrupt your workday like that. I apologize."

My heart is fucking bleeding as I look at my wife, wondering if she's falling out of love with me while I'm trying to hold on to her with all my might.

"I'm sorry," I repeat, wishing she could understand the depth of my regret. She is everything anyone could've ever wanted, and standing here with her, knowing she used to be mine... *fuck.*

"I know you are," she says, taking a step toward me, and then another. My breath hitches when she cups my face, her eyes on mine. Her gaze is searching, but there's understanding in it too.

Raya tilts her face, and then she rises to her tiptoes, her lips brushing against mine softly, once, twice, and then she kisses me. I groan, my hand instantly wrapping into her hair, my entire body reacting. My wife melts into me, and *fuck*, I've missed this. That honey taste, her soft curves, and the way she makes me feel so fucking *alive*.

We're both breathing hard by the time she pulls back, and I struggle to loosen my grip on her. "I'm still yours," she whispers, before leaning in and kissing the edge of my mouth. "Even when it hurts, even when it's tough."

My forehead drops to hers, and I swallow hard, overwhelmed by my feelings for her. No one knows me like she does, no one understands my needs without me having to say a word. No one but her.

"Let me take you somewhere tomorrow. There's something I want to say, but not here, not like this."

Her gaze roams over my face, and then she nods. Relief washes over me as she throws me the sweetest smile. Does she know there's nothing I won't do to earn more of those smiles?

Sixty-Five

RAYA

"Where are we going?" I ask as Lex parks in front of the hangar. He holds my hand tightly as we walk to his helicopter together, his expression different from usual. He seems nervous, and it's so unlike him that I'm not sure what to make of it.

Lex is never nervous, no matter what the stakes are. He seems to always be calculating the odds of a scenario playing out a certain way, and nothing ever rattles him because of it. If he's this nervous, it must be because he's found himself in a situation with too many factors he can't control.

"You'll see," he murmurs, strapping me in the way he did when he took me gliding. It seems like a lifetime ago, and so much has happened and changed since then. I'd felt so hopeful back then, and something about tonight fills me with that same feeling.

Last time, I watched the view, but this time, I can't tear my eyes off my husband. He's wearing black slacks with a white shirt, the sleeves rolled up to expose his forearms. Lexington is sexy in everyday life, but right now, when he's in his element? Irresistible.

He promised me he'd change, and it's clear he's genuinely

trying in a way he never did before. The difference in his behavior is stark — he wears his remorse on his sleeve, not letting his pride get in the way of saving our marriage. I just wonder if it's enough, if it'll last. It's easier to modify behavior for a single purpose, in this case, in order to make amends. Will it last when he's achieved his goal?

The sun begins to set all around us, and I look around wide-eyed as Lex lands his helicopter on top of the tallest building in town — a Windsor owned commercial building, with a rooftop bar at the top. He smiles as he reaches for me, his hands wrapping around my waist as he lifts me out like I don't weigh a thing.

"Wow," I whisper, my gaze roaming over the golden shades around us as the sun sets. The bar is empty, most of it cleared to allow Lex's helicopter to land. The roof is filled with soft fairy lights, and yellow flowers of all kinds, a soft breeze making my hair dance. "Beautiful."

"Yeah," Lex sighs, and I look up to find him staring at me, seemingly mesmerized. Heat rushes to my cheeks, and I look away, flustered.

Just like on our very first date, he moves so we're standing side by side, watching the view. "It's still true, you know? Maybe even more so now than then."

"What is?"

He reaches for me, his touch hesitant as he places his index finger underneath my chin. "Your eyes still keep me more captivated than anything else ever could, and I'm still very much under your spell."

He remembers.

Lex offers me his hand, and I raise a brow as I take it. "Raya, if I dared you to dance with me, would you?"

I nod, unable to deny him when he looks at me like it'd devastate him if I said no. The sound of a violin has me looking over my shoulder, my eyes widening when I notice a string quartet standing in the corner, playing live music for us.

I bite down on my lip, my heart racing. I can't believe he did this for me. The fairy lights, the hundreds of flowers everywhere, and the setting sun… this is beyond romantic, and I can't quite tell what he's thinking. He still seems every bit as nervous as he was before.

Lex pulls me close as we fall into step together, the two of us dancing the same amended version of the foxtrot as that night, the one I've come to consider ours. "I've given you a dare, so let me give you a truth too. I've always loved seeing the city in this beautiful golden shade," he murmurs, the two of us dancing across the rooftop. "But nothing beats the way the setting sun caresses your face, the way it makes your hair look a couple of shades lighter, and the way it brings out your eyes, turning them into molten gold."

My gaze roams over his face, and I try my hardest to read him, to no avail. "That's not how the game works," I tell him, my tone teasing.

Lex twirls me around, my yellow dress swaying. "No?" he replies, his eyes on mine. "Then ask me, Raya."

"Truth or dare?"

"Dare."

My heart skips a beat as my arms slide around his neck. "Lift me up the way I like," I murmur, my gaze roaming over his arms. I grin at him as I raise a brow teasingly. "You look like you could actually do it."

He chuckles and places his hands on my waist, his eyes twinkling as he lifts me up above his head effortlessly, slowly turning me around, the biggest smile on his face. His expression shifts into something akin to wonder, and he slowly lowers me back down, holding me against his body, his arms wrapped around the back of my thighs. He looks up at me, his gaze tormented.

"Why did you bring me here?" I ask, my hands on his shoulders.

He gently lowers me to the floor, our arms still wrapped around each other. "To answer a question you asked me once."

I raise a brow, and he draws a shaky breath. "Remember when

I took you gliding and told you that I wanted to share the things I love with you? You asked me what I loved most of all, and I didn't have the courage to tell you the truth."

My heart begins to pound erratically, and he cups my face, our eyes locked. "I love you, Raya. More than anything — more than flying, more than breathing. I love you with every fiber of my being, with all I am, all I'll ever be."

My eyes widen, and he smiles ruefully. "I'm sorry it took me so long to admit it, to give you what you need. I know it's not enough, that it's too little, too late —"

I rise to my tiptoes and cut him off, my lips finding his. Lex freezes for a split second, and then he's kissing me back, instrumental music all around us and the stars above us. He pulls me close, his touch filled with desperation, like he's scared this moment will disappear if he lets go.

I tilt my head, and he parts my lips, kissing me in the way I've been craving. I've missed him more than I realized, more than I care to admit. Lex groans as he deepens our kiss, and my hand slides through his hair, my touch needy. "I love you," he whispers in between kisses, over and over again, until his forehead drops against mine, both of us panting. "I love you, little fairy."

I pull away a little to look at him, my hand on the side of his face. "I love you too," I whisper, my heart aching. "I think I always will, but Lex... love isn't the problem between us."

Sixty-Six

Raya

I raise a brow in surprise when I walk into the house on a Thursday afternoon to find the scent of my mother's lamb biryani permeating the air. I head into the kitchen and find Lex standing behind the stove, his hair a mess and the sleeves of his shirt rolled up.

"I don't need your help, Lola," he says, sounding frustrated. "I just need saffron."

Lola wheels through the kitchen and shakes her head, seemingly insistent on helping nonetheless. "I don't think we have saffron, Lex," she says, sounding oddly sad.

He sighs. "My mother-in-law said she doesn't always use it, but that it's nicer with it. What do I do? I just want this to be perfect."

I smile to myself, my heart warming. It's been three weeks since he asked me for a chance, and every single day, Lex has done what he told me he would — he's done all he can to be the best husband he can be, to trust me even when it isn't easy, and to relinquish the control he's always held onto so tightly. He handed over all his security measures to Silas, making it impossible for him to monitor me himself, and when we go to my parents' house, he no longer brings extra security, even though doing so still triggers nightmares at times.

And then there are the little things. He cooks for me most evenings, and he makes me coffee at the office every morning. Once a week, new flowers appear on my desk, and Celeste told me he spends hours choosing and binding them every time. Each bouquet is yellow, and each time, the accent flowers change. So far, he's given me yellow peonies for new beginnings, sunflowers for lasting happiness, and yellow tulips to symbolize hope. He never told me what the flowers meant, and had Celeste not deciphered their meaning for me, I'd never known.

"I'm sure it *is* perfect."

He whirls around, his silicone spoon dropping to the floor, making a mess. "Raya." He looks shocked to see me and glances at his watch, clearly not having expected me. He no longer tracks my movements, and it still throws him off to not always be aware of where I am. Every time I catch him by surprise, there's a hint of discomfort in his eyes, but genuine delight always wins out shortly after.

I bite back a smile as I walk up to him. His gaze roams over my body hungrily, like he can't help but commit every inch of me to memory. The way he looks at me drives the butterflies in my stomach wild. It's different these days — he looks at me like I'm his whole world, like he'd do anything for a chance to be near me.

Lex reaches for me as soon as I'm within reach, lifting me on top of the counter as Lola cleans the mess he made on the floor. "I wanted to surprise you," he says, parting my legs to stand between them, his hands on my waist. "Do you remember when you told me that your mom's lamb biryani is your favorite dish? She taught me how to make it for you. I'm not sure it's any good though. I tried to make it exactly how she taught me, but I forgot to add saffron."

Lex's breath hitches when I slide my hand around the back of his neck. "Biryani takes hours to make. How long have you been in the kitchen?"

He shrugs. "It's fine. I took the day off for it. Besides, I spent a few hours in my lab this morning, so it's not like I've been standing in the kitchen all day."

He's been doing that a lot lately — disappearing for hours every day to work on a project he won't tell anyone but my father about. It's got the entire company in uproar, and he doesn't even realize it. I was told that each time he disappears to work on something in private, he comes back with a new revolutionary car that ends up making Windsor Motors a fortune. Every day, more articles written by industry experts appear, all of them attempting to guess which features Lex might put in his new car, and when the release date might be. All the while, he seems blissfully unaware of all the rumors as he works on his new car with Dad.

"Can I have a bite?" I ask, and he smiles sweetly as he reaches for a spoon. Our eyes lock as he feeds me a spoonful of the best biryani I've ever had, and I groan in delight.

"You like it?" he asks, his whole face lighting up.

"Told you," I murmur, grinning. "I knew it'd be perfect."

Lex grins as he puts the spoon down on the counter and places his hands on either side of my hips. "I'm so glad you like it. Now I just need to find a way to make you the perfect cup of masala tea. I don't really know what the deal is with that, you know? I've tried it countless times, but it never tastes like your mom's. Maybe I should just build a tea machine that can perfectly replicate hers, because every single cup I make just tastes different. There's no consistency at all, and I can't figure out what's going wrong."

I smile at my husband, my heart beating loudly as I cup his face and lean in to kiss him. Lex freezes for a moment, and then he's kissing me back, his touch slow, filled with intention. His hands move to my hips, and he holds on tightly as he pulls me to the edge of the counter, until our bodies are flush.

The way he wants me is so empowering, so reassuring. "Raya," he whispers against my lips. "I love you."

I inhale shakily as the words wash over me, soothing my soul as I pull away a little to look at him. I've never seen my husband look so tormented, so pained. His breath hitches when I grab his shirt, our eyes locking as I undo the top button, and then another, until his shirt falls open.

"Again," I whisper. "Tell me you love me again."

He cups my face, drinking me in. "I love you, Raya Indira Windsor."

My heart soars at the words, and I smile involuntarily, leaning in for another kiss. Lex buries a hand in my hair the moment my lips meet his, his touch tinged with desperation. "I love you," he whispers in between kisses, over and over again, mending my broken heart.

He groans against my mouth when I push his shirt down his arms, his lips never leaving mine as he shrugs out of it. My husband waits for my next move patiently, never asking for more than I'm willing to give, but he moans in delight when I undo the button on his trousers.

He pulls away to look at me, making a soft, needy sound when I grab his hand and place it on my bare thigh, underneath my skirt. Lex bites down on his lip, our eyes locked as he slides it between my legs. He groans when he realizes I'm wet, and he looks at me like he can't quite believe I still want him. Lex pushes my panties aside, and his head falls back as his eyes fall closed for a moment, a possessive smile on his face. "Fuck, you're so wet for me, baby."

He slides his fingers over me, his eyes on mine as he teases me. I moan when he slips two fingers inside me, my hips moving involuntarily. It's been so long, and I want him more than I care to admit. "Please," I whisper.

He nods and wraps his free hand in my hair, keeping my eyes on his. "There's nothing I wouldn't do for you, you know that?"

he whispers, his thumb caressing me in that way I like. "Nothing I won't do to make you smile, to keep you looking at me this way."

My hips begin to move against his fingers, and his expression shifts. "Show me my favorite sight," he pleads, curling his fingers inside me. "Please, Raya. I need to see you come for me."

He watches me as I slowly unravel for him, our eyes locked as my muscles begin to contract. "That's it," he whispers, looking enchanted. "Come for your husband, little fairy." I moan his name, and it feels more intimate this time. I feel more vulnerable. My heightened emotions just make it an even better experience than ever before.

Lex slowly pulls his fingers out of me, his eyes widening when I lock my legs around his hips and pull him closer. He looks at me with a hint of insecurity, and I smile as I reach for him, my hand sliding into his trousers to wrap around his cock. "I want you," I whisper. "I've missed you."

He inhales shakily as he lines himself up and pushes just the tip in before grabbing my face, his gaze roaming over me. "I miss you too, baby. Every second of every day."

Lex pushes into me slowly, his eyes never leaving mine as he takes me, pushing inch after inch into me. He looks tormented, like he's desperate for me, but he takes it slow nonetheless, like he wants to savor the moment, commit it to memory.

"I want this with you forever," he whispers, grabbing my hips. "I will always be yours, Raya." He pulls out almost all the way, only to thrust back into me, our eyes locked. "Forever and always. I will love you for as long as my heart beats, and longer still."

I moan as he takes me slowly, his eyes never leaving mine as he continues to tell me that he loves me, over and over again, his touch as filled with desperation as his words are.

Sixty-Seven

Lexington

I stare at the date on my watch, my heart heavy. Four weeks seemed like a lot of time, but in the end, it flew by. I tried so hard to be the husband Raya deserves, only to realize that I can't be. My best isn't enough — it never will be. Not for something as incredible as my wife.

"Is everything okay?"

I look up to find my little fairy standing in the doorway to our living room, her gaze filled with concern. She's so fucking precious, and fuck, there's no way I could ever be what she needs. We both know it.

"Yeah," I murmur, my heart aching more with each beat. I offer her my hand, and she takes it with a smile. "There's something I want to show you."

Raya nods and entwines our fingers. She smiles at me in that way I love, and bitterness unfurls in my stomach. That's probably what I'll miss most — the intimacy between us. Her sweet smiles, the way she laughs at my silly jokes, and the way she sighs just before I kiss her.

It kills me to know someone else will find out that her feet are ticklish, and that she likes honey in her coffee but ginger in her tea. Another man will learn that running a finger down her spine makes her shiver, and that she hates mornings but loves sunsets.

He'll have everything that used to be mine. My wife's long hair brushing against his face in the morning, and his old college t-shirts covering her body. Her little whimpers when she doesn't want to wake up just yet.

I tighten my grip on her hand as I lead her to our garage, my chest hollow. She'll take my heart with her when she leaves, and I almost wish I never knew what it's like to be hers, to be loved.

Raya gasps when she spots the yellow supercar I spent the last few weeks building, her name in small metal letters on the back. "I named it after you," I murmur. "It's fully solar powered, thanks to your dad's generosity. He let me apply some of his ideas to this car for you, turning it into the first-ever solar supercar to ever exist. It's thoroughly tested, but it isn't a commercial vehicle."

"Wow," she whispers. Her eyes sparkle with such pride, and fuck if it doesn't humble me. No one has ever believed in me the way she does, supported me quietly and without question. "This is incredible, Lex. I can't believe you named it after *me*."

"How could I not, when it's your car?" I smile as I hold up the key, the handle shaped like a heart, the initials RW on it. Even the key is bespoke, but it's the only hint of the Windsor name I've put on any aspect of the car.

She stares at me in disbelief. "You're joking."

I shake my head and gently cup her face, my throat tight. "All yours," I murmur. *The car. My heart. All of it.*

Raya grins as she takes the keys from me, her eyes filled with reverence as she walks around it, assessing every last detail with wonder. She's lavish with her praise, seemingly genuinely delighted by my gift.

"I hope you smile like that every time you drive it," I murmur as she strokes the hood of the car with her fingers. "I hope it'll make you think of me every once in a while."

Her gaze snaps to mine, and she raises a brow, but she doesn't say anything as she opens the door. "Join me," she says, her voice softer now.

I nod and sit down in the passenger seat, my heart bleeding. Raya's eyes roam over the interior, and all the while, I just watch her. "What's this?" she asks, her finger tracing the small button with a Psi logo on it.

"It's a direct line to Silas Sinclair. If you're ever in trouble, press that. It'll alert him, and it'll have the full force of both his and the Windsors' private security rushing toward you to ensure your safety, no matter where you might be." I hesitate then, looking away. "I won't be notified. It's not a way to track you, and though this car is tied into our security measures just like all our other vehicles are, I don't have access to the data. The button is just a safety measure."

She nods, her expression unreadable. The way she's looking at me is new, a mixture of understanding and wonder, all at once.

Raya's hand trembles as she gently touches the button shaped like a fairy's wings. "What does this do?"

My heart begins to race, and I turn to face her, our eyes locking. "It'll bring you back to me...whenever you want, no matter where I might be. In the event I'm not in the country, it'll take you back to this exact location, allowing you to bypass any security measures. The button itself is keyed to your thumb, so it wouldn't work for anyone but you. I want you to know that you'll always have every right to me. I'll always be yours. I'll always be waiting."

My wife studies me, and then she presses the button. "Little Fairy Protocol activated," Pippy says. "I am locating Lexington Windsor now, Raya," she adds, starting the car. "As soon as his location has been pinpointed, I will drive you to him. Please sit back and wear your seatbelt."

"She called me Raya. Not Mrs. Windsor."

I nod as I glance at her empty ring finger. "Yeah, I fixed that for you."

"Lexington Windsor appears to be with you, Raya. As such, I cannot drive you to him. I do apologize. Deactivating Little Fairy Protocol."

I grab her hand and sigh, my thumb brushing over where her ring used to be. "This car contains all the research and materials you'll need to revolutionize the industry, to make all your wildest dreams come true. You don't need me for any of it, Raya. I won't use my company, my knowledge, or even my money to control you, to forcibly keep you by my side. It's not what I want. Not anymore."

"Lex," she whispers. "What are you saying?"

My thumb brushes over my wedding ring, and I force a smile for her. "Our time is up, little fairy. You gave me four weeks to prove to you that I can be the husband you need, and I tried, baby. But with each attempt, it only became clearer that I'm not the one for you. You deserve real love — a coincidental meeting, a dinner date that doesn't end up in the papers. You deserve a man without demons that compete with you for his attention... someone that isn't *broken*."

I hesitate, my hands shaking as I reach for her dashboard and take out the papers I stored in there. My eyes fall closed briefly before I hand them to her, wishing with all my might things could've been different. "I signed them, Raya. I'm sorry for taking so long to accept what you already knew. I love you, little fairy, but you're right. Love isn't the problem."

Raya stares at the papers, and then she looks up at me, her gaze unwavering. "What if I don't want coincidental meetings? What if I want spilled shots and rounds of truth and dare? What if I want to wear wigs and mess with the press? What if I want to be the one you fight for, the one that stands by your side as you continue to heal and grow? What if you're all I want, Lexington, flaws and all?"

I stare at her in disbelief, and Raya smiles at me as she cups my face. "I love you, Lex. Every single thing about you, but especially the way you kept your word, the way you tried not just to make amends, but to change for the better, forever. You say I deserve true love, but if that isn't true love, what is? I love you, but more importantly, I *choose* you — forever and always. Will you let me? Let me choose you, Lex."

She smiles when I can't quite find the right words to say. My gaze roams over her as I try to comprehend what she's saying. She wants me? Despite everything? "Just say yes," she whispers.

"*Yes*," I reply, my voice breaking. "Choose me, Raya. Please, choose me."

She brushes the back of her fingers over my jaw and nods. "I do. I always will. Every single day, Lex. Forever and always."

Sixty-Eight

LEXINGTON

My nerves are entirely out of control as I take Raya's hand in mine, still a little in disbelief that she's here with me. I gave her everything she married me for, everything she needed to save her father's company, yet here she is.

With me.

By *choice*.

Week after week passed, and still she stayed. Even through moments of weakness, through nightmares that made me distance myself from her for hours on end, she's shown me grace, endless patience. My wife made me realize I didn't even know what love was before her.

"Where are we going?" she asks as I open the car door for her.

I smirk at her as I lean in to buckle her in. "You'll see." Our eyes lock, and she smiles at me as she slips her hand around the back of my neck and kisses me, nearly making me forget all about my plans.

She whimpers disappointedly when I pull away, her gaze roaming over my face leisurely. There's something so fucking thrilling about the confidence in her eyes. She knows I'm hers and revels in it. I know the feeling all too well.

Raya places her hand on my thigh when I join her in the car, my heart pounding wildly. "Give me a hint?" she pleads. "You've been acting weird all morning, you know? I'm really curious what you're up to."

I chuckle, unable to resist that adorable voice she puts on when she wants something from me. "I'll take you to see a pretty sight."

She pouts and throws me a mock glare. "That's not a clue, and you know it. You said that last week and then carried me to the mirror in our dressing room."

I smirk as I think back to the incredulous look on her face that day, and the way she burst out laughing. She squeezes my thigh, likely also reminded of the way I made her watch herself come shortly after, my fingers buried in her pussy and my hand on her throat.

"It *was* a pretty sight, and I'll admit that what I'm showing you today won't be as pretty, but I think you'll enjoy it, nonetheless. I hope so, anyway. I'm really not too sure."

My tone must have given away my nerves, because her touch turns soothing as she strokes my thigh. "It doesn't matter where we go, Lex. I'll be happy so long as I'm with you."

I glance at her, and it just hits me then. She genuinely means it. Raya has never been one for grand gestures — she loves home-cooked meals and milkshakes, tinkering with tools and dancing. She loves our life as much as I do, but that doesn't mean she doesn't deserve grand gestures, too. She deserves the world, and I'll give it to her if I can.

"I love you," I murmur, my heart overflowing as I grab our joined hands and raise them to my lips to kiss her knuckles. "I love you so much it hurts."

She grins at me as I park the car. "I love you more."

"Impossible."

Raya looks around curiously as I open the door for her. "Where are we?"

I take her hand and pull her along, enjoying the way she's just buzzing with excitement. She's so fucking precious, and fuck, there's nothing I won't do to ensure she'll always be this happy. There will never be a day that I'll take for granted the right to stand by her side, to call her mine.

"Oh my god," she whispers, gasping when she sees the hot-air balloon that's waiting for us. I chuckle when she does this little jump, and then she glances over her shoulder, her eyes filled with joy. "You're taking me on a hot-air balloon ride?"

"I thought it might be a nice change of pace versus the planes and helicopters we're always on. Everything in our lives moves so fast, but this moment, today... I want it to last."

Something shifts in her expression, and her smile softens as she grabs my hand as we walk in together. She leans over the edge as we begin to rise into the air, and I position myself behind her, my arms caging her in on either side.

"Wow, there are just so many flowers everywhere," she says excitedly. "And the sun is about to set. It'll be so beautiful."

I smile to myself, my heart racing. "Not as beautiful as you," I whisper before pressing a soft kiss to her cheek.

Raya laughs, but deep down, I think she knows I'm serious. Nothing holds a candle to her, not even the golden glow of the setting sun, or the thousands of flowers that I planted for her by hand, underneath us. Nothing beats seeing my wife look at me with love in her gorgeous brown eyes.

"This is incredible," she murmurs. "I'll never get enough of watching the sunset, but this has got to be the prettiest sunset we've ever witnessed. All these beautiful yellow flowers look even more stunning now."

I press a kiss to her shoulder as we continue to rise higher, and then she gasps. "Wait, the flowers spell something!" she says excitedly, and I grin as I catalogue her expression, enjoying every single second with her. "Is that... is that my name?"

I draw a shaky breath, trying my best to control my nerves as we continue on our flight path. Raya gasps when we reach the exact vantage point I'd been aiming for, a huge cluster of white flowers spelling five words I've been meaning to say, their lighter color making them contrast with the yellow flowers that surround them.

Raya gasps and turns to face me, and I smile shakily as I take a step back and drop down to one knee, a ring box in hand. She stares at me in disbelief when I open it to reveal a custom-made Laurier ring, set with a yellow diamond I bought for her at auction.

"Raya, my little fairy," I say, my voice shaking. "I am not a man of many words, and for weeks, I've been trying to think of what I'd say to you today. It was an impossible task that left me feeling defeated, because the truth is that no words could ever be sufficient to explain how I feel about you. I can't begin to tell you what you've done to me, *for me.* You are my sun, Raya, and everything I am, everything I'll ever be, revolves around you. It always will. You've changed me, healed me, and you continue to inspire me to be a better man. There is nothing in this world I'd want more than to spend the rest of my days with you, doing everything in my power to make you just a little happier than you were the day before. If you let me, I'll do all I can to fill your days with laughter and sunshine, with joy and home-cooked meals, with your favorite tea and honeycomb coffees. There is nothing I wouldn't do to put a smile on your face, to make you happy." I take a deep breath, trying my best to keep my hand from shaking. "Raya Indira Windsor, I love you more than words will ever be able to convey. Will you make me the happiest man on this earth and marry me? Of your own accord this time?"

"*Yes,*" she says, a tear rolling down her face. "I'd choose you a thousand times over, Lex."

I slip the ring onto her finger, but she barely even glances at it. Her eyes are locked onto mine, pure happiness radiating off her. She looks so shocked, and fuck, the way she smiles makes me feel like I'm on top of the world. It's better than flying, better than anything I've ever known.

"I love you," she says as I rise to my feet, her arms wrapping around my neck. "Forever and always."

"I love you more," I murmur against her lips, before kissing her and sweeping her off her feet. She laughs, and the last broken fragments of my soul click back into place. Underneath us, the flowers spell: *Raya, will you marry me?*

Sixty-Nine

Raya

"Do you think he'll be able to find it?" I ask Sierra as I point out where in my mehendi my artist hid Lexington's name. It's customary to hide your husband's name inside your bridal henna design somewhere, and I'm glad I get to experience it myself.

"I'm not sure. It's so dark," she says, squinting at the inside of my wrist. "But I'm sure he'll have fun trying."

I shake my head at her admonishingly, and the rest of the girls burst out laughing. They're all in pretty light yellow and gold lehengas for our wedding, and they look gorgeous. Raven has outdone herself, not just with the bridesmaids' outfits, but with the entire limited edition range she let me collaborate on, allowing me to make every single one of my traditional attire dreams come true. All our guests will be in Indian designs of their own choosing today, all of it RWC.

I look around the room in the most beautiful resort I've ever been to, my heart filling with love as I take in all the laughter and excitement. Zane, Celeste, Xavier, and Sierra collaborated on the acquisition of this resort, and they won't admit it, but I know they did it for me. It's just like I once described to Sierra — a grand palace on the water, shades of white everywhere. It's the epitome of luxury and a perfect blend of cultures.

"Ready?"

I look up in surprise when all my brothers-in-law walk in, my eyes widening. Lex and I color coordinated, but they're dressed in my pale-yellow shade when they should've been in a much darker mustard shade to signify they're part of Lex's family. I gasp when they carry in a Doli — a traditional bridal carrier in white shades with countless fresh yellow flowers on it in all kinds of colors.

"We were told the bride's brothers get to carry her into the venue," Ares says, grinning. "So here we are."

My eyes fill with tears, and the girls instantly begin to fuss over me. "Don't cry," Faye says, her voice trembling.

Val narrows her eyes at me and shakes her head as she straightens out the train on the maroon heavy bridal lehenga Raven designed for me, complete with stunning floral embroidery and diamond embellishments. "Don't even dream of ruining your makeup," she warns me, a sweet smile on her face. "It took hours to do, and if you make Lex wait for much longer, I'm worried he'll come find you himself."

Celeste nods in agreement and catches a stray tear, while Mom and Sierra begin to instruct the boys. I can't believe this is really happening. This truly is the wedding of my dreams, and I feel so loved. I'd wondered if getting married again would make me feel strange, because I wouldn't have the people I consider my family by my side. I should've known they'd never part with me, not even for a few hours.

Mom helps me into the Doli and gently smooths out my dupatta, my veil, for me, her eyes dazzling with pride. Today is a dream come true for her, perhaps even more so than for me. I'm glad I got to give her this — her traditions, a wedding as she thinks it should be.

"The girls and I will go ahead," Mom says, knowing she should've been at Dad's side, in the venue. "Faye is going to play the piano for you as you enter. It'll be beautiful." I grin at her and nod, happy that she's so happy today, when she was filled with concern during our first ceremony.

"I love you, sweetie," Mom says as she straightens my wedding jewelry, making sure I look perfect.

I smile at her, my heart overflowing. "I love you more, Mom."

She brushes the back of her fingers over my temple and sighs happily, before turning and escorting the girls out.

"We're ready when you are, sweetheart," Dion tells me. I nod, and Ares, Dion, Luca, and Zane each hold on to one side of the palanquin, and I gasp when I'm lifted into the air. The boys chuckle, their eyes sparkling with the same pride I just saw in my mother's eyes, and my heart overflows with happiness.

"I'm excited for Lex to see you," Luca says, grinning. "But I'm just as excited for you to see him. He looks really good."

I blush, unable to help it, and Ares sends me the sweetest smile. These men are all so genuinely happy for Lex and me, and it's just so surreal that I get to call them my family.

All our guests rise from their seats, and I smile broadly when I see countless familiar faces, including Adam and Halima, Celeste's brother, Silas and Alanna, Leia and Adrian, Aria and Grayson, Amara and Noah, Archer and Serenity, and so many more. Everyone we love seems to be here, and my heart soars. Today truly is a celebration of love — not just between Lex and me, but everyone in attendance. I've never felt more blessed, more grateful.

The boys gently lower me to the floor, and I look up to find my dad offering me his right hand, tears in his eyes. He smiles at me, looking exactly the same way I feel — overwhelmed by emotions, but happy.

His grip on me is tight as he leads me to the altar, another beautiful structure built almost entirely from flowers, a fire in the middle. Lex rises to his feet, Mom's priest by his side, and I stare at him wide-eyed. He looks incredible dressed in a gold and maroon kurta. The butterflies in my stomach go wild when he just stares at me like he can't quite believe what he's seeing. He looked enchanted during our first legal ceremony, but this? This is the look I've always dreamed of. When I asked him if he'd ever marry me again, this is what I imagined.

Lex offers his right hand, and Dad sniffs as he places mine on top of Lex's, giving me away. Mom rubs his arm when he struggles to let go, and Lex looks at Dad reassuringly. "You'll never lose her," he promises. "You're just gaining a son."

I bite back my tears and nod at Dad, who steps back. He loves Lex just as much as he loves me, so I didn't think today would be as hard for him as it is, but having to give me away again seems to hit him just as hard as it did the first time.

Mom pours water over both of our hands, and the ceremony begins as Lex and I are seated next to each other. Sierra comes in to tie my dupatta to Lex's, her hands trembling. She's holding back tears today too, and I squeeze her hand before she steps back again, as focused on the ceremony as everyone else.

Lex pays close attention to every single thing the priest says, taking note of every ritual that I know he's already learned by heart. All the while, I stare at my husband, wondering how I got this lucky. He never stops trying, never stops learning and growing. Every day, he truly tries to be the best partner he can be, never quite realizing that he's already the man of my dreams.

Toward the end of the ceremony, Lex is asked to put sindoor on me, along the parting line in my hair, and a veil is lifted over us, giving us a moment of privacy. "You know how I told you I didn't believe in fate when we first met?" he whispers as he applies the sindoor, marking me a married woman. "I changed my mind. Meeting you, marrying you... none of that could've been anything short of fate. You, Raya, are my destiny."

I smile at him, my heart skipping a beat. "And you are mine," I whisper. "I love you, Lex. Forever and always."

His gaze roams over my face, like he's trying to drink me in, like he can't get enough. "I love you more, Raya. I always will."

Epilogue

THREE YEARS later

Lexington

"You look beautiful, little fairy," I murmur as I take in the long golden dress my wife is wearing.

She grins up at me, despite her obvious nerves. "You look amazing too," she says, her hands running over my white shirt before she places them on my suit jacket.

I smirk and raise a brow teasingly. "It's an *authentic* Raven Windsor Couture suit."

Raya bursts out laughing, her nerves fading away as her head falls back, and I just stare at her, fucking mesmerized. "You'll never let me live that down, will you?"

"Nope," I murmur, pulling her closer, my lips settling just below her ear. My wife gasps and places her hand on my chest, drawing my eyes to the rock on her ring finger. Her gaze heats when I grab her hand and kiss her fingers just below her wedding and engagement rings, loving the way both look on her.

She bites down on her lip when she feels me harden against her, and then she shakes her head. "We can't be late tonight," she whispers, before rising to her tiptoes, her lips brushing against my ear. "But I dare you to dance with me tonight, in private."

I grin from ear to ear when she pulls back, our eyes locking. "I can't believe you're mine," I whisper, still in disbelief. Three years since our second ceremony, our real one, and I still can't quite wrap my mind around the fact that she chooses to be with me.

"I know the feeling," she murmurs, rising to her tiptoes to steal a quick kiss.

I'm filled with pride as I offer my wife my arm. "This is your night, baby. In case I haven't said it yet, it's a true honor to stand by your side tonight, and every night. I am so proud of you. You have no idea."

She looks at me like she completely understands how I feel, and my heart flutters when she kisses my cheek. "I love you," she says, and I sigh happily. "Thank you for always being there, for supporting me endlessly and selflessly. This isn't just my night, Lex. It's ours."

"I love you more," I tell her, right before we walk onto the stage to unveil LWM's first-ever fully solar powered midrange car. The safety testing and mass production phases took years, but we're proud of what we've created, and knowing we're taking a giant leap toward sustainability for the whole industry is more rewarding than any other career milestone I've ever experienced. Like every other good thing in my life, I owe it all to my wife.

"Good evening, everyone," I say, addressing the packed crowd that's gathered, all of my siblings and all the Kingstons in attendance, every one of them dressed in various shades of yellow. "It is my honor to unveil the newest, most innovative car that we, at Lewis Windsor Motors, have ever created. I dare say it is our most groundbreaking vehicle yet, but it would not exist without my father-in-law, Bob Lewis. Please, will you join me on the stage?"

Raya holds out her hand when her father takes a hesitant step toward the stage, shaking his head. He still can't deny his daughter a thing, and I grin as he makes his way to us, his hand wrapping around hers. He retired last year, handing the company over to Raya and me. Every Monday he still drops by to help a little here and there, and Raya and I still spend most weekends at her parents' house, even though we no longer need to. Her parents are such an important part of our lives, and neither of us would be standing here today, unveiling something so extraordinary, without Bob.

"My father was the visionary behind this incredible invention," Raya says, squeezing her dad's hand. He looks visibly emotional, and I smile at him reassuringly. "Lex and I simply executed that vision. Please do us the honor of unveiling our latest car, Dad."

He looks at me like he can't believe we're truly stepping aside when we've worked so incredibly hard on this car. He's a little like Raya in that way — he doesn't always realize how loved he is, how much devotion he inspires just by being himself. I nod at him reassuringly, and he inhales sharply before pushing the large red button on the stage's podium.

The middle part of the stage begins to spin slowly as the car rises from a car lift underneath, and he stares at it, mesmerized. I can't imagine what it must be like for him to finally see all his hard work come to fruition. This car will be widely available at every single one of our retailers starting tomorrow, and we're expecting to sell at least 200,000 worldwide. It won't be long before our competition follows suit, and eventually, we'll see more zero emission cars than not, all thanks to Bob Lewis.

"We named it The LWM Lewis," I announce, "after the man who invented it. It is fully solar powered, and we've engineered it to work even in areas with little sun. For those of you who aren't quite comfortable with a fully solar-powered car just yet, we've made sure hybrid versions are available too, and those will be chargeable in the same way as your current electric cars. We are, however, fully confident that you'll never need to charge it. The option is simply available to you for your comfort."

Relieved murmurs cascade through the room, and Raya smiles at me knowingly. One of the biggest challenges she foresaw was handling people's resistance to change. It's not uncommon for people to be wary, and we know we'll have to win consumers' trust as we introduce something so unknown. In another year or two, they'll no longer need that safety net, and we'll start to see real progress as a society.

I stand back as my wife takes over and explains the features of the car. Bob moves to stand next to me as we both watch her in awe. "Thank you," he says.

I frown and shake my head. "Please don't. I'm really sorry we weren't able to launch this fully under the Lewis Motors brand. Since it's such an unprecedented car, I just couldn't get safety approval as quickly as I'd hoped. This was meant to be yours, and I'm sorry I couldn't—"

"—no," he cuts me off, smiling. "Thank you for making my daughter so happy. I almost didn't let you marry her when I came to see you that day in your lab, and you told me you weren't sure you could love her."

I tense as I think back to that day. "What made you change your mind?"

He grins then. "The way you looked when you said her name. You looked tormented, like only a man in love could. I knew, even then, that you'd taken a teaching position in an attempt to get to know her. The way you felt about Raya was written all over your face. Even if I hadn't let you, you'd have found a way to make her your wife."

I grin as I glance back at my wife. "I'd already bought that yellow diamond on her finger," I admit. "I didn't even know why I'd bought it. It was too much for an arranged marriage, but I saw it, and I knew I'd end up giving it to her someday."

Bob chuckles and wraps an arm around my shoulder. "And here you are, my boy. Happy at last."

I grin back at him and nod. "Happy at last."

"Lex?" Raya says, offering me her hand. "Now that the

announcement is over, we'd better go and open the dance floor. Will you dance with me?"

I grin, as I entwine our fingers. "With you? Always."

Want more of Lex and Raya? Download the following scenes; a deleted poker night scene featuring all the Windsor boys and Xavier; a deleted scene in which Raya finds out she's marrying Lex; and a spicy bonus scene. You can download these extra scenes on on my website catharinamaura.com/bonuses or by scanning the following QR code:

More from Catharina Maura

Ares and Raven: The Wrong Bride

The man Raven has always loved is engaged to her sister. But when her sister leaves him at the altar, she's asked to step in and marry him instead.

Luca and Val: The Temporary Wife
When the secretary he thought he hated suddenly quits her job, he realizes he'll stop at nothing to make her his — especially if it means getting out of his arranged marriage by marrying her instead.

Dion & Faye: The Unwanted Marriage
Despite resisting for years, Dion Windsor can't escape his engagement to alluring pianist, Faye. Seeing her with another man makes him realize he's done running. Time is up, and whether she likes it or not, she's his, as long as the secrets he holds don't destroy her...

Zane and Celeste: The Broken Vows

Childhood rivals turn into star-crossed lovers, until tragedy tears them further apart than ever before... Forced back together through an arranged marriage neither wants, they learn that not everything is what it seems.

Sierra and Xavier: Coming Soon

Silas and Alanna: Bittersweet Memories

When her boyfriend breaks her heart, Alanna goes after his older brother in a quest for revenge. It would have been simple — if he wasn't also her new boss. As they spend time together, she realizes he knows her better than he should. He knows about the memories she's lost.

Trigger Warning

This book contains sensitive themes, including but not limited to the following:

- Threat of firearm usage
- Portrayal of behavior caused by post traumatic stress disorder